An excerpt from *One Summer of Love*

Laney leaned in to kiss Nolan's cheek—a simple show of gratitude.

But her sudden movement startled him and his firm lips met hers.

The inadvertent kiss took them both by surprise. They pulled away and silently regarded one another.

Laney's pulse raced and her heart beat wildly. It was an honest mistake for which she should apologize. Yet her only thought was that she'd really, really like to kiss Nolan again. Intentionally this time.

She raised a trembling hand to his face. His beard tickled her palm, and his chest rose and fell heavily with each breath. But he didn't pull away. Laney leaned in closer. This time, Nolan closed the space between them. His firm lips crashed against hers, and his arms circled her waist.

And she knew in that moment that if Nolan Valentine invited her into his bed, she wouldn't say no.

Sebastian's eyes drifted closed, and the tension in his back and shoulders seemed to ease.

Nolan had practically blackmailed him into spending the next three months here in town. But perhaps his brother was right. Magnolia Lake was a good place for him to get some much-needed rest.

"Sebastian?"

He opened his eyes and stared, blinking. Was the woman standing before him real? Or was she a figment of his imagination, where she seemed to reside since their meeting a year ago?

"Evelisse?"

"You remembered." She offered a playful smile, her brown eyes twinkling.

He studied the plump lips painted a deep pink shade. Scanned the black, ribbed turtleneck sweater and tan leggings that hugged her curves. The briefest image flashed through his brain of those black, knee-high riding boots dangling over his shoulders.

Sebastian swallowed hard, his throat parched. "Of course, I remember."

His response hadn't come out the way he intended because her countenance fell, as did her slim shoulders.

Shit.

He'd uttered four words and already he'd pissed her off.

It's not what you say, Sebastian. It's how you say it.

REESE RYAN

ONE SUMMER OF LOVE
&
SNOWBOUND SECOND CHANCE

HARLEQUIN

DESIRE

HARLEQUIN®
DESIRE™

Recycling programs
for this product may
not exist in your area.

ISBN-13: 978-1-335-45778-3

One Summer of Love & Snowbound Second Chance

Copyright © 2023 by Harlequin Enterprises ULC

One Summer of Love
Copyright © 2023 by Roxanne Ravenel

Snowbound Second Chance
Copyright © 2023 by Roxanne Ravenel

Harlequin Enterprises ULC
22 Adelaide St. West, 41st Floor
Toronto, Ontario M5H 4E3, Canada
www.Harlequin.com

Printed in U.S.A.

CONTENTS

ONE SUMMER OF LOVE   9

SNOWBOUND SECOND CHANCE   227

Reese Ryan writes sexy, emotional stories featuring thirty-plus-somethings finding love while navigating career crises and family drama.

Reese is a native Ohioan with deep Tennessee roots. She endured many long, hot car trips to family reunions in Memphis via a tiny clown car loaded with cousins.

Connect with Reese via Facebook, Twitter, Instagram, TikTok or at reeseryan.com. Join her VIP Readers Lounge at bit.ly/VIPReadersLounge. Check out her YouTube show, where she chats with fellow authors, at bit.ly/ReeseRyan Channel.

Books by Reese Ryan

Harlequin Desire

The Bourbon Brothers

Savannah's Secrets
The Billionaire's Legacy
Engaging the Enemy
A Reunion of Rivals
Waking Up Married
The Bad Boy Experiment

Valentine Vineyards

A Valentine for Christmas
One Summer of Love
Snowbound Second Chance

Visit the Author Profile page
at Harlequin.com for more titles.

You can also find Reese Ryan on Facebook, along with other Harlequin Desire authors, at Facebook.com/HarlequinDesireAuthors!

Dear Reader,

I love writing about big families with complicated dynamics and complex personalities. Set those stories in a diverse small town where quirky, familiar characters resurface, and it's like the perfect layered dish bursting with unique flavors.

In *One Summer of Love*, Nolan Valentine, the CFO of Valentine Vineyards, is the ultraserious, überfocused eldest brother responsible for the new winery's bottom line. He's opposed to hiring an enologist. But from the moment Nolan encounters beautiful, brilliant scientist Delaney Carlisle, he finds himself at a loss for words. The candid, opinionated single mother has ambitions for herself and her young daughter, so she only plans to spend one summer in Magnolia Lake. But when she and Nolan—two STEM nerds with a love for superheroes—make a surprising connection, each is forced to reevaluate their plans for the future.

Thank you for joining me for the passion, secrets and drama of my Valentine Vineyards series. Got a question or comment? Visit reeseryan.com/desirereaders. While there, join my VIP Readers newsletter list for book news, giveaways and more.

Until our next adventure!

Reese Ryan

ONE SUMMER OF LOVE

For my amazing readers.
You encourage and inspire me.
I am ever appreciative of your continued support.
I hope you enjoy Nolan and Laney's love story.

One

"You got fired, Laney? You were only there for a week. How is that possible? Besides, you don't get fired. You get bored and move on." Her older sister, Savannah Carlisle Abbott, sounded more shocked than disappointed.

Delaney Carlisle gripped her cell phone as she paced the floor of her small luxury apartment in Upstate New York. She chewed on her thumbnail. It was a habit she frequently reminded her nearly eight-year-old daughter not to indulge in. Yet, despite being thirty-five, it was her immediate reaction to stress.

Laney had a perfect, if wildly varied, employment record. The thought of having to sit in an interview and explain that she'd been summarily dismissed and escorted off the premises after just four and a half days…

Well, it hurt her pride, to say the least.

"Sweetie, I'm not judging you, I'm just…worried. This doesn't sound like you. I'm wondering if it has anything to do with Derrick showing up in your life again after all this time," Savannah said gently. "I know you said you're fine with it—"

"And I *am* fine with it." Laney sucked her wounded digit, the coppery taste of blood filling her mouth. She'd nibbled her thumbnail to the quick at the mention of her ex, Derrick Holden, who also happened to be her daughter Harper's father.

Until six months ago, Laney hadn't seen or heard from Derrick Holden for nearly nine years. They'd been on the verge of getting engaged when she'd gotten pregnant. When she'd decided she wanted to keep the baby, the meticulous plans they'd made — to travel the world on a dime and volunteer with global organizations that mattered most to them — were shot to hell.

Derrick had been willing to risk dysentery, malaria and a host of tropical diseases to take care of needy children across the globe. He was far more risk-averse when it came to taking care of his own child.

On every other point of disagreement in their relationship, they'd compromised like two sensible adults. But there was no compromising on this. She wanted to keep and raise their child. Derrick didn't.

It was the hardest thing she'd ever had to do, but Laney wished Derrick the absolute best and returned his promise ring. They'd made love one last time, both of their hearts broken. Then they'd parted ways. She hadn't seen or heard from Derrick Holden since. Until six months ago.

Derrick messaged her through a social media app to say hello and to ask about *their* daughter.

Their daughter? Laney's cheeks burned just thinking about it.

Harper wasn't *their* daughter. She was Laney's daughter. Laney's life. Her entire world. Unless she'd somehow missed the part when Derrick was there for diaper changes, breastfeeding, potty training and the joys and challenges of raising a girl who was far too clever for her age.

After she'd gotten over the initial shock of hearing from her ex, Laney had decided to just ignore the message. But Derrick kept messaging her. And when he'd sent a pleading message that read, "Please, Laney. I just want to meet our brilliant, beautiful daughter," Harper, who'd been playing a game on her phone, had seen it.

Once her daughter, who'd been asking about the identity of her father, had seen the message, Laney couldn't very well keep Harper from her father without coming off as the Wicked Witch.

"You don't sound fine, sweetie." Savannah's voice could barely be heard over the sound of her not quite two-year-old daughter, Remi, repeating the word "Da" in the background. "Ever since Derrick weaseled his way back into your lives, you've been distracted and on edge."

"I'm not distracted, Vanna. I've been busy." Laney relaxed her suddenly tense shoulders and tried to take the edge off her tone. "And that isn't why I got fi—"

Laney inhaled deeply, unable to say the word without the tears starting all over again. "They let me go because I brought it to their attention that the way they treated their immigrant workers and their farm animals was negligent and practically criminal."

"You did the right thing by speaking up. They sound like monsters," Savannah reassured her. "I'm sorry this happened to you."

"Their product was shitty anyway." Laney rifled through her medicine cabinet for the triple antibiotic ointment.

"Then why did you take a job with them?"

"There aren't a ton of enology jobs in the area." Laney squeezed some of the ointment onto the thumb she'd bitten a chunk out of. "Besides, the worse the product, the more my work can create a demonstrable improvement."

"That's my little sis." Savannah sighed. "Always looking for a scientific challenge."

Laney ignored the comment. "My concern now is what to do about my apartment. It's the final month of my lease. I'd planned to renew it, but without knowing where I'll end up working…" Laney sank onto the sofa again.

"Can't you do a month-to-month lease until you figure things out?" Savannah asked.

"The area is suddenly in high demand. The management company won't accept anything less than a two-year lease."

"You do realize that with the inheritance Grandad left you and the shares you own in King's Finest, you don't have to work if you don't want to, right?"

"I'd be bored to death without a job." Laney dragged a hand through her thick natural curls. "Besides, I promised Grandad I would follow my passion. And enology is it. It's the perfect intersection of my love of biology and my fascination with winemaking. I just need to find a position with a winery small enough to need me but big enough to afford me."

"Okay, Goldilocks. But while you're looking for a position that's just right, why don't you spend the summer with us here in Magnolia Lake? We'd love to see you and Harper."

"I agreed to let Harper spend two weeks in Seattle with her father."

"What? You're going to let…" Savannah paused, and Laney could swear her sister was counting. "All the more reason you should stay with me and Blake for the summer. That way, you won't be alone and obsessing about whether Harper is okay."

Her sister knew her well. That was exactly what she'd be doing while Harper was away.

"I would, but maybe you've forgotten that you're all out of spare bedrooms," Laney reminded her sister. "And I am not spending the entire summer on that pull-out sofa in the den slash playroom again," she added before Savannah could suggest it.

Laney loved her young nephew. But being awakened early in the morning by little Davis demonstrating his skills on the mini drum set his uncle Cole had bought him definitely wasn't her idea of a vacation.

"Fair enough. We'll rent you a place for the summer."

"Renting a furnished apartment for the summer is a great idea." Laney stood, surveying her apartment. She was already making a list of the things she'd need to do: pack up her stuff, put her furniture into storage, book plane tickets. "But I'll pay for it. I just need you to make the arrangements."

Laney wrapped up her conversation with Savannah, then grabbed her purse, hurrying out to pick her daughter up from school. She couldn't wait to tell Harper that they'd be spending the summer in Magnolia Lake.

Nolan Valentine eased onto a lounger on Duke and Iris Abbott's patio. Sharing a meal with his family's new-found relatives had become a regular thing in the eight months since his father—Abbott Raymond Valentine—had connected with them and purchased the local winery that had once been owned by the family of Nolan's biological grandmother.

His family, owners of what was now Valentine Vineyards, was still coming to terms with the realization that their father had been adopted and that they were related to the Abbotts—owners of the world-renowned King's Finest Distillery and various other entities. Like the King's Finest Family Restaurant they'd opened several months earlier.

Nolan finished the last bite of the steak his cousin Blake had grilled to absolute perfection. It was melt-in-your-mouth delicious and so were all the sides that had gone with the meal, most of which were favorites on the menu of the Abbotts' new family-style restaurant. He set his plate on the table beside him and hoped he wouldn't crash with his mouth hanging open.

"Nolan, there's something I want you to hear." His father stood over him, voice lowered.

Nolan glanced over at the table where his sister, Chandra Valentine-Brandon, the CEO of their winery, sat with Blake's wife, Savannah, and Nolan's younger sister, Naya. Their heads were together, and they spoke quietly.

"Looks like a business meeting." Nolan studied his father's features, so much like his own. Same eyes, mouth and forehead. But his nose he'd gotten from his mother, who'd abandoned him and his three oldest siblings when he was just six years old. The twins had come along later from his dad's second marriage. "You said we weren't talking shop today. In fact, you *insisted* on it."

"I know." Ray Valentine shoved his hands into his pockets. "But Savannah came to me, and it's too good an idea to pass up."

Nolan hoisted himself from the lounger that felt like a warm hug and a night of good sleep. He followed his father to the table at the far corner of the patio and slid into the lone empty chair, situated between his dad and Chandra.

"All right. What's this big news I need to hear?" Nolan shifted his gaze to Savannah.

"It's more of a proposal," Savannah said.

"And an opportunity for us." Chandra rubbed her protruding belly. His sister was about six weeks away from giving birth. Her husband, Dr. Julian Brandon, the town GP, had been hovering over her all afternoon, as if he expected her to give birth at any moment.

It would be the first child for both of them, and it showed.

"So let's hear about this *opportunity* and how much it's going to cost us." Nolan surveyed their faces, making it clear he knew why he was invited into this conversation.

Whatever Savannah was proposing was going to cost them quite a bit. As the CFO of Valentine Vineyards, they wanted his blessing. Not that they wouldn't proceed without it. He'd been overruled by the family before. At least, the members of the family who ran the winery: his father, Chandra, Naya and him.

His brothers were otherwise occupied. Sebastian was the CEO of Valentine Textiles—the once family-owned firm they'd sold to a California conglomerate. Alonzo worked for an ad agency in New York. And Nyles was being… Nyles. Currently, he was a club promoter for some new spot in Miami Beach.

"Don't be a tightwad, Nolan." Naya sifted her fingers through her blond box braids and tugged them over one shoulder. "You haven't even heard the proposal yet."

Savannah's hazel eyes twinkled in the sunlight. "You really do remind me of Parker," she said, referring to her husband Blake's brother.

Nolan's father and sisters, who'd also noted the similarities between him and Parker, chuckled.

So maybe he did have a very analytical brain that required detailed explanations and an ordered universe and he wasn't much of a people person. But he hadn't quite risen to the level of Parkerhood in those regards. Still, it seemed pointless to make note of those differences.

"I asked if you all have ever considered bringing on an enologist," Savannah continued.

"An enologist?" Nolan frowned.

"That's a scientist who oversees the production of the winemaking process from beginning to end and supports their recommendations with careful data analysis."

"I know what an enologist is." Nolan kept his voice even, not wanting to seem impolite. "And I can see the value of adding one to our team. Valentine Vineyards is certainly more profitable than it was when we acquired it eight months ago, but not profitable enough to justify the salary of a good enologist." Nolan pulled a soft cloth from his pocket and cleaned his smudged glasses.

His father put a hand on his shoulder. "You know how much I appreciate your thoughtful, analytical opinion, Nolan."

Code for: But I'm not going to take your recommendation.

"You make a very valid point, and I realize that is traditional corporate thinking. But I'm no spring chicken, son. If I want to see this vineyard thrive in my lifetime, we need to take a more aggressive approach to growing the business," his father said. "Is taking on a considerable salary risky? Yes. But with the sale of the textile firm, I can afford to take that risk."

"I realize you can afford it, Dad. But those are your personal funds. We shouldn't be siphoning money from your personal account to hire a new employee, especially when we can't even be sure that hiring them will have any real impact on our bottom line," Nolan said calmly. "I understand how much the winery means to you and how important it is to you that it becomes a success.

But Valentine Vineyards needs to be self-sufficient. Not slowly draining your personal finances." Nolan settled his glasses evenly on the bridge of his nose.

His father, Chandra and Naya all looked disappointed, but no one countered his point. It was an argument that even his sisters couldn't disagree with.

When Chandra agreed to join Nolan and Naya at the winery, the three of them spoke privately. They would give this winery their all. Try to make it everything their father wanted it to be. But they wouldn't allow Valentine Vineyards to drain their father mentally, emotionally or financially.

Yes, the old man was sitting on a considerable mint after the sale of their textile firm. But no matter how large a filled bucket was, a hole in the bottom would eventually drain it dry.

Savannah's hazel eyes danced, and her lips curved in a smug smile. "What if I could get you a temporary summer contract with an outstanding enologist? That would give you a chance to kick the tires without making a huge investment or a long-term commitment."

"That would be perfect." Nolan's father clapped his large hands together.

"I love the idea of trying this out short-term. You evidently have someone in mind." Chandra shifted in her seat and rubbed her belly again. "So who is it?"

"My younger sister, Delaney Carlisle."

Nolan's brows furrowed with an involuntary frown.

Someone going this hard to get their younger sibling a job... It never worked out well, in his experience. The few times he'd fallen for it, he'd later been forced to fire the younger sibling, which inevitably damaged his relationship with the person who'd recommended them.

"Look, Savannah, I can appreciate that you want to help your sister," Nolan said.

"I do want to help my sister, and I'd love it if she relocated here to Magnolia Lake. I don't apologize for that. But I'd also really like to help you. You have a history with this winery, just like my family had history with the operation that eventually became King's Finest Distillery. So I get how important this is to you, Ray. What you're doing with the winery is amazing. And I know that Laney…my sister…could help you achieve the aggressive goals you've set for yourselves."

Savannah leaned in closer and lowered her voice. "I understand how it feels to be an outsider in this family. To feel the need to measure up to what Joe, Duke, Blake and his siblings have achieved. At least talk to Laney. She'll be here for the summer anyway. And if you choose not to work with her, I promise not to take it personally." Savannah raised her right hand.

Nolan's father and sisters grinned as they shifted their gaze to him. *Game. Set. Match.*

Nolan sighed. "Fine. I don't see the harm in talking to her. Unless she's as persuasive as you are, Savannah."

Everyone at the table laughed, and Nolan couldn't help chuckling himself.

He'd talk to this woman. See if she was as brilliant as he'd heard. But even if she was, Nolan couldn't imagine committing to more than one summer with Delaney Carlisle.

Two

Laney stepped out of the black hybrid BMW SUV she'd purchased used a few years back. One of the few luxuries she'd permitted herself since they'd come into money a little more than five years ago. She surveyed the lovely little villa at the front and a smattering of buildings on the rest of the property.

The blacktop in the parking lot seemed fairly new. And while the building was lovingly worn, it was clear that the Valentine family had been doing some renovation to the main villa and outlying buildings.

The villa conveyed a romantic, old-world feeling. Like she'd traveled to another place and time. Her sister was right. There was lots of potential there. They just needed to tap into it.

Taking on a project like this could be overwhelming, especially for a family of novices. Branding and marketing weren't her thing. But she knew biology and chemistry. And thanks to her studies and apprentice-ships the past few years, she'd learned a great deal about the making of a good wine. So she was intrigued by the prospect of spending her summer lending her expertise to the Valentines, rather than pouting over her firing and the fact that her daughter now wanted to spend two weeks with her ex.

Laney smoothed her skirt down over her lean hips and stood tall. Then she made her way to the front door of the villa where she was scheduled to meet members of the Valentine family.

She closed her eyes, sucked in a deep breath, then opened the front door. Dejah, a beautiful young woman with smooth, dark brown skin, greeted her and escorted her to the great room of the villa where a tall, hand-some older man and two younger women awaited her.

"You must be Mr. Valentine. It's a pleasure to meet you, sir." Laney extended her hand to the older man.

"I am indeed. But please, call me Ray." He beamed.

Ray introduced her to his daughters: Chandra, the CEO, and Naya, who handled events and public re-lations. Then the Valentines proceeded to lay out the history of the winery and why its success was so im-portant to them.

It wasn't long before the tightness in Laney's shoul-ders eased and she was chatting amicably with the Val-entines. Ray, Chandra and Naya were all so different. But the love between them was evident, and they were warm and inviting. She liked each of them, and she admired that they were trying to build a legacy for their family that honored the parents Ray had never known.

As a child who'd lost her own parents well before she had any real memory of them, she understood Ray's deep need for a connection with his late parents. Ray's drive reminded her of her own sister, Savannah, whose determination to find out the truth about their family's connection to the King's Finest Distillery had nearly landed her in jail and destroyed the romantic relationship she and Blake had been building.

"Sorry I'm late. My meeting went much longer than I'd anticipated." A man rushed into the room, his glasses in one hand and a cleaning cloth in the other as he wiped them.

"That's all right, son. It gave us a chance to give Ms. Carlisle here—"

"Laney," she interrupted. They'd been warm and informal with her, and she wanted to be the same.

Ray smiled broadly. "It gave us a chance to give Laney here a little history on the vineyard and a bit of an overview of our plans for it. We haven't talked about her background or specific qualifications yet. Figured you'd want to be here for that."

"I would." The man slid his glasses back on. He extended his hand and opened his mouth to speak. But his eyes widened, then he blinked. Yet, he didn't say anything.

Laney wasn't sure whether she should be flattered or insulted by his reaction. But she *was* taken aback by her own reaction to Nolan Valentine. A subtle warmth spread beneath Laney's skin as she assessed the surprisingly handsome man's horn-rimmed eyeglasses and the devilish glint behind them. She managed to refrain from fanning herself in response to the heat that crawled up her neck and exploded beneath her cheeks. Instead, she widened her smile, sprung to her feet and shook the man's offered hand. "I'm Delaney Carlisle, Savannah Abbott's sister. Pleasure to meet you."

"Yes, of course. I mean...of course you're Savannah's sister. I can see the resemblance. Not of course it's a pleasure to meet me." He shook his head, as if silently chastising himself for rambling, then drew in a deep breath. "I'm Nolan Valentine, CFO of Valentine Vineyards. Pleased to meet you, Ms. Carlisle."

A shiver ran down Laney's spine and her palm tingled where his skin met hers. She honestly wasn't sure what she'd been expecting of the man her sister had described as "a little intense." But the man with the sexy-professor-with-a-secret-sex-dungeon vibe who currently held her hand in his surely wasn't it.

Nolan Valentine was handsome with his dark brown skin, well-trimmed beard and his hair worn in low-cut curls. He stood no more than three or four inches above her height of five foot five. Still, with his commanding gaze, something about the man's presence felt...*imposing*. Maybe it was those dark eyes of his that seemed to peer right through her.

"Which type of vats are you purchasing?" Laney gently tugged her hand from Nolan's, unsure if he'd planned on relinquishing her hand voluntarily and even less certain that she really wanted him to. "Steel, oak, concrete?" she clarified when he seemed bewildered by the question.

"Steel. It's what the Richardsons were using prior to our purchase of the winery. And it's what our wine-maker, Maria Rayburn, seems to prefer," Ray inter-jected.

"You have a woman winemaker." Laney nodded as she absorbed that bit of information. "Impressive. There aren't a lot of women in the industry. Thankfully, that's beginning to change. And I'm glad to hear that you're open to shaking things up a bit. Like, perhaps, consid-ering the use of oak vats."

Nolan frowned and there was a collective gasp in the room.

"I'm not suggesting you switch all of your barrels to oak. Steel does have certain advantages." Laney swept her gaze from one Valentine to the next, lingering on Nolan's dark brown eyes a bit longer than she proba-bly should. "But aging the wine in oak barrels can add dimensions of character. Wood's porosity permits the wine to breathe, lending to a softer taste, which some wine drinkers prefer. And the evaporation oak barrels permit concentrates the wine, making subtle flavors a bit more pronounced."

"Won't aging the wine in wood barrels have a no-ticeable impact on the taste?" Chandra shifted in her seat and rubbed her large belly, as if her unborn baby was also outraged by Laney's proposal and needed to be soothed.

"Oak can certainly lend tastes to the wine. Depend-ing on the type used, the aging vessel can add notes of caramel, cinnamon or nutmeg to the finished product, just to name a few. Depending on what you're looking for, that can either improve the taste of the wine or provide additional varieties. Since you've expressed a desire to expand your offerings, it's something to consider." Laney returned to her seat and folded her hands in her lap. "Sorry, I didn't intend to ruffle any feathers. But if you're considering adding an enologist to your team, I assume you're looking for ways to improve and expand the process."

"Yes, we are, of course. That is exactly the kind of recommendation we're looking for." Ray indicated that Nolan—who still stood staring at Laney with one thick, neat eyebrow lifted—should have a seat beside Naya on the opposite sofa. "And now that everyone is here, why don't you tell us a little about yourself and what made you so interested in wine."

Laney drew in a deep breath, her mouth curving with a sad smile. "My grandfather raised my sister and me. He was really sick the last few years of his life. Growing up, we didn't have much. But in those last few years... Well, we had everything we needed and more. He was able to gain access to medicine and treatments that gave us more time with him." Laney glanced down at her hands and fought the urge to nibble on her thumbnail.

She would always be grateful for the additional time she got to spend with her grandfather. Due, in large part, to Joseph Abbott's generosity in paying for the best doctors and treatments money could buy.

"He knew he didn't have much time left. So he wanted to spend his final years traveling to wineries all over the country. I went with him whenever I could. We visited wineries in California, Tennessee, Virginia and North Carolina. Then we spent two weeks at wineries in Italy and France." Laney smiled at the memory. "I learned a lot about the process of winemaking and sampled the goods. I came to understand why my grandfather was so fascinated with wines."

"It's wonderful that you got to spend that time with your grandfather." Chandra's smile was pained, and Laney couldn't help wondering about the story behind it. "Is that when you decided to go into winemaking?"

"That's when I realized how much I'd fallen in love with the process of winemaking and the science behind it," Laney said. "But it was my grandfather's final words to me that prompted me to shift my career. He said he wished he'd spent his life doing work he loved. Something that truly made him happy. And he made me promise that I would do just that. Not long afterward, I abandoned my plans to get a PhD in microbiology at an Ivy League school and moved to Upstate New York to enroll in a viticulture and enology program instead."

"Interesting career choice," Nolan muttered.

Naya elbowed her brother in the ribs and Ray and Chandra cut their eyes at him.

Laney held back a giggle at Nolan's frankness and his family's reaction to it.

"Agreed." She nodded. "But neither career was going to make me filthy rich. I went into this line of work because I'm passionate about it. And because I enjoy impacting the winemaking process in a way that both improves the winery's bottom line and brings joy to consumers of the final product."

Ray, Chandra and Naya nodded enthusiastically, all of them smiling.

Nolan didn't look impressed by the story of Laney's career epiphany. But there was *something* in his momentary gaze. Attraction? Desire? Her breath hitched slightly, and her pulse quickened at the possibility. But before she could give the matter further thought, Nolan cleared his throat and pulled a pen and a wrinkled piece of paper from his shirt pocket. He unfolded it.

"All right, Ms. Carlisle." Nolan shoved his glasses up the bridge of his nose. "Tell us about this enology program you attended in Upstate New York."

Savannah had warned her Nolan would be the toughest nut to crack.

Laney crossed her legs in her black pencil skirt, noting that his attention followed the movement and lingered a beat on her calf as it bounced.

Naya nudged her brother with her elbow, startling him. Nolan returned his gaze to the paper in his hand. He tugged at the collar of his light blue dress shirt, buttoned all the way up, as if desperate to loosen it.

The spark of attraction she felt toward Nolan... It was *definitely* mutual.

Laney smiled. Winning over Nolan "The Pessimist" Valentine was going to be fun.

Nolan studied the lengthy list of interview questions he'd prepared for Ms. Delaney Carlisle. General questions to determine her knowledge of wines. Per-

formance questions to discern if she actually knew how
to perform the job she was applying for. Behavioral
questions to determine if Laney was a problematic diva
who'd make the next three months a living hell.

He tried his best to ignore how beautiful Delaney
was or the shapeliness of the leg that bounced impatiently as he laid out a complicated question. Tried
not to be thoroughly impressed by each of her well-
thought-out answers, often substantiated by verifiable
data, a recent article or anecdotal evidence from her
studies and internships over the past few years. And he
tried not to be charmed by the amusement in Delaney's
lovely brown eyes and the way her full, berry-tinted lips
quirked with the hint of a smile when she'd answered a
question particularly well. As if she was teasing him.

Delaney was beautiful, extremely competent and
supremely confident in her knowledge and abilities
without coming off as insufferably arrogant. There was
something Nolan found incredibly sexy about that combination of characteristics. Or maybe it was that combination bottled in the ridiculously enticing package that
was Ms. Delaney Carlisle. No wonder rogue thoughts
about how good she smelled, the softness of her skin
and images of him taking Delaney into his arms and
kissing that damn smirk off her face kept commandeer-
ing his unusually uncooperative brain.

His problem, not hers.

On paper, at least, Delaney Carlisle was damn near
perfect. But this was a huge step for his family's winery, so he needed to be sure.

"Okay, son. I think we've covered just about every

possible scenario." Ray raised a hand before Nolan could launch into another question.

"And then some." Naya rolled her eyes. "Seriously, I'd be surprised if Laney even wants to work here after all that," she muttered loudly.

"Fine." Nolan glowered at his younger sister but conceded to his father's request that he formally put an end to his grilling of Delaney. "Nothing more from me, then."

"Great," Chandra said a little too enthusiastically. "Then I think that'll do it, unless you have any questions for us, Laney."

"No, I think Nolan's questions covered just about every situation imaginable." Laney barely held back a grin. "But I'd love to see the space, if that's possible."

"We did plan to give you a tour of the vineyard and the winery." Nolan's father frowned, glancing down at the expensive watch the six of them had bought him for Christmas. "But Chandra, Naya and I have a meeting in town about the possibility of starting a Christmas market here in Magnolia Lake. Perhaps Dejah could give you a quick tour of the place."

"No, you guys go ahead. I'll do it." Nolan stood. His face warmed beneath the curious, wide-eyed stares of his father and sisters. "I'm not attending the meeting, and it is my fault our chat went longer than expected."

Naya shared a look with Chandra and their father, who nodded reluctantly. Naya sighed quietly. "Fine. Nolan can show you around. Any question he can't answer, Dejah can. Her family previously owned the winery."

There was a flash of surprise on Delaney's face in response to that bit of information. But the micro expression disappeared before Nolan could even be sure he'd seen it.

"That would be great. Thank you for the opportunity." Delaney stood and exchanged handshakes with Ray, Naya and Nolan, then turned to Chandra, who was still seated.

"It was a pleasure to meet you, Laney." Chandra struggled to get up from the sofa. Their father helped her up, but the old man couldn't resist a good chuckle at his eldest daughter's plight. This earned him an elbow in the side from the irritated mother-to-be. Which only made their father laugh harder.

Chandra ignored her father's teasing and gave Laney a warm smile and handshake. "We'll contact you later this week, if we have any follow-up questions."

"Actually, I'll have very limited availability for the next few days." Laney withdrew her hand, then straightened her glasses. "I have to make a quick trip to Seattle. I'll be gone through the weekend, but I'll be back early next week."

"Another interview?" Nolan asked.

"No." Laney turned toward him, a pained look on her lovely face. "I'm taking my daughter to Seattle to spend two weeks with her father."

"Oh." There was so much pain in her voice that Nolan instantly felt like a jerk for having asked. "I'm...sorry?"

His father and sisters gave him the evil eye and he shrugged. What was he supposed to say? The subject was clearly a sore one and he felt bad for having brought it up. Apologizing felt like the right thing to do.

Per the hiked eyebrows and folded arms of his two sisters, he'd apparently chosen wrong.

"There's no need to be sorry." Delaney tucked her wild natural curls behind her ear, and for a fleeting moment, Nolan couldn't help imagining his fingers tangled in her brown curls as he pulled her mouth to his.

"Not a problem. Any questions we have can keep until your return. Either way, you'll hear from one of us by the end of next week." His father patted Laney's shoulder. "Have a good trip. We'll chat soon."

"Before our little tour, may I use your restroom?" Laney looked to Chandra and Naya.

"Actually, I was headed in that direction myself." Chandra rubbed her belly and arched her back. "I'll show you where it is. Nolan can meet you back in the front lobby when you're done."

Nolan silently nodded his agreement. But he couldn't help watching the gentle sway of Delaney's hips as she accompanied Chandra in the direction of the recently updated public bathrooms in the villa. He shoved his hands in his pockets and sighed quietly.

Delaney Carlisle wasn't anything like he'd envisioned. She shared several of her sister's features. Their mouths and noses were quite similar. But Delaney's eyes were a dark, coffee brown while Savannah's were hazel and seemed to change with the light. Delaney was a few inches shorter than her sister. And while both women wore their natural curls, Delaney wore hers in a wild, free curly afro whereas Savannah's hair was nearly always pulled into a sleek bun or high ponytail. And while Savannah was all soft curves, Laney's hips and thighs managed to look both curvy and strong.

He shuddered, his brain instantly envisioning what it would feel like to have those strong, lean brown thighs wrapped around him as she lay beneath him.

Raymond Valentine cleared his throat, stirring Nolan from his temporary daze.

Nolan's face and neck heated with embarrassment, as if his father had been privy to the Technicolor vision of Delaney Carlisle beneath him in his bed that had momentarily hijacked his brain. He headed toward the kitchen. "I'm going to grab a cup of coffee."

"I could use one before this next meeting." His father trailed him to the kitchen. He leaned against the counter, waiting silently as Nolan grabbed a mug and popped a pod into the coffee maker. "So… What do you think of Ms. Valentine?" he asked just as Naya joined them in the kitchen.

His younger sister snorted, and their father shot her a warning look. Naya folded her arms and rolled her eyes but didn't say anything.

"She's knowledgeable. Competent." Nolan shrugged. "And she seems…nice enough."

"If that's not the understatement of the year," Naya muttered.

"And what exactly is that supposed to mean?" Nolan demanded.

"It means you were staring at her like she was a gourmet meal and you hadn't eaten in a year."

"I was not—"

"Actually, you were, Nolan. And you were rambling." Chandra joined them in the kitchen and sank into her seat. She nibbled on a piece of Danish she'd brought in for breakfast that morning. "Which was surprising. You're usually much subtler than that about your interest in a woman."

The three of them stared at Nolan, as if daring him to deny it.

"Okay, maybe I was a little thrown off. I'm not quite sure what I was expecting—" That was a lie. He'd known *exactly* what he was expecting. A number-crunching lab nerd in a white oxford shirt with a pocket protector displaying an array of pens and not a single ounce of glamour. It was a horrible stereotype, and he was ashamed of himself for it. "—but Delaney was a bit of a surprise."

"Why?" Chandra pressed. "Because she's not only whip-smart with an impressive knowledge of wine-making and is completely unintimidated by your whole thousand-questions routine, she's also sweet, funny and—"

"Fucking hot." Naya shrugged when three pairs of widened eyes turned toward her. "What? We were all thinking it. I just said it."

Chandra gave their younger sister her best *Behave* glare, then turned back toward Nolan. "I was going to say sweet, funny and a little bit of a smart-ass."

"It's like she was tailor-made for you." Naya grinned.

"Even if that were the case, I'm not looking to get involved with anyone." Nolan shrugged, drinking more of his coffee. "Besides, it sounds like Laney's situation is…complicated. She has a daughter and an ex she has some sort of difficult relationship with. Been there before. Hard pass."

Nolan stood abruptly before he could see the pity on the faces of his father and sisters. The sudden end of his marriage also ended his relationship with the three children he'd loved and had raised as his own for five years. Her decision—not his.

It was still a sore point for him. And the only thing worse than the pain of losing his relationship with the kids was seeing his family pity him over it.

He'd promised himself he wouldn't get involved with anyone with children again. So it was a good thing Delaney Carlisle—the first woman he'd felt this kind of intense attraction to since the divorce three years ago—was strictly off-limits. It was better that way for both of them.

Three

Laney shifted her weight from one foot to the other as she made small talk with Dejah Richardson in the lobby of the Valentine Vineyards main villa. The younger woman was polite as she answered Laney's questions about the winery. But she wasn't exactly giving off warm, genuine vibes the way Chandra and Naya had. Laney could swear she detected a hint of latent resentment in Dejah's tone and expression. But she honestly couldn't blame the woman.

When Savannah had first gone to work for the Abbotts, she'd excelled at her job, had been highly personable and gotten along with everyone—including the Abbott family. But Savannah had joined King's Finest believing the Abbotts had swindled her family out of their half of the distillery and she'd been determined to prove it. So despite her broad smile and cheerful demeanor, Savannah had been seething with resentment.

That, she imagined, must be what Dejah Richardson was feeling. Could the woman have a nefarious motive for staying on at the winery after Ray Valentine bought it?

Laney pushed the idea out of her head.

Her love of comic books and murder mysteries was beginning to make her see everyone as either a hero or a villain.

"Sorry for the wait, Ms. Valentine." Nolan suddenly appeared in the lobby, clenching a disposable coffee cup. His expression fell somewhere between a frown and a smile. Like he wasn't quite sure which was appropriate.

Laney restrained a giggle. There was something about handsome, too-smart-for-his-own-good and way-too-serious Nolan Valentine that was…adorable. The man needed to learn how to relax and loosen up a bit. Starting with that top button. Seriously, it was June in Tennessee. Who buttoned their shirt all the way up to the top when they weren't even wearing a tie?

Nolan Valentine, apparently.

Laney sank her teeth into her lower lip, and her gaze quickly scanned the buttons on his shirt. Her impish brain and long-neglected libido left her wondering what lay beneath that shirt.

"Not a problem," Laney assured him. "It gave me a chance to chat with Dejah and to get to know more about the winery—from an employee's perspective."

Dejah frowned, the expanse between her brows furrowing momentarily when Laney had referred to her as an employee. The woman recovered quickly, her expression returning to neutral.

Nolan didn't seem to notice. He nodded thoughtfully, then held up the cup in his hand. "We thought you might like a cup of coffee. But no worries if you don't—"

"I'd love one. Thank you." Laney accepted the steaming cup.

"I didn't know if you'd like cream and sugar. So I brought those, too." He opened his palm to reveal the items.

"Both, please." When Laney accepted the packets from Nolan, her fingers raked his palm. She was sure she could feel electricity dancing along her fingertips at the incidental contact.

Nolan's eyes widened, and he quickly withdrew his hand, as if he'd been shocked.

So maybe the spark of attraction she felt wasn't a one-way street. But he was her potential boss. So exploring the tingle in her fingertips that had crawled up her arms and made her heart skip a beat was not an option.

It was a shame, really. Harper would be leaving for Seattle soon. Then Laney would be something she hadn't been in eight years: kid-free. Not that she planned to get involved with anyone during her summer in Magnolia Lake. Still, it might've been fun getting to know Mr. Serious and teaching him to loosen up a little.

Laney thanked Nolan, then added the cream and sugar to her coffee while Nolan asked Dejah to have someone bring a golf cart up front.

"I thought we'd begin with a tour of the vineyards and the surrounding property before it gets too hot. Then we can tour the lab space and the winery itself."

"Sounds perfect." Laney glanced at her watch. "I have about an hour before I need to leave. I have to meet the leasing agent at the town house I'm renting for the summer."

"Then we'd better get started." Nolan set a timer on his wrist. He opened the front door and gestured for her to go ahead of him. They climbed into the waiting golf cart, and Nolan headed toward the vineyards. They rode in silence a few moments before he spoke again. "I hope you don't think I was giving you a hard time in the interview."

"You were being thorough. If it was my family's livelihood at stake, I would've done the same." Laney studied the expanse of land coming into view. The vineyard was bigger than she'd first thought. The rows of vines were surrounded by a tree-covered rolling hillside. The landscape was serene and verdant. Calming. A beautiful place to live or work.

"The vineyard is lovely this time of year," Nolan said, as if he was inside her head. "When I lived on the property, I'd often have my morning coffee out here or on the upstairs balcony that overlooks the vineyards.

"You no longer live on the property?" Laney regarded his handsome profile.

Warm brown skin. Strong nose and jaw. Full, kissable lips. And eyes like inky depths, always assessing the people and things around him. Nolan was even more handsome than she'd initially believed. And the crisp, clean scent of his cologne with subtle hints of smoky bourbon, velvety peach and sweet, juicy orange made her want to slide a little closer to him on the leather bench of the golf cart. She gripped the armrest on the outer edge of the cart instead, planting her butt firmly in place as she surveyed the vineyard.

"Rented a place a couple months ago," he confirmed.

"So you were committed enough to lease a rental, but you're not quite ready to put down roots and buy a place." The words left Laney's mouth before she realized she was saying them aloud rather than just thinking them. She turned to Nolan, whose dark eyes had narrowed. "I'm sorry, I shouldn't have said that...out loud."

Nolan turned back to the dirt road ahead. His mouth curved in a reluctant smile and he chuckled, shaking his head. "Do you always say *exactly* what you're thinking, Ms. Carlisle?"

"Laney," she corrected him. "Honesty is the best policy, right?" She shrugged. "I like to be straightforward with people, and I'd prefer it if they were the same with me. I find that it reduces misunderstandings and eliminates mixed signals, which are the worst." Laney straightened her glasses.

"Mixed signals *are* the worst." Nolan sighed, and Laney was sure there was a long story behind it. "And you were right. I am confident in my family's ability to make this venture work. But the pragmatist in me is taking a wait-and-see position on staking roots here. A two-year lease seemed like a happy middle ground."

The tension in Laney's shoulders eased. She was glad he didn't seem insulted by her observation.

"You did quite well in there today, Ms. Carlisle," Nolan said. Laney wasn't sure if calling her that was his way of keeping things formal and distant or if it was a test to see how she'd react. "I was quite impressed. Any objection I might've had to hiring someone for this position...just know it wasn't...isn't...about you. I simply question the wisdom of making such an investment at this stage in the company's financial growth."

"Well, *Mr. Valentine*, I hate to cite trite clichés, but you have to spend money to make money. And I assure you, I'm worth every cent."

"I have no doubt of it, Ms. Carlisle." Nolan gave her a quick glance before returning his attention to the path ahead. His smile seemed more genuine and the tension in his broad shoulders seemed to ease. "Now, on to the tour. Welcome to Valentine Vineyards."

They rode through the acres of vines in neat rows, snaking between wooden posts. Workers on riding mowers mowed the spaces between the rows of vines. Others were busy weeding. Nolan noted that their vineyard would incorporate a mix of old-world winemaking techniques with the use of some of the latest technology and processes.

Valentine Vineyards was already in the midst of converting to a fully organic operation, despite some resistance from the winemaker, Maria Rayburn, and Carlos Montoya, the vigneron who managed the crews who planted, maintained and harvested the grapes.

"I'm glad you're already convinced of the benefits of going organic and of the need for sustainable planting and harvesting." Laney nodded. "The less time I need to spend convincing a client to adopt these two philosophies, the more time I can spend on gathering data and doing research and development."

After a tour of the vineyards, they headed back toward the winery.

"What are those buildings for?" Laney pointed to two groupings of small cabins.

"Those casitas were once used to house seasonal immigrant workers. They haven't been used for that purpose for some time."

"Do you have plans for them?"

"My sisters think we should convert them to guest quarters." Nolan parked alongside a large industrial building. He shrugged. "I'm not necessarily opposed to the idea."

"But the pragmatist in you believes you all should take a wait-and-see approach before investing in renovating the casitas." Laney tried to restrain a smile.

"Something like that." Nolan climbed out of the golf cart and Laney did, too.

She smoothed down her skirt and blouse, both of which had gotten wrinkled during the ride. When she glanced up, she met Nolan's heated gaze. Laney's skin warmed and her belly fluttered. She responded with an awkward smile.

"This is where we make the wine." Nolan gestured to the building in front of them abruptly. "I'll show you around."

They toured the winery, which housed several machines like destemmers and grape crushers. Commercial wine presses for both white and red wines. Hoses and pumps for transferring wine or must—a soupy mixture of skins, seeds and stems—to larger containers. Large steel tanks where the wine was stored while fermenting. Rows of casks and racks for storing the bottles.

"This is the current lab area," Nolan said, his tone apologetic. "I know it's not very impressive. But if we invest in hiring an enologist, we'd also invest in expanding and updating the lab." He glanced around the space, then shoved his hands in his pockets. "Again, we're talking about a substantial investment."

"I understand the expense involved, Mr. Valentine." Laney turned to him. "But given the ambitious plans your father has for Valentine Vineyards, it's a necessary investment, whether you choose to bring me on or not."

Nolan rested his chin on his fist, his dark eyes assessing her. "I suppose you're not wrong."

"Well, that's nearly as good as being right, so I'll take it." Laney propped a hand on her hip and tried to hold back a grin. She checked the time on her fitness wearable. "Thank you for the tour, Mr. Valentine. Would you be so kind as to point me in the direction of the parking lot?"

"Of course." He gestured toward the door. "I'll walk you there."

They walked in silence, her body increasingly aware of his and the electricity that crackled between them.

Or was that all in her head?

It couldn't be. Because she could feel the heat emanating from his skin as his deliciously subtle scent drifted over her in the narrow hallway leading to the main floor of the winery. Her internal temperature spiked, and her belly fluttered. Laney inhaled quietly.

Get it together. This is an interview—not *a blind date.*

When they emerged in the sunshine, Laney sighed quietly. She glanced around, surveying the idyllic vineyards and the majestic mountains in the distance. Laney had a warm feeling about Valentine Vineyards, the family who ran it and the workers who labored behind the scenes.

Laney had come on this interview not caring much either way about getting the position. Yes, it was in her field, which she loved. But it was mostly something to do for the summer so she wouldn't go stir-crazy worried about Harper being in Seattle without her. A stopover on the journey to wherever she and her daughter would end up next. But now that she'd met the Valentines and had gotten a chance to tour their operations and learn of their plans for the future, she honestly wanted the job.

She was excited about the prospect of working with the Valentines for the summer as they tried to redeem the legacy of their family who'd once owned the winery. Family they'd never gotten to know. Something about such a noble mission truly moved Laney, and she wanted to be a part of it. Even if it was only for the summer.

They walked across the gravel toward the paved lot where Laney's SUV was parked. She stopped and turned to him, flashing him her brightest smile.

"It was a pleasure to meet you, Mr. Valentine." Laney extended her hand, shaking Nolan's much larger one, which seemed to swallow hers. "Please thank your father and sisters for me. I really enjoyed our chat today and the tour, of course."

Nolan held her hand a few moments after their hands had stilled. Then, suddenly aware of his repeat faux pas, he released her hand and took a generous step backward. Laney could swear his cheeks and forehead were glowing red beneath his brown skin.

"I…uh…will. Of course." Nolan rubbed the back of his neck and cleared his throat. "Someone will be in touch soon. Goodbye, Laney."

She nodded, her mouth curving with an involuntary smile at Nolan's use of her nickname.

Maybe she'd broken in Mr. Serious the tiniest little bit.

Laney practically floated toward her SUV, the heat of Nolan's stare warming her back.

Yes, indeed. She hoped to hear more from Nolan Valentine soon.

Nolan stood on the newly poured concrete walkway, unable to pull his gaze away from Delaney's alluring curves as she strutted across the newly repaved parking lot. Her full hips and heart-shaped bottom were making his heart skip a beat.

Nolan sighed quietly. He *really* liked Delaney Carlisle.

Professionally, she was highly qualified, experienced, had innovative ideas and wasn't afraid to speak her mind. But Nolan was just as drawn to her personally. Laney was extremely intelligent, stunningly gorgeous, spirited yet playful and *fascinating*. He'd been mesmerized by her anecdotes about traveling Europe with her very young daughter and her grandfather who'd been ticking items off his bucket list at the end of his life. He'd enjoyed hearing her stories about growing up on a small farm in West Virginia.

Laney seemed so sweet and genuine with everyone she met. And she wasn't the least intimidated by Nolan's straightforward manner, which some considered brusque. She'd maintained her cheerful demeanor and happily chatted on, unbothered by his prying questions, gruff responses and refusal to call her by her preferred sobriquet.

And she'd made him laugh. Often. Despite his trying his best to hide his amusement.

From what he'd heard about Delaney, he wasn't surprised by her depth of knowledge or her practical experience. What he hadn't expected was that she'd also be so open and down-to-earth. Nor had he expected her to smell like a field of flowers or that he'd feel warm and tingly when her hand touched his. That he'd instantly become preoccupied with thinking about how it would feel to capture her full lips in a kiss or to palm that curvy bottom as he pulled her body against his.

Nolan rubbed his forehead and groaned. He liked Delaney Carlisle…too much.

But he was a management professional. So he'd maintain a *professional* demeanor and keep his wayward thoughts and wandering eyes to himself.

Nolan tipped his chin as Laney waved and drove off in her black luxury SUV.

Wrong time, wrong place. Story of his life.

If he'd met Laney Carlisle any other place, he'd have walked her to her car and asked her out to lunch. But if his family's eager faces were any indication, Laney would be the newest Valentine Vineyards employee. Temporary or not, that meant Delaney Carlisle was off-limits.

Four

Nolan toweled off after doing twenty laps in the pool, grateful that this pool—the second, smaller pool in his newish community—had lanes reserved for lap swimming. School was out. So occasionally getting splashed, being the inadvertent target of a wayward water gun or having a beach ball land in his lane while he was doing laps was inevitable. Still, it was much quieter than the main pool at the front of the community of luxury townhomes.

He folded his towel neatly and set it on the chair beside him to discourage anyone from sitting there. Then he put on his glasses and picked up his battle-worn copy of *Atomic Habits*—one of the nonfiction books he read at least once a year.

"No! Stop it! Don't do that!"

Nolan looked up from his book in the direction of the distressed shriek. It was a little girl wearing aqua blue eyeglasses and a hot pink Ghost-Spider swimsuit with aqua blue straps and matching ribbons at her hips. Her hair was parted down the middle in two large afro puffs. The tawny skin of her cheeks and forehead were flaming red.

The girl was obviously furious about something, and she was making a beeline for the exit.

Nolan swept the area with his gaze. No one was near the girl. So she didn't seem to be in any danger. Still, he watched through the wrought iron gates surrounding the pool as she stomped toward a spot on the outside of the fence where a group of boys stood, looking down at the ground. There was thunder in the little girl's eyes as she shook her finger at the boys.

"Get away from him, right now. He didn't do anything to you. He's minding his business, so you should mind yours." The little girl stooped and lifted something from the ground.

A rock maybe? No, it was a turtle. Though the frightened reptile had retracted its head and legs. She had zero fear of the animal as she cradled it to her chest and stared the boys down.

"Who died and made you the boss?" The largest of the boys stared her down, shoving his fingers through his dirty blond hair and sizing her up with his gray-green eyes. "What makes you think you can tell us what to do? I'll throw rocks at that ugly thing if I want to."

"No, you won't, Edgar." Nolan was standing, his arms folded and his chest puffed out. "Not unless you'd

like your mother to hear about your ungentlemanly behavior here today. I'm sure she'd be very disappointed."

"I…uh… Mr. V," the boy stammered, his eyes suddenly wide. "I… I mean… We were just teasing. We
weren't going to hurt her or the turtle. Honest."

"Liar!" The little girl propped one fist on her hip
and something about the gesture seemed so familiar.
"You were throwing rocks at him. You only stopped because I made you… *Edgar.*" Little Ghost-Spider practically sang the boy's name, her head and neck rocking
as she did.

Edgar's face had gone beet red and he slouched, as if
trying to make himself as small as possible. "I…uh…
Does my mom really need to know about this, Mr. V?"

"Not if you promise never to do anything like this
again and apologize." Nolan tipped a chin toward the
little girl whose expression was still filled with fire and
ice. "Right now."

"Sorry," Edgar muttered.

"That didn't seem much like you meant it," Nolan
noted with one brow raised. "And I meant all of you
should apologize."

"We're sorry," all three boys said in unison, their
gazes lowered.

"I don't want your sad little apologies." The girl evidently wasn't in a forgiving mood. Her tone and expression conveyed disgust. "You should apologize to
the turtle. He's the one you were attacking."

"Sorry, turtle," the boys muttered, as if they'd suffered no greater indignity in their young lives than
being forced to apologize to a reptile.

"Boys, if you want people to like you, try treating them and all forms of life with respect. You wouldn't want someone to treat you, your little sister or your pet dog this way, would you?" Nolan eyed young Edgar, who he knew had all three.

"No, sir." The boy's eyes welled, and he looked genuinely ashamed of himself.

Nolan hoped Edgar was sincere and that they'd all learned a lesson. "Good. Go on, then."

The boys walked off with their tails between their legs. One of them elbowed the ringleader. "I told you it was a dumb idea, *Edgar*."

The little girl suddenly squealed, dropping the turtle—who'd extended its head and limbs, as if realizing it was suddenly safe. It had surprised little Ghost-Spider, who'd evidently taken her love of superheroes to heart.

The turtle started to crawl toward the road.

"Oh no. If he goes into the street, someone is going to run over him, I know it. We have to stop him." Her big eyes pleaded with him.

We?

Nolan sighed quietly. Apparently, he hadn't just become the rescuer of bullied little girls. He'd become the patron saint of turtles with no sense of direction and a death wish. But if this fiery little sprite had been willing to sacrifice herself to save this turtle, helping her was the least he could do.

He went to grab his shirt, but it was dripping wet. An inadvertent victim of children splashing each other with water on the side of the pool. He cursed under his breath, shoved his feet in his sport slides and exited the gate nearest where the little girl stared in horror as the turtle made it as quickly as its limbs would carry it toward the road.

Nolan picked the turtle up by the sides of its shell, being sure to keep his hands away from its head. His first pet had been a turtle, and he'd learned the hard way just how much a bite from those snapping jaws could hurt.

He scanned the line of trees along the back edge of the property. There was a small stream back there. It was likely where the turtle had strayed from. He'd return him there and hope the reptile had learned its lesson about the cruelty of the big, ugly world outside the safety of those trees.

He was about halfway to the stand of trees when he realized the girl was on his heels. Nolan halted and she nearly crashed into him. He swung around.

"Look…hon…"

"Harper," she said indignantly as she shoved her glasses up the bridge of her adorable little nose.

"Harper," he said, "won't your parents be looking for you? Do they even know you're out here? They'll probably be worried."

Harper frowned, then glanced over her shoulder at the enclosed area around the pool. She surveyed the space, then turned back to him, her arms folded. "But I saved him. I want to help you take him back home."

"I applaud you for what you did today, Harper. It was brave of you to stand up for another living thing being harmed. I'm sure your parents will be very proud of you. But I doubt they'll be very happy about you—"

"Harper! What on earth are you doing out here?" A woman in a floppy hat, shades and a swim cover-up that hugged her curvaceous frame and highlighted the glowing brown skin on her shapely legs quickly approached. Her flip-flops slapped the grass angrily and her beach bag thudded against her hip with each step. "You know the rules about talking to strangers. Who on earth is—"

"Laney?"

"Nolan?"

They spoke simultaneously.

"Is this where you're renting a place for the summer?" Nolan asked.

"Yes. We moved in this afternoon. Why is my daughter out here with you, and why are you holding a turtle?" Laney draped a protective arm over Harper's shoulder.

The little girl, whose confused gaze went from her mother's face to his and back again, responded before he could. "You know Mr. V?"

"Mr. Valentine," Laney supplied, removing her sunglasses. "Yes. We met this afternoon at that job interview I went to."

"Your new boss is cool, Mommy," Harper said excitedly. "I rescued a turtle from these mean boys who were throwing rocks at it, and he came to save me from the big one who was a total bully. I had it under control, but it was nice of him just the same," Harper added in a loud whisper, her brown eyes twinkling.

He couldn't help laughing. God, this one was just like her mother: think it, say it.

Laney tried to subdue a grin as she squeezed Harper's shoulder. "Well, then what do you say?"

"Thank you, Mr. Valentine!"

"My pleasure. And Nolan is fine." He shifted the turtle, who had gotten bored with the entire conversation.

"Mr. Nolan." Laney gave her daughter a pointed look, then shifted her gaze to his. She seemed to be taking him in below the neck for the first time. "I… uh…you're not wearing a—"

"My shirt got soaked. Kids with those damn high-velocity water cannons," he muttered. "And our friend here—" he lifted the turtle "—decided to make a mad dash for the road."

"It's a turtle." Laney raised an eyebrow. "How quick of an escape could he possibly make?"

"A lot faster than the rate at which my shirt would dry," he assured her, and all three of them laughed.

"The villains have apparently run off." Laney glanced around. "So what are you two doing now?"

"We don't want him to get run over by a car or anything, Mommy," Harper said. "So Mr. Nolan is taking the turtle to the woods. I wanted to come so I could say goodbye, but Mr. Nolan said you probably wouldn't like that."

"And he was right." Laney gave her daughter a stern look, but then her expression softened. She stroked her daughter's cheek. "If anything ever happened to you…"

"It didn't." Harper wrapped her wiry arms around her mother's waist. The move made the back of Laney's swim cover-up rise a little, flashing more of her luscious thighs. "I'm fine."

"This time. But we're going to have another discussion about stranger danger just the same." Laney wagged a finger.

"Yes, Mommy. But now that you're here, can we go with Mr. Nolan to return the turtle to the woods?" Harper pleaded.

"Of course, darling. Sounds like a fun adventure." Laney grasped her daughter's hand and tipped her chin. She met Nolan's gaze, as if she was trying very hard not to catch a glimpse of his bare chest. "Lead the way."

"Actually, maybe we should grab some water to make sure our friend here stays hydrated." Nolan carefully examined the reptile's skin.

"I've got some." Laney produced a bottle of water from her bag.

"Perfect!" Harper gripped her mother's hand. "Now let's get turtle back home. His mommy is probably missing him, too."

Laney and Nolan shared a smile and something about it made his heart skip a beat.

God, this woman is gorgeous.

"We should hurry." Laney cleared her throat. "Mr. Nolan is probably very cold out here without his shirt."

Harper giggled as she tugged her mother toward the trees ahead.

Nolan clenched his teeth to restrain a laugh.

Delaney Harper was a handful, and so was her mini-me.

They set the turtle loose in the woods, wetting him down with half the bottle of water and creating a puddle the turtle could sip from with the rest of it. Then they returned to the pool. Nolan headed back toward his chair and Laney and Harper followed.

"Can we sit here with you?" Harper asked.

Nolan hadn't considered that they might want to hang out with him. It would be awkward given that Laney was a candidate for employment, and he was already far too taken with her. But saying no would make him seem incredibly rude. So what choice did he have?

"I…uh…sure," Nolan stammered.

"Sweetie, it looks like Mr. Nolan was sitting here quietly reading a book before he was interrupted by your little turtle adventure." Laney squeezed her daughter's hand and gave him a polite smile. "He'd probably like very much to be left alone or maybe he's here with friends."

"I'm not," Nolan said a little too quickly. He cleared his throat, his face feeling flushed. "Those are my things on that chair."

"See? We can't leave him here all alone, Mommy." Harper seemed heartbroken by the prospect of him being lonely.

But he wasn't lonely…*exactly*. He had his work and his family. He wasn't alone. He was just…very, *very* single.

"If you're sure you don't mind. I know this is really awkward when you're in the midst of deciding whether or not you'll hire me." Laney frowned, seemingly as uncomfortable as he was about the whole thing. But having her say it aloud made it feel slightly less so.

"You're the best, Mommy. Of course they'll hire

you," Harper said so sincerely Nolan felt like a heel for considering not hiring Laney.

Still, he kept his mouth shut as he removed his things from the lounger beside him. He hung his wet shirt on the back of his chair. The other items he set on a little table situated between his chair and the one Harper had claimed for herself.

Nolan tried to return to politely reading his book as Laney applied Kinlò sunscreen to her daughter, but Harper chatted on happily about her big trip to Seattle, asking him if he'd ever been there.

"I haven't."

He'd been few places outside of Nashville. He'd even gone to college at Fisk, where he'd gotten joint bachelor's and master's degrees in a program connected to Vanderbilt—both based in Nashville. But he wasn't about to admit that to an elementary-school-age child who'd traveled Europe before the age of five.

Harper continued chatting a mile a minute, as Laney carefully applied sunscreen to her own arms and legs. Nolan tried his best not to look at her, giving her chatty little mini-me his full attention instead.

Still, he couldn't help glancing at her in his peripheral vision. Noticing how smooth her creamy brown skin appeared and how shapely her calves and thighs were. When Laney stood and tugged the tunic over her head and tossed it onto the chair, Nolan sucked in an audible breath.

She was beyond gorgeous in a black two-piece suit that showed off her toned belly. A tattoo of the sun centered on her navel.

He suddenly found himself gasping for air. Was he hyperventilating?

"Are you okay, Mr. Nolan?" Harper put a hand on his shoulder and studied him with her wide, brown eyes.

"I...uh...yes. Yes, of course. I'm fine. Thank you, Harper." Nolan picked up his book and buried his nose in it. But not before he caught a glimpse of Laney rubbing sunscreen on her stomach with a deliciously impish grin.

Nolan's skin heated and his heart thumped in his chest as he imagined all of the ways he'd like to get acquainted with the incredibly enticing Laney Carlisle.

Five

Laney felt the tiniest bit of guilt about Nolan practically hyperventilating when she whipped off her swim cover-up a little more dramatically than necessary. But he'd recovered rather quickly, and now she couldn't seem to restrain the wicked smile that he'd no doubt noticed, too.

What was it about Nolan Valentine that made her feel playful and silly and slightly audacious? She enjoyed getting a rise out of the straitlaced CFO and making him reveal a little of himself. The vulnerable, tender flesh beneath the armor he wore on the outside.

Laney recognized the gleaming, shiny armor Nolan had donned to protect his heart. Because she'd been wearing a suit of it herself. Only hers was dinged up and worn out. And she'd been slowly but surely shedding pieces of it for the past few years.

She had her daughter to thank for that.

Laney had built an iron fence around her heart after the devastating breakup with Derrick. But giving and receiving unconditional love from her daughter had slowly opened the heart that had once been rusted shut.

Maybe she'd never love anyone again the way she'd once loved Derrick. But for the first time in eight years, she entertained a tiny glimmer of hope that she could have what her sister had. A solid relationship with a man who loved her deeply, two beautiful children and a big, welcoming family.

Despite Savannah's inauspicious introduction to the Abbotts, they loved her now. All of them, even crotchety old Parker. And they treated her like she was one of their own.

She loved that for her big sister. But Laney wanted a little of that for herself.

Not that she was angling to make Nolan hers. After all, she was only in Magnolia Lake for the summer. Still, there was something appealing about the man.

Nolan was her flavor of brainy without behaving as if everyone else around him was somehow deficient. He was adorably awkward and a bit of a dork like her. But then *quelle surprise*! The man looked damn good bare-chested in athletic slides and swim trunks with his feet propped up on the lounge as he pretended to be reading instead of ogling her.

Okay, so yes. Maybe a vision of her licking whipped cream off those toned pecs of his had flashed through her brain. But it wasn't as if she planned to do anything about it.

"Ready to get into the pool, Mommy?" Harper asked.

"Absolutely!" Laney smiled at her daughter, who was wearing a swimsuit with her favorite superhero of the moment: Ghost-Spider, Spider-Woman Gwen Stacy's alter ego.

"Are you coming, Mr. Nolan?" Harper bounced on her toes.

"Thank you for the invitation, Harper." Nolan smiled politely. "But I got my laps in before you two arrived. I'm going to do a little reading, then head back to my place."

"You'd rather read than swim with me and Mommy?" Harper looked at Nolan as if he'd sprouted an additional head. She turned to Laney and loud-whispered, "Who brings a book to the pool?"

"Lots of people," Laney said loud enough to be heard, realizing Nolan had surely heard her daughter's comment. "There's a reason beach reads is an entire category."

"Really?" Harper scratched her head. "Adults are strange," she muttered as she walked toward the shallow end of the pool.

"Sorry about that," Laney said. "She's seven, almost eight. The world seems pretty simple to her right now."

"I understand. At least, I comprehend that life feels simple for the average seven-year-old. That just wasn't my personal experience." Nolan's eyes hinted at a deep pain Laney knew well. Loss at an early age.

"How old were you when you lost your mom?" Laney asked.

Nolan's bitter laugh surprised her. "I didn't exactly *lose* my mother. She just…left."

He grimaced. "I was six years old at the time. So that was more than thirty years ago."

"Well, it was a loss, just the same." Laney sank onto the end of the lounger beside Nolan and placed a gentle hand on his forearm. "I'm sorry you had to grow up without your mother. No matter how long it's been… The pain never really goes away. It just dulls a bit."

Nolan replaced his bookmark and closed his book. "You lost your mother, too?"

Laney removed her hand from his arm. Her shoulders tensed. "Savannah and I lost our parents in a fire at our apartment when I was five and she was nine. My grandfather raised us."

"I'm sorry, Laney." Nolan's voice was as gentle as a caress.

Why did that make her feel incredibly vulnerable?

"I should go." She stood, wrapping her arms around her middle. "I'm surprised Harper has been so patient."

"Looks like your daughter has made a few friends." Nolan nodded toward where Harper sat on the concrete cross-legged, giggling with three other little girls and playing a card game.

"So much for our swim date." Laney folded her arms in a mock pout. "I've been stood up by my daughter. I should've brought a book, too. What are you reading anyway?"

Nolan held up a worn copy of *Atomic Habits*.

"Not typical beach-reading fare," she remarked. "But self-improvement is never a bad thing."

She sank onto the seat beside Nolan, fully aware it was Harper's chair, not hers.

"True." Nolan didn't glance up from his book, but Laney could swear his neck and shoulders tensed.

Laney took the opportunity to sneak another glimpse of the defined muscles of Nolan's arms and shoulders.

Maybe he wasn't going to enter the Mr. Universe competition anytime soon, but Nolan Valentine clearly took care of his body. The hard chest and toned, firm abs he'd been hiding beneath that buttoned-up dress shirt earlier were impressive, to say the least.

Suddenly warm, Laney picked up her bag and rummaged through it for another bottle of water. Even from where they sat, she could hear her daughter asking the other girls rapid-fire questions. What were their names? Where did they live? Had they ever been to Seattle?

A slow grin spread across Nolan's face.

"What is it?" She should be minding her own business and allowing Nolan to read in peace, but Laney couldn't resist asking.

"It's obvious where Harper gets her inquisitive nature."

"As my grandfather would say, she got it honest." Laney grinned, too. Her heart overflowed with love and pride as she watched her daughter.

"And that fierce spirit of hers..." Nolan regarded her through the sun-darkened lenses of his eyeglasses. Laney couldn't see his eyes clearly, but something about the way he looked at her warmed her skin and caused her belly to flop. "Did Harper get that honest, too?"

"Yes," Laney said after what felt like far too long.

Her synapses weren't firing on all cylinders for some reason. If she had to guess why, it would probably have something to do with the package of man candy coolly assessing her. "But from her aunt Savannah, not me."

"I could definitely see that." Nolan chuckled, returning his gaze to his book. "So Seattle… Do you go there often?"

"It'll be our first time." Laney's throat tightened at the question.

"So Laney's dad moved there recently?"

"About a year ago. When he moved back to the States for good."

"He lived overseas?" Nolan had given her his full attention again.

"He worked on the front lines for an NGO in famine-stricken areas of Africa and Asia. Eventually worked his way up to a leadership role. He felt he could do more good that way."

"But he chose to move back," Nolan prompted, lazily glancing down at his book again, as if only mildly interested in their conversation.

"His father had to have open-heart surgery. It made him realize that he'd been giving everything he had to the rest of the world and neglecting his own family."

There was a lingering silence between them. A question he wanted to ask her but wouldn't permit himself to.

Suddenly, there was a rumble of thunder in the distance.

Laney hopped to her feet and looked toward the sky studying the dark gray clouds that were moving in, then looked over at Harper and her friends, who were still playing happily.

Nolan was already on his feet, gathering his things. He slipped his partially dry shirt over his head. "It's going to storm. They'll be closing the pool soon."

"I know." Laney stuffed her things into her bag and slipped on her cover-up. "Harper will be disappointed, but we can come back another time."

Laney gathered her daughter, who pouted over the interruption of her pool time. Nolan held her bag while she cajoled her sullen daughter into her swim cover-up and shoes. Then the three of them left the pool along with everyone else.

"Well, I'm headed in this direction," Nolan said.

"So are we," Harper said. "You can walk with us."

"Sure." Nolan surveyed the darkening sky. "Why not?"

They walked toward their houses with Harper chattering the entire way about her new friends, her upcoming trip and the new Spider-Man movie Laney had promised to take her to for her birthday in a few weeks.

"This is us," Laney said when they arrived at her street. Each street had four townhomes on it—two on each side.

"Really?" Nolan's eyes widened. "I'm on the very next street. Which unit are you in?" he asked.

"The one on the end on this side." Laney pointed to her right, still stunned that she and Nolan were living in the same community and so close. Which was beginning to feel less and less like a coincidence. "Which house are you in?" She asked.

Nolan stared at her in disbelief. "I'm in the unit on the end right behind yours," he said. "Guess that makes us—"

"You're our neighbor?" Harper practically squealed. "Awesome! Right, Mommy? Now you have a new friend here, too."

Laney and Nolan shared an uncomfortable smile and agreed for Harper's benefit.

Nope. Definitely not a coincidence.

As soon as she got inside and put Harper to bed for the night, she was going to call her sister. Because Savannah Abbott had some serious explaining to do.

Six

It was two days later and Laney was still fuming at her sister for failing to mention the town house she'd reserved for her was directly behind the one Nolan Valentine was leasing. Savannah hadn't had an ounce of shame about it. In fact, her sister thought it was hilarious.

"I knew you two would get along well," Savannah had practically crowed. "And just in case Nolan tried to put a stop to his family hiring you for the summer… Well, I figured it would be a lot harder for him to do that when the two of you were neighbors."

"They haven't hired me yet," Laney had reminded her sister. "And perhaps they won't."

"They will. Trust me," Savannah said confidently. "And they're going to want you to stay on beyond the summer. So you should think about it, Laney." Savannah's voice softened. "I miss having my sister living so close. And remember how we always wished we'd had aunts and uncles and cousins growing up? Well, our kids do. Don't you want them to grow up together?"

Laney heaved a quiet sigh. Of course she wanted their children to be close. But life wasn't ever that simple.

"There's Daddy!" Harper bounced on her heels excitedly as a green all-electric imported sedan parked at the arrivals curb of the Seattle-Tacoma International Airport.

Laney's shoulders tensed as she regarded her ex, whose brilliant smile made his handsome face light up like a Christmas tree when he saw their daughter.

She should be over the surreal shock of seeing her grad school sweetheart again. He'd flown out to Ithaca to see Harper once a month for the past six months. Yet, she still felt tension in her shoulders and a knot in her gut whenever she saw Derrick.

Derrick got out of the car and hugged Harper, who'd jumped into his arms the moment he'd set foot on the curb.

"Daddy! I missed you so much!" Harper squeezed her father's neck.

"I missed you, too, sweetie." Derrick hugged her tight. "I'm so glad you're finally here."

Laney gritted her teeth to keep from making a loud *humph* sound.

Derrick had been absent the majority of Harper's life. He'd suddenly appeared like some superhero. And now he'd become the center of her daughter's life. So yes, she was slightly bitter.

Laney eased off the tension in her jaw before she cracked a molar.

"God, you look more beautiful every time I see you, Lanes." Derrick's big brown eyes were filled with an affection she didn't want and he had no right to feel. He set Harper down and gave Laney a hug.

For Harper's sake, she accepted it. But she didn't hug him back.

"Thank you so much for letting Harper come to Seattle. I can't tell you how much this means to me and to my parents."

He whispered the words in her ear, so only she could hear them. If he'd done it to diffuse her anger, it'd worked. Because now she was telling herself she should be grateful Derrick and his family wanted to be in Harper's life. Because that was what her daughter wanted, too.

"You're welcome," she whispered back, extricating herself from his grip.

He released her reluctantly, then turned his attention to Harper, who was brimming with happiness.

"When do I get to meet Grandma and Grandpa and my cousins?" she asked.

"They're waiting for us at the house, and they can't wait to meet you in person. C'mon. You two go ahead and get in while I put your luggage in the trunk." Derrick opened the two passenger doors.

Laney started to object; to tell him she was more than capable of loading her own luggage into the car. But she'd been doing all the heavy lifting for the past eight years. The least he could do was load her luggage.

Now, if she could just get through the weekend without telling Derrick exactly what she thought of him, everything would be all right.

Nolan drummed his fingers on his desk and stared at the file with *Delaney Carlisle* handwritten neatly on the tab.

The decision to hire Laney had been unanimous, even if his vote had been reluctant. Not because he thought hiring Laney was a bad investment. Because it put an end to any thoughts he'd entertained of getting to know Laney better.

Nolan enjoyed their brief encounter at the pool. It was the first time in months he'd been truly interested in someone. So, of course, she was the one person he shouldn't be interested in.

"You still haven't called her?" Naya leaned against the doorway in a tailored, sleeveless jumpsuit. Her short natural hair was dyed purple and worn in a curly faux hawk. She shoved her hands in her pockets. "I told you I'd be happy to make the call."

"No, I'll do it." Nolan leaned back in his chair, wishing he'd closed the door to his office on the second floor of the winery. Then he would've had time to put away the file before his nosy younger sister entered the room. "I had a few things to take care of first."

"Things like staring at that folder while you drum your fingers on the desk?" Naya slid into the seat on the other side of his desk. "Seriously, Nole, you have *zero* game face. It's the reason you never win on poker night."

His sister wasn't wrong about that. Good thing they only played for low stakes at the monthly poker night that consisted mostly of family and friends. Naya was the lone regular female participant.

"Obviously, you're feeling some kind of way about making this call. Is working with Laney going to be an issue for you?" Naya's expression had gone from teasing to concerned. "Because as fantastic as we all believe Laney will be for Valentine Vineyards, this shouldn't feel weird or uncomfortable for you."

"Why would it be?" Nolan pulled his shoulders back. "I'm attracted to Laney, sure. But it's not like we had a previous relationship."

"You sure? Because it sounds like you two are turtle-rescuing pool buddies." Naya's dark brown eyes glimmered. He could tell she was trying to restrain a smile.

"We're neighbors who happen to be friendly. It's a small town." He shrugged. "And any attraction I might've felt for Laney... It's already long forgotten."

"You're a horrible liar." Naya rolled her eyes. "But whatever. Are you gonna call her, or should I?"

"I'm calling her right now. Happy?"

He picked up the landline phone on his desk and carefully dialed the number on Delaney's résumé. He drummed his fingers on the desk while feigning a look of disinterest and hoping to God that the call went to her voice mail.

No such luck.

"Hello?"

"Hello, Delaney. This is Nolan Valentine, from Valentine Vineyards."

"Yes, Nolan. I know who you are."

He could hear the smile in her voice. Picture it on that gorgeous face of hers.

"I trust you haven't encountered any more intrepid turtles trying to make a break for it."

God, there was the most adorable lilt in her voice.

It instantly elicited an involuntary smile from him. His sister made kissy faces. Nolan frowned at Naya, who stifled a giggle. He cleared his throat and straightened his tie.

"No. No, I haven't." Nolan avoided his sister's gaze. "The reason for my call, Laney, is I…that is… *We* would like to offer you a ninety-day contract as an enologist here at the winery. At the end of the contract, we can both assess whether we'd like to continue the relationship…the working relationship, that is. Between you and the vineyard, not between me and you specifically, of course."

Stop talking. Naya mouthed the words to him and he realized he'd hardly come up for air.

He stopped rambling and drew in a deep breath.

"At the salary I requested or the one you proposed?" Laney asked carefully.

"We'd like to split the difference and reassess at the end of the contract."

There was silence on the other end of the line.

"Sounds fair," she said finally. "I won't be back in town until late Sunday night. Would it be all right if I started on Wednesday? I have a few things I need to take care of."

"Of course." Nolan felt an unexpected sense of relief

at Laney's acceptance. "I'll email the offer letter and a link for you to begin completing the paperwork online." He gave Naya a thumbs-up and she pumped her fist.

"That's sounds…"

"Hey, Lanes, I promised Harper and her cousins I'd take them out for ice cream. Wanna come? My treat," a man's voice said cheerfully.

Lanes? It was definitely the ex and it sounded like their relationship was *extremely* friendly.

"Just a moment." Laney muted her phone, then returned a few seconds later. "Sorry about the interruption. That sounds good. I'll look for your email and complete the paperwork on Sunday. It'll give me something to do while I'm waiting at the airport."

"Great. Then enjoy your trip and have a safe flight back."

"I will, thank you. Oh, and Harper says hello."

Nolan couldn't help smiling. "Tell Harper I said hello and that I hope she has an amazing time in Seattle."

When Nolan glanced up at his sister, she gave him a knowing smile.

"Oh my God, you are so fucked." Naya grinned.

"What are you talking about?"

"You're crazy about both of them. One afternoon at the pool and they've both got you wrapped around their little fingers, don't they?" Naya seemed endlessly amused by this.

"I'm not wrapped around anyone's finger." He sent the email to Laney, as promised. "I learned my lesson the hard way."

Naya scooted to the edge of her seat, her elbows leaning on the desk. Her expression had morphed from teasing to pitying and it made his skin feel tight and itchy.

"I know the divorce was devastating. But you can't just close yourself off to the possibility of ever finding love again, Nolan," Naya said gently. "It isn't healthy."

"But I can establish rules to reduce the chance of it happening again. Don't date anyone I have to work with—in any capacity. Don't get involved with someone whose ex is still very much in the picture. And don't date anyone with kids." Nolan ticked each item off on his fingers. "If I got involved with Laney, I'd be breaking all three of those rules. Besides, Valentine Vineyards isn't a dating service, Naya. We're hiring Laney as an enologist. Not as my potential love match. So please leave my nonexistent love life out of this, all right? I'm content with my life the way it is."

He was irritated that his sister was meddling, but he knew she meant well. Still, he hated to see the pity in his sisters' eyes whenever the subject of his divorce came up.

"Why don't you let Chandra and Dad know Laney has agreed to our terms?"

"Fine. I'll go." Naya stood, making it clear she realized this was his not-so-subtle way of getting rid of her. "Love you, Nole."

"Love you, too."

Nolan heaved a quiet sigh when he was finally alone again. He couldn't help wondering about the man whose voice he'd heard, presumably Harper's father. Laney's ex.

Working with Laney was all the reason he needed

to dismiss any ideas of getting to know her better outside of work. But an ex who called her a cutesy name like *Lanes*?

Nolan rubbed the back of his neck and shook his head. He'd played that game before and he'd lost his heart. He was never going to make that mistake again.

Seven

"Did you get the job, Mommy?" Harper bounced on her toes.

"I did. You were right, sweetheart."

"Yay!" Harper wrapped her arms around Laney's waist and hugged her. "Now you'll get to work with your friend Mr. Nolan every day."

A knot tightened in her stomach.

She'd been thinking about that from the moment Nolan offered her the contract.

Laney was excited to accept the position. She loved being on vineyards and was fascinated by the science that went into making the perfect glass of wine. But she couldn't help feeling a bit disappointed that accepting the position meant putting an end to whatever might have been brewing between her and Nolan.

She was really starting to like the man.

She'd have to work with Nolan every day. Would likely run into him around the community and at the pool. And she'd have to pretend she wasn't incredibly attracted to him.

Pretending of any sort was *not* her forte.

"Lanes, you okay?" Derrick's hand on her arm startled her from her thoughts.

"I'm fine." She gently pulled away. "Where's Harper?"

"Harper went to tell her cousins we're going for ice cream. She told you that, but you were a million miles away. You sure everything is okay?"

"I'm fine, just thinking. I have ninety days to convince them to add an enologist to their staff."

"*An* enologist," Derrick repeated. "Not necessarily you."

"That's right." Laney thought of her sister's plea for her to accept the position, if they offered it.

Magnolia Lake was an adorable little town, and its inherent small-town charm was growing on her. But she planned to relocate to a city with multiple vineyards and educational opportunities for her daughter, who was gifted in math and science.

She hadn't had access to good STEM programs when she was Harper's age. And Laney wanted her daughter to have all the advantages she hadn't enjoyed. So despite Magnolia Lake's appeal, staying didn't seem like an option.

"Once your contract ends…maybe you and Harper could move here to Seattle."

A vein in Laney's temple throbbed, and her hands

were shaking. "Until six months ago, you couldn't care less about your daughter. Now you're trying to dictate where we live?"

"That isn't true, Laney." Derrick's eyes were filled with regret. "I *never* stopped thinking about you or about our child."

"Yet you never reached out to me. Not until you thought your dad was dying, and *he* wanted to meet his granddaughter."

"I was afraid you'd never forgive me. That you wouldn't allow me to see our daughter without an ugly court battle. And I wasn't going to put you or her through that." Derrick massaged his neck. "My dad's health scare gave me the courage to reach out to you. But I've thought about you and our child every single day since you walked out of my life. This might feel sudden to you, but it isn't to me. I've been hoping to reunite with you and Harper for a very long time."

"We aren't Peaches and Herb, and we're not *reuniting*," Laney said. "This is about you developing a relationship with our daughter. Understood?"

"Of course." Derrick winced, as if her rejection had wounded his soul. "That's why I'm asking you to consider moving to Seattle. I don't want to miss any more of Harper's life. I want to be there for science fairs, school plays and ballet recitals. To bandage her knee when she falls or feed her chicken soup when she's sick…"

Derrick dragged a hand through his short curls and heaved a sigh. When Laney didn't respond, he continued.

"I know that raising Harper on your own hasn't been

easy. Going forward, I want to be there for both of you. Because I love Harper with all my heart." Derrick pressed a hand to his chest. "And after all these years, I still love you, too, Lanes."

Had he just said he still loved her?

"You do *not* get to sweep back into our lives and—"

"You're still hurt and angry. I get it, Lanes. I do. But like it or not, we're a family now. I just want to do everything I can for both of you. Like securing Harper a spot at a prestigious girls' school with a STEM-education focus. There's a long waiting list, but the dean owes me a favor. I'm sure I could get her in."

She knew exactly which program he was referring to. There was a two-year waiting list. Could he really get Harper in by calling in a favor?

"There's still a matter of my work," Laney said.

Derrick smiled. "I've been telling the dean at our university about the vintner and enology program you attended in New York. Given the increased interest in winemaking here in the region, I've convinced him the program would be a great addition to our offerings."

Laney shrugged, wanting to hear more, but not wanting to seem too eager.

"Dean Moss would love to chat with you to learn more. And between us, he asked if I thought you'd be a good candidate to consult with if the university decides to establish its own program." His dark eyes sparkled. "You've always loved teaching, Laney. If this works out, you could shape the program from the outset, and you'd be a shoe-in as a professor. It'd give you the best of both worlds, teaching and enology."

Derrick looked like he was waiting for a cookie or at the very least a pat on the head. But she wasn't about to tell him that a top-notch STEM school for their daughter and the chance to teach enology were, in fact, her ideal situation.

"I appreciate your eagerness to be a part of Harper's life but—"

"Will you at least consider moving to Seattle?" Derrick pleaded.

"We're moving to Seattle with Daddy?" Harper squealed, then turned to her cousins.

All three girls shouted for joy as they held hands and jumped up and down.

"No, Harper, I..." Laney sucked in a frustrated breath and glared at Derrick.

Harper and her cousins had run to tell their grandparents the news. Her daughter would be so disappointed when she discovered they weren't moving to Seattle.

Laney could strangle her ex.

"You did that on purpose, Derrick."

"I didn't, I swear. But it's good to know this is what Harper wants, right?"

Laney rolled her eyes. "You promised me ice cream. I want a triple-scoop banana split with whipped cream, nuts and cherries. *Now*."

Derrick chuckled. "I'll buy you the entire damn ice cream stand, if that'll make you stay."

"It won't." She stormed past him, purse in hand.

Laney thought about her sister back in Magnolia Lake, about Valentine Vineyards and about Nolan as she rode in the car in silence. She wanted to dismiss

Derrick's suggestion, but she couldn't ignore the pure joy on her daughter's face—reflected in the side mirror.

She still had no idea where her daughter would go to school in the fall. She needed to make a decision soon.

Nolan had spent the past two days up in Nashville helping his brother Sebastian, CEO of Valentine Textiles.

The sale of their once family-owned textile firm had been completed a few months ago. Sebastian had agreed to stay on after the California conglomerate that purchased the firm had offered him the role of CEO. They liked the optics of a Valentine sitting at the helm. It made employees and investors less nervous about the conglomerate's acquisition of the firm. And since Sebastian had hoped to become CEO someday, taking the position made sense for him, too. But Bas didn't seem happy in his new role. Something Nolan thought it better not to mention.

Valentine Textile's new CFO had been struggling, so as a favor to Sebastian, Nolan, the company's previous CFO, had spent the past two days trying to bring her up to speed.

Honestly? The appointee seemed less than qualified. She was a sister or cousin of someone in the conglomerate. So Bas hadn't had a choice in her selection.

Nolan had returned last night, just in time for Delaney's first day at the vineyard.

Not that he was excited about seeing Laney again. Okay, he was. But more importantly, he was eager to see if this expensive experiment would bear fruit.

His family wasn't at the villa, so he strolled over to the winery. He passed the lab area, which would be Laney's domain. The space was nowhere near adequate if they were going to hire on an enologist full-time. But they'd spruced up the space a bit and brought in a few new pieces of equipment. His first job that day was to acquisition a new desk and chair for Laney.

As he approached his office on the second floor, he heard his sisters' voices and the rumble of his father's laughter.

"What are you all doing here?" Nolan walked into his office.

"Ta-da!" Naya's eyes gleamed as both she and Chandra, with her burgeoning belly, swept their arms dramatically toward the far corner of his office. "Surprise."

Nolan studied the desk and chair set up with a lamp, phone and desk blotter. The table that was once there had been moved to the side and was stocked with a single-cup coffee maker and different types of coffee and teas. A brand-new water dispenser sat beside the coffee station.

"I love it." Nolan had been saying for months that there should be a coffee and water station on the second floor so he didn't have to go to the first floor where he was inevitably drawn into a lengthy conversation with Maria, their winemaker, or one of the other employees. It often sidetracked his day.

"But you didn't need to replace the desk. I hardly use it."

"Exactly," Chandra said. "You've often said this could be a shared office space—like the one Naya and

I share over at the villa." His sister rubbed her belly with one hand and held on to her back with the other.

"If one of the guys comes onboard, we could definitely do that," Nolan agreed.

"We were thinking the same thing." Naya handed him a fresh cup and smiled.

Nolan accepted the steaming mug, his Spider-Sense tingling. He sipped the premium coffee. But then the realization hit him like a punch in the gut, startling him.

He splashed coffee on the tiled floor.

"Tell me you didn't set this office up for Delaney."

"You said it was too large for one person," Chandra reminded him.

"And her desk is *way* over there." Naya gestured dramatically. "You two will be sharing a much bigger space than the one Chandra and I share."

"But if you'd like more privacy, we can always install partitions around her desk," Chandra added.

"And you're asking me this ten minutes before she's due to arrive?" Nolan set the mug down on his desk. He eyed his sisters, neither of whom had an ounce of shame about it.

"We thought it'd be a nice surprise." Naya shrugged innocently.

His sister could be described as a lot of things; innocent was not one of them. Even as a toddler, she'd been a schemer.

"No, what you thought is that, given how little time I have to react to your 'surprise,' I'd give you a pass."

"I was as skeptical as you are about this entire setup. I still have my doubts," his father admitted. "But your sisters make excellent points about why it makes sense for you and Laney to share an office. You're the person she'll be working with most closely and the person most skeptical about the viability of her position." His father ticked each reason off on his fingers. "Your offices should be relatively close."

"*Relatively* close," Nolan repeated. "Not practically sitting on top of each other." Why did just saying those words make his temperature rise?

"You're being dramatic, son." His dad gestured across the large space. It was at least two times as big as Naya and Chandra's shared office. "That being said…" His father got up from Nolan's chair. "I agreed to this setup on one condition. You had to okay it. If you're not, we'll set her up at the little desk in the lab and do our best to make her comfortable there."

Nolan frowned as he scanned the room. He enjoyed his solitude, but he couldn't bear the thought of Laney at the rickety old desk and chair in that cold, drab laboratory.

Chandra sensed that his defenses were down. She crept in closer. "It would only be for a few months. After that, Laney will either move on, or we'll invest in a modern lab space for her, complete with office."

"Surely, you can share the space for a few months, son."

"Besides, Laney will probably spend most of her time down in the lab, in the winery or out in the vineyard," Chandra noted.

"Three months." Nolan held up three fingers. "Then she's out, one way or another."

His father patted his shoulder and smiled. "Thank you, son. Now, we'll let you get to work. Your sisters and I are conducting Laney's orientation. There will be pastries over at the villa and we're ordering in sandwiches from Magnolia Lake Bakery later today."

Nolan took his seat behind the desk and turned on his laptop.

"The three of you are handling her orientation, huh?" Nolan tried to sound nonchalant. "You didn't include me?"

Chandra and Naya exchanged knowing looks, and his younger sister giggled.

"You've been out of the office for two days, son. We assumed you'd be busy catching up. Didn't want to impose on your time."

Oh, so now they're concerned about imposing?

"Like you said, I am the person she'll be working with most closely. So—"

"Actually, I'm the person our new *enologist* will be working most closely with." Maria Rayburn, their winemaker, poked a thumb to her chest as she leaned against the open doorway and frowned. "I hope you've scheduled time for Delaney to meet with me today."

Maria's dark eyes narrowed as she scanned the room. She wore a short-sleeve Henley shirt, broken-in jeans and well-worn boots. Her dark, wavy hair was pulled back into a low ponytail, as it had been nearly every day since Nolan had met the woman.

The room's temperature rose instantly. Partly because Maria's obvious irritation put them all on edge. Partly because heat seemed to radiate off his father, whose fascination with their winemaker had become increasingly obvious to his children, if not to the object of his affection.

"Of course." His father stood taller and straightened his tie. "I was just coming to see you, Maria. Laney can spend a couple of hours with you either after our catered lunch for everyone or at the end of the day. Up to you."

"After lunch is fine. I only need five minutes to say what I need to say." Maria folded her arms. "Don't worry, I'll show her the ropes and cooperate with this little experiment, as promised." She perked up. "Is that coffee?"

"It is." Ray gestured toward the coffee station. "Help yourself."

Chandra, Naya and Nolan watched as their dad joined Maria at the table and chatted with her as they made their individual cups of coffee.

"This congregating-in-my-office thing…not gonna work," Nolan said just loud enough for his sisters to hear.

The phone on Nolan's desk rang. He answered it on speaker. "Yes, Dejah?"

"Our new employee has arrived. Shall I send her over to her new office?"

Nolan could hear the smirk in Dejah's voice. He chose to ignore it.

"Please ask her to have a seat in the great room. My father and sisters will be over soon," Nolan said calmly, as if he didn't have a single reservation about sharing his space with the gorgeous Delaney Carlisle.

"Will do." Dejah ended the call.

"You sure you're good with this?" Chandra asked.

"I'm fine." Nolan nodded toward his sister's burgeoning belly. "You'd better get started. It's gonna take you a while to get over there."

Chandra smacked his shoulder with her open palm. Even through his shirt, it stung.

"Ouch!"

"That's what you get for making fun of a pregnant woman." She shook a finger. "Just four more weeks until this baby is out," Chandra muttered as she left the room. "Then I dare someone to say something smart. I'll take on all of y'all."

"Quit pissing off the pregnant lady," Naya scolded. "Now I'm gonna have to make her some tea and rub her feet."

Nolan chuckled. Just about everyone in their family had been on foot-rubbing duty at some point over the last few months. Thankfully, her husband, Julian, was more than happy to rub her feet and back. Which probably explained how the two of them had ended up with the surprise baby they were expecting in four short weeks.

Nolan tried his best to bleach the thought from his brain. He did not want to think about his sister and Dr. Julian Brandon, the town's general practitioner, beyond the fact that the man, nearly a decade her junior, seemed to be good for Chandra. And the two of them seemed very happy.

Honestly, he was a little jealous. He just hoped that Chandra and Julian's marriage wouldn't suffer the same fate every other marriage in this family had, including his own.

When his father and Maria finally sauntered out, Nolan shut the door behind them to enjoy his remaining moments of solitude and tried not to think about the gorgeous woman who'd commandeered his brain.

Eight

Delaney nibbled on the last of the bear claw she'd nabbed from the leftover pastries from that morning. She'd completed some additional paperwork and got set up with her shiny, new company-issued laptop.

As a contractor, she'd been prepared to use her own computer. But the Valentines had been concerned about sensitive company data being accessed on an outside laptop. So she'd agreed to use theirs.

She'd enjoyed her time with Chandra and Naya and the lovely welcome luncheon they'd arranged. It'd been the perfect chance for her to get to know all the other employees. Even grumpy winemaker Maria. But one member of the staff had been notably absent.

Nolan hadn't attended the luncheon. Nor had they crossed paths since she'd arrived.

Laney had endured her torturous ninety-minute meeting with Maria, in which the woman had essentially told her not to ruin her perfectly good system for making wine.

It was clear there would be a lot of asking for forgiveness rather than permission in Laney's future.

Then she'd returned to the villa where she spent another hour chatting with Raymond Valentine about his vision for the vineyard.

Laney liked Ray. In fact, she liked the entire Valentine family, including Nolan, who hadn't bothered to show his face.

Laney hadn't expected him to make a big deal about seeing her again. But she thought he'd at least pop in to say hello. After all, not only did they work together, they were neighbors. And after their encounter at the pool, she thought they were at least friendly. But maybe Nolan was just being polite. That would explain why she hadn't seen Nolan at the pool since, despite going every day she'd been in town. Admittedly, in hopes of encountering him again.

"Now that we're all done, why don't I escort you to your office?" Ray stood and grabbed the last apple fritter.

"I think I remember the way back to the lab." Laney followed Ray out of the kitchen, where they'd had their little tête-à-tête. Unlike his daughters, he preferred not to have an office. Said he'd spent far too many years seated in one during the time he was the CEO of the textile firm his family had sold recently.

"That's great." The handsome older man smiled

broadly. Laney noticed for the first time how much Nolan favored his father. "But we wanted you to have a better space to input data and compile your reports. Come on, I'll show you what the girls have arranged."

Laney was intrigued.

She was perfectly fine with the lab space, even if it felt a bit rustic. Honestly? She'd worked in spaces that were far less luxe than that. But she certainly wouldn't mind a better office if one was available.

Laney joined Ray on the short walk to the winery. Already she was beginning to recall the names of several of the winery and vineyard workers she'd met.

As they headed toward the back of the building, Laney was hit with a sudden moment of panic. What if she had to share an office with Maria, the winemaker?

Laney was thrilled to see another woman in the industry. She really was. But Maria didn't seem nearly as happy about Laney being there. In fact, the woman seemed threatened by her presence.

It shouldn't be shocking. She'd encountered pushback from winery employees before. Still, the idea of sharing office space with a woman who clearly didn't want her there caused a knot to tighten in Laney's gut.

They took the back stairs to the second floor. Ray rapped on the frosted glass window of an office door that was likely older than she was.

"Come in." Laney recognized Nolan's voice right away. And though she hated to admit it, a part of her was excited to see Nolan again.

Ray ushered her inside.

"You remember my son Nolan," Raymond said with

a hint of sarcasm. A seeming dig at Nolan for not showing up for the welcome luncheon.

"Of course." Laney nodded with a smile. "Good to
see you again, Nolan."

"Likewise." Nolan stood, reaching across the desk to
shake her hand. "Sorry I wasn't able to make it to the
welcome luncheon. My call with the successor to my
position at the textile firm, who I'm apparently mentor-
ing, went long." Nolan clearly wasn't happy about it. "I
trust all went well on your trip to Seattle."

"It did. Thank you for asking." Laney tried to restrain her smile and to pretend she hadn't felt electricity
dancing along her palm when Nolan grasped her hand.

"And this…is your office space." Ray gestured toward a minimalistic setup in the corner. The simple
desk, which held only the things she required, suited
her perfectly. And it was quite similar to the no-frills,
neat-as-a-pin setup on Nolan's desk.

Had he put together this space for her?

"I…um… I'll be sharing an office with Nolan?"
Laney glanced between the two men.

Ray practically beamed while Nolan looked less than
thrilled.

"I prefer to think of it as your individual offices
being adjacent." Ray chuckled.

"Nolan, you're okay with this?" Laney turned toward
him, searching his dark eyes. The slight frown and the
lines spanning his forehead made it clear Nolan wasn't
onboard with this plan. So it was unlikely that he'd set
up her desk.

"I'm fine with it," Nolan said after an incredibly

long pause and a stern look from his father. He gestured across the space. "There's plenty of room for both of us."

"See? Nolan's absolutely fine with it. But if he gives you any problems, just let me know." Ray flashed his brilliantly white teeth and patted her shoulder. He finished the last of his apple fritter and wiped his hands on a napkin he swiped from the coffee center. "Well, I'm off. Nolan here will take good care of you, Laney. But if you need anything, anything at all, Chandra, Naya and I are a phone call away. You'll find our numbers on the company directory posted on the wall beside your desk. Again, we're thrilled to have you here. I'd better head out. I'm meeting my brother Joe for an early dinner. See you tomorrow."

"Please tell Mr. Abbott I said hello," Laney called to the man's retreating back.

No matter how many times the Abbott family patriarch had told her to call him "Grandpa Joe" like all his grandchildren and their significant others did, she couldn't help addressing him formally. To her, he would always be the benefactor who'd given them more time with their grandfather by getting him cutting-edge care. Joseph Abbott had radically changed her and Savannah's lives by writing a huge check and doling out company stock to them and to their grandfather in appreciation for his contributions to the development of the King's Finest recipes.

As soon as Ray closed the door behind him, an awkward silence descended over the room. They stood there staring at each other. Then they both attempted to speak at once, followed by both going silent again.

She honestly wasn't sure which of them was most awkward.

"You go first. Please." Nolan gestured toward her with a soft smile—the first genuine one she'd seen from him that day.

Laney stepped forward, her chin tipped and her shoulders pulled back. She cleared her throat. "I appreciate you permitting me to share your office space, but it seems it's not what you wanted nor expected. I'm practically fine with—"

"Laney, I said I'm okay with sharing the office." Nolan folded his arms over his broad chest. A chest she'd seen totally bare less than a week ago.

She tried to rinse the image of Nolan naked from the waist up from her brain with the same intensity with which she rinsed the chlorine from her skin and hair after a swim.

"I heard the words coming out of your mouth, Nolan." Laney took a few steps toward the imposing desk that stood between them. "But, your facial expressions and body language tell a very different story."

"You caught that, huh?" Nolan sighed heavily, then removed his smudged glasses. He tugged his shirttail from his waistband to clean the lenses, but Laney frantically waved a hand.

"Don't! You'll scratch the lenses," she cautioned. She'd ruined an expensive pair of eyeglasses doing the exact same thing.

"As you can see, they're in desperate need of—"

"Yes, I can see that." Laney straightened her own glasses as she studied the cloudy lenses. "It's a wonder you can see out of these things." She set her purse on Nolan's desk and rummaged through it. "Do you mind?"

Nolan looked confused, but when Laney held out her open palm and impatiently wriggled her fingers, he understood. He frowned but sighed quietly and handed over his eyeglasses.

Laney produced a bottle of anti-fog spray. She lightly sprayed the lenses, then gently wiped them with a microfiber cloth. She held the glasses up to the light. "Oh my."

"What is it?" Nolan squinted without his glasses.

She'd never seen him without them. He was even more handsome, only because she could see more of his face. Laney's skin suddenly felt warm as Nolan leaned across the desk to get a better view of the glasses in her hands.

"These little lines on each lens… They're not dirt. They're deep scratches from doing what you were just about to do—wiping your glasses with abrasive materials that create fine gashes. There are several on each lens." She returned Nolan's glasses, and he examined them closely.

"I see them now." He slipped his glasses on. "I'll be more conscientious about how I clean them in the future."

"Good." Laney wasn't sure why such a basic interaction had made her heart dance. "Now… You seem like a very private person, so it clearly wasn't your idea that we share this office."

"No, it wasn't," Nolan admitted. She found his honesty refreshing, even if it meant a hit to her ego. "In fact, my family sprung this on me this morning. I've been in Nashville the past two days."

So that's why he hadn't been at the pool. At least, she'd hoped that was why.

"I was a bit irked about the office-sharing. That's the real reason I didn't come to the luncheon," he admitted. "I willingly agreed to this arrangement, but my brain needed some time to process the change to my routine."

A man who was self-aware and preferred honesty over deception. Nolan Valentine was beginning to look even more appealing.

"Thank you for being so candid, Nolan." Laney hiked her purse on her shoulder. "But there's no need to disrupt your routine when there's a perfectly good office space downstairs. I'll be away from my desk most of the time anyway." She shrugged. "I'll just tell your father I prefer working in the lab."

"You don't need to do that." Nolan shook his head. "I'm fine with sharing this space. But I appreciate your consideration," he added. "Now, I'm expecting a vendor call soon. But if there's anything you need, let me know.

Laney thanked him, trying her best to rein in a smile. Then she put her purse in the bottom drawer of her desk and got settled into the office she'd be sharing with Nolan Valentine.

Nope. Not a big deal at all.

So why did she spend the rest of the afternoon sneaking glances at the man and remembering how good he looked in nothing but swim trunks and a pair of athletic slides?

Maybe her sister was right. She needed to get out more. Start dating.

When Laney sneaked another peek at Nolan, he was staring in her direction. He turned his chair toward the window behind his desk and continued his phone call.

Nope. Not awkward at all.

Nine

"So, we're two weeks in. How are things going with you and your new *roommate*?"

Nolan glanced up from his laptop at the sound of his younger sister's voice. She was accompanied by Chandra, who looked like she was going to give birth at any moment.

"Very funny." He pointed at Naya, who cackled as she made a beeline for the coffee station. "We are *not* roommates. We're officemates, thanks to the two of you."

"You're welcome." Naya curtsied, as if she were visiting the Queen of England. "Ooh! Who made lemon bars?"

"Somehow we got on the discussion of our favorite bar desserts," Nolan said. "I mentioned that lemon bars were mine and—"

"She whipped you up a batch?" Chandra was easing into one of the chairs on the other side of his desk in what felt like slow motion.

"She didn't 'whip me up a batch.' Our conversation reminded her how much she liked lemon bars and that she hadn't made them in a long time. So she baked some and brought them into the office. Not just for me. For everyone. Laney left a plate at the coffee station downstairs, too." Nolan could hear the defensiveness in his own voice. He cleared his throat.

"Good. Then I'm definitely going to have another one," Naya mumbled around a mouthful of lemon bar. "They're delicious, Chan. You have to try one." Naya handed a lemon bar wrapped in a napkin to their older sister.

Chandra, who seemed slightly out of breath, leaned back in the chair and rested the napkin on her belly, as if it was a plate.

Nolan shook his head and chuckled.

"We appreciate your commitment, sis. But are you sure you shouldn't be at home resting with your feet up or something?"

Nolan's first niece was due in little more than two weeks, but Chandra refused to go on maternity leave until after the baby was born. She'd already been pregnant when she'd accepted the role of CEO of Valentine Vineyards. And it seemed as if she was determined to prove to all of them that pregnancy wouldn't slow her down.

"Too much to do." Chandra pinched off a piece of the lemon bar and popped it into her mouth. She made a sound akin to a cat's purr. "My God, this is good," she muttered before returning her attention to Nolan. "Once Autumn is born, I'm going to give her one hundred percent of my attention. But until then, I want to make sure that everything is in place for the three months I'm taking off."

"Three months, huh?" Nolan could envision his sister and the baby popping in frequently "just to visit." "Okay. Sure. But in the meantime, do not go into labor on my very expensive antique chairs." He gestured toward the two leather chairs he'd acquired at an estate sale just up the road.

"I'll do my best, but I can't make any promises." Chandra picked up the rest of the bar and nibbled on it, gesturing to Naya to bring her another. "Your niece is the one in control here."

Naya handed Chandra a second lemon bar, then bit into another of her own as she sank onto the other leather chair. "You still didn't answer my question. How are things going with you and Laney?"

"They're going...*fine*." Nolan's face and neck suddenly felt warm.

Why did he get all tongue-tied and flummoxed at the mere thought of Delaney Carlisle? Around her, he reverted to an awkward schoolboy with a crush. Which made it difficult to focus and get his work done without sneaking looks across the room. Not to mention when she'd bend over the coffee station to make herself a cup of coffee each morning.

Nolan adjusted in his seat, his body responding to the memory of Laney's deliciously curvy bottom bent over that table. And now he couldn't stop imagining bending her over his desk, hiking up her skirt and taking her from behind.

He swallowed hard and clutched at his suddenly too-tight tie. "Just...*fine*," he repeated.

Chandra and Naya both laughed.

"Well, that told us absolutely nothing and yet everything we needed to know," Chandra said to Naya in a loud stage whisper.

"Exactly." Naya grinned.

"What does that even mean?" Nolan wasn't sure he wanted to know. But he couldn't stop himself from asking.

"It means A, you're impressed with Laney's work and have zero complaints about her," Chandra said.

"And B, you're *totally* into her," Naya supplied. Both his sisters giggled.

Sometimes he envied his brother-in-law, Julian, who was an only child.

"You two need to stop with the whole matchmaking thing." Nolan wagged a finger at his sisters. "Laney is my...*our*...employee who also happens to be my office-mate *and* neighbor. Thanks to the two of you."

His sisters congratulated themselves for his current situation by bumping fists followed by a simulated explosion.

Chandra shifted upright in her chair with some effort. "The point is that having Laney monitoring the sugar levels of the grapes, the pH level of the soil and collecting data on the wine we're about to begin bottling, it's already making a difference. And I can envision a hundred different ways that information will be useful to us at harvest time and beyond."

"Also, you're *totally* into her," Naya repeated, brushing crumbs off her navy wide-leg pants that looked more like a skirt when she was standing. "You can't keep your eyes off of Laney. And you're not nearly as grumpy and contradictory with her as you are with us."

Nolan paced the floor behind his desk.

"That's because even when I want to be mad at her—like when she used the last caramel vanilla cream coffee pod and didn't even restock it—I can't be. Because she'll say something cute or funny or utterly fascinating." He stopped and pointed an accusatory finger at his two sisters. "It's like you two told Laney to act all nerdy and adorable and I'd be putty in her hands."

"We did no such—" Chandra was saying.

"Your sisters never said that." Laney stood just inside the door in an oversize white lab coat, the sleeves smudged with dirt. She straightened her slightly askew glasses. "I assure you."

"Awkward," Naya whispered loudly and made a face that indicated as much.

"Laney…" Chandra struggled to her feet with the help of Naya, who also stood. "We were just talking about what a difference you're making around here."

"And about how amazing these lemon bars are." Naya finished the last bite of her second or third one. "You *have* to share the recipe for these."

"Gladly." Laney smiled at Naya politely before turning her attention to him.

Nolan straightened his tie and swallowed hard, his

throat suddenly parched. He reached for his open bottle of water and it tipped over, splashing the papers on his desk.

Naya gave him a handful of napkins and helped him blot the mess.

He chugged what little was left in the bottle.

Smooth, Nolan. Really smooth.

"Well, we were just about to head out. Right?" Naya looped her arm through Chandra's.

"Right. Dad and I have a chat scheduled to review your acquisition requests for the lab before we meet with your penny-pinching roommate here." Chandra nodded toward Nolan, who was doing his best impression of a spider on the wall who'd gone still, hoping not to be noticed.

"Thank you," Laney said. "Please let me know if you need any additional data to justify the proposed purchases. I can get you—"

"No." Chandra held up a hand. "You've supplied us with plenty of data, research and case studies. I think we're good."

Nolan tried his best to hold back a smile. Delaney Carlisle was nothing if not thorough.

"I might've gone a little overboard." Laney peeked through her thumb and forefinger. "I wanted to ensure you had all the data you needed."

"And we appreciate your diligent efforts." Chandra gave Laney a reassuring smile. "Like I said, you're good for this place. And we're all glad you're here."

Laney nodded her thanks. Her brown eyes twinkled, and a slow smile spread across her beautiful face. Nolan couldn't help smiling, too. A smile that emanated from deep in his gut and warmed his chest. After his sisters left the room, he glanced over at Laney. She glared at him with one hip cocked like the hammer of a revolver aimed directly at him.

Shit.

"So… You think I'm *nerdy*?" Laney folded her arms over her chest, drawing his gaze to the swell of her breasts and the hint of cleavage visible in the V-neck shirt she wore beneath her open lab coat.

"You don't?" Nolan responded with a nervous chuckle, relieved when he noticed Laney was holding back a grin. "Because I see absolutely nothing wrong with being a nerd. I was the president of my local chapter of blerds—Black nerds—group," he clarified, "for two years. I'm still a card-carrying member."

"I know what a blerd is, Nolan," Laney said. "I've been a member of an online blerd organization for years. But with caring for my daughter and grandfather and then school, I haven't been very active." She nervously prattled on, and he found it delightful and captivating. Just like that button nose and shy smile of hers. And those dimples, which were now in full effect. "Wait! That means you also think I'm *adorable*." She practically sung the final word, looking incredibly satisfied with herself.

It was like she was in his head. It was scary but also somehow endearing.

Nolan pushed up his glasses.

Damn his sisters.

Even when they weren't actively behind the matchmaking, they were in his head and had him doing their bidding.

"Your words, not mine, Carlisle." Nolan shoved his hands in his pockets. "I'd describe you as brilliant, insightful, resourceful and damn annoying."

Laney cocked a hip, those devilish eyes of hers dancing as she turned those dimples up a notch. "I think I like that description even better."

Great. He couldn't even insult this woman.

"Well, I just came up here to make a fresh cup of coffee." Laney strode toward the coffee station

He sucked in a quiet breath, his eyes drawn to the swell of her picture-perfect derrière.

Ç'est si bon.

It was one of the few phrases he recalled from several semesters of French.

Nolan kneaded the back of his neck. "Isn't there a coffee station downstairs?"

"The flavor selections are better here." Laney made herself a fresh cup, then grabbed a lemon bar before sauntering toward the door. "This *nerdy, adorable* woman has work to do. If you need me, you know where to find me."

"Yes, in *my* office," Nolan grumbled. Laney had already left the room, but he could swear he heard her laugh from down the hall.

Nolan heaved a sigh, annoyed that his sisters had eaten most of the lemon bars Laney had made for him… or rather for *them*. He popped a caramel vanilla cream pod into the coffee maker, put his mug underneath and pushed the brew button.

"And I will *not* be needing you, Delaney Carlisle. I assure you," Nolan muttered beneath his breath

"That's when you know a woman has really gotten into your head son." His father slapped his shoulder and chuckled. "When she has you standing here talking to yourself."

Nolan's face heated, but he didn't bother arguing the point. Better if he just ignored the comment altogether.

"When did this coffee station become so popular?" Nolan grabbed his steaming cup of coffee and stepped aside so his father could make a cup for himself.

"Since you got a much prettier and far less cranky roommate who also happens to bake legendary lemon bars." His father chuckled. "Speaking of which… May I?" His father gestured to the plate with just two bars left. They were all out downstairs."

"Help yourself," Nolan said through gritted teeth as he added cream and sugar to his coffee.

His father picked up a bar and nibbled on it, murmuring with pleasure before practically inhaling the square and then shifting his gaze longingly to the lone remaining piece.

Nolan lifted the plate, extending it toward his father, who accepted it gratefully.

"Anyway, I just stopped by to see how things were going with you and—"

"Okay, what is going on with you all?" Nolan griped, then sighed when his father raised one of his white-and-silver eyebrows, as if to say, "Who you think you talking to?" "Look, I'm sorry if I sound crabby. But you're the third person in twenty minutes to ask that. Things are fine with Laney. It's still too early in the game to make any snap judgments, but so far you all were right." Nolan shrugged. "I'm impressed with her. And it seems just about everyone else is, too."

"*Almost* everyone." He nibbled on his second lemon bar, as if trying to savor every last crumb. "Our wine-maker isn't too happy about the data analysis Laney is doing. Numbers she's accustomed to pulling. I've been trying to convince Maria that Laney is here to comple-ment her role as winemaker, not to usurp her. She didn't seem that convinced."

"She'll come around." Nolan took his seat behind his desk, not thoroughly convinced, either. "Or maybe this trial run doesn't look so shiny after the initial hon-eymoon glow, and we decide not to move forward with it." Nolan shrugged, sipping his coffee.

Raymond Valentine gave him that silent stare he em-ployed whenever he thought one of his kids was trying to bullshit him. "Right. Catch you later, son."

Nolan closed the office door behind his father, thank-ful to finally get a moment of peace. But as he opened his document and began reviewing sales figures, he kept glancing over at Laney's empty desk.

His father was right. Laney was definitely in his head. And though he knew he shouldn't, he couldn't help wishing she was in his bed.

Laney returned from a walk through the vineyards with Carlos Montoya, the vigneron who managed the workers who planted, maintained and harvested the grapes. Carlos had been polite. But he hadn't much liked Laney when she'd started working at Valentine Vineyards two weeks ago.

She realized it was about the work she'd been hired to do and that the man likely didn't have anything against her personally. Still, there'd been a definite chill in the air whenever they'd chatted.

One afternoon, Laney had suggested acquiring some new harvesting equipment. Carlos had shaken his head and muttered under his breath, "A los tontos no les dura el dinero."

A fool and his money are soon parted.

"Él que no arriesga, no gana," she'd replied, her pronunciation suspect, at best.

He who doesn't risk doesn't gain anything.

"Senorita, habla usted español?" The handsome older man's face and neck, weathered by the sun, had gone beet red.

"Un muy poco." Laney had peeked through the tiniest space between her thumb and forefinger and smiled. "Estoy aprendiendo con mi hija. Usamos Duolingo para aprender español."

"Ah." Carlos had nodded approvingly. "And how old is your hija?"

Laney had shown Carlos photos of her nearly eight-year-old daughter on her phone. Carlos had given her tips on how to form a circle with her lips when she pronounced the U sound in Spanish and how to make her tongue hit the roof of her mouth in order to roll her Rs.

Since then, Carlos often spoke to her in slow, deliberate Spanish. He encouraged her on the words and phrases she got right while gently correcting the words she got wrong and the pronunciations she botched. And that afternoon, for the first time, he'd agreed with one of her suggestions instead of responding with his usual: "But we have always done it this way, senorita."

Maybe that was why Laney felt like she was floating on a cloud when she glided through the door, located directly across from Nolan's desk. He wasn't there; nor was he at the coffee station. Laney hated to admit it, but she was disappointed not to find him there. And if she was being particularly honest with herself, she'd have to admit that part of the euphoria she'd been feeling that afternoon had more to do with the fact that Nolan had told his sisters that he found her adorable.

Adorable wasn't really what she'd been going for. She'd prefer him to find her gorgeous or devastatingly hot. But the point was there was at least some mutual attraction between them, even if, because he was her boss, he didn't want to admit it.

Seriously, had it been so long since she'd been on a date that she was excited that a man she liked had the mildest interest in her? An interest he had zero intention of acting on? Laney plopped down in the chair behind her desk. She really needed to get out more. Perhaps go on an actual date.

But in the meantime, maybe she could revive one of her old hobbies. It would give her something to do besides hanging out at Blake and Savannah's place when she wasn't working.

Laney checked her watch. It was the end of the workday. She considered staying a few more minutes to see if Nolan returned. Just because the polite thing would be to say goodbye. But after ten minutes of waiting, she realized she was being silly. Nolan certainly wouldn't stay just to say good-night to her.

Laney retrieved her purse from her bottom desk drawer and lifted it onto her shoulder, then headed for the door. Her phone rang. It was a number she didn't recognize.

She sat on the front edge of her desk, answering it on speaker since she was alone in the office with the door closed. "Hello."

"Hi, Mommy!" She could hear the grin in Harper's voice.

"Sweetie, is everything okay? Whose number are you calling from?"

"Mine!" Harper practically squealed. "Daddy bought it for me as an early birthday present."

"Your father bought you a phone, Harper?" Laney shot to her feet and dropped her bag on the desk. "But you're only seven—"

"Almost eight!"

"You don't need a phone, Harper," Laney said calmly as she rubbed the sudden tension in her temples. "We've talked about this. I promised to get you a phone when you turned ten."

"I know," Harper said sheepishly. "But all my cousins have phones. I was the only one who didn't have one. So Daddy bought me one. It's really pretty, Mommy. It's pink with sparkly crystals on it."

"Harper." Laney uttered her daughter's name through gritted teeth as she squeezed her eyes shut and tried to massage away the tightness spreading across her forehead. "Is your dad around? I *really* need to speak with him right now."

"Okay, Mommy." Her daughter sighed. "But first, I need to ask you something important."

"It would've been nice if you and your father had asked me about buying you a phone *before* he got it." Laney folded one arm over her chest as she stared at the wall behind her desk. She counted to ten in her head, then sighed heavily. "Never mind. I'll talk to your dad when he brings you home this weekend. What is it that you wanted to ask me, sweetheart?"

Harper's lengthy pause broadcast the seriousness of the question before she uttered a single word. "I don't want to come home."

"What?!" A knot tightened in Laney's gut and her heart pounded in her chest. "What do you mean you don't want to come home?"

"Two weeks went by so fast. Can I stay two more weeks? Daddy said it was fine if you said it was okay, because I don't have school yet. Besides, we're moving here anyway, right?"

"I…uh…" Laney faltered, unable to recite the response she'd planned.

I promised to consider moving there, and I have. But I don't think Seattle's the right place for us.

She couldn't make herself utter the words because it wasn't true. She hadn't given the possibility of moving to Seattle fair consideration like she'd promised.

And why hadn't she?

Currently, her only other prospect was to stay in Magnolia Lake, where they had family, but her job was only temporary and none of the nearby schools had the advanced math and science programs Harper was accustomed to. Was she really going to let the minor awkwardness of occasionally encountering her ex make her miss out on a situation that could be ideal for both of them? Either way, she wouldn't lie to Harper about it.

"I promised to consider moving to Seattle, and I will," Laney said calmly. "But I haven't made my decision yet. And you, young lady, are supposed to be coming home this weekend."

"We don't really have a home right now," Harper noted. She wasn't wrong. "We're just hanging out in Magnolia Lake with Auntie Vanna for the summer. But this summer I'd really, really like to spend some time with Dad and my grandparents and my cousins. *Please.*"

Laney could already visualize the sad, brown, puppy-dog eyes that accompanied her daughter's plea.

"Pretty please?" Harper continued. "What if we move back to New York? It'll be a long time before I get to see any of them again," she added, panic rising in her daughter's voice.

Laney frowned. "But, pumpkin, next weekend is your birthday."

"I know," Harper said sheepishly. "And I know we were going to do something at auntie's house. But I've never gotten to have a birthday with Daddy and I'd—"

"Okay, Harper." Laney forced a smile, hoping it carried through the phone. "If that's what you really want for your birthday."

"I do!"

Laney blinked back tears. "Then if it's okay with your father—"

Harper was calling her father, and even the sound of her calling him *Daddy* grated her nerves.

"Laney? Hi, I didn't realize Harper had called you. You're probably still at work."

"You should've called me *before* you purchased my seven-year-old daughter a phone." Her voice was tight.

"Harper said you planned on getting her a phone, so I—"

"When she was ten, Derrick. Not now. Or did your little princess leave that essential point out of the conversation?"

"Ouch. Sounds like I've been duped. I'm sorry, Lanes. I didn't mean to—"

"Never mind that for now. When did you two cook up this idea about Harper staying another two weeks?" Laney demanded.

"This isn't some conspiracy, Lanes, I swear. I planned to call you later tonight to talk to you about this myself. I had no idea Harper was going to spring it on you. But yes, I'd like more time with her. We all would. My parents can't get enough of doting on her. My brother and sister and their kids adore her. Harper is funny and fearless and whip-smart." He chuckled softly. "God, she reminds me so much of you."

Laney wanted to yell. To tell him what nerve he had to make such a request. And that she didn't want his little compliment. But instead, she did what she always did. Tried to keep the peace for her daughter's sake.

"Fine. Harper can stay another two weeks. Just don't forget her birthday is next—"

"Saturday. I'm on it. Now that we've gotten the green light on her staying, my mom and sister will be in full party mode. I think they're more excited about throwing a birthday party for Harper than she is."

"I should go," Laney said after an awkward silence settled over line.

"Of course." Derrick was silent a moment, then spoke again. "Lanes, you've done one hell of a job raising our daughter alone. I can't thank you enough for the sacrifices you've made over the past eight…no… nine years. Harper is an amazing little girl. I'm grateful you're allowing me to be her *dad*." He stressed the word. "Don't ever think I'm oblivious to how tough it must be for you with me coming back into your lives like this. From the bottom of my heart, thank you."

Derrick's words were tender and filled with emotion. And despite all of the angry things she wanted to yell at him, she couldn't voice any of them. Instead, she said something that truly surprised her.

"I'm glad you decided you were ready to be Harper's dad, Derrick. It's what Harper has wanted so badly these past few years. But if you ever break her heart the way you broke mine—"

"I won't, Laney. Trust me. I realize I can't change the past, but I promise you I will spend the rest of my life trying to make it up to Harper and to you."

"You don't need to make amends with me, Derrick. Just be the father Harper deserves and we're fine."

"But are you fine?" he asked.

"What is that supposed to mean?" Laney frowned, as she rummaged through her purse.

"It means while I know only Harper is my responsibility, you're her mother. We'll always have that connection. So, I can't help worrying about you, too." He paused. "You're an amazing mother, but I can't help wondering if *you're* happy."

Now he was concerned with her happiness?

"No need to wonder. I'm fine." Laney drew in a shaky breath, her jaw clenched. "Now, don't forget to take lots of photos at the party and videoconference me when you sing 'Happy Birthday.'"

"I will. Promise." There was sadness in his voice and a hint of what she could swear was pity. "Enjoy your kid-free summer, Lanes. You deserve it. We'll talk to you soon."

Laney stared at the phone long after Derrick had ended the call.

She should be grateful her daughter's father was a decent, caring human being. But all she could think was: How dare he act like he suddenly cared about her?

"So…that's the ex, huh?" Nolan's voice startled Laney, and she nearly jumped out of her skin.

Laney swiveled toward him so quickly she nearly twisted her ankle. Her heart raced.

"When did you come back to the office?"

"A few minutes ago." He shrugged.

"I'm sorry, Nolan. I would never have answered the call on speaker if I'd known you were here. I thought I was alone." Laney cleared her throat. "How much of that did you hear?"

"Enough to know you're not happy about him buying Harper a phone or about them guilting you into letting her stay another two weeks."

"Oh." She lifted her purse onto her shoulder, wishing she could sink into the floor.

"The ex… He seems like a pretty decent guy." Nolan sat on the front edge of his desk. His hands were shoved into his pockets.

"He is," Laney acknowledged

"Yet, things didn't work out between you," Nolan hedged. The unasked "What happened between you two?" hanging in the air between them.

If he wasn't comfortable asking her the question directly, she wasn't about to answer it.

"It's a story that's better told over barbecue and a beer," she said.

"You're a beer drinker?" Nolan raised an eyebrow, then nodded. "You're full of surprises. I saw you as more of a wine snob."

"I can be that, too." She smiled. "Good night, Nolan."

"Wait." He followed her to the door. "You have a little something on your face."

"Where?" Laney wiped the area Nolan indicated, but apparently didn't get it.

"Here." He pulled a handkerchief from his pocket and leaned in closer, wiping her cheek.

His skin didn't touch hers. Yet, there was something inherently intimate about the gesture. His warm breath mingled with hers. His delicious scent enveloped her. And she could feel the heat of his hand through the fabric.

Laney's face and neck heated, and her breath came a bit faster. Her gaze met his, and for a moment, she couldn't help hoping he'd lean in and cover her mouth with his. Resolve the lingering question in her head: What would it feel like to kiss Nolan Valentine?

It was evidently something she'd go to her deathbed wondering about.

"Looks like lipstick," Nolan said.

Laney glanced at the burgundy smudge on the handkerchief, then at her fingers.

"Crap. The cap came off a tube of lipstick at the bottom of my purse. It probably destroyed the lining of my bag." Laney wiped her fingers on a napkin, then tossed it in the trash. "Thanks, Nolan. I'll take the hankie and wash it. Bring it back as good as new."

"That isn't necessary," he said.

Laney held out her open palm, her fingers outstretched, making it clear she wasn't taking no for an answer. He tried to hide his amusement as he deposited the fabric in her hand.

"Good job, by the way, on establishing common ground with Carlos. It'll go a long way toward earning his trust and the trust of his workers." Nolan returned to his desk. "See you in the morning."

"Thank you." Laney picked up her purse and phone. "See you tomorrow."

Laney made her way through the winery, now much quieter than at the height of the day. Her heart danced in her chest and her skin still tingled where Nolan had wiped the smudged makeup from her face. Yes, she was being incredibly silly about the crush she had on her boss. But it had been a long time since she'd felt so giddy about someone. So even if nothing would ever come of it, she would hold on to these moments just the same.

Ten

Nolan stood on his back patio and stacked the last of the coals in a pyramid atop a few pieces of loosely balled-up paper in his barbecue pit. Now all he needed to do was wait fifteen or twenty minutes until the coals turned white-hot. No lighter fluid required.

Nolan grabbed his beer and took a swig. It was a slow Saturday afternoon and he'd promised his sisters that he wouldn't go into the winery or work at home. That he'd truly take the afternoon off and enjoy himself. He was doing his best to do just that. But it had turned into more of a cleaning and organizing day.

He'd taken everything out of his refrigerator, pantry, kitchen cabinets and linen closets, wiped down the shelves, discarded anything he didn't need, then returned everything to its proper place. Because everything needed to have its right and proper place. Otherwise, it threw off his carefully arranged world.

That meant no fruit in the veggie drawer. Only dairy items in the dairy compartment. All of his shoes neatly lined up in the designated shoe bins near the door and in his closet. And no feelings of attraction toward an employee.

The former items he had well in hand, as his tidy dwelling made clear. But the latter he was failing at miserably. Three weeks of sharing an office with Delaney Carlisle and he was a little more smitten with the woman every day.

Who even said *smitten* anymore? Nolan sighed, drinking more of his beer. Maybe his grandmother had been right. He was born with the soul of a ninety-year-old man.

The slamming of a screen door followed by Laney's melodic laugh captured Nolan's attention. He glanced over to where she'd emerged on her back patio in her bare feet, a pair of cutoff denim shorts and a V-neck T-shirt. She held her phone in one hand and a watering can in the other.

Nolan stepped back to where the vegetation hid him from her view but permitted him to watch her. Not that he made a habit of doing so. It was something he'd discovered completely by accident. Though he may have taken advantage of this vantage point a time or four.

Laney stood on her toes as she watered the hanging plants on her porch, revealing a swath of her toned abdomen and the tattoo around her navel. Then she bent to water the plants that framed her patio. Her cutoff shorts hugged her round bottom and highlighted her thick, toned thighs.

A shudder of desire rippled through Nolan. He sank his teeth into his lower lip as his dick stirred in appreciation for Laney's figure: a classic work of art. Nolan found the need to adjust his stance.

Get a fucking grip. She's an employee.

He did *not* date employees. A rule he'd pushed to include in the employee handbook. Nolan had witnessed, firsthand, just how messy things could get. He'd met his ex-wife when she'd worked for one of the charitable organizations Valentine Textiles had sponsored.

He'd been outvoted by his father and sisters, who all felt that, in such a small town, dating a coworker was inevitable. But if he started dating an employee… It would prove they'd been right, and he'd been wrong. And he wasn't. No good came from dating a coworker.

Laney started to sing "Happy Birthday" loudly and off-key. He couldn't help smiling. But even across their yards he detected a hint of sadness in her expression.

When Laney had finished singing, she blew a kiss at the screen and said, "I love you, honey." Then her tone and expression changed as she continued speaking, saying something he couldn't hear.

She was undoubtedly talking to the ex. He knew that expression well. Laney ended the call abruptly, then plopped down on a sofa on her patio. Her shoulders were shaking, and even though he couldn't hear her sobs, she was clearly crying.

Nolan rubbed his forehead and sighed. Whatever was going on between his employee and her ex was none of his concern. He should just stay in his yard and mind his own business. But the thought of Laney crying her eyes out on the other side of that fence tore a hole in his chest.

Maybe he *should* stay out of it, but he couldn't.

Nolan checked the grill. In another ten minutes, it would be ready to go. He set a timer on his fitness wearable, took a deep breath, then set out toward Laney's yard.

He rapped on her back fence with his knuckles.

"Yes?" Laney sounded both puzzled and alarmed. "Who is it?"

"It's me, Laney. Can I come in for a minute?"

She didn't answer right away, but he could hear her sniffling. "Yes, of course. Come in, Nolan."

Nolan entered the yard with an awkward wave and made his way up the path toward Laney. "Hey, I don't mean to pry but I happened to be outside grilling and I noticed that you seemed…upset. I just wanted to make sure you're all right."

Laney dragged a finger beneath one teary brown eye and sniffled. "I'm fine," she said unconvincingly.

"With respect, you certainly don't seem fine.". When she didn't respond, he sank onto the cushion beside her. "I heard you singing 'Happy Birthday' to Harper. Is this your first time being away from her on her birthday?"

Laney nodded, wiping at the silent tears streaking down her cheeks. "Is it that obvious?"

"It's obvious you love and miss your daughter," he said gently.

"Everyone keeps telling me I should be enjoying my

freedom. But for the past eight years and nine months, Harper has been my entire life." Laney shrugged. "I can't stop worrying about her. Is she brushing her teeth every morning and again before bed? Is she putting on sunscreen before she goes out to play? Is she wearing her bonnet at night and detangling her curls?"

Laney placed one foot on the sofa and wrapped her arms around her raised leg while extending the other. Nolan couldn't help staring at her toes. She'd gotten a pedicure sometime between now and when she'd arrived at work in sandals the day before.

Nolan drew in a deep breath. He was distracted by Laney's toes and even he had to admit it was just fucking weird.

It took herculean mental effort to tear his gaze away from her artfully designed toenails, the miles of smooth, brown skin worthy of its own damn cocoa butter commercial and thighs thick enough to star in a two-piece with biscuits and a side of red beans and rice.

"Is it how long she's been gone that's bothering you? Because it feels bigger than that."

Laney's attention snapped to his abruptly. She seemed both impressed and annoyed by the accuracy of his assessment.

Laney heaved a sigh and smoothed back her hair pulled into a high afro puff secured by a silk scarf. "The truth is, I'm a little resentful to find myself competing with Derrick for my daughter's love. It's always been just the two of us. Suddenly, he comes out of nowhere and…" Laney let her words fade. "It's hard to compete with the shiny, new, fun parent when you're the rule enforcer, a.k.a. the fun killer."

"Rules are important. They're meant to protect us." The words were meant to provide solace to her and a warning to himself. "But that probably isn't something an eight-year-old is keen on hearing," he added when Laney narrowed her gaze at him.

"No, it isn't." She sighed.

"So Harper's relationship with her father is a new one," Nolan observed casually.

He totally wasn't prying.

"Yes." She hesitated, as if deciding just how much she was willing to share with him. Then she continued. "I was in grad school when I got pregnant with Harper. Derrick and I had plans to travel the world making a difference in areas of drought and famine. Harper was a surprise. I decided to keep the baby. He wanted to forge ahead with the life we'd planned so diligently, but having a young child wouldn't have permitted us to do that. Compromise wasn't an option, so we went our separate ways. I held no ill will over his decision. At another point in my life, I might've made the same choice. I'm not resentful that he chose to walk away. I'm resentful that after years of doing this on my own, he waltzes in and seems to be crushing this whole dad thing while I struggled for years to figure out motherhood. I'm still figuring it all out."

"That can't have been easy for you," Nolan said. "It was generous of you to allow Harper to go to Seattle to see her dad."

"I have to admit, he's been working hard the past

six months to build a relationship with Harper and to earn my trust." Laney sighed. "I still wasn't ready to be away from her for two weeks. But Harper wanted to go so badly, and Derrick has done everything I've asked of him and more. So I let her go." She shrugged.

"Sounds like Harper is in good hands. Besides, she's tough—just like her mom. She's going to be fine." Nolan nudged her arm with his elbow and smiled. "I trust your judgment, Laney. You should trust that you made the right call, too."

"The next time I try to acquisition a piece of equipment you don't see the need for, I'm going to remind you that you said you trust my judgment." Laney's sexy lips turned up in a teasing smile, and her eyes danced.

"And that's why you never become friends with the people who work for you." Nolan chuckled.

"Oh, is that what we are? Friends? Good to know." Laney stared off into the distance, still smiling.

What was he going to say? No? Instead, he deflected.

"So what are the birthday girl's plans for her big day?"

Laney's smile suddenly disappeared, and she was on the verge of crying again.

What the hell had he done wrong?

Before he could ask, the timer went off on his wrist.

Shit. He couldn't leave her on the verge of tears again when he'd clearly upset her somehow. But he couldn't leave his grill unattended any longer, either.

"Go." Laney sniffled. "I'm fine. Really."

And Santa is real, and pigs can fly.

Nolan stuffed his hands into the pockets of his basketball shorts and studied Laney.

"I'm grilling tonight. Nothing fancy. Just a couple of steaks and some brats. Maybe a few beers. But you're welcome to join me."

Laney stared at him, her brown eyes blinking. "You're inviting me to a barbecue at your place." She pointed to him and then to herself, as if needing to make his invitation crystal clear.

"Yeah. I was. I mean… I am," he stammered. "But please don't feel obligated in any way. If you'd rather not, I completely understand."

"A cookout for two sounds much nicer than the pity party for one I had planned. Thank you, Nolan. Give me a few minutes to lock up, and I'll be right over."

"Great." Nolan hoped he sounded more confident than he felt.

His invitation had been genuine. Yet, he hadn't expected her to say yes. Part of him was thrilled that she'd accepted. Another part of him was in full-blown panic about spending an afternoon alone with the stunningly gorgeous but decidedly off-limits enologist who, even in cutoff jeans and with tear-stained cheeks, was everything he'd ever dreamed of and more.

Nolan nodded, then returned to his backyard.

A couple of hours of polite conversation while keeping his hands and his eyes to himself. Surely, he could manage that.

But his heart, trying its best to pump its way right out of his chest, was already calling him on that lie.

Eleven

Laney didn't bother knocking as she entered Nolan's back gate. He was already expecting her. Besides, if she stopped to knock, she might find a reason to return to the comfort of her own back patio.

She still couldn't believe the stodgy CFO who seemed to prefer his alone time had come over to check on her. She was even more shocked he'd invited her to his place for a cookout. Laney had gone out to lunch with Chandra and Naya a few times since she'd begun working at the winery. She'd even gone out to lunch with Ray and Maria. But Nolan had maintained his distance. Laney hadn't even seen him at the pool, no matter how many times she'd tried to run into him there "accidentally."

Nolan had seemed surprised by her acceptance of his invite, too. Had he invited her over just to be polite?

Laney shook off the thought and made her way up the path to where Nolan was checking on two T-bone steaks and a few brats on the grill.

"Mmm… That smells good." Laney smiled. She lifted the cloth grocery bag on her shoulder. "I'd already made a salad and my first attempt at lemon icebox pie," she said cheerfully. "So I thought I'd bring them."

"Thanks." Nolan put the lid on the grill, wiped his hands on a towel, then led her into the kitchen. "That's one of my favorite pies."

She remembered. It'd come up in their random discussion of desserts one day. But it was better not to mention it.

"My God, this place is spotless." Laney glanced around at the clean, uncluttered countertops and sparkling appliances. The entire place smelled like lemons and sunshine.

"Today was cleaning day." He shrugged when she looked surprised. "I promised my sisters I wouldn't come into the office or work from home."

"So you cleaned your house instead?" Laney did her best to hold back a grin. The man's desk was organized, neat as a pin and dusted regularly. Unsurprisingly, his home mirrored it.

"I should've removed my shoes." She glanced down at her feet.

"It's fine. Really." Nolan placed a warm hand on her elbow, sending tiny jolts of electricity up her arm. "Why don't I take these?"

Nolan set the covered wooden salad bowl on the table and put the lemon icebox pie in the refrigerator. "Would you like a beer? I only have imported pale ales." He indicated one of those mix-and-match six-packs grocery stores often offered. The kind she preferred, too. It gave her the chance to try out new flavors.

When she selected a light-bodied Belgian beer, Nolan chuckled to himself. He handed her a bottle opener.

"What?" Laney popped the top, then tossed it into the trash.

"That's the one I would've picked for you." He grinned proudly.

Laney sipped her beer, then pointed the longneck toward Nolan. "You made a couple of educated guesses about me, Valentine. Don't gloat."

"Whatever you say, Carlisle." Nolan headed toward the back patio and she followed.

They settled onto opposite ends of the outdoor sofa.

"So about this story you said required beer and barbecue…" Nolan sipped his beer.

Laney chugged from her bottle, then shrugged. "I've already told you most of what there is to know about me and Harper's dad."

"Okay. Then tell me why it upset you when I asked about Harper's plans for today?"

Laney frowned, then gulped more of her beer. "This is going to make me seem petty and ridiculous. I acknowledge that."

"No judgment." Nolan held up a hand as he turned his body toward hers.

She did the same, then sighed. "Harper is a huge superhero fan."

"Kind of figured that." He smiled.

"What you may not know is so am I. We've been tracking the making of one of the major studios first releases featuring a Black super heroine. Some of the movie was filmed on location in Upstate New York, not too far from us. We were both so excited to learn that the film was opening on the weekend of Harper's birthday. It felt like kismet, you know?"

Laney frowned, her eyes stinging again. But this time she refused to let the tears fall.

"So you'd planned to take Harper to the opening of the movie for her birthday." Nolan's words didn't convey any of the judgmental or placating tone she'd expected.

"Yes, but we weren't just going to attend the movie," she noted. "I bought the VIP experience, including costumes. And I'd planned a spa day for the two of us."

"You kept the spa appointment, I see."

"I did. How'd you—"

He indicated her freshly painted toes rather than her manicured nails. A distinction she found…*interesting*. It warmed her body in places she'd rather not think about while sitting this close to her boss, whom she already had an unhealthy crush on.

"Oh," was all she could manage. She took another sip of her beer. "Anyway, it was supposed to be this big surprise. When she asked to stay longer, I figured we'd see it together when she came back but…" Laney let the words die, not wanting to get riled up again.

"But your ex is taking her today." Nolan frowned.

"He isn't just taking her to see the film. *That's* where they're having Harper's birthday party. She's already wearing her costume." Laney huffed, then waved a hand. "Like I said. I know it seems petty and childish of me to be so upset about it. I should be happy Derrick is giving our daughter an amazing experience she'll always remember. But it's been kind of our thing these last couple years. Then Derrick swoops in and steals what should've been *our* moment."

"Which probably feels like a metaphor for how he's hijacked your relationship with your daughter." Nolan's dark eyes were soft and kind, as was his voice.

Laney nodded, not trusting herself to reply.

On the surface, Nolan was this grumpy exec who did everything by the book and kept to himself. But beneath that spiny exterior, the man was so much more compassionate and perceptive than Lancy could ever have imagined.

Nolan had come to her daughter's aid, and then firmly but kindly handled those bullies—one of whom was another employee's son. He'd been understanding when she'd been upset about Harper asking to stay in Seattle longer. Then he'd shown her compassion and genuine concern by checking on her. He'd even invited her over, so she wouldn't be alone and moping, when he likely would've preferred to spend a relaxing day alone.

If she hadn't already had a crush on Nolan Valentine, today would've sealed the deal. Nolan was brilliant and handsome and kind. Laney couldn't remember the last time she'd shared this kind of connection with someone. Someone she was comfortable talking to and who genuinely seemed to understand her. Someone her daughter liked, too. But Nolan was her boss. Getting involved wouldn't be a good look for either of them.

They drank their beers in silent companionship. Laney appreciated that Nolan was kind and supportive in a way that didn't feel overwhelming. Just being there with him was enough to soothe her frayed nerves and wounded heart. And he seemed to understand that.

"Know anyone who'd want a couple of overpriced movie tickets for later tonight?" Laney finished her beer and set it on the table.

"Confession." Nolan set his beer on the table, too. "I was a huge superhero nerd growing up. Still have a ton of comic books in storage in Nashville. But after college, life got really busy, and I got away from it. Until I met Marian's three kids and…" Nolan winced, then flashed a rueful smile. "They were into comics and superheroes like I was at their age. I was an absolute goner."

Laney could practically feel the pain and loss radiating off Nolan. She wanted to reach across the sofa and hug him. But instead she asked, "How old were they?"

"Three, five and seven. They were adorable kids— two boys and a little girl. Didn't take long before they had me wrapped around their little fingers." He smiled fondly. "Everything was superhero all the time. Took me back to my own love of comic book characters. We didn't miss a single movie, comic book release or local Comic-Con."

"Please tell me that you're talking cosplay and that there are photos out there somewhere of you wearing tights and a cape."

God, had she just said that aloud?

But as she studied him now, she couldn't help wondering how Nolan's strong arms and chest would look in a tight shirt. And she was pretty sure the ass she'd caught glimpses of around the office would look exceptional in tights.

Laney resisted the urge to bite her fist. She settled for discreetly sinking her teeth into her lower lip instead.

"I'll never tell." Nolan chuckled, his dark eyes dancing as he flashed her that smirky half grin that made her tingle all over and wonder about the taste of his full lips.

"Sounds like you had a great relationship with the kids. I'm guessing with their mom not so much." It was something Laney had wanted to ask about for a while, but she hadn't managed to twist their conversations into territory that made the question relevant. She wouldn't pass up the opportunity to ask him now.

Nolan picked up his bottle and took a long, slow sip before setting it down. He was likely trying to determine the politest way to tell her it was none of her business.

"Things were good for a while. But pretty quickly I think we both became more invested in 'us' the pseudo family unit than 'us' the couple. We dated for a year. Got married. And the marriage lasted for five years. But Marian was still in love with her kids' dad. And he was always looming over our relationship. Once we got married, and she was seemingly over him, her ex suddenly returned to their lives. Started showing up to see the kids regularly. Calling my ex often, supposedly to discuss one issue or another involving the kids." Nolan rubbed his forehead as if trying to soothe his furrowed brows. "I was blindsided when she asked for a divorce. But in retrospect, I guess I shouldn't have been."

"I'm sorry," Laney said.

"Don't be." Nolan mustered a brave smile that barely lifted the corners of his mouth. "It was for the best. Not being able to see the kids is the only thing I regret. Their dad…who my ex went back to…didn't want me to have contact with them anymore… After that, I pretty much avoided the things I'd done with the kids. It felt too painful." He shrugged. "So I didn't know about the movie."

"Then I'm sorry for bringing it up. I didn't mean to upset you."

"You didn't," Nolan said. "You reminded me of something I once loved. This movie is groundbreaking. We should celebrate and support it." He sipped his beer again, looking less tense than he had a few moments earlier.

"We?" Laney cocked her head. "As in…"

"I'm really not being very clear today, am I?" Nolan rubbed the back of his neck and chuckled. "I'm just saying, rather than eating the tickets, I think you should go. This movie is just as important to you as it is to Harper. And if you need a theater companion, I'd be happy to go with you…as friends, of course."

"The movie is in three hours and the theater is thirty minutes away," Laney noted, stunned that Nolan was volunteering to go to the movie with her.

"The steaks and brats won't be too much longer." Nolan glanced down at his watch. "Gives us plenty of time. If you'd like to go," he added. "If you'd rather not or if you have someone else in mind—"

"I'd love it if you went with me," she said quickly. "It'd be fun. Thanks."

"Great." He finished the last of his beer and stood. "I'd better check on the food. Then we can eat, and I'll still have plenty of time to grab a shower and wash off this grilling scent before we go."

Laney stood there staring a Nolan. The image of

Nolan standing in the shower naked, lather streaming down his back and chest, was burned into her brain.

She was going on a movie date with her boss, whom she'd been thirsting over from across the office. And now, she couldn't get the thought of him naked and wet out of her head.

"Everything okay?" Nolan transferred the perfectly grilled bratwursts to a tray.

"Just…peachy." Laney stood, folding her arms over her chest and hoping he hadn't noticed the beading of her nipples through the thin material of her shirt. "Mind if I have another beer?"

"Not at all," Nolan said. "Help yourself to anything you'd like."

Even you?

Laney drew in a sharp breath, then ducked inside the kitchen. She pressed her back to the wall and released a slow breath.

They were rational adults. Workmates with similar interests. Friendly neighbors. She could certainly handle a few hours alone with the man without lusting over him and imagining those large hands of his on her hips, his lips on her neck, him hovering above her in his bed.

Or could she?

Laney fanned herself, her skin suddenly feeling flushed.

Why did Nolan have to be so damn likable and easy to get along with when being with him clearly wasn't possible?

Still, she couldn't help entertaining the idea of them being together in her head.

Twelve

Nolan pulled his black Jaguar XF out of the movie the-ater parking lot, and though he knew he shouldn't, he couldn't help sneaking another glance at Laney.

The woman was absolutely stunning. Seemingly more so each day.

Laney had been gorgeous, fresh-faced and natural, in the T-shirt and cutoff shorts she'd worn earlier. But then she'd gone back to her place to shower and change. He'd nearly tripped over his own feet when he got out of the car to open the door for her. Because she'd taken his breath away.

She'd emerged from her town house in a flirty little blue sundress that managed to be both beachy with a summer vibe and elegant enough for an evening on the

town. The midthigh hem of her dress and strappy plat-
form sandals showcased her lean, shapely legs.

He'd been obsessed with the miles of glowing brown
skin on her arms and legs ever since.

"So… I've met your sisters," Laney said. "Tell me
about your brothers. Why aren't they part of the business?"

"They are. They just don't realize it yet." Nolan
chuckled. It was something Naya often said and more
and more he realized it was true. "Sebastian took on
the role of CEO at the textile firm our family owned
for generations, but recently sold. Alonzo, the eternal
playboy, works in advertising in Manhattan. Naya's
twin, Nyles, is trying his hand as a promoter at a club
in Miami Beach he recently invested in. My brothers
haven't quite bought into my dad's vision yet. But he's
determined to build Valentine Vineyards to a point
where all of his children are eager to be a part of it.
We often consult Sebastian, Alonzo and Nyles, tap-
ping into their specific areas of expertise on matters
regarding the vineyard. It's Dad's genius way of slowly
reeling them in."

"Is it working?" Laney asked.

"I think so. If I had to guess, I'd say that Sebastian
is the one who is the most disillusioned with his career.
Uneasy lies the head that wears the crown. Especially
when you're basically a puppet king for a shadowy conglomerate," Nolan said.

It had looked as if Sebastian had aged a couple of
years. His brother had been popping antacids during

Nolan's recent trip to Nashville. He was worried about Sebastian's health.

"So there is you, Chandra, Naya, Sebastian, Alonzo and Nyles." Laney ticked them off on her fingers. "I can't even imagine what it must've been like growing up in such a big family. It was just me and my sister and my grandfather. Savannah sort of had to handle both big sis and mom double duty. Which, even now, I can't help feeling guilty about. Like she missed out on part of her childhood by helping to care for me."

"It was the same with Chandra." Nolan rubbed the back of his neck. "That's why we're thrilled to see her so happy about her marriage and the baby. She deserves this."

"I feel the same about my sister. She's done so much for me. She's still mothering me—the way Chandra sometimes does with you." Laney's voice was filled with emotion. "But I admire the love between you, your sisters and your dad. It's sweet. Honestly? I'm a little jealous. When I was a kid, I always wished I had a big family."

"Losing a family member—whether through death or abandonment—it has a lifelong impact on you," Nolan acknowledged, fighting the urge to reach over and squeeze Laney's hand. "When Chandra moved to California several years ago, we all slowly drifted apart. So it's nice to feel connected with my family again."

"Okay. I have to know what you were all like as kids." Laney turned toward him as much as her seat belt would allow. "Starting with you."

Nolan glanced over at this incredibly beautiful

woman who had him mesmerized. He could easily talk to Laney for hours. Despite the fact that he was an introvert who cherished his solitude and usually found it difficult to deal with chatty people. Or to talk about himself like Laney was asking him to do now. But there was something so easy and comfortable about being with her. He wished they'd met anywhere other than the vineyard.

He forced a smile, then told her fond stories about him and his five siblings that made them laugh. As Nolan pulled into their community, he realized it'd been the best day he'd had in a long time.

"We didn't get to have our pie," he noted.

"No, we didn't." Laney seemed as happy as he was for an excuse to continue their evening.

"Nightcap?" Nolan asked, trying to rein in a grin. "I'm not sure what wine or beer goes with lemon icebox pie, but I'm sure I have something that'll do."

"I'd like that," Laney said.

Nolan pulled into his attached garage and parked. Maybe extending his night with Laney was a bad idea. But he just wasn't ready for their night together to end.

Laney slipped off her shoes at the door, just as Nolan did, even though he insisted she didn't need to. Hands washed, she took out the pie and cut it while he opened a German Riesling that had been chilling in his wine fridge.

He poured them each a glass and they sat on the back patio beneath the star-filled sky and talked about…everything. He'd said it was only fair that she share embarrassing stories about her and Savannah when they were kids. So she complied. They talked about their families. Their careers. Their favorite foods. Their shared love of great wine. The places she'd traveled and the places he hoped to travel. And with each passing moment, Laney felt more drawn to Nolan.

"Is it really nearly midnight?" Laney shot to her feet after glancing at the time on her phone. She'd enjoyed herself so much that time had gotten away from her. "I had no idea it was so late. I honestly didn't intend to kidnap you the entire day."

"You didn't kidnap me." Nolan stood, too. He shoved his hands into his pockets and flashed her a sheepish smile. "I invited you over for a cookout, then invited myself to be your date…*companion*…for tonight."

"Still, it's late and I should go. I'll walk across our backyards. No need to start the car."

"I'll walk you over," he said. "Let me grab our shoes."

"Nolan, wait…" Laney placed a hand on his arm. She tried to ignore the jolt of electricity that seared her palm. "Today was tough for me. If you thought I was being melodramatic about it, you never let on. And it was sweet of you to give up your day of peace and solitude, so I wouldn't feel so alone. It means a lot to me that you'd go out of your way to turn what started off as a miserable day into one of the best days I've had in a while. Thank you."

Nolan's dark eyes twinkled in the moonlight. He stared at her a moment, like there was something he wanted to say. "It was my pleasure," he said, finally.

"I know you want everyone at the winery to think that you're this hard-ass. But the truth is you're as gooey and sweet on the inside as the cinnamon rolls from the Magnolia Lake Bakery." Laney enjoyed teasing Nolan far more than she should.

"I don't know if I'd go straight to sweet and gooey." He chuckled. "But I'm glad you enjoyed today. I did, too. Maybe we both needed a night out and a little conversation beneath the stars." Nolan glanced up at the sky.

Laney leaned in to kiss Nolan's cheek: a simple show of gratitude. But her sudden movement startled him. He turned back toward her, and his firm lips met hers.

The inadvertent kiss took them both by surprise. They pulled away and silently regarded one another.

Laney's pulse raced and her heart beat wildly. It was an honest mistake for which she should apologize. Yet, her only thought was that she'd really, *really* like to kiss Nolan again. Intentionally this time.

Laney's teeth sank into her lower lip when Nolan's gaze dropped to her mouth. She raised a trembling hand to his face. His beard tickled her palm, and his chest rose and fell heavily with each breath. But he didn't pull away. Laney leaned in closer. This time, Nolan closed the space between them. His firm lips crashed against hers, and his arms circled her waist.

Laney understood all of the reasons they shouldn't be doing this. But she'd liked Nolan from the moment she'd met him. And she'd spent the past few weeks wondering how it would feel for him to kiss her and to hold her in his arms like this. So she couldn't tear herself away, even if she should.

Nolan pulled her closer, molding her lower body to his. His lips glided over hers. When she parted her lips on a soft gasp, Nolan swept his warm tongue—tasting of her homemade lemon pie and the bottle of Riesling wine they'd shared—between them. And she knew in that moment that if Nolan Valentine invited her into his bed, she wouldn't say no.

Nolan kissed the edge of the incredibly kissable lips that had driven him crazy for weeks. His eyes had been drawn to them every time Laney spoke. Stealing glances at her mouth was a habit he'd tried, unsuccessfully, to break.

And now that he was finally kissing Laney, his body was filled with heat and deep longing for this woman he'd been silently pining over for weeks. Imagining what it would be like to kiss her this way. To take her to his bed and show her just how much he wanted her and all the ways he could worship the body he'd been adoring.

He swallowed the gentle murmurs that intensified along with their kiss. His thumb caressed the soft skin of her arched back as he inhaled the deliciously sweet scent that had been teasing him since she'd gotten into his car freshly showered. A citrus grove surrounded by a field of fresh flowers.

Nolan loved the feel of her soft lips gliding against his. The taste of her mouth. The way her body with its undulating curves melded into his. But in a brief moment of clarity, he recognized he shouldn't be kissing her.

Delaney was an employee, and the work she was doing for their vineyard was important. Critical to the growth and success of Valentine Vineyards, which his father wanted—seemed to need—so desperately. He wouldn't be the reason this experiment failed.

Nolan pulled away, his chest heaving as he tried to catch his breath and get his head back on straight.

"Laney…" He swallowed hard as he studied her wild eyes and kiss-swollen lips. "I'm sorry, but we can't."

"No, I'm sorry. I shouldn't have…" Laney's lashes fluttered. Her eyes cast downward as she pressed a hand to her lips. "I should go. Let me get my things."

She hurried inside, a blur of sky-blue fabric and shimmering brown skin.

Nolan stood there frozen, dragging a hand down his face. Unsure of what to say or what to do. He'd really messed this up by kissing Laney. Not just because she was an employee. Because he liked Laney as a friend. He enjoyed spending time with her.

"I've really fucked this up," Nolan muttered beneath his breath.

"You really fucked what up, Nolan?"

"Naya? What the hell are you doing here?" Nolan asked in a loud whisper. "And where's—"

"Laney?" Naya folded her arms and cocked a hip. "She was escaping out of the front door just as I was about to knock on it. Said she was walking home, but I insisted we'd drive her. She's waiting in the living room looking like a feral rabbit desperate to escape," Naya responded in a loud whisper of her own. She smacked Nolan's arm hard. "What the hell did you do to upset her?"

"I didn't do anything."

"Nolan." Naya hiked an eyebrow, her expression calling bullshit on his claim of innocence.

Nolan sighed heavily, glancing over his sister's head at the doorway, then back again. He pulled her farther away from the door. "Laney and I spent today together. It wasn't a date," he noted in response to Naya's widened eyes. "It was two neighbors, who are also coworkers, hanging out. No big deal."

"Except?"

"Except… She kissed me a moment ago. And I kissed her back. But then I came to my senses and reminded her that dating isn't an option for us." He groaned quietly.

"Why not?" Naya asked.

"You know why, Nye."

"There's nothing in the employee handbook prohibiting dating. No thanks to you." She poked a finger in his chest. "And you obviously like each other so—"

"No, Naya. End of discussion. And again… What are you doing here?"

"Right." His sister's expression shifted from being ready for a full-blown argument to one bursting with excitement. "It's Chandra. She's been in labor for the past few hours. We've been trying to call you, but your phone is off."

"Shit. I turned it off while we were in the movie theater. I must've forgotten to turn it back on. It's still in the car. Is Chandra okay?"

"She's fine. Just beyond ready to get this baby out of her." Naya smiled. "We'll get to meet our niece in

just a few hours. Since we had some time, I promised
Dad and Chan I'd try and track you down. They were
both worried."

Nolan narrowed his gaze at his sister.

"Okay, I was, too, knucklehead." Naya shoved him
with her elbow. "Don't ever scare us like that again.
As soon as we get to the hospital, I'm gonna add tracking to your phone. Now, c'mon. Let's go. If I miss the
birth of my niece because you couldn't remember to
turn your phone back on after your movie date, I'm seriously going to kick your ass."

Naya hurried back inside, where Laney was hovering near the garage door like she was a cornered rabbit
plotting her escape.

"Laney, I'm sorry about this," Nolan said.

"There's nothing to be sorry about." She gave him a
dead-eyed smile that broke his heart a little. "We'd better go before you two miss the big moment."

"Exactly what I was saying." Naya slipped her arm
through Laney's. "You look super cute tonight, by the
way."

"I'm glad someone thinks so." Laney glanced at
Nolan momentarily, before returning her attention to
Naya.

Was his sister seriously hitting on his date, just to
prove a point?

*She is not your date. She is not your date. She is
not...*

"I'll drop Laney off and meet you at the hospital."
Nolan narrowed his gaze at his sister.

Translation: Not funny. Quit fucking around.

Naya grinned, amused to no end.

"Actually, I'll just sit in your drive and wait. That way you can follow me back to Gatlinburg. If you can keep up. And don't forget to turn your phone back on." Naya hit the garage door opener. "Good night, Laney. See you at the office on Monday."

Laney said good-night, then climbed into the passenger seat of Nolan's car as soon as he unlocked it. She put her seat belt on and stared out the window, as if she couldn't bear to look at him.

Nolan turned his phone back on, then pulled out of the garage. He made the short drive over to Laney's, then turned to her.

"I had an amazing time with you tonight, Laney. And, obviously, I'm attracted to you. But I can't risk blowing this for my dad. This vineyard means everything to him."

"I'm clear on your position, Nolan. No need to explain. See you in the office on Monday." She got out of the car. "Thank you again for tonight. I had a really nice time."

Laney hurried up her walkway. She fumbled with her keys at the door before finally stepping inside and turning on the light. She waved goodbye, then shut the door.

Nolan cursed himself for being an idiot. Then he rubbed his throbbing temple. Maybe Laney had kissed him first, but this was all his fault. Despite telling himself otherwise, everything about tonight had felt like a date. Should he really be surprised it had ended in a kiss?

He slowly backed out of Laney's drive and then fol-

lowed his lead-foot sister in her black Audi A5 Prestige
Cabriolet convertible back to the hospital in Gatlinburg
to await the birth of their first niece. Trying his best to
forget about the best kiss he'd ever had and the woman
who'd burrowed her way beneath his skin.

"So do we want to talk about the whole Laney Carlisle thing?" Naya rocked their brand-new niece, Autumn Sienna Brandon—the first of a new generation
of Valentines.

The girl slept peacefully in his sister's arms. Her
parents were fast asleep after twelve exhausting hours
of labor. The proud, first-time grandfather had gone
home to get some sleep.

"No, *we* don't." Nolan stared at his niece with her
sepia-brown skin, jet-black curls and a nose like her
father's. "Mostly because it's none of your business."

"I'm glad you and Laney are dating. She's perfect
for you."

"We are *not*—" Nolan halted his objection.

What was the point? Regardless of what they called
it, his day with Laney had been tantamount to a date.

"I wouldn't be super obvious about it, but there's
nothing that says you two can't date."

"Stop hogging the baby." Nolan sank onto the sofa
and reached for his niece.

Naya deposited the sleeping newborn in his arms,
and Autumn settled against his chest.

"Cole and Ren's wedding is Saturday, and neither
of you has a date. You should go together. It makes
sense, right? Parking will be limited, and you're neigh-

bors. Why not carpool? Besides, I helped Renee and her mom create the seating chart. I put you two next to each other anyway."

"Enough with the matchmaking, Naya," Nolan whispered.

"The movie date and making out on your back patio… I ain't have nothin' to do with that." She yawned. "I'm simply suggesting that you two ride to the wedding together. I'm not asking you to propose, Nolan. Don't do it for me. Do it for the environment." His sister managed to say that last bit with a straight face.

Nolan didn't respond. Thankfully, Naya dozed off, her head resting on his other shoulder. The room was quiet except for the breathing of the sleeping baby, her exhausted parents and meddling aunt.

Maybe his sisters were right. Whatever was happening between him and Laney seemed worth exploring. Carpooling to his cousin Cole's wedding was the perfect way to start.

Thirteen

Laney strolled into the office as nonchalantly as possible on Monday morning. She flashed Nolan a bright smile and exchanged greetings.

She dropped her purse in her bottom desk drawer, then made herself a cup of coffee. "Did Chandra have the baby?"

"Meet Autumn Sienna Brandon." Nolan stood beside Laney and showed her a photo of Chandra holding the baby in her arms while the proud father, Julian, held her in his. "I'm officially an uncle now, and my dad is annoyingly happy about finally being promoted to grandfather. So be prepared... He'll probably corner you at some point and show you about fifty photos of my niece doing absolutely nothing."

"I'm thrilled for him." The tension in Laney's shoulders eased. She added creamer and sugar to her coffee. "And send my congratulations to the proud parents. I'll whip up a batch of those lemon bars Chandra likes so much."

"She'd like that." Nolan stared at her with a slight frown. Like there was something he needed to say but couldn't quite find the words.

"If this is about the other night," Laney said quietly.

"It isn't. Not exactly." Nolan stood taller. "I wanted to talk to you about Cole's wedding this weekend. I assume you're going."

"Yes. Why?"

"I'm going, too. And I was just thinking that…" Nolan inhaled deeply, and for a moment, Laney was worried he might hyperventilate. "The parking lot at the venue isn't very big. So I was thinking… There's no point in us both driving."

Laney considered his suggestion as she stirred her coffee. If they could share an office eight hours a day after their unfortunate kiss, sharing a car ride a few miles up the road seemed harmless enough.

"Carpooling sounds like a great idea. And don't worry. I promise not to kiss you this time." Laney held up a hand.

"Oh…well, good." Nolan almost sounded disappointed. He straightened his tie. "We can iron out the specifics after my meeting with Maria this morning." Nolan grabbed his cup of coffee and laptop, then left.

Laney sank onto her chair and sighed.

Nolan Valentine was a riddle wrapped in a mystery inside an enigma if ever she'd seen one.

When she'd first come to the winery, he didn't seem to like her. Then he'd come to tolerate her but remained distant. Then he'd been all concerned and friendly. Even a little flirtatious. But when she'd kissed him, he'd completely backed off saying they couldn't do this. Now he was inviting her to carpool to Cole's wedding?

Laney blew out a long breath and shook her head. No one could accuse Nolan of being boring and predictable. That was for sure.

Laney picked up the phone and dialed her sister to tell her she needed to go shopping for Cole's wedding after all.

"You're actually considering moving to Seattle?" Savannah stopped looking through the racks of clothing at the expensive department store. She propped one hand on her hip.

"I am." Laney kept sifting through the overpriced dresses, avoiding her sister's stare.

"Why?" Savannah put a hand on her shoulder, forcing Laney to meet her gaze.

"Because this is what Harper wants."

"Harper is eight, Laney. She also wants her own pony and a diet that consists of nothing but chicken nuggets and Rice Krispies Treats. You've never had a problem saying no to an unreasonable request." Savannah folded her arms.

"Is it *really* unreasonable that she wants to get to know her dad? That she wants to grow up with her grandparents, aunts, uncles and cousins?" Laney asked.

"Because I would've given anything for the chance to have that when I was her age."

"I know." Savannah pushed back her loose dark brown curls. "But our situation was different, Laney. Our parents died. They didn't abandon us, then show up eight years later ready to play parent of the year."

"I realize that." Laney tried not to sound as deflated as she felt. "But that isn't Harper's fault. I won't rob her of the opportunity to get to know her father, if that's what they both want. Whatever your feelings about him, Vanna, Derrick is a good dad."

"Maybe he is." Savannah shoved dresses on the rack angrily. "But I don't like Derrick showing up out of the blue and acting like he has the right to dictate your lives. Or that you're allowing Harper to believe that you two just lost touch. Derrick *chose* to walk away." Savannah's expression softened. "It isn't your job to buy into some revisionist history that makes him seem like a hero just for showing up in his daughter's life."

"I know." Delaney resumed her fruitless search.

"Harper has the right to know why her dad hasn't been in her life. It isn't fair that she believes it's been some nefarious plot of yours to keep them apart."

"Maybe she does have the right to know." Laney selected a dress for a closer look, then put it back. "But now, when she's finally connecting with her father, certainly isn't the time to tell her. He isn't a bad guy, Vanna. He made a choice back then, and so did I. I don't fault him for that."

"You always approach things calmly and objectively. You remind me so much of Dad." Savannah's eyes filled with tears. "I wish you'd really gotten to know him. To know them both."

"Me, too." Laney fought back tears.

And that was why she wouldn't do anything to sour Harper's relationship with Derrick. Laney knew how painful it had been growing up without her parents.

"I appreciate you wanting to give Harper the world. But what about what you want?" Savannah sifted through the garments on a nearby rack.

What she wanted was for Nolan Valentine to kiss her again and to invite her to his bed. But her life rarely played out exactly as she'd wanted.

"This consulting opportunity Derrick arranged is something I would never have anticipated at this stage in my career," Laney said.

"You're saying you're not qualified?" Savannah frowned. "I find that hard to believe."

"I'm confident in my qualifications, but most institutions would require more experience for a pivotal role like this. And if this opportunity wasn't in Seattle, and had been arranged by anyone other than Derrick, I'd already be on the next plane there, and you'd be cheering me on," Laney said. "So why should I let my issues with Derrick prevent me from exploring such a golden opportunity? One I might never see again?"

It was the sensible choice. And Laney always tried to make important decisions based on logic rather than emotion. But she couldn't deny her growing attachment to Magnolia Lake. Savannah and her family were there. She loved the community and her job at the winery. Then there was her growing relationship with Nolan.

But the job was temporary, and Nolan had made it clear there would be nothing more than friendship between them. So other than her sister, what was keeping her there?

"Do you always have to be so damn reasonable, Laney Carlisle?" Savannah groaned. "Just once, can't you be petty and a little vindictive?"

They both dissolved into a fit of giggles in the middle of the luxury department store.

Savannah hugged Laney. "Whatever you decide, you know I'll support you. Even if it breaks my heart."

"I know." Laney smiled. "Now, can we hit Pause on this dress hunt and get something to eat?"

"That's a decision I can definitely get behind." Savannah's dimples were on full display as she slipped her arm through Laney's and led her out of the store.

"Harper's education is an important consideration," Laney explained after they'd placed their order at an Italian restaurant. "She's gifted in math and science, and I want to nurture that. She's spent the past couple of years in enrichment programs."

"Magnolia Lake is expanding. And Renee, Zora and I are working to create a community school that would accommodate children with a range of learning styles. That would include a typical education model and options for children on the autism spectrum, like Ren's son Mercer, as well as an advanced track for children like Harper," Savannah explained excitedly.

"That's an impressive undertaking," Laney said. "Why didn't you mention it before?"

"We wanted to do the necessary research and build a solid case before we presented the idea to the rest of the family. Initially, we considered establishing a small private school. But then we realized what an impact we could have on the town we love by making it a community school instead. Zora is spearheading the project with support from me and Renee. We want to have the school up and running by the start of the next school year. So if you did decide to stay…"

"You've covered all the bases, haven't you?" Laney loved her sister, and it'd been nice spending the summer in Magnolia Lake where they could have moments like this in person. Was it really possible that Harper could attend school with her cousins and still be challenged academically? "But no pressure, right?"

"Oh, I'm applying all the pressure I can." Savannah sipped her coffee, which she drank every chance she got now that she was done breastfeeding Remi. "I promised to support you, no matter what you choose. I never said I was abandoning my campaign to make you stay. Derrick isn't the only one with a few tricks up his sleeve."

That was her sister, all right. Savannah knew exactly what she wanted, and she was determined to make it happen. Laney wished she were more like her older sister in that regard.

"So… How are things going with you and Nolan?" Savannah asked.

"What?" Laney coughed and sputtered, her eyes wide. She nearly choked on her water.

"Well, well." Savannah raised a brow.

"Naya obviously told you about the incident at No-lan's place."

Incident? Is that how she was referring to the kiss now? Like it was a safety issue or a mugging?

Now Savannah coughed and sputtered. She set her coffee mug down on the saucer with a clink. "What happened at Nolan's place, and when was this?"

Oops.

"It was nothing. Really." Laney brought her sister up to speed on everything that had happened, ending with Nolan's confusing invitation to carpool to Cole's wedding.

"For the record, sweetie, that isn't nothing. That sounds like a whole lot of *something*," Savannah teased. She dipped a piece of the warm, crusty bread their server set on the table into a plate with a blend of olive oil and fragrant herbs.

"Okay, fine. It's a *little* something. But by the time I figure out whatever the hell this might be between us, I'll be long gone." Laney dipped a piece of bread into the oil, too. "Maybe it's for the best. Nolan is my boss, and he's Blake's cousin. If we dated, it'd be weird, *right*?"

Savannah's hazel eyes lit up. "Honestly? You two go together like peanut butter and jelly. I realized it the moment I met him."

"Is that your official admission that renting me a place across from his backyard was a bold-faced attempt to get the two of us together?" Laney pointed at her sister.

"I have no idea what you're talking about." Savannah shrugged. "But this explains your frantic call about finding the perfect dress."

Laney's face warmed, but she wouldn't confirm or deny Savannah's conclusion. "So, about this dress..."

"Now that I understand the situation, I've got just the shop in mind." Savannah grinned, and Laney could practically hear the gears turning in her determined sister's head.

Laney was thankful the server chose then to bring out their plates.

Nolan Valentine already took up way too much space in her head. She needed to put her hurt pride over his rejection aside and focus on the career opportunity of a lifetime. The one that would take her to Seattle at the end of the summer, if all went well. Then she wouldn't need to think about Nolan and what might have been between them.

Fourteen

Nolan sat at his assigned table at Cole and Renee Abbott's wedding reception, nursing a Bourbon Peach Smash and admiring Laney's form. The woman looked exquisite in an elegant, yet seductive one-sleeve dress as she danced with one of the locals. The vibrant orange hue popped against Laney's deep brown skin.

Nolan's jaw had practically hit the floor when Laney had stepped out of her house in the formfitting dress. The fabric hugged her curves and the ruching made her bottom look like a sweet, juicy, summer-ripened peach. The nude heels made her legs look incredibly long while still giving him maybe an inch of height on her. She was wearing some shimmery body lotion that sparkled in the light, and tonight she'd opted to wear contacts rather than her usual glasses.

Nolan was more than a little taken with Delaney Carlisle. She was the most beautiful woman in the room aside from Renee, the bride. He was still kicking himself for not accepting her invitation to dance.

"Laney looks hot tonight." Naya slipped into Laney's vacant chair beside Nolan.

"Didn't anyone ever teach you it's rude to openly lust after someone else's date?" Nolan took another sip of his cocktail.

"Thought you weren't on a date?" Naya smirked.

"We aren't. I'm her ride."

But for the past week, he'd thought of little else but that kiss and how much he'd enjoyed the day they'd spent together.

"That's bullshit, and we both know it." Naya picked up Nolan's drink and sipped it. "Oh, that's good. What is this?"

"It's a Bourbon Peach Smash and it's yours."

Naya raised the glass in thanks, then took another sip.

"Now, since you two obviously *are* on a date, why don't you do something novel, like… I don't know… dancing with her yourself? In that dress, every available man and a few women will be lined up to dance with her."

"I don't know, Nye. I really do like Laney, but there's a lot to consider. I have baggage. She has baggage— whom she happens to have a kid with. She works for us. The woman breaks all my dating rules." Nolan rubbed his jaw, stealing another glance at Laney. "Yet…"

"I've never seen you so enamored with someone."

Naya placed a gentle hand on his arm. "She obviously likes you, too."

"I know Laney kissed me, but… I'm not sure she sees me the same way I see her. And to be honest, I'm not sure I'm ready to get involved like that again."

"You'll never know until you try." Naya straightened his tie. "Besides, I think you're underestimating Laney's feelings for you. Have you not noticed how often she glances over here?"

They both looked toward Laney, who happened to catch his eye. She flashed him a bashful smile, then returned her attention to a guy who looked a lot like that country singer they played on the radio there all the time.

"Laney is talking to country superstar Dade Willis right now. And while he's making eyes at her, she keeps stealing glances at you. If that woman isn't into you, I don't know who is."

Nolan considered Naya's words. Maybe his sister had a point.

"Show her there's more to you than spreadsheets and expense projections, Nole. If you don't, you'll regret it." Naya stood, squeezing his shoulder. "I'm going to get my drink. When I get back, you'd better not still be sitting here."

Nolan groaned in response to his bossy younger sibling. But he couldn't take his eyes off Laney. When two other women came up to Dade, Nolan made his way across the room. He grabbed a bottle of water and handed it to her.

"I know it isn't your favorite Malbec," Nolan said. "But it's important to stay hydrated."

"Thank you, Nolan." Laney's brown eyes glittered with amusement.

His heart beat wildly, and his pulse raced.

Why couldn't he stop staring at those glossy, full lips with just a hint of peach tint? Wondering if the lips that had tasted like fresh berries when he'd kissed her before tasted like an orchard peach tonight?

Laney sipped some water as a slow song started to play.

Nolan cleared his throat. "Dance with me?"

"I thought you couldn't dance." Laney drank more of her water, then capped the bottle.

"Didn't say I couldn't dance." Nolan extended his open palm to Laney, and she placed her hand in his. He twirled her before slipping an arm around her waist and settling into a slow sway. "I said dancing isn't my thing. Not anymore."

"That's a shame. You're not bad." Her playful grin lit up the room and made his heart swell. "You said you don't dance *anymore*. Why'd you stop?"

"My ex and I took ballroom dancing classes together for a fraternity brother's wedding. We enjoyed it, so we joined one of those dance studios. I guess I don't like dancing anymore because—"

"It reminds you of her." Laney leaned into him, her warm gaze level with his.

For a moment, it felt as if the entire world had faded away and it was just him and Laney on that dance floor, in that town, in the whole of existence. And he could barely fucking breathe, let alone think of anything but leaning in for another taste of those sweet lips that had teased and tortured him for the past few weeks. Lips that had tasted like fresh berries, sunshine and a little slice of heaven.

If Laney thought his sudden inability to speak strange, she didn't let on. Instead, she leaned in a little closer, smiled sweetly and continued.

"When Derrick and I first split, everything reminded me of him. It didn't happen right away, but one by one, I reclaimed the experiences that had once brought me joy by doing them anyway. I needed to associate new memories with those places or activities. Otherwise, I was permitting my past to steal the future joy those things could bring me."

Nolan finally found words again. "Never thought of it that way."

Delaney Carlisle had taken him completely by surprise. Because Nolan had honestly begun to believe that his dream woman—brainy, beautiful and just nerdy enough to get his offbeat sense of humor—just didn't exist. Yet here she was, standing in his arms dancing with him and staring at him like maybe she felt the same way about him, too.

But his life had never been that simple. So he couldn't help looking for the trapdoor that would open and swallow his hopes and dreams whole—like a killer whale swallowing a seal pup.

"Speaking of associating new memories with past experiences... I really enjoyed our movie date the other night. It reminded me how much I enjoyed going to a sci-fi or action film on opening weekend. I'd convinced myself that I'd just outgrown the experience. But that wasn't true. It was my way of walling off painful memories."

"Then I guess it was a moment of growth for both of us." Laney's dark brown eyes lit up with a warmth that made him feel as if he was floating on the warm Caribbean Sea. "Wait… Did you just refer to it as a *date*?"

"I did." Nolan led Laney to a more isolated area. The light was even dimmer there than on the dance floor. "I know I said it wasn't a date then or tonight."

"But now?" Laney's gorgeous skin practically glowed, and she could barely restrain a lopsided smile. The same smile she flashed when they debated something at the winery, and he'd realized she was right. And while she often finished his sentences, she seemed to be enjoying this moment far too much to let him off the hook.

Nolan loosened his tie a little so he could breathe. "What if I wanted them to be?"

Laney's mouth spread into a full-blown grin. "If you'd asked, I would've said yes."

Nolan smiled. "Does that mean we're officially on a date now?"

"Looks that way, Valentine." Laney's eyes danced with amusement. "I hope to see more of those fancy moves because I do not want to dance with Len Dawson and those two left feet of his again. My poor toes can't take it."

And just like that, he was obsessed with those

painted toes of hers. He didn't even need to look down, the image was already branded on Nolan's brain.

"There are a couple things we should address," Nolan said.

"The whole you're-my-boss thing?" Laney was clearly enjoying this.

"Yes. More importantly, I'm part of the management team at Valentine Vineyards. So as much as I like you, Laney, I can't let that temper my decisions about what's best for the company."

"I'd be disappointed if you did." Laney smoothed down his tie. "Your sense of logic, fairness and propriety are among the things I like most about you. Seeing you in those swim trunks didn't hurt, either." Her melodic laugh made his heart flutter.

"And it can't seem as if I'm showing favoritism because of our relationship. So I'd like to be discreet about this." He gestured between them.

"So you're proposing we continue the *we're just friends and totally not dating* facade for everyone else's benefit. Sounds like fun, and it would drive our sisters crazy."

"That's the best part," he whispered conspiratorially, and she laughed.

"So does that mean I shouldn't lean in like this and…"

Laney's soft, warm lips tasted like the sweetest, juiciest peach he'd ever had. When she pulled back and glanced around with a naughty smile, he was breathless and desperate for another taste. Missing the softness and warmth of her body pressed to his.

"This'll be fun." Laney grinned. But it was immediately followed by a serious tone and expression. "This undercover dating thing… You're not looking for anything serious, right?"

Open trapdoor. Cue the baby seal being swallowed whole.

"Definitely not," Nolan said in a voice that indicated he definitely did. "Been there. Done that."

"Perfect." Laney's smile seemed sad. "I need to talk to the bride and groom, but I'll see you on the dance floor."

Nolan heaved a quiet sigh, a knot churning in his gut as he watched Laney walk away.

Laney glanced over at Nolan. The cabin of his black, top-of-the-line Jaguar XF had been silent since he'd pulled out of the parking lot of the wedding barn. Laney's heart was racing and there were a million things she wanted to say. Beginning with asking Nolan if she'd just imagined that he'd asked that they consider tonight an actual date. But before she could speak, he slipped his hand into hers while driving.

It was a very un-Nolan thing to do for a man who almost always drove with his hands firmly at ten and two o'clock. Which made it all the more meaningful to her.

Laney's shoulders relaxed and she tried not to grin like a giddy schoolgirl after her first kiss. Though to be fair, when she'd kissed Nolan the other night, it had been her first kiss in quite some time.

"So… I've been thinking," Laney said.

"Uh-oh." Nolan chuckled. "Whenever you say that

at the winery, it's accompanied by spreadsheets, a case study and an expensive acquisition request."

Laney laughed. "True. But not this time. This time, I was thinking, if you don't already have plans for tomorrow, we could maybe do a movie marathon. Catch you up on the Marvel and DC movies you've missed over the past three years and fill in some of those story gaps. Then the movie we saw last week will make a lot more sense to you."

"You want to spend the entire day watching movies with me?" Nolan seemed amused by the proposal.

"You're lucky I'm such a cheap date." She laughed. "Besides, since we're trying to be undercover about this whole thing, hanging out at my place seemed like a good idea."

Nolan nodded, his smile widening. "Yeah. That sounds great. I'll bring the wine, and if you want, I can throw something on the grill."

"Perfect!" Butterflies danced in Laney's stomach. She was over the moon about sitting on her sofa with Nolan watching sci-fi flicks for hours. Savannah was right. She needed to get out more.

How would she ever get over being socially awkward if she wasn't being very social?

"So what time are we doing this movie marathon tomorrow?" Nolan asked.

Suddenly a wave of guilt hit Laney. She had an informal interview the next morning with Derrick's friend—the dean of his university in Seattle. She'd opted not to tell Nolan. She didn't want the Valentines to base their decision on whether she would be available beyond the summer. If Laney decided to move to Seattle, she would help the family find a qualified enologist, if they chose to add one to their team.

But Nolan had made it clear that he wouldn't allow their relationship to compromise his business decision about whether they would keep her on at the winery. It was a reminder to her to do the same. She needed to make her relocation decision based on what was best for Harper's happiness and education and for her career.

Laney would base her decision to stay or to go on logic and reason. She wouldn't be swayed by the fact that she was shamelessly craving Nolan, who looked like a three-course meal *plus* a snack in a tailored, athletic-cut three-piece gray suit, a crisp white shirt he'd managed not to get a speck of food on all night and a solid black tie. Nor would she be swayed by the fact that every day it felt like she was falling for the man a little more.

"One o'clock," she said, finally. Laney turned her attention to the road ahead, her shoulders suddenly tense. "I have an appointment earlier in the day."

"Around here? On a Sunday morning?" Nolan's words felt more like an observation than a question. So she treated them as such.

Still, Laney couldn't help the guilt that ate away at her, making her palm, pressed to Nolan's, suddenly feel itchy.

"That'll give me time to go for a morning swim, then take breakfast to my sister and Julian and visit my niece," Nolan said.

"That's sweet of you, Nolan." Laney regarded him with a smile.

There was something incredibly attractive about a man who cared so deeply for his family. Especially his mother and sisters. She was an absolute sucker for them. In fact, she'd met Derrick in the campus bookstore when he'd asked her opinion while he was picking out university T-shirts and mugs as gifts for his sisters and parents.

"Chandra pretty much gave up her childhood, helping to raise us after our moms walked away. Chandra, Sebastian, Alonzo and I have a different mother than the twins," Nolan clarified. "There's not a lot we wouldn't do for her."

"I feel the same about Savannah."

Laney understood that deep sense of love mixed with guilt and the resulting sense of obligation to an older sibling who'd sacrificed so much. That's why this decision was hard. She didn't want to disappoint Savannah, who wanted so badly for her to stay in Magnolia Lake. But she'd promised their grandfather that she'd pursue a career she loved. Achieve all the things she dreamed of. She couldn't do that if she stayed, and that realization broke her heart.

"I also have a date proposal," Nolan said tentatively. "And before I ask, you need to know that I won't be the slightest bit insulted if you say no." He squeezed her hand.

"Noted." Laney nodded. "What do you have in mind?"

"You know how you talked about not letting past experiences steal your future joy? Well, I've been sitting on this invitation to a charity gala for an organization I sit on the board of: The Nashville Natural History Museum. Marian and I went every year. In fact, working on the gala is how we met. She was the executive director of the museum at the time. She moved on to a corporate position a couple years ago, but I haven't had the nerve to attend. And since you're into science and biology, I thought…"

"I'd love to go with you to Nashville, Nolan," Laney said. All the noticeable tension in Nolan's arm seemed to ease. "But Harper is coming back this Friday. So I'll need to make arrangements for her to spend the night with my sister. When is the gala?"

"In three weeks. I thought we could drive up the night before and spend some time exploring Nashville. Make it a weekend. Separate rooms, of course," he added, clearing his throat. "You're my guest, so I'll pay for your room."

"You don't need to do that, Nolan."

"It's the least I can do."

"If you insist," she said. "Sounds like a lovely weekend. I'm looking forward to it."

They resumed their comfortable rhythm of chatting about mundane things. Stories of them growing up with their siblings. College experiences. Odd coworkers, etc. Laney was disappointed when she realized Nolan had parked in her driveway.

Nolan held her hand as he walked her to the door. Neither of them spoke as they climbed her front porch.

"Laney, I didn't say it before, but you look stunning

tonight. When you walked out of that door, you honestly took my breath away. I'm pretty sure my heart stopped for a microsecond." Nolan put a hand to his chest, then shoved both hands into his pockets. "Until tonight, I always thought those were just metaphors."

"The dress was my sister's doing." Laney placed a hand high on her belly and glanced down at the midi-length bodycon dress that clung to every one of her curves. She hadn't been sure it was the best choice, but Savannah insisted that with the right foundation wear, the dress would look flawless, and she'd have Nolan and every man in the place eating out of her hand.

Thank God for Spanx.

Also, why did her sister *always* have to be right?

"Well, the incredibly beautiful woman inside that dress… That's all you." Nolan rubbed his bearded chin, his eyes sweeping admiringly down her body and land-ing momentarily at her feet before meeting her gaze again. "I really like the hair, too." He nodded toward her hair pulled back into a sleek bun with an off-center part. "It shows off your gorgeous features. Hands down, you were the most beautiful woman in that room tonight who wasn't wearing a wedding dress."

"That's kind of you to say." Laney took a few steps forward.

In her nearly three-inch nude Kahmune sandals in the shade Kumasi—which actually matched her deep brown skin tone—Laney was nearly as tall as Nolan. But she liked that his height was closer to her own. That she didn't have to crane her neck all the time the way she had when she was dating Derrick.

"You look quite dashing tonight, Mr. Valentine." Laney smoothed a hand down the lapel of the handsome gray suit Nolan wore. The athletic cut of the most certainly bespoke suit highlighted the strong chest and biceps that lay beneath the lightweight wool.

Nolan slipped his arms around her waist, pulling her a little closer. "I'll give my tailor your regards."

Before she could manufacture a witty comeback, Nolan leaned in and captured her lips in a soft, easy kiss that built slowly. As if he was savoring every moment of it. And when she parted her lips, Nolan swept his tongue between them, deepening their kiss.

The cooling sensation of the mint he'd popped in the car contrasted with the warmth of his tongue and the heat spreading down her spine, making her feel slightly weak at the knees. When he cupped either side of her face and tilted her head, she slid her arms beneath his open jacket and snaked them around his waist.

The chorus of "Cover Me in Sunshine" by P!nk and her daughter Willow Sage Hart startled them both.

Nolan pulled away, his eyes searching hers before pressing another kiss to her mouth. "That's Harper, right?"

Laney nodded, breathless. "She's calling to say good night."

"You should answer that." He nuzzled her neck. His voice, low and sexy, vibrated down her spine.

"I'll only be five minutes if you'd like to—"

"It's okay, beautiful." Nolan traced her cheekbone with his thumb. She could swear that her cells were transforming into putty one-by-one, beginning with her knees, which barely seemed to be able to hold her up. "I'll see you tomorrow afternoon. Tell Harper I said hello."

The phone had stopped ringing. But Laney knew her daughter. Harper would call back any second. She fumbled in her purse for her keys and opened the door, giving Nolan another quick kiss goodbye before going inside.

Back pressed to the door, Laney groaned, her heart still racing. When the phone rang again, it startled her, despite expecting the call.

"Harper, sweetie, hello," Laney said before her daughter could speak.

"You sound a little out of breath." Derrick's voice startled her.

"I was just coming into the house from a wedding reception. Savannah's brother-in-law's wedding was today."

Why did she feel guilty about telling Derrick—who had no right to know her personal business—that half-truth?.

"Where's Harper?"

"She's brushing her teeth." Derrick lowered his voice. "But before I bring her on, I wanted to ask if you'd consider letting Harper stay for the rest of the summer. Or at least a couple more—"

"Yes." Laney hadn't been able to say it quickly enough.

"You're sure?" Derrick seemed stunned.

"I'm sure." Laney unstrapped one shoe, then the other and padded into the kitchen. Why did kissing

Nolan make her hungry for…mint chocolate chip ice cream? "I realize how special this time together is for both of you."

"Thank you, Laney. I know how much you miss Harper."

"I do," she said, meaning it. "But I'm doing my best to take everyone's advice and enjoy my first kid-free, hot-mom summer."

"I can't thank you e— Wait…your *what*?"

"Is that Mommy? Mommy, Daddy and I want to ask you something…"

Laney put that one improv class she'd taken to use as she feigned surprise at Harper's request. Then they said their good-nights.

She'd already been enjoying her summer. Hanging out with Savannah and her family. Evenings at the pool. Her work at Valentine Vineyards. And getting to know Nolan. But now that they'd agreed to a secret summer fling, her summer was about to get much more interesting.

A knock at the door startled Laney. Had she left something in Nolan's car?

Laney opened the door. "What's wrong? Did I forget—"

Before she could finish the question, Nolan's lips were on hers. He ravished her mouth, with a desperation that warmed her chest and set her skin afire. One hand was pressed to her low back; the other cradled her face possessively.

Nolan kissed Laney with the same sense of urgency she felt. Like it was now or never.

Fifteen

Nolan had been sitting in Laney's driveway for five minutes, regretting declining her invitation to come in. Willing himself to start the ignition and make the short drive to his place.

But it was as if he'd been physically incapable of starting that car and driving away when what he'd wanted more than anything was to take Laney to bed. To live out all of the erotic fantasies that had been playing in his head for the past few weeks. To show her how much he wanted her; how much he needed her.

As he kissed Laney now, his tongue gliding over hers as he cradled her face, he couldn't imagine ever going back to his life as it was before she'd walked through the doors of that winery and turned his world upside down.

Long before he ever laid a hand on her. Long before he'd ever considered kissing her or touching her this way.

"These lips—" he whispered between kisses "—and these hips—" he dropped his hands below her waist and squeezed her bottom "—have been teasing me all fucking night." Nolan kissed her greedily as he backed her against the wall.

"I was beginning to wonder if you'd noticed." Laney's impish grin and heated gaze ramped up his desire. Made him feel like his temperature was rising and his skin had grown too tight.

Electricity danced along Nolan's spine, and his heart thudded in his chest. His dick grew painfully hard pinned between them as he ravished her sweet mouth and his hands roamed her soft body. He wanted desperately to taste her.

"I want you, Laney," Nolan whispered roughly. He nipped at her earlobe and kissed along her jaw. Nuzzled her neck, inhaling her addictive floral-and-citrus scent. Then he kissed the bare shoulder that had been calling to him all night. "I want you more than I've ever wanted anyone in my life. And I want you *now*."

Laney cupped his jaw and met his gaze. She dragged a thumb along his lower lip. "I want you, too, Nolan."

Her sultry voice ratcheted up the desire that made him ache for her touch.

Nolan molded her body to his as he kissed her again. He loved the way she melted beneath his touch, her knees wobbly and her breath hitching.

When Delaney Carlisle entered a room, she shone from within as brightly as the Olympic torch with her vibrant personality, sparkling brown eyes and conta-gious laughter. But the tiny spark she revealed to the world was a glimmer of the blazing inferno beneath the surface. A blaze that burned so hot it had been capable of igniting the cold, dark depths of his frozen heart. Something he'd begun to feel impossible. But right now, his biggest dilemma was how to peel off the painted-on dress that had sent his pulse racing all night. Because he honestly didn't think he could wait long enough to get her up to bed.

Nolan kissed his way down Laney's neck and down her chest. Then he dropped to his knees on the living room carpet and kissed the fabric covering her belly, her stomach rising and falling with each breath. He dipped lower, his hands gliding up her outer thighs beneath the dress, lifting the fabric as he went.

Laney placed her hands on his shoulders, to steady herself. Her chest heaved from their heated kiss. "Oh my God, Nolan. You aren't going to… I mean…right here?"

Nolan's mouth curved in a sly grin as he kissed her now-exposed inner thigh. He shoved up the hem of her dress high enough to slip one leg over his shoulder, then the other.

Laney gasped as he pressed her against the wall and shifted her weight onto his shoulders, his hands beneath her ass to steady her. She pressed her palms flat against the wall, her breathing rapid and shallow.

He kissed his way up her thigh, then over the damp, black fabric shielding her sex. God help him, three snaps held the fabric in place.

"A bodysuit," he muttered.

Why did he find the fact that Laney was wearing a strapless bodysuit so fucking hot?

He popped open one snap, then the next and the next. A little thrill shot down his spine with the sound of each snap giving way. He inhaled deeply, appreciating the scent of her arousal. Nolan kissed her bare, glistening skin, eliciting tiny moans that grew more vocal as he laved her swollen sex with his eager tongue. Laney dug her shoulders into the wall, her back arching as he feasted on her salty-sweet skin, bringing her closer to the edge.

"Oh my God, oh my God, oh my God..." she muttered again and again. "Yes, yes, yes!"

One hand dived into his hair as Laney moved against his mouth. Suddenly, she froze, his name on her lips and her sex pulsing. He lapped at her salty-sweet skin. Loving the feel and taste of her. His mind going immediately to how good it would feel to be inside this woman who had a gift for making him feel a kaleidoscope of emotions. All of the feelings he typically stuffed down and pretended weren't there. But with Laney, he couldn't. More importantly, with her he didn't want to hold back any part of himself. He wanted to give her everything.

Nolan ran his tongue along her glistening center, loving the way she shivered in response. Finally, her breathing started to slow. He set one of her bare feet onto the floor, then the other as he stood, his own breathing still labored. But he didn't pull down the fabric hitched above her hips. Instead, he turned Laney around, his hardened length pressed to her gloriously bare bottom. Even through the fabric of his pants and underwear, having her bare ass rubbing against him made him hard as steel, aching to be inside her.

He lifted her hands above her head, pressing her palms flat to the wall as he lifted the dress, gliding it and the bodysuit up over her hips. He slid down the side zipper of her dress, tugging the top of the dress down to her waist and freeing her full breasts, leaving Laney nearly naked with her arms up and her hands pressed to the wall.

It was the most erotic thing he'd ever seen. His dick throbbed and his heart raced. Nolan kissed Laney's shoulder blade and used his foot to spread her stance a little wider. He slipped two fingers back and forth through her wetness. The other hand reached across the front of her body, squeezing her firm breast and teasing the already hardened peak as she lay back against him moaning softly.

"Delaney Carlisle, you are the sexiest woman I have ever known. I honestly can't get a fuckin' 'nuff of you," he whispered roughly in her ear as his fingers moved inside her.

Laney whimpered in response, her body languid.

Nolan stepped back, pulling Laney away from the wall enough for her to bend over slightly at the waist, changing the angle of his fingers inside her. Permitting him to reach the spot that made her cry out in pleasure and beg for more.

He dropped his other hand from her breast, placing it between her thighs and strumming her eager clit as his fingers moved inside her. Until she was squirming and begging, telling him how close she was again. And when she came hard, she leaned back against him, her legs trembling.

Nolan could not care less about the wetness on the pant leg of his expensive suit. All he knew was that he wanted...*needed*...to bring her to orgasm like that again. This time, he needed to be inside her.

"You okay, beautiful?" Nolan wrapped an arm around her waist, taking on the bulk of her weight as she breathed heavily. He nuzzled her neck and stroked her bare hip with his free hand.

"Okay?" Laney smiled slyly with her eyes still closed and her head against his shoulder. "Nolan, you have a real gift for understatement, don't you?"

Nolan chuckled, then kissed her tantalizing lips, which tasted of the frosting from Cole and Renee's wedding cake. He trailed kisses along her bare shoulder.

Laney practically hummed, her dark eyes finally fluttering open. "Can you grab a bottle of wine and a couple of glasses and meet me upstairs?" Laney pulled the top of her dress up and Nolan tugged the bottom back down over her hips.

"I would love to meet you upstairs, Laney." Nolan wrapped his arms around her waist and kissed her neck. "But first I need to make a quick trip to my place to grab—"

"Condoms? I grabbed a box last week." Laney laughed in response to his wide-eyed expression. "Don't look so surprised." She poked him in the gut, then kissed him again. "After last week I calculated that there was a better than fifty-fifty chance we'd end up needing them." She shrugged. "I didn't want to be caught ill-prepared."

"No, we definitely wouldn't want that, would we?" Nolan chuckled, he brushed his lips over hers before kissing her again. "You go ahead, sweetheart. I'll be up shortly."

Nolan watched appreciatively as Laney climbed the stairs. Even half-zipped and in disarray, the dress made her ass look like a museum-worthy work of art. He was incredibly grateful to whoever had designed the dress for the sexy vision of Laney climbing those stairs, which would forever be burned into his retinas.

He went into the kitchen, grabbed a bottle of Malbec—the full-bodied Argentinean wine Laney preferred—and opened it. Then he grabbed two crystal Syrah wineglasses, turned out the downstairs lights and made his way upstairs, determined to show Laney just how good they could be together.

Nolan entered the main bedroom, dimly lit by a bedside lamp. The shower was running in the adjoining bathroom and his heartbeat quickened at the thought of Laney naked, water sluicing over her soft brown skin.

He swallowed hard and set the wine bottle and glasses on the small table between the two chairs. Nolan removed his jacket and loosened his tie. He poured half a glass of wine for each of them and took a seat.

Until Laney had introduced him to it a few weeks ago, Nolan had never tried Malbec. He gently swirled the reddish-purple liquid in his glass, careful to hold it by the stem and not the bowl, so as not to raise the temperature of the wine. Nolan tipped his glass, inhaling the notes of blackberry, plum and black cherry finished with a hint of tobacco from aging in oak barrels. Then he took a deeply satisfying sip of the wine.

The Malbec was bold in some ways while nuanced in others. Much like Laney. She could be serious and focused about her work one minute and crack some silly joke the next. She was a tree-climbing tomboy by day and a glamorous goddess who could bring any man to his knees by night. Laney was like a highly addictive drug, and he simply couldn't get enough of her.

So why had he agreed to a temporary relationship when what he really wanted was to explore the possibility of a future with her?

Maybe because the way she'd phrased the question made it seem that a short-term fling was his *only* option.

The sound of Laney clearing her throat as she stood in the bathroom doorway pulled him out of his haze. He set his glass down roughly and moved to stand.

"No, don't get up." Laney held up a hand as she sauntered toward him wearing only a fluffy white towel secured by a precarious knot. Her hair was still pinned up. "You're exactly where I want you."

As Laney walked toward Nolan, her hips swaying, it felt as if time itself had slowed. Her eyes locked with his as she straddled him, planting her knees on either side of his hips. She cradled his face and planted soft kisses on the corners of his mouth, then directly on his lips. Laney licked at the seam of his lips, then glided her minty-sweet tongue between them, gliding it against his.

Her fingers made quick work of the buttons on his shirt as his dug into her bare bottom. He worked with

Laney to remove his dress shirt and undershirt. Watched as she trailed sensual kisses down his neck and chest. His body tensed with each deliciously slow kiss or teasing lick of his heated skin that cranked up flames of desire already burning inside him.

"Do you have any idea what you're doing to me right now? How hard it's been to sit across that office from you and pretend I wasn't imagining this?" Nolan gently gripped her chin, dragging her mouth back to his. He wrapped his arms around her as he kissed her greedily, his tongue searching hers. Until he felt like he might burst with desire for this woman.

Nolan gripped Laney's firm bottom, which was testing the limits of that towel, and stood. She wrapped her legs around him as he carried her to her bed and deposited her there.

Laney opened a bedside drawer and set the unopened box on top of it with an almost bashful smile. She loosened her towel, then dropped it to the floor before climbing beneath the covers. When she released her hair from the bun, those wild curls he simply adored sprang free. And when she lay back, the way her curls spread out on her silk pillowcase mimicked the rays of sunshine surrounding the sun inked on her brown skin. And for him, Laney Carlisle was just that. Much-needed sunshine that had turned his life upside down and given him reason to smile.

Nolan shed his remaining clothing and sheathed himself. Then he climbed into bed and resumed their heated kiss. Nolan spiked his fingers into Laney's soft hair that smelled of coconut and vanilla. He kissed her with a desperation he honestly hadn't ever felt before. He trailed feverish kisses down her neck and shoulder. Through the valley of her breasts and down her belly. Then he spread her open with his thumbs, kissing the glistening space between her thighs and lapping at her swollen folds.

Nolan relished every sigh, every hitch of her breath. The way Laney dug her heels into the mattress, legs trembling and back arched, when he'd sucked on her distended clit, bringing her to orgasm again, his name on her tongue as she gripped the sheets.

He kissed his way back up her body, his head peeking from beneath the cover. Nolan's glasses, foggy and crooked, didn't prevent him from enjoying the look of utter satisfaction on Laney's face as she lay back on the pillow, breathing heavily. She gripped the back of his neck, pulled him to her and kissed him long and hard, without hesitation.

There was something exceedingly hot about the way she'd kissed him. If he hadn't already been painfully hard and desperate to be buried inside her, the unhesitating glide of her full, lush lips against his—which tasted of her—would have driven him over the edge.

Nolan grabbed his aching length, pressing it to her entrance, savoring the delicious sensation as he slowly sank inside her depths. Laney's short fingernails dug into his back as she arched hers, as if impatient for him. He moved his hips, slowly at first, as he resumed their kiss. He ground his pelvis against the needy, swollen bundle of nerves, driving Laney to higher heights until she was trembling beneath him. Until the pulsing of her sex pulled him over the edge and he was calling her name, his forehead pressed to hers.

Nolan tumbled onto his back and stared at the ceiling, huffing as he tried to catch his breath. The world seemed to be spinning; a kaleidoscope of light and colors filled with a pleasure and passion he'd never known.

But as he lay there, staring at the ceiling, his chest rising and falling, he couldn't help wondering how sex would change things between them and what would happen next.

Sixteen

Laney lay on her back, her breath coming in shallow bursts as she stared at the ceiling. Nolan lay beside her doing the same, neither of them speaking. Her skin felt warm and tingly as her heartbeat and the pulsing of her sex slowed. Her brain was floating contentedly in a foggy bliss.

She was sated, yet ravenous for him again. Dreamy and euphoric, yet apprehensive about the impact sleeping together would have on their relationship. In the quiet of her bedroom filled with only the sounds of their collective breathing, a growing awkwardness bloomed in the silence.

Everything about their night together had been amazing. She wouldn't allow their shared social ineptitude to ruin it. One of them just needed to say...*something*.

Laney sucked in a deep breath, her heart starting to race again.

Just tell him how you feel. How hard can that be?

"Nolan, that was *beyond* amazing." The words rushed from Laney's lips before she could talk herself out of saying them. She rolled onto her side, propping her head on one fist as she met Nolan's gaze.

His nostrils flared and his sensual lips pulled into a sexy, lopsided smirk that managed to do things to her every single time. It was the expression he wore most often in the sensual dreams she'd had about him. When she'd imagined the two of them together like this. Only tonight had exceeded even her wildest dreams.

"*You* were beyond amazing." Nolan cupped her cheek and pressed another kiss to her lips—his still tasting of her. Something she'd found surprisingly erotic. In fact, nearly everything about Nolan Valentine was surprising.

Nolan was sweet and charming, despite his no-nonsense, seemingly gruff exterior. He was sincere and funny—often without trying. He understood her in ways no one else did—not even her sister. And after a single night in bed together, he'd shown her an unexpected side of himself that had also revealed an unexpected side of hers.

Had she forgotten how much she enjoyed sex and intimacy? Or did she just enjoy it so much more with Nolan? Or maybe it had just been a really long time since she'd been with anyone she didn't have to restock with batteries, and it was playing havoc with her sense of perception.

Laney traced a finger down his sternum, reveling in finally getting to touch the body she'd been thirsting over since she'd seen him in his swim trunks at the pool. "Tonight was…unexpected," she said.

"Was it, though?" Nolan raised a teasing brow as he dragged his thumb over her lower lip. "You stocked up on condoms."

Laney laughed. "That was more delusional hopefulness than a plan to seduce you. Besides, that's not what I meant. What surprised me was how amazing it was… how incredible we were together."

"You assumed the number-crunching nerd would be mediocre in bed?" Nolan dropped his hand from her face and frowned.

"It's not that I expected you to be substandard." Laney's heartbeat spiked when Nolan's frown deepened.

Fuck. She was making this after-sex conversation exponentially awkward.

He climbed out of bed suddenly, "I need to take care of this."

Laney watched Nolan, who was gloriously naked, as he stalked away and disappeared into the bathroom, providing her with an incredible view of his muscled ass.

She bit her lower lip and sighed. Nolan Valentine wasn't six feet tall with bulging biceps and a washboard belly. But he was fine, in every sense of the word. And his intense sex appeal had as much to do with his brilliant mind, huge heart and deep sense of empathy as it did with his handsome face, toned body and prowess between the sheets.

And she'd just hurt his feelings. Something she truly hadn't intended to do.

Why can't you just be normal?

Laney put one of the pillows piled onto the bed over her face and screamed into it.

She was really, really, *really* bad at this. Maybe it would've been better if they'd just lain there in silence.

No. That wasn't the answer. She just needed to think about what she wanted to say and then say it. *Clearly*, this time.

The toilet flushed and she could hear water running at the sink.

Laney sucked in a deep breath, counted to four, then released it.

As soon as Nolan emerged from the bathroom, Laney sat up, pulling the covers up around her chest. Nolan seemed to be debating whether to climb back into bed or get dressed.

"When I said you surprised me, I wasn't talking about any of those silly stereotypes, Nolan. I meant you're very straitlaced and proper. All about following the rules. So I didn't expect that you'd be a dirty-talking cunnilinguist with a gift for bestowing multiple orgasms and a penchant for having sex upside a wall while fully dressed."

Laney could hear herself rambling but couldn't quite stop herself. She needed him to understand how much tonight had meant to her. How glad she'd been that he'd been the one she'd finally broken her hiatus on sex with.

"And you made me remember that I'm not just a scientist and a mom. That I'm a sensual being who de-

REESE RYAN 189

serves to have amazing sex and…you know…maybe likes being a little adventurous in bed."

The tension in Nolan's face eased. The wide smile that spread across his face warmed her chest and made her stomach flip. Suddenly, he dissolved into a full belly laugh as he climbed back into bed. He tugged her down, so she lay flat on her back. Then he hovered over her.

His dark eyes twinkled in the dim light cast from the bedside lamp. "That's it. Your official nickname is Tisi."

"Tizzy? As in nervous, distracted and easily excited?" She studied his face.

"No. T-I-S-I. Think it, say it." Nolan pressed a kiss to her lips and all of the fluttery feelings low in her belly returned.

"My grandfather always said honesty was the best policy." Laney managed the words between the heated kisses Nolan peppered the corner of her mouth with. She glided her hands to his back, pulling him closer. Needing more of the skin-on-skin contact she craved.

"Agreed." Nolan trailed heated kisses down her neck. "I like that I know *exactly* what you're thinking in real time. That I never have to worry that you're saying one thing when you're actually feeling something else."

"Was that an issue in your last relationship?" Laney regretted her question the moment Nolan's back tensed beneath her fingertips. He ceased the delicious kisses that made her feel warm and tingly. "I'm sorry, Nolan. I understand if you don't want to talk about it."

"No, it's fine." Nolan lay on his back and gathered her to his chest. He kissed Laney's forehead and her heart expanded with the deep affection and protectiveness she felt toward this man. "It's been a while since I really talked about my marriage and why it fell apart."

"Was that your last relationship?"

"Yes." Nolan twirled a lock of her hair around his finger.

"How long ago was the divorce?" Laney asked.

"Three years. It was a rough breakup, so I haven't been in a rush to start anything new."

"I'm sorry things didn't work out, Nolan." Laney stroked his stubbled cheek. Her heart broke for him and the pain he'd endured.

A slow smile lit Nolan's eyes. He kissed her lips. "I was, too, then. I'm not sorry now. Because I wouldn't have met you. And that's something I'd truly regret."

She was probably grinning like an idiot, but Laney didn't care. Hearing Nolan articulate exactly what she felt… She couldn't have been happier.

Laney kissed Nolan hard, her tongue searching his.

Nolan gripped her bottom, pulling her into him as their kiss grew more frantic. Her beaded nipples ached, sensitized as they glided against the coarse hair on his hard chest. He reached for the bedside drawer where she'd stashed the remaining condoms.

"No." Laney grabbed his wrist. "Let me."

Nolan's eyes danced with heat and a hint of amusement. He gestured toward the drawer with a sly smile. "By all means."

Laney reached for one of the strips and tore off a foil packet, ripping it open. Her hands trembled slightly as she slowly rolled it down his length. When Nolan moved to flip the two of them over, she pressed his shoulders to the mattress and kissed him hard again. Then she gripped his length, pumping it a few times. She lifted onto her knees on either side of his hips and pressed the thick head of his dick to her entrance, sinking down onto him.

She sighed contentedly at the sensation of Nolan filling her, loving his wide-eyed look of amazement and the hunger in his hooded gaze as she mounted him and started to move her hips. Laney leaned forward, her hands pressed to his chest as he gripped her hips, his fingers digging into her flesh as he moved against her.

"Oh God, Nolan. I'm so close." Laney's hips moved faster, a sheen of sweat forming on her forehead. She was out of breath, her legs felt weak and the air-conditioned room suddenly felt so damn hot she thought she might burst into flames.

Nolan pulled her mouth down to a bruising kiss, his fingers trailing down her spine.

"I've got you, baby," he whispered, his lips brushing her ear, and his beard abrading her skin.

She was overwhelmed with the opposing sensations, feeling him everywhere at once. And there was something about Nolan Valentine uttering those four words: *I've got you, baby.* She felt both a heightened sense of arousal and a deep sense of comfort.

Before Laney could register what was happening, Nolan had flipped her onto her back without breaking their connection. He kissed her ear. "I'm gonna bring us both home."

Nolan lifted one of her legs onto his shoulder as he moved inside her, his pace slow and steady, at first.

But as she got closer to the height of her arousal, his hips thrust harder and his pace increased. Her breathing quickened as he ground his pelvis against hers, further sensitizing the tight, needy bundle of nerves and bringing her closer to the edge.

Laney gripped his shoulders, her short nails digging into his skin. Suddenly, her stomach tensed and her sex pulsed as she called his name. The most delicious sensation filled her body as she came hard around him. Nolan slid her leg from his shoulder and kissed her. He flipped her onto her stomach, entering her from behind.

He held her hands above her head with one strong hand as he moved inside her. The other hand gripped her breast, his thumb and forefinger squeezing her already hardened nipple. The familiar sensation low in her belly began to build again despite the fact she was sure it was impossible for him to bring her to orgasm again.

Nolan kissed her neck and shoulder, his hips thrusting until she was practically floating. She called his name, her throat hoarse and her sex pulsing. Finally, he arched his back, whispering her name again and again, as he emptied himself inside her.

They lay together spent, trying to catch their collective breath. Laney was exhausted. Her body was sated, and her mind was still spinning with a euphoric sense of bliss. But it was more than that. Laney felt a deep sense of connection to Nolan. The thought of losing this newly found joy and contentment before they had the chance to discover where this could go made her chest ache and her eyes sting with unshed tears.

When Nolan returned from the bathroom, he slipped

into bed and cradled her body against his, her back pressed to his chest. He kissed her shoulder. "Is it all right if I stay?"

Laney tried not to smile too broadly as she settled into his embrace. "I'd love it if you stayed, Nolan."

Nolan pulled her closer, and it wasn't long before he'd drifted off to sleep.

It'd been a perfect night. And Nolan was perfect for her.

But she was staying in Magnolia Lake for one summer.

Derrick had arranged the perfect opportunities for their daughter's education and her career. How could she possibly walk away from such an ideal situation? And how could she break Harper's heart when she was looking forward to living near her dad?

She couldn't.

The pain of that realization burrowed deep in her gut and made her heart ache.

If all went according to plan, they'd be moving to Seattle before the end of summer. But until then, she would enjoy the deep sense of happiness she felt being with Nolan and enjoy their one summer of love.

Seventeen

Nolan stared in his hotel room mirror and huffed in frustration as he unfastened his black bow tie and began his third try at tying the damned thing.

He'd never had this much difficulty putting on a bow tie before. But tonight, the first attempt had been uneven; the second crooked. His third attempt was at least presentable.

He was distracted, knowing that Delaney was on the other side of the bathroom door preparing for the gala.

Nolan had offered to get Laney her own room, but she'd insisted it was a waste of money. She planned to spend as much time as possible in his bed. He hadn't been able to cancel that second reservation fast enough.

They'd arrived in Nashville the previous evening, driving up after work. He'd taken Laney to the rooftop bar L.A. Jackson. They'd had beer queso and gourmet burgers and shared a bottle of German Riesling. Laney was fascinated by the stunning night view of the city while Nolan couldn't help admiring Laney in her little black dress. Her curls were piled atop her head, and she wore only a hint of makeup. After dinner, she'd pulled him onto the dance floor and they'd danced to early 2000s throwback music spun by the DJ.

They'd spent an incredible night together in their room, then woke up early and had breakfast in bed. Earlier in the day, they'd visited the Frist Art Museum and explored the city before returning to their room with just a couple of hours to spare before the gala at the natural history museum. They were supposed to be taking a nap. Instead, they'd made love, and now they were both rushing to prepare for the gala being held at the museum not far from the hotel.

Tonight would be their sixth outing together. They'd agreed to a transitory relationship. Yet, the more time he spent with Laney, the more he found himself falling for her. He needed Laney to see that his interest in her went beyond the physical. Because she was special. As rare as a shooting star or a natural red diamond—only two or three dozen known to exist.

Delaney was exceptionally intelligent, remarkably proficient, incredibly attractive and the most fun person he'd ever been with. She truly got him and wasn't put off by his eccentric habits and curious nature. With Laney, Nolan had been able to relax and enjoy life. He found himself smiling...*often*.

So despite the voice in his head constantly reminding him of how things had turned out last time he got involved with a woman with children and a looming ex, Nolan couldn't help believing that there was the potential for more between them. Because spending time with Laney made him happy and more hopeful than he'd ever been. It was a feeling he desperately needed to hold on to.

Nolan glanced at the rose-gold-and-black Asorock Ambassador watch on his wrist. Then he smoothed down his white shirt and slipped on his navy tuxedo jacket. Suddenly, Laney stepped out of the bathroom and Nolan's eyes widened. His heart beat wildly, and his jaw practically hit the floor.

"Wow." Nolan pressed a hand to his chest as his gaze swept the length of her body. The woman was beyond stunning in a deep red strapless, floor-length gown that hugged her hips, then gradually widened at her feet. Her toes, painted a sparkly candy apple red, peeked from beneath the hem of the dress in glittery, silver sandals. "Laney, you look incredible."

"Thank you," Laney said with a playful bow of her head. Then she poked him in the gut. "Also, don't sound so surprised, Valentine. You've seen me dressed up before."

He had. And yet, she continued to find ways to surprise him.

"I was putting on my jewelry. I could use your help." Laney held up a bracelet. "Would you mind?"

Nolan studied the platinum tennis bracelet with at least ten carats of diamonds.

"This is an exquisite piece." Nolan slid it onto Laney's wrist and secured the clasp.

"Thank you." She put on matching diamond earrings. "They're extravagant birthday gifts from my grandfather not long after Joe Abbott wrote him that first check and gave him…us…stock in King's Finest." She touched the diamond solitaire around her neck. "I adore all three pieces but rarely find occasion to be draped in diamonds out in the vineyard or in the carpool lane. As you've probably guessed, I'm not usually a gala kind of girl."

Laney's bashful smile lit her eyes. Nolan fought back the urge to glide his fingers through her thick curls and kiss her full, lush lips.

"I'm honored you made an exception for me." Nolan extended his elbow. "Shall we?"

"We shall," Laney said with a teasing lilt. She swiped her clutch off the dresser, then slid her arm through his.

As they stepped on the elevator together, her subtle floral-and-citrus scent washed over him. His heart beat as wildly as the West African djembe drums street musicians had been playing in the park earlier that day. He was falling hard for Laney.

Was it possible she felt the same about him, too?

Delaney Carlisle felt like a little girl playing dress-up. She had her sister to thank again for selecting the perfect outfit. A dress Laney would've thought too ambitious. Yet, she had to admit the dress looked amazing on her. Or did she look amazing in the dress? She honestly wasn't sure which was most accurate. Either way, she felt like an African warrior queen and a Disney princess all rolled into one. And she had the bold red strapless mermaid gown with a small train to thank for it.

Laney's cheeks glowed with heat and her pulse raced every time she thought of Nolan's expression when she'd stepped out of the bathroom in that dress. He'd been so handsome in his navy tuxedo, white shirt and black bow tie. Part of her had hoped Nolan would suggest they skip the gala and spend the rest of their weekend in Nashville locked away in their room. But he hadn't. And while she was enjoying the elegant museum setting, the premium hors d'oeuvres and top-shelf champagne, what she enjoyed most was being on Nolan's arm.

She loved watching the quiet, reticent man turn on the charm and talk business with CEOs and fellow executives. Laney realized how much effort it required and how draining it could be when being a social butterfly didn't come naturally. It made her admire Nolan all the more.

Laney enjoyed the unexpected little conversations where she and Nolan shared seemingly insignificant details about themselves. Like the individual brushstrokes that formed the timeless masterpieces created by impressionists like Monet, Renoir, Cassatt and Matisse, each small revelation slowly created a fuller picture of who Nolan was. And the more she got to know him, the more she adored him.

She only wished they'd gotten to know each other under different circumstances.

Laney had grown fond of Magnolia Lake. She understood now how her sister had fallen in love with Blake Abbott, his family and the town and then stayed. Because Laney found herself in a similar situation. She adored Nolan and his family, and she'd really come to enjoy life in the town of Magnolia Lake. It would be a great place for Harper to grow up. But Dr. Genobli had made her an incredibly lucrative offer to come to Seattle and help create an enology and vintner program.

She'd gotten her dream job offer, Derrick had found the perfect school for Harper and her little girl would get to grow up surrounded by her paternal family.

Laney had been handed everything she'd wanted on a silver platter. How could she pass up opportunities that had been handcrafted for them?

Still, Dr. Genobli had given her a generous period to consider the offer. She had yet to accept it, but she hadn't rejected it, either.

"Everything okay?" Nolan's eyes were filled with concern.

"Yes, of course. Why?"

"You suddenly seemed far away. Like something is weighing on you." He lifted their clasped hands and tenderly kissed the back of hers. "Are you sure you're all right?"

Laney's belly fluttered. Was it a reaction to the sweetness of Nolan's gesture or manifestations of guilt over not telling him she was considering moving to Seattle?

"I'm fine, thank you." Laney hoped her smile didn't look as disingenuous as it felt.

"I know you're probably bored to tears right now," he whispered in her ear. "I need to talk to a few more people. But afterward, how about I give you a private tour of my favorite exhibits?"

Laney nodded, her belly fluttering again. "I'd love that. Thank you."

Nolan kissed her cheek, then turned just in time to

greet a man he introduced as the CEO of a quickly growing software company. He clutched her hand as he spoke to the other man. As if he needed the physical connection as much as she did.

Laney couldn't help staring at the handsome, surprisingly sweet man standing beside her.

She really, *really* liked Nolan.

Right person, wrong time.

Laney heaved a sigh at the truth of those words. Despite her painted-on smile, it broke her heart that at the end of the summer, she'd have to walk away from Nolan and start a new life thousands of miles away.

Until then, she was determined to enjoy every single moment they had together.

Laney loved seeing the museum through Nolan's eyes as he excitedly shared special details about each of his favorite exhibits. A shark exhibit featuring ancient fossils and life-size models of various sharks. A hall of dinosaurs with a nearly complete Tyrannosaurus rex skeleton, a variety of fossils and a few life-size models. An exhibit featuring an array of gems, crystals and minerals, including an exceedingly rare red diamond. The connected planetarium. She was disappointed when the announcement came across the PA that dinner would begin soon.

They made their way toward the rotunda, where they would have dinner among fossils, casts and models of past and present oceanic creatures.

"Is there a bathroom around here?" Laney asked. "I'd like to wash my hands before dinner."

They descended the lovely marble staircase with its

decorative metalwork railings. The bathrooms were on opposite sides of the staircase.

Laney made a quick trip to the restroom and washed her hands. Then she opened her purse, pulled out her matte lipstick and touched it up, allowing the kiss-proof formula to dry.

"That's a beautiful shade of lipstick and what a gorgeous dress." A woman exited one of the stalls, then washed her hands.

"Thank you." Laney grinned. "It's not my usual style, but tonight I felt adventurous. Let's hope it pays off." She winked and the woman laughed.

"You be sure to let me know." The woman chuckled. "My relationship could use a little magic right now."

"I hope you find it." Laney flashed the woman a sad smile. "Enjoy your evening."

"You, too." The woman put her hands beneath the dryer, and it whirred on.

Laney exited the restroom and walked over to Nolan. The deep affection in his expression as he watched her approach made Laney's heart expand.

Leave it to her to finally find her dream guy only to discover her dream job thousands of miles away. Life could be surprisingly kind and cruel with the same stroke.

She and Nolan had very little time left to spend together. She couldn't afford to waste it by being coy about what she wanted. And what she wanted was to spend the rest of the night in bed with Nolan.

Laney pulled Nolan into the shadows behind a large marble pillar. She smoothed down the black lapels on his navy tux. "Any chance we can skip dinner and spend the rest of the night in our room?"

Heat flickered in Nolan's hungry gaze. He gave her a kiss that was soft and sweet, yet filled her body with heat. Her nipples beaded and there was the sweetest ache between her thighs. For a moment, she nearly forgot they were barely shielded by the shadows in a public space. And for a moment, she didn't care.

Nolan groaned, his expression filled with apology. "I need to at least make an appearance through dinner. But after that—"

"Nolan?"

The voice calling Nolan's name seemed vaguely familiar to Laney. But the sudden tension in Nolan's back as he dropped his hands from her face indicated the voice was all too familiar to him.

Nolan's movements were stiff as he turned toward the source of the voice. "Marian?"

"Marian? Your ex-wife Marian?"

Laney hadn't meant to say the words aloud. But *holy shit*. It was the woman she'd been chatting with in the restroom about how her magical dress was working, implying that the dress would get her some action tonight. She would pick tonight, of all nights, to get chatty and overshare with a stranger in the restroom.

"Yes." Nolan turned back to Laney, cupping her cheek.

He might've been stunned to see his ex at the gala. But the look in Nolan's eyes was all the reassurance she needed.

He was here with her, and that was the only thing that mattered.

Eighteen

The moment Nolan recognized Marian's voice, his forehead tightened, and his temple throbbed.

What the hell is Marian doing here?

Nolan sighed quietly. It didn't matter. What mattered was he was here with Laney. Given the tension in Laney's shoulders and the fact that she seemed to be holding her breath, he needed to reassure her of that.

Nolan stroked Laney's cheekbone with his thumb. A silent reminder that he was thrilled to be here with her. Encountering his ex didn't change that.

That adorable smile of hers slowly spread across her face, and his heart melted. Laney's brown eyes twinkled, and her shoulders relaxed.

Nolan slipped an arm around Laney's waist. "Good to see you again, Marian."

He'd said it because it seemed like the polite response to seeing one's ex-wife after three years. Not because he actually welcomed this wholly unexpected and immensely awkward interaction.

"You, too." Marian's glance shifted from him to Laney. "I didn't realize… I mean, I wouldn't have…" She paused, as if needing to start over again, then offered a forced smile. "It's good to see you've moved on."

He wasn't so sure he had…until Laney.

"Marian, this is my date, Delaney Carlisle. She's a consultant currently engaged by the vineyard my family recently acquired." That sounded much better than admitting he was dating the woman who worked for his family.

"I see." He didn't miss the message behind Marian's squinty stare.

Got involved with another woman you worked with, huh?

Apparently, it was his MO.

"We chatted in the bathroom briefly." Marian extended a hand to Laney. "I'm Marian Lester, Nolan's ex-wife, as you've probably already surmised."

"Delaney Carlisle. Pleasure to meet you." Laney shook his ex's hand, then turned to him. "I should go ahead and make sure they get our meal selections right."

"You don't need to—"

"I know." She lowered her voice to a whisper, her soft lips brushing his ear. "But this is your chance for resolution. And maybe you need that more than you realize."

Laney's warm gaze and reassuring smile made his

heart swell. She gave him a quick kiss, said goodbye to Marian, then headed up the stairs.

Nolan watched Laney ascend the staircase, then turned toward Marian.

"I appreciate what Laney was trying to do, but I can't imagine that there's anything left for us to say to each other, Marian. You pretty much said all you had to say the night you took the kids and walked out." Nolan shoved his hands into the pockets of his navy tuxedo pants. "I'm glad to see you're doing well, and I hope the kids are, too. But I should get back to my date."

"What if we aren't okay?" Marian clutched Nolan's elbow as he turned to walk away.

Nolan frowned, glancing down at where she touched his arm.

Marian withdrew her hand. "What if I realize now that going back to Douglas was a terrible mistake?"

"Then I'm sorry to hear it." He'd once cared deeply for her. It gave him no pleasure to learn she was unhappy. Because that meant the children might be, too. "It was hard to accept it when you abruptly ended our marriage. But now I realize it was the right move. We both deserve to be with someone who truly makes us happy."

"And does Delaney make you happy, Nolan? Or is this thing with her just a fling?"

"This isn't about me and Laney, Marian. It's about me and you. Because my answer would be the same, even if Laney wasn't in the picture," Nolan said calmly. "There will not be a reboot of our story. *Ever.* Good night."

Nolan turned on his heels and made his way up the marble staircase two steps at a time, eager to return to Laney. Every step he took toward the table where Laney sat chatting with their tablemates with the biggest of smiles, he felt lighter and happier. In fact, since she'd come into his life, he'd been the happiest he'd ever been.

He offered his fellow guests a cursory greeting, then sank onto the chair beside her.

"You're out of breath." Laney cradled his cheek. "Did you run the entire way? You didn't need to hurry. I'd understand if you needed—"

"You," Nolan whispered, turning to kiss her palm, oblivious to the stares of everyone else at their table. "The only thing I need is you."

Nineteen

Laney stood in front of the floor-to-ceiling windows overlooking the Nashville skyline in the darkened hotel room. She was wearing one of Nolan's T-shirts, luxuriating in the comfort of being wrapped in Nolan's arms as he stood behind her barefoot in nothing but his pajama pants, kissing her neck.

She'd honestly never felt so content, so at ease, so… loved.

Lancy sighed, then took a deep sip from her glass of Malbec and stared out at the flickering lights of the Nashville skyline. It was a beautiful night. But what had made this night…this weekend…so magical was spending it with Nolan.

After dinner, they'd returned to their room and made love. In the bed. Over the sofa. Beneath the rainfall showerhead. Her body ached and was exhausted in the best ways. But being with Nolan was exhilarating. They had so much in common. And they'd spent the weekend talking about everything from their childhoods and families to work and their shared love of winemaking and fascination with all things science.

When Nolan shared the details of his conversation with Marian, her first reaction had been to reassure him that it had been his ex's loss, not his. And she'd meant it. But now she felt a deep sense of guilt.

The only thing I need is you.

It had been such a sweet, beautiful moment. And yet, it broke her heart. She felt the same. But how could she say no to Seattle?

And what if Nolan was meant to encounter Marian again at the gala because the two of them were supposed to be together? To be a family? Wasn't it selfish of her to ruin his second chance at forever when she'd be gone in just a few weeks?

"Is everything all right?" Nolan asked.

"This weekend has been amazing. I've enjoyed every moment we've spent together." Laney set down her wineglass and turned to face him. "I'm sorry if I seem…distracted. It's just that…" The words caught in her throat.

"What is it, sweetheart?" Nolan stroked her cheek.

Laney leaned into him, eager for the comfort of his body. She sucked in a deep breath, her throat suddenly dry and a knot tightening in her gut.

Just say it.

"What if you and Marian are meant to be together,

and I'm somehow interfering with your destiny?" Laney asked.

"I told you, this wasn't just about you, Laney."

"How can you be so sure?" She paced the floor. "If I hadn't been here tonight, maybe things would've gone differently, and you'd be on your way to becoming a family again."

Her stomach churned at the thought that she might selfishly be ruining Nolan's happiness. Because despite seeming a bit prickly on the outside, Nolan Valentine was a truly amazing man. He deserved joy and contentment. Laney couldn't bear the thought of him missing out on a lifetime of happiness for one summer of love with her.

"Laney, sweetheart. Come here." Nolan held her, halting her frantic pacing.

She laid her head on his shoulder, breathing in his comforting scent as her erratic heartbeat slowed.

"This isn't really about Marian at all, is it?" Nolan asked finally, his voice gentle.

Laney tried to pull away, but Nolan cradled her cheek. His voice was kind, his expression open. Something he'd worked at. Because his natural tendency was to be closed off. It was his way of protecting himself from being hurt by anyone who got too close.

And wasn't that what she was doing—hurting him?

"Whatever it is, Laney, I can handle it." His attempt at a smile did little to reassure her. But Nolan was right. What she was about to say shouldn't be a surprise to him. Because they'd agreed that this was just a fling. That they wouldn't get serious.

"Why are you so eager to push the narrative that Marian and I are meant to be together? Is that your way of telling me—"

"I've been offered my dream job," Laney blurted. She lowered her gaze, avoiding the disappointment in Nolan's eyes. "I didn't apply for the position. I was recommended for it," she felt the need to clarify.

"Oh. Wow." Nolan stepped back. He dragged a hand across his forehead, looking stunned. Like a person being interviewed by a reporter after some inexplicably terrible thing had happened to them. She felt like a flaming garbage bag of a person for being the reason for that pained look on his handsome face.

"That's great news, right?" Nolan attempted a smile, but it looked more like he had gas. He reached out for her hand, but didn't step closer, and she missed the comfort of being wrapped in is arms. "Tell me about this perfect job."

"I'd be working for a top-tier private university developing the curriculum for their brand-new viticulture and enology program. And I'd get to head up the department once it's established." Laney's words were rushed. Her heart thundered in her chest.

"Sounds like an exciting opportunity. One I know you'll excel at." Nolan was saying all the right things, but his tone was flat and there was pain reflected in his eyes. He faced the window, arms folded, and stared out at the darkness. "So where is this great opportunity?"

"Seattle." The word felt like glass in her throat.

Nolan's eyes widened with recognition. "Your ex recommended you for the job."

"Derrick works at the university."

"Are the two of you—"

"God, no." Laney waved a hand. She needed Nolan to know this wasn't Marian all over again. She wasn't walking away from him to reconnect with her ex. She didn't want a second chance with Derrick. She wanted to stay in Magnolia Lake and explore this amazing connection she and Nolan shared. "That ship has sailed."

"For you, maybe," Nolan said.

He wasn't wrong. Derrick wanted them to pick up where they'd left off. For the three of them to be a family. The very thing he hadn't wanted nine years before.

"He didn't really do this for me at all. Derrick wants to spend more time with Harper and for her to get to know his family, who all live in Seattle. And he found a spot for Harper at a great school with advanced math and science. Connecting me with this opportunity… It's a means to an end as far as Derrick is concerned."

"And what about where you're concerned?" Nolan's voice was a pained whisper.

"I wouldn't ever have imagined that I'd get a shot at something like this at this stage in my career." Laney sank onto the sofa and dragged her fingers through her hair. "And this school… I couldn't possibly find a better situation for Harper. And then for it to be in the same city with her grandparents and cousins…"

"And with her dad," Nolan noted.

Laney's head throbbed, and her heart felt like it was ripping in two.

Neither of them spoke for a moment.

"The timing is awful, I know. I didn't expect to fall

in love with Magnolia Lake. Nor did I expect to feel the way I do about you, Nolan. Leaving Magnolia Lake isn't what I want. But when you assess the situation objectively… It's an ideal academic opportunity for Harper and an exciting career opportunity for me."

Nolan sank onto the sofa, too. The space between them felt as wide as a football field.

Laney rubbed her arms against the sudden chill that swept over her.

"So you've already accepted the job?" Nolan sounded deflated.

"I asked for time to think it over. They expect to hear from me by Monday."

"But you haven't accepted the position, yet," Nolan continued. "Why?"

It was a fair question. One she didn't have an answer for. Or maybe she just hadn't been willing to admit the truth. Not even to herself.

Nolan sighed softly, then moved to sit beside her on the sofa. He threaded their fingers and the two of them sat in silence for a moment before he spoke again.

"You don't have to approach every decision in life like a math equation, Laney." He stroked the back of her hand with his thumb. "What you want matters, too. You said you don't want to leave Magnolia Lake. Why?"

She studied the pained look on Nolan's face, her own heart breaking at the thought of never seeing him again. And the answer was evident.

She'd fallen for Nolan Valentine and for the little town of Magnolia Lake. And she couldn't bear the thought of saying goodbye to either of them.

* * *

Nolan waited patiently for Laney's response. It was foolish of him to expect her to say that he was the reason she couldn't bear to pack up her things and move to Seattle. Yet, that was *exactly* what he wanted to hear.

But in true Laney fashion, she responded to his question with one of her own.

"What would you do if you had an opportunity that was exactly what you wanted, but it came at the wrong time in your life?"

"How am I supposed to answer that, Laney? As your friend? As your lover? As the CFO of Valentine Vineyards?"

"Honestly."

"That isn't as simple as it seems."

Laney drew her feet onto the sofa and laid her head on his shoulder. "Why not?"

"Because I'm the selfish asshole who'd do anything to make you stay. Like telling you that we plan to offer you the position as enologist—at your requested salary. But I'm also the man who loves you enough to tell you that you should go for this opportunity, if it's what you really want." Nolan sighed. "Which guy would you prefer to hear from?"

"First... I want to hear from both." Laney stared at him with widened eyes. "Second... Did you just offer me a job *and* tell me you love me without taking a breath?"

"I did, and I do. Very much." Nolan scrubbed a damp palm down his leg. "I think I fell in love with you the moment I met you, Laney. I tried to convince myself it wasn't possible. And I just kept falling in deeper until I couldn't deny it any longer."

"Why didn't you say something before now?"

"You said you weren't looking for anything serious. I didn't want to scare you off. I'm not saying this just to make you stay. I guess the realization just hit earlier tonight."

Laney climbed onto his lap and kissed him. Her soft, sweet lips glided over his. Then she smiled softly as she cradled his cheek. "I know you well enough to know you'd never say you loved me if you didn't, Nolan."

"Good. I hope you also believe me when I tell you, more than anything, I want you and Harper to be happy." Nolan choked back the flood of emotions he hadn't expected. "Obviously, I'd hoped that would be here with me. But if chasing your dream takes you to Seattle, I'll find a way to be happy for you, Laney. Eventually." He forced a wan smile. "But until then, I don't care if it makes me selfish. I want to spend every single moment I can with you. Because being with you has made this the most amazing summer of my life."

Delaney was as bright and warm as the sun. She'd brought light to the darkness he'd been floundering in since his divorce and thawed the frozen tundra that once was his heart. Nolan dreaded the empty ache he'd feel the first time he walked into his office and Laney's things were gone. Hated knowing his bed and his heart would be cold without Laney in them.

"I love my life in Magnolia Lake. I'm near my sister. I love my job and the quirky family I work for." Laney laughed through her tears, and Nolan couldn't help laughing, too. "I love being a part of what your family is creating at Valentine Vineyards. But most of all, Nolan, I want to stay in Magnolia Lake because I love *you*. I don't want to walk away from this. Not when it's the happiest I've been in a long time, too."

"What about Seattle being the logical choice?" He should shut his mouth and be grateful Laney was choosing to stay. But he needed to know she'd thought this through. That she wouldn't wake up one day and regret missing out on her big opportunity because she'd chosen him over her dream job.

"There are two instances in my life when I made a decision with my heart instead of my head. The first was my choice to become a mother. The second was my decision to switch to a career I loved. They're the best decisions I've ever made, and they've brought me so much joy. And in a way, they both brought me to you. So I'm following my heart and doing what makes me happy, just like I promised my grandfather."

Nolan heaved a sigh of relief. He kissed Laney and held her tight. For the first time since Laney had told him about the possibility of her moving to Seattle, he felt like he could breathe. "I'm glad you'll both be staying in Magnolia Lake. I'm only sorry it'll break Harper's heart."

"She'll be disappointed, but she's a resilient kid. And she loves her family here, too. She'll adjust. The most important thing is that her dad will be in her life, and I get to have you in mine. And that makes me incredibly happy."

"Me, too." Nolan kissed her again, something he'd

never tire of. "Now, if we're going to continue this relationship, I do have one condition."

"You've got conditions already, huh?" She cocked an arched brow. "Okay, let's hear it."

"I don't want this relationship to be our little secret anymore. I want everyone in the world to know how much I love you, Laney. Starting with those meddling sisters of ours."

"I suppose it's only fair since they were absolutely right about us being perfect for each other." Laney laughed, tugging Nolan to his feet. "But we can wait until we get home to let them gloat. Tonight, I have other plans."

Laney whispered the most gloriously filthy thing in his ear that required chocolate syrup and the can of whipped cream she'd stashed in the bar fridge. His body reacted instantly.

If he was lucky enough to spend the rest of his life with the ever-fascinating Delaney Carlisle, it would never be enough.

Epilogue

Laney's shoulders tensed slightly as she surveyed the vehicles parked on the street and in Duke and Iris Abbott's driveway. There was a full house for their annual end-of-summer cookout. She was both excited and nervous. Today, she and Nolan were finally telling their families about their relationship.

"Are you ready for this?" Nolan found a spot and parked his car.

"I am." Laney took a deep breath and then released it. She gave Nolan a quick kiss.

The mood was disrupted by the giggles of the eight-year-old in the back seat.

"Kiss him again, Mommy!" Harper had taken off her seat belt and leaned forward. Her adorable little face poked between the front seats.

Nolan smiled shyly, and Laney could practically feel the heat radiating from his cheeks.

"She'll eventually get bored with us, I promise." Laney kissed Nolan again, then opened her car door. She opened Harper's back door, too. "Come on, you." Laney tweaked her daughter's nose. "Everyone is waiting to see you."

That momentarily shifted her daughter's attention off the fact that Mommy had a boyfriend now—a song she'd been singing for the past two days to the tune of "Bills, Bills, Bills" by Destiny's Child.

"I can't wait to see them, too." Harper practically bounced on her heels as she took Laney's hand on one side and then grabbed Nolan's on the other.

Nolan seemed pleasantly surprised by Harper's gesture, and Laney couldn't help smiling.

Harper had been pouting and distraught over not moving to Seattle. That had lasted all of three days. Because that's when she'd sat her daughter down and explained that she and Mr. Nolan were dating now. Laney had been concerned about how Harper would take the news, but her daughter had been thrilled.

Harper shook off her blues and was obsessed with the fact that Nolan was Mommy's new boyfriend. Thus, the one-line song she'd been singing for the past two days.

Laney's belly fluttered as they approached the majestic home with its gray stacked stone and poplar shake exterior and a stunning view of the Smoky Mountains.

She and Nolan had agreed that they should keep their relationship under wraps until after she'd officially been offered and accepted the position as Valentine Vineyards' in-house enologist. And until she could tell Harper in person. Now that she'd ticked both items off her list, they looked forward to telling their sisters.

When Duke and Iris had invited everyone over for an end-of-summer cookout, telling everyone then seemed ideal. But as they got closer to the house, the butterflies in her stomach disagreed.

They walked around to the back patio of Duke and Iris's well-manicured backyard. The scent of grilled meat, savory side dishes, baked bread and fruit pies; the sound of a dozen different voices; and the laughter of children greeted them before they rounded the corner.

The outdoor space was brimming with the extended Abbott family: Joe Abbott; Duke and Iris; all of their children and grandchildren; the Abbotts' cousin Benji and his family; Nolan's father and sisters; and a host of in-laws and friends.

Harper took off running the moment she saw her cousins Davis and Remi, and Benji's twins, Beau and Bailey.

Nolan took Laney's hand, threading their fingers as they moved toward their families, who regarded them with grins and wide-eyed stares.

"Yes! It's about damn time." Naya tackle-hugged them, nearly tipping them over. "I knew you two would make the perfect couple."

"You were right, Nye." Nolan chuckled, slipping an arm around Laney's waist. "I owe you one."

"Yes, you do," Naya agreed. "And apropos to nothing, I wouldn't be opposed if you named your first kid together after me." Naya burst into laughter when both of their eyes went wide. "Relax, you two, I'm just kidding. Jeez!"

"She definitely wasn't kidding." Nolan uttered the words out of the side of his mouth with a polite smile still plastered on his face after Naya walked away.

"I don't know. A variation on Naya could be really cute, if not as a first name as a middle…" Laney stopped midsentence when Nolan turned to her suddenly, his mouth gaping. "What? You don't like your sister's name?"

"Yes. I do. I just… I guess I didn't realize that you wanted…that you'd consider having…" Nolan stammered, and he'd never been more adorable. "I didn't realize you wanted more children," he finally managed.

"I'm not unhappy with my life the way it is. But yes, I would like to have another child someday." Laney shrugged. "Is that a deal breaker for—"

Before she'd finished her sentence, Nolan leaned in and pressed a sweet, lingering kiss to her lips. He pushed aside a few stray curls and tucked them behind her ear as he grinned sheepishly. "No, Laney, it's definitely not a deal breaker for me."

Heat radiated in Laney's chest and her cheeks burned. Maybe it seemed premature to be discussing the possibility of having children together someday. But knowing that was just one more way in which she and Nolan were on the same page warmed her chest and reassured her that Nolan Valentine was the man for her.

"So…you two." Chandra practically beamed, bouncing gently as she cradled little Autumn, snuggled down in the fabric of the wrap-style baby carrier. "I'm thrilled for both of you." She gave each of them a one-sided hug, careful not to disturb the sleeping infant.

"Thank you, Chandra." It meant a lot to Laney that Nolan's sisters liked her. She adored Nolan's father and sisters. Even as an employee of the winery, they'd made her feel like she was a part of their family. The idea that she and Harper could someday become a part of the Valentines' big, loving family made her smile.

"Thanks, sis. For everything." Nolan squeezed his sister's arm.

He took Laney by the hand and they made their way through the crowd of friends and family offering their congrats and well-wishes for their budding relationship. An hour into the party, Laney's cheeks hurt from the deep, genuine smile that had been plastered on her face since they'd arrived. She loved Nolan Valentine. And she couldn't be happier that what had begun as one summer of romance had the potential to become a lifetime of love.

Laney couldn't wait to discover what the future held in store for them.

Nolan left Laney's side to grab himself another beer when he saw his brother Sebastian rounding the corner.

"Hey, Bas. I didn't expect to see you here." Nolan popped the top on the beer. He'd known that Duke and Iris had extended the invitation to his entire family, but he hadn't expected his brothers, who were in Nashville, New York and Miami, to actually come. "You drove nearly five hours from Nashville for a cookout?" Nolan raised a brow as he handed Sebastian, who looked exhausted, the frosty bottle of imported beer.

"It's a long weekend." Sebastian swallowed a few gulps of his beer while Nolan got another bottle from the ice chest for himself. "My assistant insisted I needed a break. She knew if I'd stayed in Nashville for the weekend, at some point, I would've ended up back at the office."

"She's right about you needing a break." Nolan pointed the longneck bottle in his brother's direction. "Dude, you look exhausted. At this rate, Dad's going to look like your younger, more handsome brother within five years."

"Ha, ha, ha." Sebastian frowned. The fine lines forming around his mouth and between his brows testified to a grimace being Bas's signature expression. "There's a lot more to being CEO, you know." Sebastian sighed, glancing over at their father, who was holding their niece and beaming like the proudest grandfather in the land. "Pop made it look easy. But it's far more involved than I ever imagined."

"More so since you're trying to dance to the tune of the syndicate that acquired Valentine Textiles, I'd imagine," Nolan acknowledged. He braced a hand on his brother's shoulder. "So don't beat yourself up if the job is a lot tougher than you anticipated, Bas."

"I'm not." Sebastian drank more of his beer. "And it's nothing I can't handle. It's just that every time I feel like I'm making some headway…things seem to change."

"Okay," Nolan said. "But if you're not happy in your current role—"

"It's work, Nole. It's not supposed to make you happy," Sebastian said.

"I disagree," Nolan said. "But since you think your career shouldn't make you happy, why exactly are you torturing yourself with this job?"

"You know I've had my sights set on being the CEO of Valentine Textiles since I was a teenager."

"Well, now that you've checked that goal off your list, you can join us at Valentine Vineyards," Nolan said. "We're just a few months away from expanding operations, so we could *really* use your expertise as our operations manager."

"I appreciate the offer, Nolan. But I'm not waving the white flag," Sebastian said. "I'm sure that by the end of the year, everything will be fine."

"All right," Nolan conceded. "But the offer stands if you ever change your mind. Now, there's someone I'd like you to meet." Nolan's heart danced when his gaze met Laney's and her eyes lit up.

"Is that you?" Sebastian bumped his shoulder against Nolan's.

He nodded. "That's Savannah's younger sister, Delaney Carlisle. She's Valentine Vineyards' brilliant new in-house enologist and the woman I plan to marry someday."

Sebastian's dark eyes widened and he coughed and sputtered, nearly choking on his beer.

"You okay?" Nolan patted his brother's back, preparing himself for an onslaught of negativity from Sebastian, who was also a divorcee. They'd both come to the conclusion that they weren't cut out for marriage.

But falling in love with Laney had made Nolan hopeful enough to want to try again.

"Then I'm thrilled for you, Nolan," Sebastian said. "I know the past few years have been rough, since the divorce. But you deserve to be happy. So I'm glad you found what you were looking for here in Magnolia Lake."

"Thanks, Bas. But you deserve happiness, too." Nolan finished his beer. "Promise me you won't let that stubborn ego of yours keep you from building a life you truly enjoy."

Sebastian heaved a sigh and nodded. "Promise."

"Good. Now, come on. I want you to meet Laney and her daughter, Harper."

They walked over to where Laney was chatting with her sister, Savannah, and her brother-in-law, Blake. Nolan introduced his brother to the woman who'd turned his world upside down in a matter of months. The woman with whom he hoped to spend the rest of his life.

* * * * *

Dear Reader,

We're made to believe that we should have it all
figured out by a certain point. But unexpected life
lessons can completely alter our paths. I enjoy
writing about characters on such a journey.

In *Snowbound Second Chance*, Sebastian Valentine
is the CEO of his firm, a job he's worked toward his
entire career. But the job is stressful and unfulfilling.
When a health scare sends him on sabbatical, he
stays at the Sweet Magnolia Inn, near his family. To
his surprise, the gorgeous innkeeper is the woman
he encountered a year ago and hasn't stopped
thinking about.

Evelisse Jemison takes a break from her floundering
acting career and returns to her hometown to take
on the role of innkeeper while her injured sister
recovers. When Sebastian and Evvy get snowed in
during an unprecedented storm, they discover the
depth of their growing feelings for each other. But
will they sacrifice what they've always believed they
wanted for something more genuine?

Want to know what comes next in my Valentine
Vineyards series? Visit reeseryan.com/desirereaders
and join my newsletter list for book news,
giveaways and more.

Until our next adventure!

Reese Ryan

SNOWBOUND
SECOND CHANCE

To my readers:
Thank you for coming along for the ride!

To my incredible husband and loving family:
Thank you for your patience
and continued support.

To K. Sterling, Leigh Carron, Belle Calhoune,
Karen Booth, Katherine Garbera, Joss Wood and
Joanne Rock: Thank you for the hand-holding,
cheerleading and genuine encouragement.
I wouldn't have finished this book
without your support.

To reader Sharon Eatmon-Roland:
Thank you for your continued readership and
support online and at reader events.
And thank you for coming up with the
perfect name for the Sweet Magnolia Inn.

One

Sebastian Valentine felt groggy. He had a splitting headache, his chest ached, and his mouth felt dry. When he raised his hand to scratch his nose, he was startled by the IV drip attached to his wrist.

He shot upright.

"Relax, Sebastian. You're okay." His older brother Nolan's voice was concerned but calm. He placed a hand on Sebastian's shoulder. "You're in the emergency room, but you're going to be fine."

Sebastian rubbed his forehead with his untethered hand and blinked, trying to recall how he'd ended up there. Then it hit him.

He'd been working alone on a Saturday afternoon—nothing unusual. Suddenly his heart raced. He had intense chest pains, shortness of breath, and dizziness. His hands had trembled so much he couldn't write. When he stood, he'd been unsteady on his feet and tumbled to the floor. A security guard making the rounds had come to see what the commotion was. Sebastian asked her to call an ambulance and then call his brother because he was pretty sure he was having a heart attack.

He grabbed his chest in a sudden panic. "Did I have—"

"No, it wasn't a heart attack," Nolan assured him calmly, settling onto a chair beside Sebastian's bed. "The doctor believes you suffered a severe panic attack. Have you had them before?"

"No. I don't think so." Sebastian eased back against the pillow and thought hard, which made his head hurt more.

"But you have been under a lot of stress in your new role as the CEO of Valentine Textiles," Nolan noted with concern.

"Comes with the territory." Sebastian shrugged, as if being sprawled out on the floor of your plush executive suite, feeling as if you were dying, was simply par for the course. "Things have been *different* since we sold the company."

Valentine Textiles had been run by generations of Valentines until Sebastian's father—the previous CEO—sold the family-owned firm to a California conglomerate a year ago. The conglomerate had appointed Sebastian as the new CEO—the job he'd had been vying for since college. But running the firm without his family and under the new organization's strict rules and unrealistic expectations was far more stressful than he'd anticipated.

"I know being CEO is what you've wanted for a long time. But bruh, this job is *literally* killing you," Nolan said. "You've aged five years in the past year."

"Not really the best time to trade insults." Sebastian stared at the ceiling.

"I'm not insulting you, Bas, I'm stating a fact," Nolan said. "You've got dark circles around your eyes, bags underneath them, some serious frown lines, and you're graying—which is a bit premature for thirty-six in our family."

Sebastian ran a hand over his head. "You think I don't own a mirror?"

"I think you're ignoring the signs that this job is killing you because you're too damn proud to admit that it isn't all you'd hoped it would be." Nolan's dark eyes seemed sad. "There's no shame in admitting that, Bas. Even if you don't want to join us at Valentine Vineyards, there are lots of other opportunities out there that won't drive you to an early grave."

A year ago, after learning that he'd been adopted by the Valentines, their father had purchased a vineyard once owned by his biological mother's family. His dad was determined to create a wine empire in honor of his biological parents. And he wanted all of his children to join him. Nolan and their two sisters, Chandra and Naya, were on board. But Sebastian and his two younger brothers hadn't joined the company. It didn't stop his father and siblings from consulting them on winery business.

"You know this is the only job I've ever wanted. I realize we aren't Valentines by blood. But we carry Gram and Pop's last name. It'd be a shame not to have someone from the family sitting at the head of the table."

"Dad didn't feel obligated to maintain the business," Nolan noted.

"And on that, we disagree." Sebastian shrugged, then coughed.

Nolan handed him a cup of water.

Parched, Sebastian drank most of it. He felt drained and a little foggy.

"If it was only a panic attack, then why the IV?" Sebastian held up his arm.

"Because you were severely dehydrated, Mr. Valentine." A petite Black woman wearing a white lab coat floated into the room and washed and dried her hands. Her dark brown locs were twisted atop her head. "It seems you haven't been taking very good care of yourself." She studied her tablet. "I'm Dr. Violet Benson, the emergency physician on duty."

"And you're sure it wasn't a heart attack because…" Sebastian assessed her carefully.

"Because we've run a complete battery of tests." Dr. Benson set her tablet down and checked his pulse with her icy fingers. "You're feeling calmer now, I hope."

"I am." This was the calmest he'd felt in weeks.

"That's because of the benzodiazepine we administered." She typed something on her tablet. "How long have you been having these symptoms? The breathlessness, shakiness, dizziness, dry mouth, and irregular heartbeats?" She read the symptoms he'd no doubt rattled off upon his arrival.

Sebastian frowned, then glanced over at Nolan, whose look of concern heightened in the wake of hearing his symptoms.

Dr. Benson followed Sebastian's gaze to Nolan's, then glanced back at him, her voice lowered. "Would you prefer we speak alone?"

"No. It's fine." Sebastian heaved a quiet sigh. "I've been having the symptoms for a while, I guess. More notably for the past month or so. But they've never been quite so...*intense*."

"The dehydration can act as a trigger, intensifying the symptoms, to the point where it feels like you're dying," Dr. Benson explained calmly. "Let me guess... you spend your day drinking countless cups of coffee but very little water?"

"Something like that." Could this embarrassing scene really have been avoided if he'd just been conscious of drinking more water? "So if I promise to stay hydrated and drink less caffeine, can I get out of here?"

"Those are factors in your panic attack," Dr. Benson acknowledged. "But so are stress and anxiety. Is your work or family life particularly stressful?"

"I'm the CEO of a firm that's in transition. For the past few weeks, I've admittedly been under quite a bit of pressure to meet some pretty exacting standards." Sebastian could practically feel his blood pressure rising.

"Are you happy in your job, Mr. Valentine?" Dr. Benson typed out more notes on her tablet.

"As much as most." Sebastian ignored the tightening of his jaw and the clenching of his teeth.

"I've seen patients younger and healthier than you in here with strokes and heart attacks because of job-induced stress. I would prefer it if that didn't happen to you." Dr. Benson rolled a stool over and sat beside him. Her voice was warm but firm. "I realize our jobs are often a huge part of our identities. But no job is worth your health and possibly your life, Mr. Valentine. If you don't make some serious changes, you'll find yourself back here again. Only we'll be having a very different conversation. Understood?"

Sebastian nodded, then listened as the doctor suggested a variety of lifestyle changes—starting with taking a break from his intensely stressful job.

"Dr. Benson was clear about you needing to make some lifestyle changes. So what are you going to do?" Nolan asked as he drove Sebastian home.

Sebastian glanced down at the prescription in his hand. "Cut out the energy drinks, cut back on the coffee, hydrate more, I guess."

"What about work?" Nolan asked.

"What about it? It's my job, Nolan. I'll figure it out."

"You heard what the doctor said, Bas. Do you have any idea how terrifying it was to get that call that you thought you were having a heart attack?" Nolan, who was usually even-tempered, sounded hurt and angry.

"You didn't tell Dad or the girls?" Sebastian had made his brother promise to keep this quiet until they knew more. When Nolan confirmed he hadn't, Sebastian said, "Good. No need to worry them. I'm fine."

"You are *not* fine, Bas. And if you let this job kill you, I swear to God I'll shake you back to life for the express purpose of kicking your ass."

Sebastian laughed, and Nolan did, too. It diffused the tension between them.

"Okay, point taken. What exactly would you have me do?"

"Take a vacation. You haven't taken one since we were all in Magnolia Lake when Dad told us about buying the winery," Nolan said.

"You call that a vacation? I'm pretty sure that's when my anxiety began." Sebastian rubbed his chest.

"Maybe it wasn't a week in the Caribbean, but it was great being together as a family for the first time in years." Nolan made a turn.

"It was." Sebastian smiled, thinking of the late nights playing cards, watching movies, and hanging out with his siblings. Something they hadn't done in ages. "But it won't be a good look for me to suddenly take a vacation in the midst of the company executing changes everyone knows I'm opposed to."

Being the CEO, in name only, of the company his family had owned for generations was the hardest thing he'd ever done. But he'd never been one to back away from a challenge.

Nolan pulled into Sebastian's driveway and parked.

Sebastian stepped out of the car, hoping Nolan hadn't noticed that he was a bit unsteady.

"Those anti-anxiety meds are sedatives, you know."

"I'm aware, Nolan. Thank you." Sebastian grabbed the banister and slowly climbed the stairs to his front door.

He'd never much liked the house. But he'd purchased it in a last-ditch effort to save his marriage five years ago. It hadn't worked. What his now ex-wife had really wanted was a husband who wasn't married to his work, and Sebastian had been. Though back then, he'd actually enjoyed his job.

Sebastian let them inside the house, which was as dark as it was cold and empty since Tiffany had packed her things and left four years ago.

"It's too late for you to drive all the way back to Magnolia Lake." Sebastian flipped on the lights in the living room and then the kitchen. "Why don't you stay in the guest room? And order whatever you want. Dinner is on me."

"We can talk about dinner later, Bas." Nolan, who was a couple inches shy of Sebastian's five-foot-ten, pushed his glasses up the bridge of his nose and frowned. "Right now, I want to discuss why you feel compelled to keep doing a job you clearly don't enjoy. Are you doing it because you really want to or because you're desperate to prove a point?"

"Kind of like Dad trying to revive the winery once owned by his maternal relatives? The winery that just happens to be in the same town as his half brother's billion-dollar distillery?" Sebastian folded his arms.

"We're not discussing Dad's issues right now," Nolan said. "We're discussing yours. Besides, Dad actually loves the work he's doing, we've made amazing strides with the winery, and he's never been healthier or happier."

"As opposed to me, floundering and apparently needing to be medicated to do my job?" Sebastian shot back.

Nolan removed his smudged glasses and massaged his eyes before replacing them. "No one is calling you a failure, Bas."

"So now I'm a failure?"

"I literally just said you *weren't.*"

"Then why mention the word at all?" Sebastian retrieved a crystal decanter of brandy from the glass bar cart in the great room.

"You probably shouldn't be drinking that with your meds," Nolan warned.

"Shit." Sebastian muttered under his breath. He set the decanter down roughly, staving off the desire to throw the damn thing.

Sebastian pulled the prescription from his pocket and slapped it on the counter.

"You have no intention of filling that prescription, do you?" Nolan sat beside him.

"I can't do my job if I'm sedated and not fully functional," Sebastian grumbled.

"That's a bullshit excuse. Plenty of folks in high-powered jobs take anxiety meds," Nolan countered. "It's called taking care of your mental health."

Sebastian didn't respond.

"And what about the doc's other suggestions?" Nolan pressed.

Sebastian grabbed two bottles of water from the fridge and handed Nolan one. "See? I'm hydrating."

Nolan scowled. "Great. But have you considered taking a sabbatical from work?"

Sebastian was just about to tell his brother where he could shove his sabbatical idea when a text message popped up on his phone.

MANDATORY meeting Monday morning at ten to discuss rolling out new company guidelines as soon as possible.

Sebastian gripped the open water bottle tightly and liquid gushed out, wetting his pant leg and the floor.

Nolan grabbed a handful of paper towels and mopped up the mess. "Not good news, I assume."

Sebastian gritted his teeth. His heart thumped, and he could feel his blood pressure rising. A band of tension tightened across his forehead.

Dr. Benson was right. He needed a break: a chance to screw his head back on straight. Besides, the new company owners desperately wanted the optics of him buying into the new policies. Policies that would negatively impact his employees and alarm vendors. If he took leave, perhaps it would delay the implementation of those changes while he figured out how to permanently derail them.

Sebastian picked up his phone and typed out a quick email. He informed human resources and the three men representing the conglomerate, which now owned Valentine Textiles, that he'd be taking a three-month medical sabbatical. He'd submit the necessary paperwork on Monday.

He showed Nolan the message. "Happy?"

"I'd be happier if you spent those three months in Magnolia Lake. Do you have any idea how chilling it was to receive that call knowing you were alone and nearly a four-hour drive away?" Nolan said.

"I don't need a babysitter, Nole."

"And I can't trust that you won't end up back at work if you stay here. At the very least, you'll spend the entire three months stewing over the situation. And if that's the case—"

"Fine. I'll come to Magnolia Lake."

"Great. You can stay with one of us."

"No, thanks."

"Why not?"

"Because Dad and Naya will drive me crazy about coming to work for the winery. Chandra and Julian are still basically newlyweds with a young infant. And you've got your girlfriend and her giggly eight-year-old daughter over all the time."

"Okay, Sebastian the Grouch." Nolan invoked the nickname Naya had given him years ago. His siblings and father pulled it out whenever they were annoyed with him. "So where exactly do you plan to stay while you're in Magnolia Lake?"

"Didn't Parker's wife, Kayleigh, say she was opening an inn there?"

Parker was one of the surprise cousins they'd met a year ago. He and his siblings helped run the King's Finest Distillery, along with their father and grandfather.

"That's right," Nolan said. "It's opening soon."

"You think they'd be open to a three-month residency?"

"I don't see why not." Nolan smiled.

Sebastian sighed. Three months would give him plenty of time to come up with options to stop the conglomerate's disastrous changes.

Evelisse Jemison punched in the security code and let herself into her boss's Hollywood Hills mansion. She clutched the dry-cleaned suits she was there to deliver and frowned at the mess in the kitchen and the great room. Her boss, Fabian Gathers, was a brilliant director. He was also a generally shitty human being who still lived like a frat boy at the age of fifty-five. He had a string of ex-wives and former personal assistants who'd attest to that. Evvy wasn't sure if the fact that she'd been Fabian's personal assistant for nearly three years made her brave, desperate, crazy, or some unholy combination of the three.

Ascending to the role of a personal assistant at the age of forty-one meant her career as an actress, which had never quite taken off, was officially in the cosmic toilet with no hope of resurrection. She'd hoped that perhaps she could establish a career behind the camera. But there weren't a ton of film production internships for women over thirty.

Evvy had taken this job because Fabian was in a bind—having just lost another assistant—and had promised it would lead to a studio job.

It hadn't.

In fact, Fabian became perturbed whenever Evvy

gently reminded him of his promise to help her find a
position with the studio. As if she was betraying him
rather than asking him to make good on their bargain.

He'd even seemed indignant whenever she took personal time off. Like when she'd attended her younger
sister's wedding back in Magnolia Lake, where they'd
both grown up. Or when she'd attended the ground
breaking ceremony of the site where her baby sis was
building an inn in memory of their mother, whose family had once owned the property.

Evvy's phone buzzed. She pulled it from her back
pocket and read the text from Fabian.

Since you're there, love, could you tidy the place up a
bit? Marla can't make it in, and you know how much I
abhor having strangers rummaging 'round my place.

Now I'm the substitute housekeeper, too?

Evvy sucked in a long, slow breath, gritted her teeth,
and unleashed a string of curse words that would've
made her grandmother demand she wash her mouth
out with soap.

She put the dry cleaning away, then donned latex
gloves as she reminded herself Fabian was an asshole
who paid extremely well. Evvy grabbed a trash bag,
then surveyed the place. It was an appalling mess: a
pigsty with a top-notch view. And what the hell was
that smell?

Evvy had nearly filled an entire trash bag by the time
her phone rang. She yanked off her gloves and answered
the video call from her little sister.

"Hey you." Despite the lingering smell Evvy still hadn't identified, she couldn't help but smile when her younger sister's face filled the screen. "What's up?"

She and Kayleigh had spent years estranged. Not because she didn't love her sister. Going to college had been Evvy's way of escaping the trauma of her father's drinking problem, her mother's enabling it, and the embarrassment and pity being the town drunk's daughter engendered.

She couldn't get out of town fast enough. And she distanced herself from everything that had reminded her of that awful pain—including her family. Now that her parents had passed only she and Kayleigh were left. They'd slowly been reconnecting over the past few years, and since her sister's wedding, Evvy had been trying really hard to be a good sister. And to make up for abandoning Kayleigh all those years ago.

"First…don't panic," Kayleigh said.

"Those are never good words." Evvy dragged a hand through her wild, coppery-red curls—a feature they had in common. She was instantly taken back to when her mother had called to say her father was dying, then a few years later when Kayleigh had called to say the same of their mother. Her spine stiffened and a knot tightened in her gut. "Please tell me you're okay."

Kayleigh hesitated. "Mostly."

"What on earth does that mean?"

"It means I took a tumble when Parker and I were out mountain biking with Cricket," Kayleigh said sheepishly.

"Did you break anything?"

"Broke my left arm in two places." Kayleigh held up her arm in a sling, then panned the phone down to her leg in a cast, propped up on pillows. Her golden retriever Cricket laid beside her. "And my right leg."

"You go mountain biking all the time. What happened?" Evvy pressed a hand to her forehead.

"Cricket was tethered to my bike and got spooked by a really aggressive squirrel," Kayleigh explained. "Parker is working from home and taking the best care of me." Her sister lowered her voice and whispered, "He's been so sweet, but he's driving me crazy."

There was a soft smile on Kayleigh's gorgeous face, despite her proclaimed frustration with her husband. A look that Evvy could only describe as love.

It was sweet, but also damn annoying, given Evvy's own relationship status.

"Let Parker take care of you and save your energy. You'll heal faster. And let me know if there's anything I can do for you." Evvy balanced her phone on a stack of plates as she carried them to the kitchen.

"Actually, there is something I could really use your help with."

"Name it." Evvy sat the phone on the counter and rinsed the first dish.

"I need you to run the inn until I get back on my feet."

"Wait…you want me to drop everything and move back to Magnolia Lake? For how long?" Evvy asked.

"Three months." Kayleigh laughed nervously.

"Parker has a huge family. Can't any of them help with the inn? Or maybe you could hire someone?"

Evvy's brother-in-law and his family were beyond wealthy. They owned King's Finest Distillery—a world-renowned maker of bourbon and other spirits. And Kayleigh's jewelry design business had really taken off, too. Surely, they could afford to hire someone to manage the inn until Kayleigh was up to it again.

"Parker's family is busy running King's Finest or their own businesses. And I hired a part-time employee before the accident. Mari is great, but she's new to the hospitality industry. She certainly isn't ready to take on a project this big alone. Besides, this inn is a legacy to mom and her family," Kayleigh continued. "At least one of us should be the face of the inn. I'm not asking you to do this as a favor, Evvy. I'd pay you. Maybe not as much as Fabian does, but I'll throw in most of your meals, the studio apartment over my shop next to the inn, the Cricketmobile—"

"Is that old thing still running?"

"It is. And I won't tell her you asked that," Kayleigh said, referring to her Jeep as if it was a person. A sensitive one, at that. "And of course, I'll cover your transportation costs."

"There is no way in hell Fabian is going to give me three months off, Kayleigh. So if I do this, I probably won't have a job to come back to." Evvy continued rinsing the dishes.

"*Good.* Because Fabian doesn't deserve you."

"I know he doesn't," Evvy acknowledged. "But movie-adjacent jobs are hard to come by in this town for forty-one-year-old women."

"Then that entire town doesn't deserve you! And it

sounds like you have no reason to stay in LA." Kayleigh leaned down to kiss Cricket's snout. The dog lay with her head on Kayleigh's lap and had likely been startled by her sister's exuberant exclamation. "Come home, Evs. We miss you."

Guilt tightened a knot in Evvy's gut. It'd been nice getting to know Parker and his family the week of the wedding. The Abbotts had gone out of their way to make her feel like part of their family. She'd even liked their extended family—the Valentines—whom she'd met on her last trip there, a year ago.

It'd been a fun trip. But she couldn't help the flush of shame in her cheeks whenever she encountered town residents who knew her family's history.

"I miss you too, sis." Evvy turned off the water. "And I want to help. But this is a big ask. Give me a couple days to consider it?"

"Of course," Kayleigh said.

"I'll think about it. Promise." Evvy turned on the dishwasher and returned to the great room. "Either way, I'll see you in a week for the grand opening."

"Okay." Kayleigh flashed her a sad smile. "Love you, sis."

"Love you, too." Evvy ended the call, sinking onto the pricey sofa. She sighed, recalling her sister's words.

It sounds like you have no reason to stay in LA.

Brutal honesty was her sister's signature trait. And though she knew Kayleigh was only trying to help, her words landed like a kick to the front teeth.

"Stop being so dramatic, Evelisse Jemison," she whispered to herself. "Things could certainly be worse."

But she glanced around, it felt like she had truly hit bottom in her career.

When had this become her life?

"No." Evvy shook her head. Kayleigh was right. Fabian didn't deserve her. Neither had her ex Calvin. That's why she'd ended their relationship a few months ago after being together nearly six years.

She needed a fresh start. And while she had no plans to stay in Magnolia Lake, she could use her time there to figure out where she'd end up next.

Two

Sebastian pulled his BMW 7 Series black sedan into the parking lot of the Sweet Magnolia Inn. It'd been two weeks since he'd landed in the emergency room. He was concerned about his health, of course. But his primary reason for taking a sabbatical was to delay the implementation of the conglomerate's misguided changes.

Camping out in Magnolia Lake would provide the rest the doctor insisted he needed and a quiet place to plan his next strategic move.

Sebastian stepped out of his car and inhaled the exhilarating mountain air. The landscaping included a mix of young and mature magnolia trees, pruned crepe myrtle trees, and a variety of bushes—some still bearing flowers in mid-October. The trill of sparrows nestled in the pine trees along the edge of the property announced his arrival.

Sebastian retrieved his luggage from the trunk and made his way toward the inn's bright orange front door. He followed the welcoming path framed by bales of hay; assorted gourds; and overflowing ceramic pots filled with pansies, violas, and mums in vibrant pops of orange, yellow, and red. Their sweet scents mingled, drifting on the subtle breeze.

He stepped inside, greeted by the aroma of freshly baked sweet bread, homemade cookies, and mulled cider with a hint of cinnamon. Sebastian's eyes drifted closed momentarily, and the tension in his back and shoulders seemed to ease. Nolan had practically blackmailed him into spending the next three months here in town. But perhaps his brother was right. Magnolia Lake was a good place for him to get some much-needed rest.

"Sebastian?"

He opened his eyes and stared, blinking. Was the woman standing before him real? Or was she a figment of his imagination, where she seemed to reside since their meeting a year ago?

"Evelisse?"

"You remembered." She offered a playful smile, her brown eyes twinkling.

He studied the plump lips painted a deep shade of pink. Scanned the black ribbed turtleneck sweater and tan leggings that hugged her curves. The briefest image flashed through his brain of those black knee-high riding boots dangling over his shoulders.

"Of course I remember you," he said incredulously.

How on earth could he forget Evelisse Jemison?

He'd met her at a soiree hosted by his cousins Duke and Iris Abbott more than a year ago. And he'd often thought of her and that incredible evening they'd spent getting to know each other.

But his response evidently hadn't landed quite as he'd intended, because her countenance fell, as did her slim shoulders.

Shit.

He'd uttered four words, and already he'd insulted her.

Why does every word you utter make the rest of us feel like incompetents who don't deserve to occupy space in your world?

His ex-wife's refrain echoed in his head.

Should he apologize? Or maybe just explain that what he meant was that how could he possibly forget someone as fascinating and beautiful as she was?

"So *you're* the SBV on the register." Evelisse scanned her phone before returning her gaze to him. Her polite tone was devoid of the genuine eagerness to see him that had been there before. She regarded him with curiosity. "Why so mysterious?"

"I didn't want my sisters getting wind of me coming to town."

"We don't typically divulge our guests' names in the local newspaper." She folded her arms, and her nostrils flared .

"But your sister is friends with my sisters."

"So you thought my sister would violate your privacy and tell your sisters that you'd booked a room with us."

The flare of her nostrils widened, and the warmth was gone from her maple-syrup-brown eyes.

"No, of course not. I just... I..."

Evelisse wasn't buying his story. *Fair.* It was complete bullshit. He had been worried Kayleigh would blab to Chandra and Naya about him coming to town.

Sebastian groaned quietly. He'd never claimed to be a people person. But his interpersonal skills were particularly inept today. He could hear his younger sister Naya's voice echoing in his head.

Take it down six notches, Sebastian the Grouch. And for God's sake, would it kill you to smile?

"My apologies if I've offended you. That wasn't my intention." Sebastian forced a smile that felt unnatural, though it was sincere. He shoved his hands into his pockets. "It's just... I love my sisters, but they can be a little intense. So I didn't want them to know I was coming."

"Apology accepted." Her steely gaze made him doubt that she actually did accept his bungling apology.

"Welcome to the Sweet Magnolia Inn, Mr. Valentine. We'll take good care of you during your stay. You can leave your luggage there. I'll have it delivered to your room as soon as we get you all checked in."

"Why?" Sebastian had made Nolan promise not to divulge his health scare to their family unless it became absolutely necessary. Let alone to relative strangers—not even extremely beautiful ones. "Did my brother indicate that I required special care?"

Evelisse stared at him as if he'd suddenly grown horns and a tail. "No. Should he have?"

"No." Sebastian gripped the handle of his luggage. "And I can handle my own bags, thanks."

"Whatever you'd prefer." Evvy shrugged, her irritation with him barely concealed.

They went through the steps of registering him at the inn. Then Evvy walked him up the elegant stairwell and to a room at the end of the hall.

"Since you'll be with us for a while, we wanted you to be comfortable. This is one of our larger, deluxe rooms." Evvy opened the door for him.

Sebastian followed her inside, taking in the brand-new room that boasted top-notch furnishings and a lavish, spa-like bathroom. The room smelled like apples and cinnamon.

"There's a basket filled with luxurious toiletries and sumptuous Egyptian cotton spa towels in the bathroom. You have a small refrigerator and microwave here and a work desk there with lots of outlets and a charging station. This room has a gas fireplace that'll keep the place warm during cold winter nights. The switch is on the wall there. And this—" she gestured toward a chaise and small coffee table "—is one of my favorite spaces in the entire inn. It's the perfect place to sip your morning coffee while you pore over your latest memoir."

Sebastian set his luggage in the corner. "You remembered I'm an avid reader."

"I did." Evelisse's cheeks flushed as if she was embarrassed by the admission. "Probably because I'm a big reader, too. But you're into nonfiction, memoirs, and the occasional legal thriller, while I'm into—"

"Suspense, thrillers, and cozy mysteries…but only if

they have a healthy dose of romance." Sebastian quietly regarded Evelisse. She was even more beautiful than he remembered.

"That's right." A genuine smile lit her deep brown eyes and stirred something in Sebastian's chest.

"I'll be going into Gatlinburg once a week. So if you need anything from the bookstore, I… I mean, *we*… would be happy to pick it up for you." Evelisse scanned the room, seemingly eager to look anywhere but directly at him.

"I brought a stack of books, so I think I'm all set." Sebastian patted the leather satchel sitting atop his rolling luggage. "I plan to get plenty of reading done during this trip."

"Then I'll see to it that you're not disturbed, Mr. Valentine."

"Time out." He formed a T with his hands. "I appreciate the professionalism, but how about if you go back to calling me Sebastian instead?" He made the effort to smile, aware that his sisters accused him of having RGF: Resting Grouch Face. Sebastian sat on the edge of the bed. "And as I recall, you go by Evvy."

"Yes, but either Evvy or Evelisse will do." Her eyes followed him as he sank onto the mattress. Her gaze shifted toward the pile of pillows at the head of the bed, and then to the floor. The flush of her cheeks deepened. "Again, welcome to the Sweet Magnolia Inn… *Sebastian*. We're glad you chose to make our home yours during your stay."

Sebastian sighed quietly as Evvy turned to leave. He'd liked her the moment they'd met. There had been harmless flirtation on both sides, but nothing had come of it. They'd both been in town for only a week, and he'd had bigger fish to fry. Like talking his father out of selling their family's textile firm and making it his life's mission to convert a broken-down old winery into their new family empire.

Sebastian had failed on both fronts, but at least his father seemed happy.

He hadn't seen or spoken to Evvy since then. But he'd thought of her often. Now that she was standing in front of him, he was apparently incapable of stringing together a single coherent sentence that didn't make him seem annoyed.

"I thought you went back to Cali," he said.

Evvy turned to face him. "I did."

"When'd you return to Magnolia Lake?" He stood, taking a few steps closer.

"A week ago. My sister broke an arm and a leg in a mountain biking accident. She'll be fine," Evvy added in response to the look of alarm on his face. "But she asked if I'd serve as innkeeper until she's back on her feet."

"How long will you be in town?"

"Until the end of the year." Evvy shrugged. "Same as you."

There was an awkward silence, their gazes locked.

"Sorry to hear about Kayleigh's injuries," Sebastian said. "But it is really good to see you again, Evvy."

"You, too." Evvy's smile was reserved. "What brings you to town for such an extended stay?"

Pressure rose in Sebastian's chest at the thought of

everything that had brought him there. He rubbed his chin. "Long story."

"Well, whatever the reason, I hope you enjoy your stay." Her tone had gone flat. She reached for the knob. "If you need anything, please let me know."

"Have dinner with me?" Sebastian jammed his hands into the pockets of his gray chinos. His heart thumped wildly when she turned back to him with widened eyes.

"Tonight?"

"I was thinking more like this weekend." Sebastian laughed nervously. "I'll be here for a while, so there's no rush."

"I'm flattered that you asked me out…*a year later*," she muttered the last part. "I would've gladly said yes then. But now, I'm the acting innkeeper. I've already turned down a couple of other offers because dating the clientele doesn't set the right precedent for my staff. So I'm afraid I can't accept your offer. I hope you understand."

"No need to apologize." Sebastian stepped backward, offering a cursory smile. "I should've asked you out when I had the chance. Have a good evening, Evvy."

"Same to you, Sebastian." There was a hint of sadness behind her smile. "But if you need dinner recommendations, I'd recommend the King's Finest Family Restaurant. And I hope to see you at breakfast. It's served from six to eleven each morning, and the coffee station downstairs is available all day."

Sebastian thanked her, then watched the gentle sway of her hips as she sashayed away. He sank onto the bed again, inhaling the remnants of her subtle floral scent.

He'd blown his chance with Evvy, but it was probably for the best. He already had enough on his plate.
Getting involved with Evvy would only further compli-
cate matters. He should be glad she'd turned him down.

So why was he anxiously looking forward to seeing
her at breakfast?

Three

"Kayleigh, when you asked me to fill in for you as the innkeeper, did you know Sebastian was staying here for the next three months?" Evvy paced the floor of the small office behind the inn's front desk.

"Sebastian *Valentine*?" Kayleigh coughed. "He's at the inn now?"

"Yes. He was the mysterious SBV on the register. You're telling me you had no idea?" Evvy asked incredulously.

"No, Evs, I swear this is the first I'm hearing of it. And I certainly didn't take a three-month reservation for someone who was only willing to share their initials," Kayleigh said. "Mari must've booked the reservation."

"Hmm." Evvy sank onto the leather chair behind the handmade desk with a live wood edge, much like the

front desk. Both were Hamilton Haus originals, cour-
tesy of Kayleigh's brother-in-law Dallas Hamilton.

"So you think…what? That I broke my leg and shattered my arm as some extreme form of matchmaking?" Kayleigh laughed bitterly. "I love you, sis. But
I'm pretty sure there are much less painful ways of
finding my sister a man. Besides, being a matchmaker
requires subtlety. We both know that isn't my gift."

It really wasn't.

"Well, look at it from my perspective. You asked
me to come for a few months. He's staying for three
months. You're friends with his sisters. And your best
friend, Savannah, just *arranged* a summer job for her
sister at Valentine Vineyards, and suddenly Laney's a
permanent Magnolia Lake resident and dating Nolan
Valentine." Evvy counted each item off on her fingers
as if Kayleigh could see them. "Can you blame me for
being suspicious about this arrangement?"

"When you put it like that, I guess not," Kayleigh admitted. "I can't believe Chandra and Naya didn't mention that Sebastian was coming to town. Chandra and
the baby were just here yesterday. Wait until I talk to
Naya later. They could've given me a heads-up."

"No! Don't!" Evvy pressed her palm to the golden-
brown wood surface. "He wants to surprise them. *That's*
why he booked under his initials."

Despite her protests otherwise, Sebastian had probably been right to book anonymously. Score one for him.

"Fine." Kayleigh pouted like she did when they were
kids and Evvy wouldn't give her another piece of her
Halloween candy. "Is Sebastian still grumpy?"

"Yes." Evvy thought of how he'd snapped at her when she'd been surprised that he remembered her name. As if the idea of him forgetting anything was preposterous. "And no."

"Okay, I'm lost."

"He was weird and standoffish when he first got here. Then he apologized for assuming you would've shot your mouth off about his visit to his sisters—"

"I totally would have…if he hadn't told me it was a secret," Kayleigh interjected, munching on something.

"Noted." Evvy wouldn't mention that to Sebastian. "Then, when I was about to leave his room—"

More coughing. "You were in his room?"

"He didn't want his luggage taken up. So I escorted him to his room and showed him all of the amenities." Heat spread through Evvy's cheeks. She was glad she'd chosen not to video call her sister.

"Show him the amenities? I'll just bet you did."

Evvy slapped a hand to her forehead and sighed. "That isn't what I meant, and you know it. I was pointing out the premium bath towels and the lounge area, for goodness sake."

"Do you normally escort guests to their rooms and give them a private tour to show off our…*amenities*?" Kayleigh burst into giggles.

"I most certainly do not." Evvy stood and paced the floor again. "But like you said, Sebastian can be really picky. He's going to be with us for a while. I wanted to get his stay off to a good start. We're new to the hospitality industry. Every guest experience is important, but especially long-term guests, which can be extremely lucrative," Evvy rattled defensively.

"You're right. I'm sorry. I was just teasing you, Evs." Kayleigh sounded mildly apologetic, but she could still hear the grin in her younger sister's voice. "So, go on. You're showing him the amenities and…"

"And then he starts making small talk. Asking when I came back and how long I'll stay."

"I like where this is going." Kayleigh munched on something crunchy.

"Right? But then I ask him about what brought him to town for three months, and he gets all cagey and mysterious about it. So I take that as my cue to exit, and I'm about to leave. But then he asks me out to dinner."

"You're kidding?"

"I am not. Honestly, I was stunned as you are. The way he was so hot and cold in the twenty minutes since he'd arrived, it was the last thing I expected."

"I guess I'm better at this matchmaking thing than I thought."

"Not funny, Kayleigh Jemison Abbott." Evvy stood at the window surveying the wooded property surrounding the inn. "And that is *exactly* why I turned down his offer."

"You turned him down? Why? You said, and I quote, 'He may be a little grumpy, but I find him fascinating. And his fine ass could definitely get it.'" Kayleigh mimicked the sound and cadence of Evvy's voice, then laughed again.

"Okay, yes, I did say that," Evvy admitted. "But in my defense, I'd sampled a lot of that Valentine Vineyards wine and had a couple of those knock-you-on-your-ass spiked apple ciders your sister-in-law Zora made. Those things really sneak up on you." Evvy rubbed her forehead. "My head is throbbing just thinking about the hangover I had the next day."

"Don't blame it on the alcohol, Evs. I was there when you two first laid eyes on each other. There were sparks and magic and shit. You two were completely mesmerized. You managed to sit together at dinner and were practically inseparable all night," Kayleigh recounted.

It had been a really fun night. When she'd first spotted Sebastian, he'd been standing along a wall scowling. But when they'd been introduced and he shook her hand…

Evvy stared at her open palm, tingling now just as it had the night she'd put her hand in his. She'd never admit it to Kayleigh, but there *was* something almost magical about that night. And while Sebastian had been a little awkward and standoffish at the beginning, his cool demeanor had quickly thawed. Once he'd relaxed a little, she'd found him to be warm and amiable. His dry sense of humor had made her laugh. They'd shared funny stories about their siblings and commiserated over their less-than-ideal childhoods.

They'd both been in town for about a week, visiting family, and she'd been so sure they'd clicked. Sebastian had asked for her number, but then he hadn't called. To say she was disappointed would be a gross understatement.

"Actually, the more I think about how Sebastian was

with you that night… I'm not surprised at all that he asked you out," Kayleigh said.

"That was more than a year ago," Evvy reminded her sister.

"It's good he didn't call you back then. You didn't have Calvin out of your system yet. You two got back together after you returned to LA. But now you're seriously done with him, right?"

"Yes, Calvin and I are over. But that doesn't mean I need to jump into another relationship. I'm content being on my own, thank you very much."

"I wouldn't call this a jump. You and Calvin broke up a few months ago."

"Sebastian isn't staying in Magnolia Lake, Kayleigh. And neither am I. What would be the point?"

Her sister hadn't been very subtle with her suggestions that Evvy should stay in town and run the inn permanently. A classic little sis bait-and-switch scenario. But this time, Evvy wasn't falling for it.

"Does there have to be a point?" Kayleigh asked. "Why can't it just be fun?"

"I didn't come to town to hook up with Sebastian Valentine." Evvy's tone was firm. "I'm here to ensure you get better and to get the inn off to a strong start, so I can hand it back to you once you're on your feet again. Are we clear?"

"Crystal."

"Great. Now, I had an idea about creating welcome baskets for long-term guests. The kind you might get when moving into a new town. It would be filled with items that'd introduce guests to a few of the premier establishments in town. Bourbon from King's Finest Distillery. Wine from Valentine Vineyards. Fancy sugar cookies from Magnolia Lake Bakery bearing the inn's logo. A gift certificate to King's Finest Family Restaurant. Fresh fruit and flowers from Lockwood Farms."

"Sounds fantastic, Evs." There was hesitancy in Kayleigh's voice. "It also sounds *really* expensive."

"They'd only go to guests who stay four weeks or more. So we can *certainly* afford it. And who knows, some of the vendors might be willing to sponsor the welcome baskets. After all, it benefits them, as well," Evvy noted. When her sister didn't respond, she said, "I thought maybe I could do a sample one for Sebastian—since he's our first long-term guest."

"Of course you did." The smirk was evident in her sister's voice.

In her head, she could hear ten-year-old Kayleigh singing, *You like him, you like him, you really, really like him*, to the tune of "I Like It" by DeBarge.

"Well, what do you think?" Evvy nudged.

"I think it's a great idea, sis. Go for it. Go ahead and make one—"

"Actually, I was thinking three."

"But we only have one long-term guest."

"I'd like to display the other two behind the front desk, so guests could buy them. That might help offset the cost of the one we're giving away."

"Okay, fine. But just remember, Miss Hollywood, the point of this venture is to *make* money, not spend it."

"I know, but long-term guests will love it, and short-term guests might be enticed to return and stay a bit longer."

"Great. I can't wait to see it. Our dinner was just delivered, so I have to go. Love you, Evs."

"Love you, too, sis. Feel better."

Evelisse pulled out a pad and pen and jotted down ideas for the Welcome to Sweet Magnolia Inn basket.

Marketing and guest relations were simply part of her job as the acting innkeeper. It wasn't as if she, personally, was shopping for Sebastian.

So why couldn't she stop smiling?

Sebastian approached the lovely little cabin off the lake that his eldest sister Chandra shared with her new husband—the town doctor—and their infant daughter. He chuckled, recalling the last time he'd stood on this porch. He'd been shoulder to shoulder with his three brothers: Nolan, Alonzo, and Nyles. They'd come there to ensure Julian didn't have ulterior motives regarding Chandra.

To his credit, Julian hadn't been intimidated by their show of bravado. He'd been patient and respectful, but he made it clear he was head over heels for their sister and looking forward to starting a life and a family with her. They were less than a year into the marriage, but so far Julian had been a man of his word. He'd made Chandra extremely happy.

Sebastian rang the doorbell.

"Hey, Bas. Good to see you." Julian greeted him with a warm handshake. "Chandra didn't mention you were in town."

"That's because I had no idea he was coming." Chandra hugged him, then accepted the bouquet of flowers and bottle of wine he'd brought.

"You didn't tell me you were coming." His younger sister, Naya, raked her fingers through the bangs of her short blond bob.

"Didn't realize I was required to report my whereabouts to you, Blondie." He ruffled her hair.

"Hey! Do *not* touch the wig, buddy." Naya took a step back and fluffed her wig. "She don't like just anybody putting their hands all up in there."

Sebastian laughed, and so did everyone else. Naya loved her wigs, gave them all names, and referred to them as if they were people. "Well, tell Veronica or Stacy or—"

"It's Phyllis, actually." Naya patted her wig and popped a hip.

"Fine. Tell *Phyllis* I'm sorry."

"She ain't deaf. Tell her yourself." Naya poked his arm.

Sebastian shook his head. He'd always been protective of his little sister. She'd been an outspoken, bisexual, Black woman growing up in a *very* conservative neighborhood. But Naya could clearly hold her own.

She was a no-nonsense woman who didn't take shit from anyone—including her older brothers. Naya was an Instagram beauty and lifestyle influencer long before agreeing to join the winery. She'd taken on the role of Valentine Vineyards' brand ambassador and events and PR manager.

But as much as he loved his little sister, he drew the line at apologizing to inanimate objects.

"Pass," Sebastian said.

Naya wrinkled her nose and sauntered off.

"Sebastian, hey. Good to see you." Nolan approached, holding the hand of his girlfriend, Delaney Carlisle, the enologist at Valentine Vineyards. Sebastian had met her at an end-of-summer barbecue thrown by Duke and Iris Abbott.

"Good to see you, too." Sebastian slapped his brother's shoulder. He extended a hand to Delaney, but she hugged him instead.

"Come say hello, sweetie." Delaney reached out to her daughter, Harper. The girl—the spitting image of her mother—sat on the floor watching Sebastian's father bounce Chandra's infant daughter Autumn on his knee.

"Hi, Uncle 'Bastian." Harper bounced up and wrapped her wiry arms around his waist, then dashed back over to the baby.

Harper calling him "uncle" had been an even bigger surprise than Laney's hug.

"She's obsessed with Autumn and the idea of having a baby sister of her own." Lancy exchanged a shy smile with Nolan. "So don't take her rushing off personally."

"I won't."

"Good." Laney smiled. "I should go help your sisters." She kissed Nolan before joining Chandra and Naya in the kitchen.

"Uncle, huh?" Sebastian nudged his brother's shoulder. "You two are moving pretty quick."

"I told you, I plan to marry that woman." A wide smile spread across Nolan's face when his eyes met Laney's. He was clearly a man in love.

Nolan and Laney were adorable together. Sebastian was happy for his brother. But there may have been a tad bit of envy alongside it.

"Thought you were just in that lovesick puppy phase again," Sebastian admitted with a chuckle. "But seriously, being in love again…it's a good look for you, Nole. You deserve this."

"So do you," Nolan said. "Speaking of which, I hear Kayleigh's sister, Evelisse, is running the inn temporarily."

"She checked me in and arranged for the delivery of the wine and flowers." Sebastian's ego was still slightly bruised over Evvy's polite rejection. "I'm not looking for anything serious, and neither is she."

"So you already asked her out."

It hadn't been a question, so Sebastian didn't respond.

"Sorry to hear that. You two being back in town at the same place and same time…" Nolan rubbed his chin thoughtfully. "I was sure—"

"We're only in town a few months." Sebastian lowered his voice. "What would've been the point anyway?"

"If you really believed that, why'd you ask her out?"

Sometimes Sebastian hated that his brother was usually right. Especially when Nolan's logic countered the fallacies Sebastian held on to so tightly. Like telling himself he didn't want or need a relationship at this point in his life.

"You do plan to make it over here before they put me in the ground, don't you, son?" Sebastian's father said.

Sebastian was thankful for the distraction from Nolan's pointed observation.

"We both know that you're going to outlive all of us, old man." Sebastian sank onto the sofa beside his father and gave him a one-armed hug. "How've you been?"

"Really good, son." Abbott Raymond Valentine glanced around the room proudly at the four of his six children gathered there. Then he kissed the slobbery cheek of his first and only grandchild. "Even better now that you're here. But tell me, to what do we owe this unexpected visit?"

"It's been a while since I've taken time off work." Sebastian shrugged, his gut twisting.

He felt bad about not leveling with his father and sisters about the health scare that brought him to town. But they were all busy with their own lives and the new winery. Why burden them further?

"So you decided to vacation here in Magnolia Lake?" His dad raised an eyebrow.

"You're always saying how beautiful it is. Besides, I wanted to spend time with my family."

"You're *voluntarily* spending your vacation here with us?" Naya appeared out of nowhere. She stood in front of them with her arms folded and one hip cocked. "Okay, what the hell is going on? Oh my God, are you like dying or something?"

"Naya!" His dad, Nolan, and Chandra all called her name at once.

"No, of course not." Sebastian narrowed his eyes at

his sister, willing her to lower her voice several decibels. "I'm fine. I just needed a little mental health break, that's all. I have the time available, so I chose to spend it with my family. So relax, all right?"

Chandra handed their father a drink, presumably bourbon and soda with lime, his preferred beverage. Then she lifted Autumn into her arms and nuzzled her cheek. "How long will you be in town, Sebastian?"

"I was thinking through the end of the year."

"Great. You'll be here for Christmas," Naya said excitedly. "But you should've given us a heads-up. I would've gotten one of the bedrooms at the villa ready."

"I'm staying at the Sweet Magnolia Inn. I checked in earlier."

"You're staying at a hotel, son? Why? We have plenty of room at the villa," his father said.

"And you're welcome to use our spare bedroom here," Julian offered, netting a warm smile from his wife.

"I appreciate it, really." Sebastian held up a hand. "But I'm going to be here for a while, so I needed a quiet place to read or tackle the occasional work project. I'm already settled in, and it's just up the road."

"The Sweet Magnolia Inn, huh?" Naya flashed him a knowing smile. "That's Kayleigh Abbott's new place. Her sister, Evvy, is running it while Kayleigh is recovering from her bicycle accident."

"I had no idea Evvy was in town until I checked in today," Sebastian said.

"Sure, bruh. Whatever you say." Naya stole their niece from Chandra, tickling the little girl's belly as she walked away.

He opened his mouth to respond, but Chandra spoke instead.

"I believe you, Sebastian." Chandra leaned into Julian, who pulled her closer, his arm encircling her waist. "The only thing that matters is that you're here. And we're all glad of that. Can I get you a glass of wine?"

"Please," he said.

"So this sabbatical of yours, son." His father lowered his voice. "What's this really all about?"

"You always say I work too hard. I finally listened. Can't we leave it at that?"

"If that's what you want. But if you need to talk—"

"I'll come to you, Dad. Promise."

His father nodded, seemingly satisfied. They fell into an easy chat.

Chandra handed Sebastian a glass of the sparkling muscadine wine that was his current favorite.

He thanked her, then took a sip. "How are things going at the winery?"

"Fantastic." Chandra beamed. "Sales are up. We're doing great business at the tasting room. And we've hosted a few small weddings."

"Things are a *lot* different than they were last time you were here," his father said. "You should come by tomorrow for a tour."

"I look forward to it." Sebastian raised his glass.

He spent the rest of the evening enjoying time with his family, getting acquainted with his new niece, and trying not to wonder where Evelisse Jemison was and what she was doing.

Four

"What's wrong?" Evvy walked into the kitchen where the inn's part-time chef, Sofie Braaten, was fussing up a storm in Norwegian. Evvy couldn't understand most of the words, but Sofie clearly wasn't pleased.

"It's that…that *man* out there. Every day, he eats the same boring breakfast: oatmeal with fruit. Every day for two weeks he eats this. This morning, I surprise him. I make this man the *perfect* Eggs Norwegian. A veritable masterpiece. He sends it back to me because he says it's too 'fishy.'" Sofie was completely outdone, her blue eyes flashing with disgust.

"Well, it is made with smoked salmon, Sofie." Evvy spoke calmly, trying to restrain a smile. Their house chef was nothing if not passionate. "Perhaps Eggs Norwegian was a bit too adventurous for Mr. Valentine."

Sofie threw her hands up in the air, followed by more cursing in Norwegian.

"Why don't you take a break? I'll make his oatmeal. All right?"

"*Ja. Greit,*" Sofie agreed quietly. She removed her apron and donned her coat. "I go for a walk now. Back in twenty minutes."

Evvy had been thinking more like ten, but whatever. As long as Sofie was happy, and Sebastian got his usual breakfast of fruit and oatmeal, it was all good. She could manage the kitchen for twenty minutes.

"If someone other than that man needs breakfast, call me," Sofie said before she disappeared through the outside door.

Evvy checked her watch. It was barely seven in the morning, and already Sebastian the Grouch had her staff in a tizzy. Sofie was madder than a wet hen that he'd insulted the meal she'd lovingly made for him. Mariana, who was their part-time server/front desk clerk, was outdone when he'd suggested that she carry his glass of orange juice in on a tray, rather than holding it in her hands. The housekeeper/porter, Daniel, was still somewhere grumbling under his breath about Sebastian showing him the *proper* way to make a bed.

She honestly didn't know if they'd make it another two weeks—let alone another two months—before a member of her staff strangled the man in his bed.

Evelisse washed her hands, tied on an apron, and took the oatmeal out of the pantry and the almond milk out of the industrial fridge.

While the oatmeal cooked, Evvy sliced up a banana,

a few strawberries, and a kiwi. Once the oatmeal was done, she served it up in a bowl, neatly arranged the sliced fruit on top, then added a handful of blueberries. She set the bowl on a saucer, removed her apron, and walked out to the dining room. Sebastian sipped his coffee, his face buried in a copy of late civil and human rights activist John Lewis's memoir.

"I was just about to send out a search party for my oatmeal," Sebastian muttered without looking up from his book.

"Perhaps you should send out a search party. Because my cook, front desk clerk, and porter are all on the verge of mutiny." Evvy set the bowl on the table and propped a fist on her hip. "I hope you know how to make beds and cook breakfast, because pretty soon, it might just be you and me around here."

"Evelisse." Sebastian missed his mouth and splashed a little of his coffee on the table. He set his cup down and blotted up the mess with a napkin.

"Sorry. I didn't mean to startle you. I brought your breakfast." Evvy gestured toward the bowl.

"Where are Sofie and Mariana?"

"Probably reviewing the want ads right now," Evvy said, only half joking. "May I have a seat?"

"Yes, of course." Sebastian dabbed coffee from the pages of his book.

"Look, Sebastian, we're thrilled to have you here at the inn," Evvy said. "But could you please go a little easier on my staff? We've got a full house, and we're all doing the best we can. I can't afford to have my staff jump ship."

"But Daniel's hospital corners weren't tucked tightly enough. I move around a lot in my sleep. I need nice, tight, precise hospital corners," Sebastian said.

"Fair enough. And I don't think he'll ever forget the importance of tucking those hospital corners tightly again," Evvy said.

"And as for breakfast this morning…" Sebastian glanced around the room, then leaned closer. "I assure you that I did not ask for fish and eggs for breakfast. Every morning, I have the same thing…oatmeal with almond milk and sliced fruit. How can a person mess that up? All you have to do is read the instructions on the box and microwave it."

"You're right. You didn't ask for an adventurous breakfast. And I apologize for that." Evvy pressed a palm to her chest. "But you sit here each morning brooding and avoiding the other guests as much as you possibly can. Sofie wanted to do something to make you feel more at home. So she lovingly prepared the meal she has such fond memories of her maternal grandmother making her for breakfast when she was a little girl growing up in Norway. Especially when she was feeling a little lonely."

"But there was fish in it…*for breakfast*," he added. "And I'm not crazy about eggs to begin with. And wait…are you saying she thinks I'm sad and lonely?" He seemed far more distressed about that than the combination of eggs and seafood for breakfast.

"What I'm saying—" Evvy placed a hand on his wrist "—is Sofie wanted to do something to brighten your day."

And overall outlook. But she thought it best not to say that part aloud.

"Food is Sofie's love language," Evvy continued. "So she surprised you with the meal her mormor always whipped up to make her feel better as a child."

"I'm sorry. I didn't realize it was a gesture of kindness. And I honestly didn't mean to insult her grandmother or her culture. Nor did I intend to hurt her feelings. It's just that I have a sensitive…*palate.*" Sebastian placed a hand on his stomach. The movement drew her attention to the sound of his hand slapping his apparently toned belly beneath that burgundy cashmere sweater. It also drew her attention to his lap and the slim gray pants that hugged his firm thighs.

Evelisse sucked in a quiet breath and tried to ignore the butterflies that flitted in her stomach whenever she was around Sebastian.

"Don't worry, I think Sofie is clear on the fact that you're not the kind of person who likes surprises, no matter how well-meaning they might be. So I assure you that it won't happen again."

Sebastian stared at her for a moment, blinking. He looked ridiculously handsome despite the ever-present scowl that had etched fine lines around his eyes and mouth.

"I should apologize to Sofie."

"It's okay, Sebastian." Evvy waved a hand. "I know you didn't intend to upset Sofie or Daniel or Mariana…"

"Mariana is irritated with me, too? What did I say to her? Never mind." He rubbed his fingertips across the furrows in his forehead. "I should just speak to all of them. Make it clear that I'm not trying to be difficult. It's just that I like what I like, and I—"

Sebastian moved to stand, but Evvy held on to his wrist, and he settled back in his seat.

"I'll speak with them." She released his arm, her palm tingling where it had touched his skin. "You should eat your food before it gets cold. I made it myself." Evvy smiled.

Sebastian studied the bowl and frowned.

"What's wrong now?" Evvy regarded the bowl carefully, too. "It's oatmeal made with almond milk and garnished with fresh fruit...just like you like it."

"I don't usually have kiwi," he noted.

"If you'd prefer not to have kiwi on your oatmeal, I'll get you a fresh serving." Evvy reached for his bowl.

Sebastian held onto the bowl possessively, dragging it closer. "You made it for me, so I'd like to at least try it."

"Is that the only reason you're trying it?" Evvy teased. "Because I will not be making your bed or bringing you juice every morning."

His genuine laugh startled Evvy. But then she laughed, too.

There was that silly fluttering in her tummy again. The same one she'd felt when she and Sebastian had spent a lovely evening getting to know each other more than a year ago.

Evvy felt the tiniest twinge of regret over rejecting Sebastian's dinner invitation. And she hated that he hadn't looked at her with an ounce of interest since then. Their daily interactions had been brief, polite, and strictly business.

Which was exactly what she'd wanted. Wasn't it?

But as he surveyed her now, there was a hint of heat in his dark eyes that made her want to lean down and taste his full lips.

Sebastian finally broke eye contact with her, delved his spoon into his bowl, and brought it to his lips. He chewed thoughtfully, then took another bite.

"Surprisingly, the kiwi is a nice addition," he said. "I'll keep it. Thank you, Evelisse."

"Good. And if you ever want to walk on the wild side, ask Sofie to toss on a handful of toasted walnuts and some shredded coconut," she whispered conspiratorially.

Sebastian's eyes widened. He put down his spoon and held up a hand. "I think this is enough adventure for now." He dabbed his mouth. "Have you eaten breakfast yet? If not, you're welcome to join me." He gestured toward the empty chair across from him.

"I appreciate the invitation, Sebastian, but I'm in charge of the kitchen while Sofie's taking a break. Maybe another morning?"

"Of course." His polite smile did little to mask his disappointment. "Thank you again."

Evvy nodded, then headed back to the kitchen, wishing she'd taken Sebastian up on his offer.

Sebastian returned to his room at the inn exhausted after a day with his family. He'd spent the bulk of the day with his brother Nolan going over the winery's financials and some of the plans his father and sisters had for the winery.

It was the kind of thing they'd frequently discussed when their family had run the textile firm together. But now that they no longer owned the firm, Sebastian had very little input on such decisions: an increasing point of contention. So it was nice to be asked for his opinion.

He'd spent the previous two hours sitting with his dad, who'd been watching little Autumn—whom Chandra brought to work. Sebastian quickly discovered the imprudence of tossing his infant niece in the air not long after she'd been fed.

Sebastian had come right back to the inn to shower, wash his hair, and change. Yet he could swear he still smelled sour milk.

There was a knock at his door. He glanced at his dry-cleaning bag on the floor by the bed. He'd been so preoccupied with scrubbing every inch of his skin and washing the sour milk from his hair that he'd forgotten to set the bag in the hall outside the door as Mariana had requested. He tugged on a shirt, then grabbed the dry-cleaning bag and opened the door. "Here you go. There's no rush getting it back."

"Good to know." Evvy was holding a large, black leather bin overflowing with goodies and wrapped in cellophane. "I'll see to it that it's taken care of. Mind if I come in?"

"Not at all." Sebastian stepped aside and let her into the room. "I thought you were Mariana. She was coming up to pick up my dry cleaning."

"I had to bring this up anyway, so I told her I'd handle whatever you needed." Evvy set the basket down on the table.

"Is this for me?" Sebastian studied·the elegant arrangement.

"Yes." Evelisse's smile lit the room and made his heart skip a beat.

"What's the occasion?" Sebastian loosened the ribbon that held the cellophane closed. "Is this a bribe to get me to leave?"

"Is that all it would've taken?" Evvy broke into melodic laughter when his eyes widened in shock. She placed a hand on his forearm, and he could swear he felt a zing of electricity. "I'm kidding, of course. It's a small token of gratitude to thank you for choosing to stay here at Sweet Magnolia Inn."

"I realize that some of my earlier requests might've made you believe otherwise, but I really am enjoying my stay. A few hospital corners aside, so far you're killing it." Sebastian nudged her with his elbow.

Her smile widened, and her gorgeous, brown eyes gleamed. For a moment he felt like he was floating, and he couldn't help wondering about the taste of the deep pink gloss on her enticing lips.

"So, what do we have here?" He pushed aside the plastic and surveyed the basket's contents. "You've been to my family's winery."

He lifted a bottle of Valentine Vineyard's sparkling muscadine wine. Not one of their most expensive offerings, but it was his current favorite.

"I did." She beamed. "I might go with the pinot or chardonnay in future baskets. But when I arranged delivery for you the day you arrived, you mentioned that this one was your favorite."

Something about Evvy recalling that detail and selecting the wine explicitly for him evoked an involuntary smile. Then again, she remembered what each of the guests liked for breakfast and how they took their coffee. It was part of her job to cater to guests. So he shouldn't read anything more into it.

Sebastian lifted a small tin and opened it. There were half a dozen individually wrapped frosted sugar cookies. Half of them were shaped like the inn and frosted in the same colors as the actual building—right down to the orange front door. The rest were made in the shape of the magnolia flower—the leaves frosted white with yellow centers and surrounded by green leaves. The tin and the labels on each cookie indicated they were from the Magnolia Lake Bakery & Café. He opened one of the cookies and bit into it.

"These are delicious," Sebastian murmured through a mouthful. "They taste fresh out of the oven."

"They were baked about an hour ago," she confirmed. "I got the idea for the basket the day you arrived, but I wanted the cookies to be shaped like the inn and the flower in our logo. That took a while to orchestrate, so…" Evvy paused, seemingly self-conscious. "What is it?"

"You came up with the idea for the basket *after* I arrived?" Sebastian smirked. "Meaning it's a custom gift for me?" He nibbled on more of his cookie. All of Evvy's seemingly random questions about foods he did and didn't like during their brief breakfast chats now made sense. The questions hadn't been random at all. She'd curated the basket to his specific tastes.

"Yes, the idea for creating a welcome basket for our long-term guests came to me after you arrived," Evvy stammered. "And since you're our first, I wanted to ensure that the basket was to your liking. But you do realize that this is a gift from Sweet Magnolia Inn, not from me."

"Okay." He did his best to hold back a grin as he rummaged around the basket, pulling out a bottle of King's Finest bourbon and a gift certificate for dinner at King's Finest Family Restaurant.

"Since you'll be making these baskets for other guests, thank you for including wine from my family's vineyard," Sebastian said.

"Valentine Vineyards makes an excellent product. As you know, I tested quite a bit of it." Her warm brown eyes twinkled. "I should go and let you enjoy your basket." Evvy swiped the dry-cleaning bag from the floor. "I'll get this to Mariana."

"Thank you for the thoughtful basket. I appreciate it." Sebastian clapped a hand to his chest. "But there's a lot here for one person. Interested in helping me polish off this bottle of wine?"

"It's a lovely offer, but I have a few more things to do before Mariana leaves for the evening. So perhaps another time. But I'd like to ask a favor."

"Sure. Anything." He rubbed his chin.

"I want these baskets to be perfect. So I'd appreciate your opinion. Give me the no-holds-barred Sebastian Valentine Report."

Why did Evvy's teasing smile make his head swim and his heart race? He wanted, with every ounce of his being, to take her in his arms and kiss that smirk off that sexy little mouth of hers.

"Yes? No?" Evvy was saying.

How long had he been in a daze while he imagined kissing this woman?

"Yes, absolutely. I can do that."

"Great. Anything else you need?"

Yes. You. Right here. Right now.

"No, I'm good, thanks." Sebastian walked her to the door and opened it. "Good night, Evvy."

She gave him a cursory smile and was gone.

Sebastian dragged a hand down his face and groaned.

What was it about Evelisse Jemison that had him completely mesmerized?

Sure, she was gorgeous in a grown-ass woman kind of way that really did things to him. And those curves... He could gladly give a TED Talk on all of the reasons he appreciated Evvy's curvy hips, thick thighs, and show-stopping bottom. But it was more than the physical attraction. There was just *something* about her that appealed to him in a way he couldn't quite explain.

From the moment they'd met, he'd felt relaxed around Evvy. As if they were old friends getting reacquainted. He didn't typically make that kind of connection with strangers. Not even ones as beautiful and captivating as Evelisse Jemison.

Sebastian put the wine in the fridge. Then he grabbed a few cookies from the thoughtfully tailored welcome basket Evvy had crafted for him. He couldn't help smiling, thinking of how perfectly she'd designed the gift basket. Even the container—a black leather bin lined with felt—had been thoughtfully selected. It was the perfect container to house his books and business magazines stacked on the table.

Regardless of how Evvy had tried to minimize the work she'd put into the gift, she'd clearly given a lot of thought to what would fit him personally. That kind of care and concern only made the woman more appealing. Which was a shame, because their moment had passed. And he had no one to blame but himself.

But if Evvy ever gave him another shot, he'd take it, no questions asked.

Five

Driving Kayleigh's old hand-me-down Jeep, Evelisse pulled up to the home Kayleigh and Parker shared. The vehicle was a decade overdue for the junkyard. But it was clean inside and out. And since the car she'd driven in LA had belonged to her boss, Evvy was grateful for the transportation.

"Thanks for keeping Kayleigh company." Parker hurried out of the open garage door and approached the Jeep before she'd turned off the engine. He seemed frazzled. An attaché was tucked beneath one arm, and he was trying to straighten his tie with the other as Kayleigh's golden retriever, Cricket, yapped in his wake.

"Where's the fire, Park?" Evvy hugged her brother-in-law, then took a moment to straighten his tie.

"I need to chat with my dad about a few things before

the board meeting this afternoon. Thanks for coming over to keep your sister company. I know you're busy at the inn, but I don't want to leave Kayleigh alone for too long just yet."

Parker's love and genuine concern for her sister made Evelisse smile.

Kayleigh and Parker had been best friends as kids. But after a falling out, they'd become mortal enemies. The childhood friends had mended their friendship while faking an engagement as part of a convoluted business deal when Parker's family had wanted to buy Kayleigh's old studio and jewelry shop. That broken-down old building had been renovated and was now the trendy, always-packed King's Finest Family Restaurant. And Kayleigh and Parker's relationship had led to love and marriage.

Evvy was glad Kayleigh wasn't alone anymore. She had a doting husband, a ride-or-die best friend in her sister-in-law Savannah and was now a part of the ever-growing Abbott Family. People who could take care of her better than Evvy or their parents ever had.

"I've got it. Just get out of here, and say hello to your family for me."

"Will do." Parker shoved his smudged glasses up the bridge of his nose. "Cricket has been fed and let out but not walked. I'll take her when I get back."

"No worries. I've got it." Evvy kissed the top of Cricket's head and patted her warm side. "Good luck with the meeting!"

She waved goodbye to Parker as he pulled out of the drive, then went in through the kitchen and made her way to the primary bedroom. Kayleigh wasn't nestled amid the pile of soft pillows perfectly placed to prop up her broken leg and cradle her broken wrist.

"Kayleigh? Where are you, hon?" Evvy called after checking the en suite bathroom and the walk-in closet.

"I'm in here!" Kayleigh responded.

Evvy followed the sound of her sister's voice to a spare bedroom down the hall.

"Kayleigh!" Evvy jogged over to help her sister, who was attempting to scoot a box across the carpeted floor with the knee scooter her injured leg was propped on. "Are you trying to break your other arm and your other leg?"

"God, you're worse than Parker." Kayleigh rolled her eyes. "It's not that serious. Besides, with this thick padding and carpet, how badly could I injure myself?"

"I'd prefer not to find out," Evvy said. "What are you doing in here anyway?"

"Since I can't go into the studio for a few more weeks, I thought I could bring the studio to me," Kayleigh said proudly. Her uninjured hand was propped on her hip, which had gotten a bit curvier during the month or so that she'd been confined to bed.

"You want to set this room up as your temporary studio?" Evvy glanced around the room, then turned her attention to her sister. "First, who on earth do you expect to drag all of that stuff from your studio here? Second, there's no way everything in your studio will fit in here. And third, doesn't that run counter to the fact that you're supposed to be *resting* so your body can heal?"

"Relax, *Mom*." Kayleigh used the same singsong

voice she'd used as a kid when Evvy had to make her do her homework or brush her teeth before bed. Usually because their actual mother was too busy coddling a grown man who couldn't seem to function without her undivided attention. "I only need a few items so I can do a little beading and metalwork."

"Did you miss the part about you needing to get some rest?" Evvy repeated.

"I have been. But if I lie around watching reruns while Parker fusses over me for much longer, I'm going to lose it, I swear."

"Seeing you all mangled and bloody like that after your accident… I think it broke Parker a little. He just wants to protect you."

"And I adore him for it. But I guess I'm still not used to allowing other people to take care of me." Kayleigh shifted her injured leg to the floor and sat down on the scooter, wincing a little. "I was on my own for a long time before my friendship with Savannah and then my relationship with Parker. So my first thought is still to do things on my own."

Guilt curled in Evvy's gut. She draped an arm over her sister's shoulder and leaned her cheek atop Kayleigh's head. "I'm so sorry I left you on your own. I was trying to outrun the past and all of the painful memories."

"I get it." Kayleigh shrugged. "Dad was a lot, and mom was—"

"Dad wasn't 'a lot,' Kayleigh. He was an angry, emotionally abusive, narcissistic alcoholic who neglected his wife and children. And Mom chose him over us."

Evvy's voice had become louder than she intended. She took a deep breath. "End of story."

There was only a slight age difference between her and Kayleigh. But Evvy had to be the adult in the house. No wonder she and Kayleigh's recollections of their parents were so vastly different.

Kayleigh's memories were soft and hazy. Greatly improved by the filter of the passage of time. But for Evvy, the wounds still felt raw and fresh decades later. She'd been glad when Kayleigh had told her the old house was being torn down to build a new community of homes. Evvy had been relieved that the dwelling where she'd experienced so much pain and anger had been decimated. As if the demolition of the structure would erase the hurt and resentment that still plagued her. It hadn't. But when her sister had called and asked her to be in her wedding... Evvy knew she had to find a way to let go of that pain.

She'd immediately booked her first appointment with a therapist, and she'd seen one regularly for the past year. But in moments like this one, those old memories still bore jagged teeth that tore at her flesh.

"I realize he was harder on you," Kayleigh acknowledged. "That they expected more of you than they did of me. I know it wasn't fair. But they were our parents, Evs. The only ones we'll ever have. Dad was sick, and Mama was just trying to do the best she could to keep her marriage together and to take care of us."

"Would you do what she did?" Evvy demanded. "Sideline your kids for a man who refused to get help no matter how many times you begged him to?"

"No, I wouldn't," Kayleigh admitted. "But Mom's

situation was very different from ours. She did what she felt was best for us. Like ensuring we both had the money for college by selling her family's land to Duke. And making arrangements for him to watch over us when she was gone." Kayleigh smiled fondly at the mention of Parker's dad. She wiped away the wetness at the corner of her eyes. "That's why we've each become the strong women we are now and why we'll never be in the position she found herself in."

Evvy faced the window that overlooked the stunning backyard and pool. She sniffled, wiping away the hot tears that streaked down her cheeks.

Her parents had been gone a long time. If Kayleigh needed to find some good in them, who was Evvy to stand in the way of whatever her sister needed to do to cope with her own pain?

"Maybe you're right." Evelisse turned back to Kayleigh and forced a bright smile. She glanced around the room. "So...a temporary mini studio, huh? Fine. I'll help you. What do we do next?"

Evvy rummaged through some chairs and tables in the basement. While she was stacking two chairs, her phone rang. "Evelisse Jemison speaking."

"Hi Evvy, it's Sebastian... Valentine."

He'd had her phone number for a year, and today he decided to use it?

"Hello, Sebastian. Is there a problem at the inn?"

"No, I just wanted to say how much I appreciated the basket. Everything I've tried in it thus far has been great."

"I'm glad to hear it. And it was my...*our* pleasure."

Evvy wandered through the basement in search of a comfortable chair for Kayleigh's makeshift studio. She spotted a stack of boxes with *Dad's Things* scribbled on them in her sister's handwriting. Evvy hadn't realized that Kayleigh had kept any of her parents' things. She opened one of the boxes and peeked inside. "Is there anything else I can help you with?"

"I'd hoped to speak to you in person, but Mariana said you were out." Sebastian's voice was deep and sexy. A shot of electricity jolted down her spine. "I had to make sure I hadn't run you off to LA again."

"Hate to disappoint you, Valentine, but I'm tougher than that," Evvy said. "I'm at my sister's place. My brother-in-law asked if I'd stay with her while he attends a meeting. And now she has me helping her set up a makeshift studio in one of the spare bedrooms."

"That sounds like a job." He paused for several seconds. "If you need a hand, I'm not busy this afternoon."

Evvy stopped digging in one of the boxes marked *Dad's Things*. "That's very generous of you, Sebastian. But you're a guest at the inn. I can't ask you to lug around tables and chairs."

"I'm not just a hotel guest, Evvy," Sebastian reminded her. "I'm Parker's cousin, and I'd like to help."

Evvy lifted the edge of the heavy table she'd selected. Dragging it up those stairs was definitely a two-person job. "Then I'd appreciate the assistance."

"Text me the address. I can be there in half an hour."

"If I text Daniel a list of items I need him to retrieve from Kayleigh's studio, would you mind bringing them?"

"Not at all. Text me when Daniel has everything ready."

Evvy thanked Sebastian and ended the call, more excited than she should be over the idea of seeing him again. Then she forwarded the list of items to retrieve from Kayleigh's studio to Daniel, hating to add to his list of duties on an already busy day. She closed one box of her father's things back up and moved it aside before rummaging through the next. Evvy pulled out a brown leather messenger bag with her father's initials stitched onto it. She ran her hand across the worn, dusty leather and swallowed hard.

It was the last birthday gift she'd bought him.

He'd grumbled that he was a plant worker. So why would he need a bag like that?

Evvy had been heartbroken. She'd slammed the door, gotten into her old rust bucket of a car, and driven off. Later, when she returned home, her father had been sober, he'd hugged her and thanked her for the bag and for the birthday card in which she'd written, *It's never too late to follow your dreams, Dad. You can be anything you want. I believe in you.* She'd included brochures and applications for enrolling in trade schools and the local community college in Gatlinburg.

It was one of the few good memories she had of her father.

Evvy hugged the bag to her chest momentarily, surprised to see that it looked like he'd actually used it over the years. She tossed the bag onto one of the chairs and lugged it upstairs, where Kayleigh was waiting.

"That's Dad's bag," Kayleigh said. "Where'd you find it?"

"In one of the boxes in the basement. I hope you don't mind that I looked through them." Evvy took a damp rag and wiped down the chair before settling her sister onto it.

"I know it seemed like he didn't appreciate your gift, but he cherished it." Kayleigh ran her hands over the supple leather and smiled. "He used it all the time after you went away to college. I think it was his way of keeping a part of you with him. Especially once you stopped coming home."

The fact that their father had the capability to be kind and loving during moments of sobriety only made her angrier about the unkind moments that had made her feel worthless.

"You really hated Dad, didn't you?" Kayleigh said.

"Honestly? I spent a lot of my teenage years wishing he'd never been born."

"If Dad had never been born, neither would we," Kayleigh reminded her.

"Back then, there were times when I wished we hadn't been." It pained Evvy to say the words she'd never admitted to her sister before.

There was anguished silence between them.

"Have you ever considered…" Kayleigh fumbled for the words. "Did you ever attempt—"

"What difference does it make now, Kayleigh? That was a lifetime ago."

"So that time we rushed you to the hospital… Mom said you ate something that didn't agree with you…"

Evvy faced the window, her eyes squeezed shut as

she thought of that night. The night she'd been so miserable and depressed and over it that she'd shoved a handful of pills down her throat and hoped never to see another day.

She wiped away tears, her back to Kayleigh, not wanting to see her sister's reaction. "I'd taken a handful of mom's sedatives."

"I'm sorry, Evvy. I knew you were unhappy, but you shielded me from so much. I had no idea it had gotten to that point." Kayleigh's voice broke. "I understand now why you needed to escape. It was what you had to do to protect your sanity. Don't ever feel guilty about having put that first. I only wish you'd told me."

"You were so scared. I remember you hugging me and crying. You clung to me for days, afraid to let me out of your sight. So maybe instinctively you knew all along." Evvy wiped away tears, sniffling again. "I stayed away because I couldn't be sure it wouldn't happen again. I kept thinking about how devastated you would've been if you'd found me. I couldn't take a chance on doing that to you, Kayleigh." Evvy finally turned to face her sister.

Kayleigh's eyes and cheeks were red, and tears streaked down her face. She reached her uninjured hand out. Evvy squeezed it, allowing her sister to pull her into a one-arm hug.

"I don't care if you were here, in LA, or in Timbuktu. I would've been just as devastated. I will always need my big sis. *Always.* So promise me that if you ever feel that hopeless and alone again, you'll talk to me about it, Evs. *Please.*"

"I promise," Evelisse said. "But mentally and emotionally, I've never been in a better space than I am now, and I have you to thank for that."

"Me?" Kayleigh wiped at her tear-stained cheeks. "How did I help?"

"By asking me to be in your wedding. You offered me a second chance at family and sisterhood. I couldn't let you down. It forced me to try therapy. That first time I came home, I needed anxiety meds. I've since learned to manage my anxiety with therapy and other strategies. But I'm also discerning enough to admit when that's not enough."

"Good." Kayleigh pulled back and smiled. "Love you, sis."

"Love you, too." Evvy wiped her eyes, eager to change the subject. "In fact, I love you so much that I just mobilized a team to help us put together your little studio today. Hopefully, it'll be done before Parker returns home."

"Really?" Kayleigh's eyes widened. "Who'd you call?"

"Daniel is collecting items from the studio. Sebastian is driving them here and helping me set them up."

"Sebastian, huh?"

"Don't start. I told you, there's nothing going on between us. He called about something else. When I mentioned what I was doing today, he wanted to help his cousins. It's that simple."

They were in for a grueling afternoon. So why was her belly fluttering in anticipation of Sebastian's impending visit?

Six

Sebastian unloaded the clear storage boxes Daniel had packed in the trunk of his BMW. Most of them contained jewelry-making supplies: wire, beads, various types of cords and leather, and an extensive set of tools. He walked up the steps to the front door of the address Evelisse had texted to him and rang the doorbell.

Before his foot hit the bottom stair, Kayleigh's dog Cricket announced his arrival. There were footsteps, and then the front door opened. Evvy was dressed more casually than he'd ever seen her. She wore a simple fitted white T-shirt beneath a too-big, unbuttoned, long-sleeve plaid green shirt and a pair of distressed skinny jeans that hugged every single one of her delicious curves.

He was pretty damn sure he was salivating over this

casually beautiful goddess who set off fireworks inside his head whenever he was around her.

"Good afternoon, Sebastian." Evvy's demure smile momentarily rendered him speechless. "Thanks for bringing Kayleigh's things."

Sebastian snapped out of his momentary daze when Evvy reached for the stack of containers. He held on to them firmly. "Just point me in the right direction."

Evvy led him to a spare bedroom. "You can set them here."

He set the boxes down, then stooped to greet Cricket, whose tail wagged. "Good to see you again, girl. Been taking care of your mom?"

When Sebastian glanced up, Evvy was staring at him with a sweet smile that made his heart skip a beat.

What was it about Evvy that simultaneously made him feel like a teenage boy with a hard-core crush, yet also more at ease? It was a paradox he couldn't explain, despite lying awake the past few nights trying to unravel the conundrum that was Evelisse Jemison.

"So where's Kayleigh?" Sebastian stood, shoving his hands in his pockets. "I was sure she'd be overseeing the project."

"She would be. But by the time she showered and got dressed, she was in some pain again. She took a pain pill, then she was out like a light. Fortunately, we drew up a plan beforehand." Evvy waved a rudimentary sketch of the room. "So I know *exactly* which pieces to bring up and where they go."

"Maybe we can have it finished before Sleeping Beauty wakes up." Sebastian extended a hand. "Can I see the layout?"

Evvy gave it to him reluctantly. "Drawing isn't one of my talents."

"It used to be one of mine." Sebastian studied the sketch.

"Why'd you stop drawing?"

Sebastian rubbed his chin. "I wanted to get an art degree. But my grandmother—the family matriarch—was adamant that I needed to get serious about life if I wanted to prove my worth to the world. Eventually, I set my sights on becoming CEO of the company. Became as stern and austere as she was, because she believed it was the only way we'd be taken seriously in a mostly white corporate world."

Sebastian was surprised by his admission. It wasn't something he had ever really acknowledged himself—let alone shared with someone else.

"I'm sorry you were made to feel that way, Sebastian. We should be able to explore and excel in any arena we choose—corporate or creative—without that sort of mental burden. It's harmful and stifling both individually and culturally." Evvy sighed heavily.

He understood how mentally exhausting it was to navigate systemic racism and painful stereotypes. And he couldn't help wondering if it played a role in the reason the conglomerate that had acquired the textile firm so easily dismissed his input.

"I hope you get a chance to sketch while you're here," she said.

"When I was younger, I was passionate about art. Losing people who were important to me at a young age made me want to find a way to permanently capture moments. But I eventually became jaded. It's been a long time since I was inspired to draw. Whatever talent I had… I'm pretty sure it's faded."

"The only way you'll find out is to try." Evvy placed a gentle hand on his arm. Her warm brown eyes met his. "And I'd love to see one of your drawings."

Sebastian froze. His brain was unable to function, and his vocal cords were suddenly tight. He returned the sheet to her and clapped his hands together. "So… the basement, right?"

"Yes." She folded the sketch and slipped it into her back pocket. "Follow me."

They dragged up a heavy vintage butcher block table—the kind people frequently converted into islands in farmhouse kitchens. Then they brought up two padded wooden barstools, a couple of task lamps, and a chaise. Last, they hauled up a short vintage bookcase. Then they carefully arranged the items he'd brought over from Kayleigh's studio.

When they were done, Sebastian gazed around the room. "This looks amazing. You've got a gift for making do with what you've got."

"It's a talent you're forced to learn growing up poor in the rural South." Her words were tinged with a hint of bitterness.

"I'm sorry. I didn't realize…"

"It's fine, Sebastian." She offered a stiff smile. "Can I grab you another bottle of water or maybe a beer?"

"A beer would be great."

"C'mon." She led him to the kitchen, and they both

washed their hands. Then she got him an icy beer from the fridge and opened it.

His fingertips touched hers when she handed him the beer. Sparks of heat traveled up his arm, and he nearly dropped the bottle.

"Parker is on his way home with pizza and more beer. I know you probably have plans with your family tonight—"

"Actually, I don't," Sebastian interjected.

Evvy's eyes lit up. "Well, since you don't have plans with your family, maybe you'd like to stay and have dinner with mine." Her cheeks flushed, nearly matching the color of the lip gloss that had been taunting him all afternoon.

"I'd love to stay for dinner." Sebastian sipped his beer.

"Great. I'll let Parker know." Evvy whipped out her phone and tapped out a message. Then she returned it to her back pocket.

When she looked inside the refrigerator, assessing its contents, Sebastian's eyes were drawn to the phone in her back pocket. More specifically, he was drawn to her full, round bottom.

He guzzled the remainder of his beer, hoping the cool liquid would bring his temperature down.

Cricket came into the kitchen, looking out of sorts with her leash in her mouth. She dropped it at Evelisse's feet and plopped down.

"Cricket, sweetie. I'm so sorry. I promised Parker I'd walk you before he got home. Once we started setting up your mama's studio, I completely forgot." Evvy glanced at her watch. "Why don't I take you for a quick walk now?"

Cricket barked, her tail wagging.

Evvy clipped on Cricket's leash, then slipped into her jacket. "I won't be gone long, and Parker will be here shortly. I can turn on a movie or SportsCenter if you'd like."

"It'll be dark soon." Sebastian glanced out the window at the receding daylight. "You shouldn't be out there alone."

"I won't be. I have Cricket to protect me." Evvy scratched the senior dog's ears. "She might be an old bitch, but she's still a bad bitch." Evvy laughed. "I suppose she could say the same thing about me."

"First…you're not old," he said. "Second, I'm coming with you."

"We'll stick close to the house, but I'll leave Sleeping Beauty a note, in case she wakes while we're gone."

Sebastian put on his jacket and waited for Evvy.

This wasn't the dinner date he'd had in mind when he'd asked Evvy out. Nevertheless, he'd enjoyed getting to know her. He was still surprised by his propensity to open up to her. So what if neither of them was prepared to start a relationship? Perhaps they could forge a lasting friendship.

But as he walked beside her in the waning afternoon light, getting to know this fascinating woman, Sebastian was deeply aware that he was telling himself a bald-faced lie.

Friendship with Evvy would never feel like enough. But given their situations, it was all he could hope for.

At the end of their evening together, Evelisse felt like she was floating as she stepped out into the cool, brisk fall air and surveyed the stars twinkling in the darkened sky.

When Kayleigh had awakened from her nap earlier that evening, she'd been beyond thrilled with her new remote studio. They'd celebrated with pizza and beers. Then the four of them watched the sixth or seventh sequel in one of those action movie franchises where the characters had more lives than the luckiest alley cat. Despite all the explosions and car chases, Kaleigh had dozed off again.

After the movie, Sebastian volunteered to help Evvy straighten up and put away the leftovers while Parker got Kayleigh back to bed.

Sebastian Valentine was quite the surprise.

Her initial impression was that of a man with a superior attitude who was surly, demanding, and accustomed to having everything his way. But the more Evvy got to know Bas, the more she could see him for who he was. Like her, he'd been deeply, irrevocably wounded by family trauma and parental loss. He'd struggled with self-identity, just as she had. And in many ways, they were both still desperately trying to prove their worth to the world.

It made her sad for both of them. But there was some comfort in realizing that someone else understood her pain in a way even her little sister couldn't. It made her sadder still that despite their growing sense of connection, the best she could hope for was friendship.

After a nearly six-year relationship that went nowhere, Evvy wouldn't torture herself like that again. If she got into another relationship, it would be with someone who was on the same page. Someone who wanted love and a lasting commitment. Someone who wanted to be with her, *and only her.*

Sebastian's prickly, porcupine-like outer shell wasn't an act, per se. But knowing what she did about him now, it felt very much like a defensive mechanism meant to protect his soft underbelly from further trauma and pain.

Evvy couldn't blame him for that. But he'd let down his defenses just enough to reveal hints of his emotional depth and nurturing kindness. Traits he seemed to prefer to hide from the world.

Was it a conscious choice made to keep people away? Or was Sebastian unaware of what he was doing?

Either way, it wasn't her job to try and fix every broken man between Tennessee and California.

After they said good-night to Parker, Sebastian walked her to the Jeep, both of them smiling, as they had been much of the evening.

"She's a classic." Sebastian nodded toward Kayleigh's old Jeep.

"That's a generous way to put it." Evvy laughed.

She turned the key but got nothing. She tried again and again.

"Wait." Sebastian held up a hand. "You don't want to flood the engine. Has it given you problems before?"

"The Cricketmobile has a lot of miles on her, so she can be a little temperamental. But she's never refused to turn over like this." Evvy stepped out of the Jeep, slamming the door behind her in disgust. This definitely wasn't the memorable departure she had hoped to make. "You go ahead. I'll have Parker call a tow truck."

"We're headed to the same place. Why don't I give you a ride to the inn? Even if you get it towed tonight, a mechanic won't look at it until tomorrow."

"Mariana is off tomorrow, so I can't afford to spend another day away from the inn. I need to handle this tonight. I just hope Mari can stay a little while longer while I wait for the tow truck. You don't need to wait with me, Sebastian. I'll be fine."

"Take my car and head back to the inn, so you can relieve Mariana," Sebastian said. "I'll wait here for the truck."

"You want me to drive your BMW?" Evvy stared at him, blinking.

"It's just a car, Evelisse." Sebastian pulled his key fob from the pocket of the dark-wash jeans that fit his toned body just right and placed it in her palm. "I'm sure Mariana is probably exhausted, so you should go. I'll find out where Parker wants to tow the Jeep."

Evvy glanced at her watch. If she left now, she'd arrive about fifteen minutes before the end of Mari's shift. Just enough time to get Mari's end-of-the-day update. "How will you get back to the inn?"

"Let me worry about that." Sebastian walked her to his car and gave her a quick rundown of all of the controls. "Go." He nodded toward the road. "I'll see you in about an hour."

Evvy thanked him again, then headed toward the inn.

Yes, Sebastian Valentine was quite the surprise indeed.

Seven

One hour had become more like two. But eventually, a driver came and towed the car to the garage owned by Julian's cousin Elias.

Sebastian had spent the long wait for the tow truck driver picking Parker's brain. His cousin was the CFO of King's Finest Distillery.

It wasn't that he doubted Nolan's capabilities. His brother had been damn good in his role as the CFO of their textile firm. But as owners of a winery, his family was finding their way in a very different industry. The Abbotts had been leaders in the alcoholic beverage industry for the past five decades.

Why not tap into their expertise?

Parker's insights into the industry and King's Finest's past failed and successful product launches were illuminating. Sebastian had typed lots of notes into his phone to share with his family when he visited the winery the next day.

After the driver left with the Cricketmobile in tow, Parker offered to drive Sebastian back to the inn. Neither man was the sort to chatter on mindlessly. They traveled mostly in comfortable silence.

"So… Evvy." Parker's words came seemingly out of nowhere. He didn't supply any additional context, as if those two words had composed a clear question.

"She's an amazing person," Sebastian said after a few moments of suddenly awkward silence.

"She is," Parker agreed. "She and Kayleigh were estranged for years. I'm grateful that they were able to reconnect and that Evvy feels comfortable coming back here to Magnolia Lake again, so—"

"You don't want anything, or more specifically, *anyone* to ruin it," Sebastian finished his cousin's thought.

A faint smile curved Parker's mouth as he stared ahead. "Precisely."

Evvy had made it clear nothing was going to happen between them. There was no need to argue the point. Yet despite that clear logic, he felt the need to push back.

"So you're saying you don't want your sister-in-law getting involved with me?"

Parker frowned, clearly annoyed that the issue hadn't been easily resolved.

"If I thought you were serious about Evelisse and you planned to stick around, I'd be all for it," Parker said. "But you aren't. So where would that leave Evvy?"

Extremely satisfied.

The words danced in Sebastian's head, but it seemed better to keep them to himself. If he'd been having this conversation with one of his own brothers, he would've lovingly told them to fuck off.

He and Evvy were two grown-ass adults who could do whatever the hell they wanted. But though he and Parker were family, they were still in the getting-to-know-you phase of their cousinhood.

"I'll keep that under advisement." Sebastian looked over at Parker, whose eyes were glued to the darkened stretch of road ahead.

Parker's eyebrows scrunched as he glanced over at Sebastian momentarily. He sighed and shook his head. "That's code for 'I'm not going to listen to a damn thing you just said,' isn't it?"

"I wouldn't put it quite like that." Sebastian chuckled. "I like Evvy. There's no point in denying that. But I've already taken my shot. She wasn't interested. End of story."

"And yet you volunteered to spend your afternoon hauling old furniture up from my basement." Parker snorted. "Sounds to me like a guy who still believes he has a shot. Besides, the way you two were making eyes at each other all evening tells a different story."

The man has a point.

He hadn't been able to take his eyes off Evvy, no matter how hard he tried.

"So wait…you're saying she was watching me all night, too?" Sebastian sounded more hopeful than he'd intended to. But when it came to Evelisse, his brain had clearly ceded control to less logic-driven body parts.

Parker gave him a side-eye as they approached the inn. He pulled in front of the walkway to let Sebastian out.

"Look, I realize that you two are adults and that I have no say in what happens. Everything I know about you makes me believe that you're a stand-up guy. When it comes to my *sister*—" Parker emphasized the word "—all I'm saying is please, don't prove that assessment to be wrong."

"Understood." Sebastian stepped out, clutching his box of leftovers, and wished Parker good-night.

He surveyed the inn, lit up against the night sky, and sighed.

Parker was right. Evvy was special. And their connections to the Abbott Family would make things awkward if things went sideways between them. So he'd just be content to consider the remarkable Evelisse Jemison as a friend.

Evvy stood in front of Sebastian's door and raked her fingers through her hair, wishing she'd stopped at a mirror before she'd headed up the stairs.

Busy taking inventory in the supply closet, she hadn't heard him return. And when he'd sent a text message to let her know he was back in his room, she was placing a grocery order. As she stood in front of his door now with her fist raised to knock, she wished she didn't look like she'd been moving dusty furniture all day.

Relax. You're returning his car key, not meeting for a date.

She knocked, butterflies fluttering in her belly as footsteps approached.

"Hey." Sebastian stood aside and let her in. He was wearing a fresh white T-shirt and a pair of gray sweat-pants.

"Hey." Evvy sank her teeth into her lower lip as she dragged her gaze up from the less-than-subtle dick print in the gray fleece. She might've even groaned and said, *Oh, mercy.* But she really, really hoped that part had only happened in her head. "Sorry I missed you earlier. Didn't mean to hold your key hostage."

"Not a problem. It gave me a chance to take a long hot shower."

Okay, now I can't stop thinking about that athletic body butt-ass naked beneath the showerhead.

Sebastian didn't seem to notice that she'd temporarily blacked out.

"My body is reminding me that I'm not in my twenties anymore." Sebastian rotated his left shoulder. The movement made the bottom of his T-shirt rise, revealing a hint of the skin low on his belly and the trail of fine hair that disappeared below the waistband.

Evvy squeezed her eyes shut, restraining the urge to bite her fist.

She was the one who'd insisted nothing would happen between them. And she was seriously regretting that decision right now.

"I can definitely relate." She rubbed at her shoulder. "But anyway, I—"

"Come here."

Evvy stared at him a moment, her eyes widened at the unexpected request. Her nipples tightened and there was an ache low in her belly in response to the command issued in a low, gruff voice that vibrated through her body.

"My ex-wife would get tightness in her back and shoulders all the time. I got good at massaging out the kinks." He wiggled his fingers. "It's been a minute since I've done this. Let's see if I still have the touch."

Evvy walked closer, then turned her back to him as he requested.

"Where does it hurt?"

"My shoulders here and my lower back here." She indicated the trouble spots.

When Sebastian put his large hands on her shoulders and gently kneaded her already sore muscles, it felt so good she nearly whimpered.

"Right there?"

"Oh my God, *yes*. Right there."

"Your shoulders are super tight." Sebastian leaned down, his voice low. "Relax, Evvy. It's just me."

An involuntary smile spread across her face, and she released a breath.

"Much better," Sebastian declared as he massaged her upper back and shoulders.

With her muscles relaxed, the kneading of his large hands felt even more divine. Evvy sighed softly, her head falling forward like a rag doll's.

"You weren't lying, Sebastian. You are *really* good at this."

"Wait until I get to your lower back." His thumbs gently massaged either side of her spine as his hands slowly glided down.

Suddenly the tension in her body started to rise again.

"Suck in a deep breath, then release it, nice and slow," he instructed, his minty breath warming her ear. "That's it." He gently rubbed at the soreness and tension in her low back.

Evelisse was about five seconds from melting in a puddle of deep and utter satisfaction when Sebastian suddenly pulled his hands away.

She fought the urge to have a complete meltdown like a toddler demanding more time in the toy aisle at Target.

"Good?" he asked.

"Orgasmic," she said dreamily. Evvy's eyes widened and her cheeks flamed the moment she heard the word come out of her own mouth. She turned to face him. "*Figuratively*, of course. Not..." She cleared her throat, her brain willing her mouth to shut up. "What I meant to say is thank you. That feels better."

Sebastian's dark eyes glittered. "Take a couple of ibuprofen and either a nice hot shower or a soak in the tub. You'll be golden tomorrow."

Now she couldn't stop imagining the two of them in the shower together.

This visit was quickly deteriorating. Time to make her exit.

"I will, thanks. Good night." She hurried toward the door.

"Evelisse?"

"Yes?"

"I think you forgot—"

"Your key." She slapped her forehead, her cheeks stinging with embarrassment. Evvy dug Sebastian's key fob out of the back pocket of her jeans and placed it into his outstretched palm, her fingers brushing his.

She was startled by the spark of electricity in her fingertips, and Sebastian clearly felt it, too.

The air was drier at this time of year as they headed toward winter. It was a simple case of static electricity. Nothing more.

So why did she still feel the zing all the way up her arm?

Sebastian cleared his throat and shoved the key fob into his pocket. Evvy's eyes were drawn to that damn dick print again, which at this point she was pretty sure was intentionally taunting her.

She pulled her shoulders back and reminded herself to calm down. They'd been together all day. So why was she suddenly acting so weird about being around him?

"Thank you again for helping me today. There's no way I could've done that alone. And I love my brother-in-law, but if I'd had to work with Parker to put that room together, he would've questioned every single furniture selection and placement. We'd have been ready to strangle each other by the end of it."

They both laughed, and some of the tension she'd been feeling eased.

"It was sweet of you to give up your afternoon to help us out. Then letting me use your car and then waiting for the tow truck… You were a lifesaver today, Sebastian. I honestly can't thank you enough."

Evvy hugged him, sinking into the comfort of his strong arms.

"You're an amazing sister, Evvy. No wonder Kayleigh adores you."

"I have a lot to make up for. I'm just grateful my sister isn't holding a grudge about the years I pulled away from her and this town." Her eyes stung, and her voice broke slightly.

"Then maybe you should cut yourself some slack, too." Sebastian stepped back, lightly grasping her arms as he studied her face. His gaze was warm and understanding. "We all react differently to the hand we're dealt. You managed the best you could then. But you're here for her now. That's what matters."

"Thanks, Sebastian. I needed to hear that." Evvy kissed his whiskered cheek.

Warmth and a subtle, woodsy, citrus scent radiated from Sebastian's freshly showered skin. Evvy wanted to press her nose to his neck and inhale the scent. Imprint it in her skin and burn it into her memory.

She pulled away, reluctantly, her gaze on his full lips. But before she stepped out of his embrace, Sebastian tipped her chin and lowered his head. His lips hovered over hers as if seeking her permission.

Evvy closed the space between them, pressing her mouth to his. She wrapped her arms around him, her fingertips digging into the dewy skin of his back beneath his T-shirt.

Sebastian cupped her cheek and angled her head. His kiss was soft and searching as if testing the waters. She tightened her grip on his waist, gasping softly at the feel of his hardened length pressed to her belly.

He swept his tongue, warm and minty, against hers. Evvy sighed softly, loving the feel and taste of him.

Suddenly, her phone rang. The custom ring indicated that the call had been forwarded from the inn.

Evvy pulled out of the kiss. Her skin felt like it was on fire, and her heart thumped loudly as her eyes searched his.

"I'm sorry, Sebastian. I shouldn't have… I didn't mean to…" she faltered, then swallowed hard. "I need to take this call. So… I should go."

"Of course." Sebastian managed a polite smile. "Good night, Evelisse."

She wished him a good night, then hurried out the door and tried to answer the call, but it had already rolled over to voice mail.

She nearly collided with one of the guests as she headed for the stairs.

"There you are, dear." Mrs. McConley glanced in the direction of Sebastian's room and gave her a knowing smile. "I was just calling you."

"No, it isn't what… I mean, I was returning one of Mr. Valentine's belongings." Evvy cleared her throat and hoped lip gloss wasn't smeared all over her face.

"Whatever you say, dear." Mrs. McConley wiggled her eyebrows. "He's a handsome devil."

Evvy wanted to curl up into a ball and sink through the floor. This was exactly why she and Sebastian needed to keep their relationship strictly business. It wasn't only her reputation on the line. It was the inn's.

"You wanted something, Ms. McConley?" Evvy tucked her hair behind her ear.

"Have you been watching the news, dear? A major snowstorm is headed this way. They anticipate that the airports will be closed for a day or two. As much as I hate to leave, we need to get ahead of this storm. Harlan was able to switch our flight to tomorrow afternoon, which means we'll need to check out in the morning. I'll understand if there's a surcharge for checking out early."

"Our first priority is your safety. After all, we want you to visit us again next year." Evvy flashed the older woman a warm smile. But beneath her placid demeanor, her heart raced and her brain was going a million miles a minute, thinking of all the things she needed to do to prepare the inn for its first major storm.

"Harlan and I have already decided to return to this charming little inn of yours in the spring." The older woman beamed. "Now, you will update our reservations, won't you?"

"I'll have everything ready before you check out in the morning," Evvy assured her.

"Good. Carry on. And in case we don't see him in the morning, do tell that handsome Mr. Valentine we said goodbye." Mrs. McConley winked, then hurried off to the honeymoon suite at the other end of the hall.

Evvy dragged a hand down her face and groaned. She glanced in the direction of Sebastian's room, then hurried down the steps.

She'd been right about not getting involved with a guest. Not even one as kind, thoughtful, and deliciously sexy as Sebastian Valentine.

She was here to do a job. She'd update the McConleys' reservation, pop two pain pills, and take a long bath while she watched the weather channel on her tablet and created a plan of attack.

Winters in Magnolia Lake and the surrounding area were typically mild in the lower elevations. It was rare for them to get the kind of storm that Mrs. McConley had described. She hoped the woman had simply overreacted to the news of an early snowstorm. Either way, she'd develop a detailed plan and be ready for the storm ahead.

Eight

Sebastian had awakened exhausted. His brain had been busy replaying his kiss with Evvy in strikingly vivid detail. He'd considered going to the gym or perhaps taking a walk in the increasingly crisp fall air to clear his head. But he'd spent the time lying in bed, staring at the ceiling and imagining what might have happened had Evvy not received that ill-timed phone call.

He got up later than usual, groggy despite the extra time in bed. The few hours of sleep he'd gotten had been fitful and restless.

Sebastian was angry with himself. Because despite the smiles and flirtation they'd shared, Evvy had been clear about not wanting to get involved. So he shouldn't have kissed her.

He hadn't helped Evelisse and Kayleigh out expecting Evvy to change her mind. He'd done it because he liked Evvy, and she'd clearly needed help. So he'd wanted to be there for her.

Then why was he feeling so out of sorts about last night?

Sebastian got out of the shower and dressed. He spent an hour reading—an activity that always helped to improve his mood. But perhaps he was also delaying his inevitable encounter with Evvy at breakfast.

It was petty and childish. He was better than that.

He and Evelisse were adults, and it certainly wasn't the first time either of them had dealt with an uncomfortable situation.

His physical attraction to Evvy was strong, to say the least. But there was a connection between them that calmed his restless soul and brought him a sense of joy. Made him laugh and put him at ease. From her reaction, she seemed to enjoy the tentative friendship they were building, too. He didn't want things to be awkward between them for the next two months when they could be spending that time enjoying each other's company instead.

Sebastian tucked his Gil Scott-Heron memoir, *The Last Holiday*, beneath his arm and made his way down the stairs. Something about the energy of the space seemed off. It was harried and anxious rather than the calm, soothing space he'd grown accustomed to and anticipated each morning.

Mr. and Mrs. McConley were at the front desk wearing coats and surrounded by their luggage. They appeared to be checking out. Other guests were in the lobby, scarfing down their breakfasts rather than leisurely sipping their coffee and enjoying the made-to-order creations the inn was known for. Everyone in the room seemed stressed, including the staff.

It was barely after eight, but Mariana already looked as if she'd run a marathon, and the buffet stacked with take-and-go convenience foods was uncharacteristically disorganized.

Sebastian nodded to another guest, who was stuffing a few of the convenience items into her purse before tugging her rolling luggage toward the door. Then he sat down with his book at his preferred table, prepared to read until Mariana came to take his order.

"Sorry, Mr. Valentine." Mariana rushed over. "Everything is a little crazy this morning. Your usual?" She'd already started writing the order on a pad.

"Actually, I was thinking I'd try the steak and eggs this morning." Sebastian glanced up from his book to find Mariana staring at him with her mouth open.

"You don't want your oatmeal?" she asked, as if he must be confused.

He repeated his order, more slowly this time. "No. I'd like the steak and eggs with the steak medium and the eggs over easy, but not runny."

"Oh, all right," she said. "Anything else?"

"Maybe one of those fresh, hot cinnamon rolls Sofie makes?" He set down his book.

"Living it up this morning, eh, Mr. Valentine?" Mariana teased as she jotted down the order. "I like it. Sofie's steak and eggs are the best. You're going to love them. Be back as soon as they're ready."

Mariana was gone before Sebastian could ask her why everyone in the inn was running around as if their hair was on fire.

He had resumed his reading when he heard Evvy's voice. She spoke in a cool, composed tone. But beneath it, Sebastian could hear the tightness of her vocal cords. And when he glanced up at her, he noted the stiffness in her posture.

Evvy was stressed about something, too. When she glanced over, her eyes meeting his as she spoke to another guest, she offered a stiff smile and a nod before returning her attention to the older man. Evvy walked toward her office but was stopped by a couple who seemed just as harried as everyone else.

Sebastian's phone rang. It was his sister Chandra.

"Good morning, Chan. Surprised to hear from you so early."

"I know. But between Autumn being fussy this morning and all the preparations we need to make for the storm, I needed to grab a minute to call you as soon as your niece fell asleep." There was tension in his sister's voice and the sound of drawers opening and closing in the background.

"What storm?" Sebastian set his book down and leaned forward.

"Meteorologists are predicting that a huge snowstorm will hit this area within the next forty-eight hours. We're running around like mad to make sure that the winery and vineyard are prepared for what could be several feet of snow."

"Here in Tennessee at this time of year?" Sebastian asked incredulously.

"I know. It's not typical. But they're using words like 'storm of the century' and referencing that huge snowstorm in Gatlinburg that happened when we were kids," she said hurriedly. "Remember how jealous we were of the kids who got all that snow and camped out in their living rooms because the power was out for a week? Well, I'm definitely not feeling that way now."

"That explains why everyone here is so stressed," Sebastian muttered under his breath. "What can I do to help at the winery?"

"So far, we have everything covered. If we need help, I'll let you know," she said. "I called to invite you to stay with either Julian and me or here at the villa with Dad and Naya. If this storm is half as bad as they're predicting, we could be without power for days. There's a generator here at the villa and a smaller one at our cabin."

"What about Nolan and Delaney?" Sebastian asked.

"Their townhomes don't have generators, so Nolan, Delaney, and Harper are staying at the Villa with Naya and Dad," she said hurriedly. "Let me know if you're coming, so I can order enough groceries to tide us over and keep everyone from turning on each other. You know how hangry you get when your blood sugar dips."

She said it teasingly, but they both knew it to be true.

"So either I can potentially spend a week knee-deep in relatives at the villa or crash at your love nest and room with my fussy infant niece? Hmm, let me see…"

"You're such an ingrate." Chandra laughed, only half

kidding. "Those are your choices, friend. But you won't have to share a room with Autumn. We have a third bedroom. We've been using it for storage, but there's a bed and desk in there."

Lovely.

"Let me find out if there is a generator here at the inn. If so, maybe I'll just stay here." Sebastian quietly thanked Mariana for the steaming cup of coffee she'd just set on the table. "Can I get back to you in a few hours?"

"I'm placing another grocery order in two hours, so you have until then," Chandra said. "And if you decide to stay, make sure you have plenty of food, lots of warm clothing, several blankets, a radio, batteries…"

"All right, all right. I get the point," Sebastian said. "I'll stay with you and Julian. Thanks for the offer. What time is the storm coming in?"

"Late tomorrow afternoon and into the evening."

"Then I'll get there tomorrow before noon. I'll stick around here through breakfast tomorrow," he said. "That'll give me time to pick up a few things."

"Well, I wouldn't wait," she admonished. "You know how it is when snow is predicted in the South. The grocery and supply store shelves are bare."

"Noted."

"Good. It'll be nice to have you stay with us for a few days," Chandra said. "And if this is all much ado about nothing, then we can have a good laugh about it on the other side. But better to be prepared. I have to go. I'll call you if we need help. Love you, bye."

When he glanced up, Evvy was reloading the convenience table. He put down his book and walked over to her.

"Good morning, Evvy," he said.

She nearly jumped out of her skin. "Good morning, Sebastian."

"Seems everyone is a little jumpy today. Because of the storm, I assume."

"Yes. They're talking storm of the century. So there's a lot to do. We have a generator here at the main building and a separate, smaller unit over at the carriage house which houses my apartment and Kayleigh's studio. So we should be fine. Not that it matters. Most of the guests are checking out to get ahead of the storm. Are you going to stay with your dad or your sister?" she asked. "Sorry. I might've overheard a little of your conversation with Chandra."

"I'm going to spend a few days with my sister, but I'm not checking out."

"I'll adjust your bill for the days you won't be staying here." She held up a hand before he objected. "Feel free to leave your things in your room. I just don't feel good about charging you for nights you won't be here."

"Thank you," he said. "But what about you and the rest of the staff?"

"Now that you're leaving, that will officially make the inn empty. I'm sending my staff home early today so they can make preparations at their own homes and ride the storm out there."

"And you?"

"I'm staying with my sister and Parker. But first, I

need to storm-proof the inn. I'll be here until a little after breakfast tomorrow."

"That's when I plan to leave, too." He rubbed his chin.

"Then you'll have to settle for me making you breakfast," Evvy said.

"I'll survive." Sebastian chuckled. "But what about the Cricketmobile? Isn't it still in the shop?"

She groaned. "I've been so busy with everything that I forgot. I'll have Parker—"

"He's probably busy, too," Sebastian said. "We're heading out around the same time, why don't I give you a ride to Kayleigh's place? Then I'll head to my sister's."

"You're sure it won't be an inconvenience?"

"It would be my pleasure." He smiled warmly, then turned to leave.

"Sebastian, wait." Evvy gripped his arm and glanced around. She lowered her voice. "About last night—"

"I shouldn't have kissed you. I got a little carried away."

"*We* got carried away," she noted, then sighed. "The truth is, I wanted you to kiss me. But I was right about it being inappropriate while you're a guest here." Evvy glanced around again. "I really like you, Sebastian, so I don't want things to be weird between us. I hope we can be friends, but I can't offer more than that right now."

"Understood." Sebastian backed away, hands raised. He forced a smile, despite the tightening in his chest.

He ate his steak and eggs and tried not to steal glimpses of Evvy, the sweetest, most beautiful woman he'd ever known.

Nine

Evvy was startled awake by a loud crash. She shot upright in her bed and gazed around the darkened room, disoriented.

The alarm clock was blinking, so the power had definitely gone out. Either it had come back on, or the standby generator had kicked on. Evvy reached for her cell phone on the charger. It was 7:15 a.m., and she'd overslept by two hours. There would be no time for her usual morning ritual of meditation, reflection, and a twenty-minute sun salutation yoga practice.

She'd begun the routine, at the recommendation of her therapist, shortly after she'd ended things with Calvin.

There'd been a notable reduction in her anxiety since she'd begun the grounding daily practice. And she'd felt a peace and calmness that made her believe she could take on anything. Even this unexpected pre-winter snowstorm. Starting her day without her routine felt unsettling. But she'd have to manage.

Evvy stepped into her slippers and shivered, already missing the layers of blankets piled on her cozy bed. She walked over to the first of two large windows that provided loads of light in the studio apartment above Kayleigh's jewelry-making studio and gift shop. She swept the curtains open and turned the blinds. Bright sunlight filled half the space. Evvy peeked through the blinds. The inn's parking lot was filled with snow.

It wasn't supposed to snow until late that afternoon. And yet it had clearly been snowing for hours. Heavy, wet snow blanketed the nearly empty parking lot and clung to the tree branches—some of which had given way beneath its weight.

She opened the blinds to get a better view.

"Oh my God!" Evvy could barely breathe. Her heart pounded in her chest, and anxiety swirled around her like a tornado slowly gathering steam. Her knees felt weak, and the familiar feelings of fear and anxiety snaked their way through her chest and twisted her gut.

A large old pine tree had fallen into the parking lot, narrowly missing the lone car—Sebastian's black BMW. What if that tree had totaled Sebastian's car? What if he'd been inside it at the time? Evvy quickly changed into a pair of old sweats and put on a jacket. She went down the stairs and looked out of the front windows of Kayleigh's shop. The snow was nearly knee-deep and still falling. She shivered at the thought of going out into the cold, wintry weather.

"Kayleigh, you're a genius," Evvy muttered, heading toward the side door, which led to the enclosed walkway Kayleigh had insisted on. The passageway connected the carriage house to the inn. The space wasn't heated, and she quickly regretted not putting on a heavier coat.

Evvy unlocked the door to the inn and stepped inside, noting the darkness and frigid temperature. She flicked the light switch and got nothing. She tried another switch and another. The power was out.

Why hadn't the standby generator kicked on? She'd find out, but first, she needed to check on Sebastian.

She made her way up to his room, rubbing her arms. It hadn't taken long for the cold to seep in. She only hoped Sebastian had been running the gas fireplace before the power had gone out. Without electricity, the wall switch wouldn't ignite the gas.

Evvy knocked on Sebastian's door. There was no answer. She knocked again.

"Sebastian, it's me, Evvy. Are you in there?"

She was about to use her master key card to enter his room when Sebastian finally opened the door.

"Evvy, what's up? I thought we said eight thirty for breakfast." Sebastian covered a yawn. His sleep-roughened voice was even sexier than his regular voice—something she honestly hadn't thought possible. He was wearing a classic *Martin* TV show T-shirt and a pair of black pajama pants that outlined all of his assets. And he didn't seem particularly happy about being awakened from a sound sleep.

"Sebastian, I'm sorry to wake you up like this, but we've got a problem."

"What's wrong?" He yawned again. "And why is it suddenly so damn cold in here?"

"That's one of our problems," she said. "The power went out last night. May I come in for a minute?"

Sebastian stepped aside and rubbed his arms.

Evvy flicked the switch next to the gas fireplace in Sebastian's room. Just as she suspected, she got nothing.

"Dammit" Evvy dragged a hand across her forehead.

"So the fireplace won't light. No worries. Just let me take a hot shower and then we can get out of here."

"That's our second problem." Evvy sighed. "We went with tankless water heaters to ensure that guests had hot water on demand. But since they don't store any heated water…"

"I have zero interest in turning into an icicle in the shower," Sebastian said. "I'm pretty much packed, so I can be ready in half an hour. I'll just wait until I get to my sister's to take a shower."

"And that's our third problem." Evvy frowned. "You clearly haven't looked outside yet."

"No. Why?"

Evvy walked over to the window, opened the curtains, and beckoned Sebastian to join her.

Sebastian rubbed his eyes and looked out the window.

"Shit." He covered his mouth and pointed. "That tree…it missed my car by that much. And where did all that snow come from? It's not supposed to start for another six hours."

"I know. Which means—"

"We're stuck here." Sebastian dropped into one of the chairs by the window, and Evvy did the same. He was pensive for a moment. "I thought you said there was a backup generator."

"There is, but for some reason, it didn't come on at the main building the way it did at the carriage house. I'm going to see if I can figure out what the problem is. Maybe it just needs to be turned on manually. But I wanted to check on you first."

"If freezing and being stranded counts as okay, then I'm great," he muttered as he paced the floor.

Evvy stood, too. "Don't worry. I'll figure this out. But in the meantime, you should grab whatever you need and come with me to the carriage house. My generator is working for now. And even if it goes out, there's a wood-burning fireplace and a tank-style water heater in my studio apartment. You're welcome to take a hot shower there. I'll be outside trying to determine why the generator isn't working."

"You're going out there alone?" he asked incredulously. "It's freezing. And look how quickly the snow is falling. Do you realize how easily you can become disoriented in a storm like this?"

"In case you haven't noticed, I'm the only person here. Unless you'd rather stay here all night and freeze to death, I don't have much of a choice."

"Give me ten minutes to get dressed. We'll go and check the generator."

"I can't let you do that, Sebastian. I'm the innkeeper." Evvy jabbed a thumb into her chest. "This isn't like when you were helping me and Kayleigh as a friend. Here, it's my responsibility to ensure the comfort and safety of the guests. I can't ask you to—"

"You didn't ask, and I'm not taking no for an answer. So you can step outside while I get dressed or you can stay for the show. Either way, I'm coming with you to check on the generator. Are we clear?" He tugged off his shirt, revealing his broad chest.

"I…you… I can't…" Evvy stammered, her heart racing. "If you insist on trudging out into the freezing cold and snow, fine. While you're getting dressed, I'll gather some things to take over to my place. I'll make breakfast there if we can't get the generator going. And if we can't—" she pointed a decisive finger at him "—you'll stay at my place until the power is restored."

"And where will you stay?" Sebastian rifled through one of the dressers and pulled out a V-neck undershirt.

Evvy hadn't thought that far ahead.

"I'll make a pallet on the floor in Kayleigh's studio. I'm sure we have sleeping bags in one of the sheds."

"I've seen the studio. The floor is cement. I don't care how good the sleeping bag is, you'll be freezing, and your back will be aching the next day," Sebastian said. "Why can't we just share your place?"

"Because you're a—"

"If you say I'm a guest one more time." Sebastian pulled a shirt down over his head. He rifled through another drawer. "We're clearly beyond that stage. At this point, we're a team. Period. All right?"

Evvy nodded. Part of her wanted to tell Sebastian Valentine off. How dare he assume she couldn't do this

on her own? But part of her was relieved. She'd been a
ball of stress and anxiety since she awoke to the sound
of that tree falling.

"I'll meet you downstairs with my overnight bag in
ten minutes." Sebastian grabbed more clothing from the
drawer, then disappeared through the bathroom door.

Too bad. I was hoping to see the rest of the show.

Evvy shut her eyes and tapped her forehead, trying
to banish the naughty thoughts churning in her brain.

Being stuck here alone at the inn with Sebastian
didn't change a thing. Despite their ill-advised kiss,
they would not get romantically involved.

Evvy repeated the words to herself as she headed to
the kitchen and gathered breakfast supplies. But all she
could think about was the kiss they'd shared and how
she wanted more.

Ten

Sebastian zipped up the black winter parka he'd had the presence of mind to pack. It was the last of his three layers of clothing. He put on the silk-lined merino wool skully that had seemed like an impulsive splurge at the time, but he now considered a solid investment. Then he lifted his leather overnight bag onto his shoulder and jogged downstairs, where he found Evvy in the kitchen with a basket filled with packages of bacon, eggs, and almond milk, and loads of fruits and veggies.

"That looks like enough breakfast for a small army." Sebastian took the basket from her and tucked it beneath his free arm.

She opened her mouth, likely to object, but didn't. Instead, she grabbed two reusable grocery bags stuffed with a variety of snacks and pantry goods and then led the way.

They went through the covered walkway to Kayleigh's shop, then up a stairway he hadn't noticed when he'd been in the shop before. Evvy opened the door, and it led to a studio apartment.

She set the groceries on the counter and began loading items into the fridge. "I'll change the bedding once we're done outside. But for now, you can set your bag down wherever you'd like. The bathroom is through there." She indicated the only other door in the space. "If you need to hang anything, the walk-in closet is off the bathroom."

"Thanks." Sebastian dropped his leather bag beside her luggage beneath the windows, which filled the space with light.

He slowly took in the apartment, which managed to feel both cozy and spacious. The footprint wasn't huge, but it made good use of the available square footage. The vaulted ceiling, skylights, and large windows made it feel bright and open. The wood finish of the ceiling with its decorative beams and one natural brick accent wall gave the space a rustic, industrial feel.

"I know this isn't anything like your room at the inn, but—"

"I love it." Sebastian smiled, taking in the autumnal decor. Fall motifs of leaves and various gourds were all around the room, from wall art to miniature pumpkins, and a variety of knickknacks that made the place feel inviting. "It's welcoming and...*you*, quite frankly."

"Thank you." The grateful smile that lit Evvy's eyes made his heart swell. "Coffee?"

"Please."

She made them two cups of coffee and handed him one. They both sipped from the ceramic mugs, the room filled with an awkward silence as they stood in the kitchen, just a few feet from her bedroom.

"So…" Sebastian clapped his gloved hands together. "Ready to check out the generator situation?"

"Let me put on something warmer." Evvy disappeared through the bathroom door.

Sebastian shoved his hands into the pockets of his parka and roamed the space. The room was warm and toasty—even without the fireplace lit. And the space smelled like cinnamon and apple cider, just like the inn.

The small kitchen had everything they'd need. A gas stove, an apartment-size refrigerator, a sink, and a small island that doubled as a breakfast bar. Two armchairs were situated in front of the fireplace, along with a coffee table. Beneath one of the windows was a window seat. Beside it was built-in shelving that housed books, photos, and more knickknacks.

Sebastian picked up a frame that held two photos. On one side there was a photo of two little redheaded Black girls laughing and smiling. The younger one had a snaggletoothed smile, and they both wore their hair in two thick braids. The second photo was of the same two girls—now gorgeous women—laughing together at Kayleigh's wedding.

"Those are my two favorite pictures of us…then and now." A soft smile lit Evvy's dark brown eyes.

"Both photos are beautiful." Sebastian returned the frame to the shelf.

"Thank you." Evvy slid on a black slouchy beanie hat with a faux fur black pom-pom at its crown. She tugged the material down over her ears. Then she zipped up her puffy knee-length black coat until the collar touched her chin. She was wearing chunky fur-lined knee boots. Evvy glanced down at herself and shook her head. Then she tugged on her mittens. "I look like the Abominable Snowman's girlfriend, so I guess that means I'm ready."

He should be so lucky.

"I need to call my sister and tell her there's no way I can make it out of this parking lot." Sebastian pulled out his phone and dialed Chandra. The call didn't go through. Neither did calls to Naya or Nolan. "Shit. Cell service is down, too."

Evelisse frowned. "You mean we can't reach anyone? What if something happens? What if there's an emergency?"

Her cheeks flushed, and her breathing was quick and shallow.

"Hey, everything is gonna be fine." Sebastian took her mitten-clad hand in his gloved one. "We're okay and we're together. We've got this. So don't worry. You're already doing great. All right?"

Evvy nodded, still frowning. But her breathing seemed to slow down. She slipped her hand from his, and they headed downstairs and through Kayleigh's studio behind the main shop.

The studio was already notably chillier than Evvy's

apartment upstairs. And when Evvy opened the door, they were met with a gust of wind that took them by surprise. The heavy, wet snow was falling rapidly, and there was at least two feet of snow on the ground.

"That's a lot of snow," Evvy said.

"And it doesn't seem to be letting up anytime soon." Sebastian studied the winter wonderland behind the studio. He put a hand on her shoulder. "Do we really need to do this right now? We could wait until the snow lets up. Then we could see what's happening better."

"I've got to get the power back on over there or I'll lose everything in the fridge and freezer. Besides, I'm worried about the pipes bursting if there's no heat."

"Okay." Sebastian sucked in a lungful of the frigid air. "The quicker we figure this out, the more time we'll have for important stuff like eating breakfast and uninterrupted reading."

"Spoken like a true introvert." Evvy laughed. The sound warmed his chest and made him laugh, too.

"Let me go first. Then you can step into my footprints. Just hold on to the back of my coat."

Evvy moved aside and the cold, wet snow whipped him in the face. She grasped the edge of his parka.

Sebastian trudged through the snow one step at a time, making sure not to get so far ahead that Evvy would lose her grasp of him. She shouted directions to the backup generator over the howling of the wind. But as they turned the corner, the reason the machine wasn't working quickly came into view.

The tree that had fallen in the parking lot, narrowly

missing his vehicle, hadn't been as kind to the inn's backup generator.

"There's our problem." Sebastian stepped aside and pointed at the mangled generator.

"There's no way we can fix that," she said.

"Afraid not," Sebastian agreed. "But we're fine over at the carriage house. Hopefully, the power will be restored at the main inn soon."

"Except I have a fridge and freezer full of food I'll need to transfer."

"Out here?"

"No. To the overflow fridge and freezer at the carriage house. I'll do that now. You just go upstairs, take a hot shower, and relax. There are breakfast bars and cold cereal in the basket on the counter. I'll make your made-to-order breakfast as soon as I'm done." Her tone and expression were apologetic.

"We're a team, remember? That's whether we're out here facing the elements or lugging a frozen ham from one freezer to another. Now come on. Let's get started."

Evvy's expression was filled with gratitude and relief. He fought the urge to hug her and reassure her everything would be okay.

When they returned to Kayleigh's studio, their clothing was cold and wet. They dusted the snow off their pants and coats and stomped the snow off their boots, leaving little puddles all over the floor.

Sebastian shook his head, thinking of Evvy's offer to sleep on a mat down here on the cold concrete floor in Kayleigh's frigid studio. But he opted not to bring it up. Instead, he was grateful that she'd agreed they should share the studio apartment.

Now his heart was racing. But there was no time to worry about sharing space or sleeping arrangements right now. First, there was plenty of work ahead.

Eleven

Evvy stood at the stove and stirred handfuls of cheese into the pot of creamy grits while she watched the news.

After they'd used rolling serving carts to shuttle all of the cold storage items over to the carriage house, they'd gone back to the inn to secure the building and leave a few water faucets on a slow drip. Hopefully, that would prevent the pipes from freezing. Sebastian had let her take a quick shower first. Then he'd planned to soak in the tub.

It was early afternoon now, so Evvy had forgone breakfast. Instead, she made buttermilk biscuits, a compound butter made with roasted garlic and shallots, and a nice-sized pot of shrimp and grits for a late lunch.

"It smells amazing in here." Sebastian emerged from

the bathroom in a T-shirt and a pair of broken-in jeans that accentuated his strong arms and impressive ass.

She marveled over how handsome he was. More so since she'd gotten to know him better.

"When we were transferring the food, you mentioned you hadn't had shrimp and grits in a while."

"So you whipped some up?" Sebastian shoved his hands in his pockets. "What'd I do to deserve that kind of service?"

"That's how we roll here at the Sweet Magnolia Inn. So don't forget to include that part in your Yelp review when you're telling the story of how you got stuck sharing my studio apartment during Magnolia Lake's very own Snowpocalypse." Evvy flashed him a playful smile, only half teasing.

"You say it as if my accommodations were downgraded." Sebastian sat on a stool at the little kitchen island. "But I don't see it that way."

She looked up from the stove, eyeing him suspiciously and awaiting the punchline. "You went from a luxurious private room to rustic living in a glammed-up barn with a roommate and a shared bathroom. I'm pretty sure that's considered a downgrade."

"If the space didn't come with a beautiful, vivacious roomie and warm, homey interior decorations—" he gestured around the space "—maybe I would agree. Yes, I had to sacrifice privacy, but I've traded it for great company. And I'd much prefer that to waiting out this storm over there in that spacious room all alone." He grinned. "Now you're adding an incredible meal to it—just because I mentioned a craving for it in passing. So no complaints here."

Evvy's face warmed and her belly fluttered. She would've expected Sebastian to be cranky and complaining. Instead, he'd been comforting and supportive. And he'd done whatever was required—even though it wasn't his responsibility.

"That's sweet of you to say, Sebastian. It almost makes it sound like you're not here because you were trapped by a snowstorm that didn't have the good manners to arrive on time." She gestured toward the television playing footage of snow-blanketed streets and snow-covered cars. "Were you able to get through to your family?"

"No." Sebastian shook his head.

"Neither can I." Evvy sighed. She wasn't worried that Kayleigh and Parker were in danger. But she could only imagine how worried her sister must be about her, thinking that she was there at the inn all alone.

Evvy hated that Sebastian had gotten stuck here, too. But he was right. Being here with someone else was far better than being snowed in all alone. So if she had to be here, a part of her was selfishly glad Sebastian was here, too.

She pulled the biscuits from the oven, then pulled out two of her fanciest ceramic bowls and spooned a generous portion of the golden cheesy grits into each. She topped them with the bacon, shrimp, and scallions mixture. Evvy placed lemon wedges on the bowls and set one at each place. Then she set out two beers, a small plate of biscuits, and a dish of compound butter.

When Sebastian ate his first spoonful of shrimp and grits, he moaned quietly and his eyes drifted closed.

"My God, this is good." Sebastian spooned more of the shrimp and grits into his eager mouth, and she was pretty sure he was humming. "You've been holding out on us. I had no idea you were this skilled in the kitchen."

"I can burn a little." Evvy sat beside him at the small island. Her thigh brushed his beneath the counter, and her skin warmed in response to the incidental touch. She slathered some of the roasted garlic and chive butter onto a still steaming-hot biscuit. "I learned to cook when I was really young to help my mother out. But mostly because the only thing my dad seemed to appreciate more than an open bottle of whiskey was a well-made meal." She shrugged. "It felt like the only thing I could do to make him proud of me."

Sebastian, seated beside her, placed his large, warm hand over hers and squeezed. "I'm sorry, Evvy. I really am."

Warmth spread up her arm from his touch, her flesh tingling, and a zing of electricity danced along her spine.

"It was a long time ago." Evvy gently withdrew her hand and nibbled on the flaky, buttery biscuit. "I know I should be over it, that I should let it go the way Kayleigh seems to have now that she's made a life with Parker and become part of his family…" She went silent, wishing she hadn't started down this road.

They had enough to worry about being stuck in a blizzard. The last thing she wanted to do was to bring the mood down.

"Childhood trauma doesn't disappear just because a certain number of years have passed." Sebastian grabbed one of the biscuits and sliced it open. "Believe me, I wish it was that simple. Then maybe I wouldn't be battling this constant internal pressure to prove that I'm not some fuckup that caused our mother to walk away."

"You're no one's fuckup, Sebastian. You're the CEO of Valentine Textiles—a company your family owned for generations."

"*Owned*—as in past tense. I worked my ass off to prepare for this role. Took every certification, earned every degree, read every leadership book…but now that I have the job…" A pained look furrowed Sebastian's brows and etched deep lines in his handsome face. "I never imagined that I'd achieve this goal, only to be relegated to being a figurehead who's all bark and no bite."

She buttered another biscuit and handed it to him. "So your hiatus from your job…it's more than just an end-of-the-year vacation. Are you considering accepting your father's offer to join the winery?"

Why did she feel so hopeful about the possibility of Sebastian staying in Magnolia Lake when she had no plans to stay herself? Maybe because if he was here, where her sister lived, she'd be assured of seeing him a few times a year.

"My family would love that. But honestly? Before I returned here, I still believed they'd all made a huge mistake. That this venture would eventually come crashing down around them. But after getting more involved with the business these past few weeks, I'm starting to appreciate the history and the charm of the old place and the generational connection my dad and siblings feel to the land."

A soft smile lit Sebastian's eyes, and Evvy was struck by how handsome he was.

"That sounds really nice, Sebastian. Was it not like that when you all worked at the textile firm together?" she asked.

"The mood there was somber and businesslike. But at the winery, things are different. The mood is lighter. *Joyful.* Valentine Textiles was a family obligation. Valentine Vineyards is a shared passion. I'll be the first to admit that working with my dad and siblings sometimes drove me up a wall. But working at the firm without them feels…"

"Joyless?" Evvy prompted.

"Soulless," Sebastian corrected her. "Definitely not the kind of atmosphere that makes you eager to get out of bed and go to work every day. And if I feel that way, you can only imagine how it's impacting the workers."

She'd been in lots of jobs with crappy management teams and soul-crushing company morale. So Evvy could relate. Her heart broke for Sebastian knowing that he'd spent his entire life preparing himself for a role he now seemed to dread.

They ate in silence as Evvy decided how to best phrase her next question. Finally, she asked, "If the job isn't what you expected and it doesn't make you happy…why stay?"

Sebastian narrowed his dark eyes as he turned on his stool to face her.

"You went to Hollywood, presumably because you wanted to become a star."

"Yes." She shrugged, spooning more food into her mouth.

"And how long have you been in LA?"

Evvy stopped chewing, heat spanning her forehead and cheeks. She'd just asked him a deeply personal question about his career. How could she then be angry when he responded in kind?

"Twenty years." She frowned, her eyes on her bowl.

"Is your career going the way you'd hoped?" he prodded.

"You know it isn't, Sebastian." She forced her eyes to meet his.

She was trying not to feel condemned by this line of questions, but that one felt damn personal.

"So why have you stayed in LA? Why do you keep going on auditions? What do you hope to—"

"Enough, Sebastian!" Evvy dropped her spoon with a clang, stood, and paced the kitchen.

Sebastian could come off as cranky, maybe even a little judgmental. But his rapid-fire questions made her feel like she was in a courtroom on the witness stand. There was no need for that.

"You don't think I know that I'm past my prime in Hollywood? That there's a good chance I'll never be anything more than an extra in an acid reflux commercial or a waitress in an indie film whose one big line is 'Coffee or tea, sugar?'" she mimicked the words in the deep Southern accent one director had insisted on. "I am fully aware my career is a bust, Sebastian Valentine. So there's no need to be cruel. And if you didn't want to answer the damn question, you could've simply said so." She huffed.

Evvy folded her arms and shifted her gaze into the distance. One minute she was dreaming of kissing the guy. The next, she'd wanted to shove him off that stool. Maybe he wasn't intentionally being an asshole about this. But that didn't make his words hurt any less.

Sebastian closed his eyes and pressed a hand to his forehead. He was an ass, and once again, his meaning had come out all wrong.

The last thing he wanted was to hurt Evvy's feelings or to make her feel as if he was judging her. He wasn't. He just wanted her to understand his point of view.

"Evvy, I'm sorry." Sebastian walked over to her and gently grasped her upper arms, prompting her to meet his gaze. "I'm not trying to make you feel bad. I admire your commitment and the bravery required to put yourself in a position to be rejected over and over again."

"And this is your idea of an apology?"

Sebastian dropped his hands to his sides and stepped back, giving Evvy space. "I'm just saying that walking away from my grandparents' company isn't as simple for me as it has been for Dad and Nolan."

After a few moments of awkward silence, he tried a different approach.

"My point is that, like you, I've invested a lot of time and effort into seeing this through. This job was supposed to be the pinnacle of my career. Instead, it feels like a joke. I got the job because no one else with the last name Valentine wanted it."

There was compassion in Evvy's warm brown eyes, but she didn't respond. So he continued.

"Are there days when I want to up and walk away? Hell, yeah. But then I think about all of the sacrifices I made to get to this point." He shook his head and sighed. "Not going to art school, the places I haven't traveled to, abandoned friendships, broken relationships, a failed marriage, choosing not to start a family. Every one of those sacrifices was a choice I made to get me where I am now. So if I just walk away—"

"What was the point of it all?" Evvy's tone was soft, her gaze compassionate.

"Exactly." Neither of them spoke for a moment, but there was clearly something she wanted to say. "What is it, Evvy?" he asked finally.

"I appreciate not wanting the sacrifices you've made to have been for nothing. But isn't the point of attaining the brass ring in your career that it's supposed to make you happy? Because the position you're in now clearly isn't, Sebastian."

The sincerity in her tone and expression quickly squashed any offense he might've taken at her words. So maybe there was something to the whole *it's not what you say, it's how you say it* argument.

"Besides, if you feel so strongly about sticking it out and making it work, what prompted you to take a three-month leave?"

He felt a twinge of guilt for the secret he'd been keeping from his father and sisters. But he wanted Evvy to fully understand the situation. Even if it meant trusting her with the truth.

"My dad and sisters don't know this, so it needs to stay between us."

"Of course." Evvy inched closer. "Is everything okay?"

Sebastian kneaded the sudden tension rising in the back of his neck.

"I've been under a lot of stress to implement new policies at the company. Policies that feel anti-worker. Things my family would never have considered imposing on our employees. They want to push out our longtime workforce because of their higher pay, so they can hire younger workers at a much lower rate and with fewer benefits. I've been fighting them on it, but now that my family no longer owns the company…"

"You don't really have a leg to stand on," she supplied.

He nodded with a long sigh. "I'd been racking my brain to figure out how to demonstrate the financial benefits of ensuring that all of our workers make a living wage. It's not just the right thing to do, well-compensated workers are invested in the company and committed to doing good work. That's why our company has remained profitable and competitive. But they were about to release a sizable chunk of our workforce to cut costs, so I was under the gun. Coming in early, staying late, and doing all kinds of research. I wasn't sleeping much or eating very well. Then one weekend, I'm in my office working, and I crumple to the floor, sure I was having a heart attack."

Evvy squeezed his forearm. "Did you?"

"No. It was a panic attack. My anxiety was through the roof. The doctor warned me that she'd seen much younger professionals have heart attacks and that if I didn't take what happened seriously and make some lifestyle changes, I'd likely be one of them."

"So you came here to recuperate?"

"That's why Nolan suggested I come here," he admitted. "The reason I agreed to it is because the company wants it to seem as if they have my complete buy-in on these policy changes. I figured if I suddenly required a ninety-day health sabbatical—"

"It would stop their plans temporarily." Evvy nodded. "Did it?"

"For now. But unless I can find compelling enough data or create some sort of leverage that would change their minds, this sabbatical is the equivalent of applying a Band-Aid to a gunshot wound." He huffed. "I'm telling you this because I need you to understand that I wasn't taking a dig at you earlier. I'm just extremely direct. Sorry if I upset you." He placed a hand over his heart.

"Apology accepted." Evvy squeezed his arm. "Now, don't let your food get cold. And if you're good, there might be homemade apple pie in your future."

"Yes, ma'am."

There was heat in her dark brown eyes as she met his gaze, and a shudder rippled down his spine. His brain immediately returned to their kiss. He tried to shake off the thought and resumed eating.

"Another beer?"

"Please." He finished off his first.

Evvy got two more beers from the fridge, opened them, and set one at each of their places. She climbed back onto the stool beside him.

They resumed their pleasant conversation as they

finished their meals while watching the news of the storm. The snow was still falling, though not as heavily as it had been earlier. Thousands of homes in the surrounding area were without power. So the power at the inn wouldn't likely be restored anytime soon.

As much as Sebastian hated that they were stuck there, cut off from their families, a part of him looked forward to spending time alone with Evelisse.

When they were done with dinner, Evvy reached for their empty bowls. Sebastian wouldn't relinquish his.

"You prepared an incredible meal. The least I can do is handle the dishes."

"You're going to clean the kitchen and run the dishwasher?" She clearly doubted his domestic capabilities.

"I am an autonomous adult, you know."

"Then I accept your offer, Mr. Valentine. And there will indeed be pie in your future."

She flashed him a flirty smile that did things to him and made him want to do things to her—like capture those soft, lush lips in a kiss, toss her over his shoulder, and take her to the bed that was a mere few steps away and seemingly taunting him.

"Now that we've settled that, maybe we should finally address the elephant in the room."

"What elephant in the room?" Evvy seemed genuinely confused by the question.

"Our sleeping arrangements." He nodded toward the queen-size bed dressed in luxe autumnal colors and motifs and piled with pillows.

Evvy glanced over at the bed and then back at him, her cheeks suddenly flushed. "Right. Well, you're the guest. You take the bed and I'll sleep in one of the chairs. Or we can haul one of the cots over from the inn, and I can sleep on that." She seemed to be talking to herself more than to him.

"I'm not letting you sleep in a chair, Evvy," Sebastian said. "Not when there is a much simpler solution." He gestured toward the bed.

"You mean...share it?" She turned on the stool to face the bed. Evvy swallowed hard, then muttered, "I can't believe I'm in a real-life only-one-bed situation."

"That's a thing?" He laughed.

"It's actually one of my favorite romance novel tropes." Evvy slid off the stool and paced at the foot of the bed. She looked at him, then looked at the bed again, as if sizing the situation up.

"You stay on your side and I'll stay on mine. I can keep my hands to myself...if you can." He flashed a teasing smile.

Evvy smoothed back her hair and sighed. "Okay. Fine."

He gathered their dishes and took them to the sink.

"Thank you for trusting me enough to tell me about your panic attack. I know that wasn't easy," she said. "Now I'm going to change the bedding and start some laundry. Let me know if you need anything."

Sebastian watched as Evvy walked off, her generous hips swaying.

He was in so much trouble. But he was a man of his word. So he'd keep his hands to himself, as he'd promised. But if Evelisse Jemison kissed him again, all bets were off.

Twelve

Evvy returned from the bathroom in a pair of soft, warm pajamas that were anything but sexy. She expected to find Sebastian in bed fast asleep after the long, eventful day they'd had. Instead, he was at the kitchen table finishing another piece of apple pie piled high with whipped cream.

"I guess it's safe to say you like my pie." Evvy laughed.

"You can cook for me anytime," he assured her.

She didn't cook much anymore, particularly since her breakup with Calvin several months ago. Every night she'd dragged her ass home after a day of catering to her needy boss, eager for someone to take care of her. Even if that meant picking up a flame-broiled burger or a packaged salad at a drive-through window. She simply didn't have the energy to spend thirty minutes to an hour preparing herself a healthy meal. But she'd enjoyed whipping up a meal for herself and Sebastian.

Seeing how much he'd appreciated her cooking had only prompted her to make something else for him… thus the warm apple pie with a flaky homemade crust and just a hint of tartness from the Granny Smith apples.

"Tired of the Snowpocalypse coverage already?" Evvy nodded toward the television Sebastian had turned off while she was in the other room getting dressed for bed.

"Got tired of them repeating the same coverage and replaying the same video clips." He shoveled the last bite of pie into his mouth and did that appreciative humming again.

Her heart swelled. What chef didn't relish watching someone enjoy their food? Especially when that someone was a notoriously picky eater who'd practically licked his plate clean. But when that person was also a broad-chested human god who was devastatingly handsome with mysterious dark eyes and a sexy little smirk aimed directly at her…well, it just didn't get better than that.

Evvy surveyed the still-made bed.

"You haven't picked a side," she noted.

"Which side do you usually sleep on?"

"The side farthest from the door." She pointed to the right side of the bed.

"Then I'll take the left side." Sebastian rinsed his

plate, then put it in the dishwasher. He grabbed the book he'd been reading.

They stood at the head of the bed on their respective sides, sharing an awkward smile before climbing in.

"Do you mind if I read a little?" Sebastian sat against the upholstered reclaimed wood headboard her sister had made.

"Not at all. I planned to do the same. I'm exhausted, but too wound up to go right to sleep." Evvy picked up the latest addition to author Sharon C. Cooper's Atlanta's Finest romantic suspense series.

"See? Not so bad, right?" Sebastian didn't look up from his book. "And this way, no one freezes to death in their sleep or wakes up with a bad back."

"You were right. We're both sensible adults who understand boundaries. And there's plenty of room in this bed for both of us."

Within an hour, Sebastian was snoring softly on his side of the bed.

Evvy set her book on the nightstand and turned off the light.

She was about to snuggle beneath the covers, but Sebastian's light was still on, and he was slumped against the headboard in what looked like an awfully uncomfortable position.

Evvy should just leave him be and grab her eye mask. But that would require leaving the warm, toasty bed. Wouldn't it be easier to lean over and turn out Sebastian's light?

She planted one hand in the middle of the bed on the imaginary line that demarcated their individual spaces.

With the other, she reached across Sebastian to turn off the lamp. But it was farther than she anticipated, and she wobbled slightly. She braced one hand on his shoulder so she wouldn't topple face-first into his lap.

Sebastian was startled, and his eyes opened with surprise. His sudden movement caused her to lose her balance. She lunged forward, her chest crashing into his. He grabbed her hips to keep her from toppling onto the floor but studied her with a scowl.

"The light," Evvy squeaked before Sebastian had the chance to ask why the hell she was accosting him in his sleep. "You dozed off with the light on. I reached over to turn it off, but you fell asleep in this really awkward position..."

"So it's my fault I woke up to you trying to give me a lap dance?" There was a hint of amusement in his dark eyes despite the deadpan delivery.

"Of course not! I was just explaining why... God, why can't I stop looking at your lips?" Evvy clapped a hand over her mouth.

Please tell me I didn't say that last part aloud.

But the deepening of Sebastian's grin and the flare of his nostrils indicated she had. He cupped her cheek, his gaze drawn to her lips.

"Probably for the same reason I've been mesmerized by yours all night." He leaned in closer, his whiskered chin grazing her cheek. "I can't stop thinking of our kiss and wanting another taste of those lips."

Evvy's skin heated, and electricity rippled down her spine. Her nipples beaded, and there was a steady pulse between her thighs. Her breathing was rapid and shallow. She couldn't seem to form words or find the strength to pull out of Sebastian's gentle hold. But the truth was, she had no desire to extract herself from his grip. She wanted to lean into it. To get another taste of the mouth she couldn't stop watching whenever he spoke, too.

"I… I…" She swallowed hard, still unable to manage a coherent sentence.

"I promised to keep my hands to myself, Evvy." Sebastian's lips grazed her ear, and he slid a hand up the skin of her back beneath her loose pajama top. "But you're making it incredibly hard for me to be good." His breath warmed her neck.

Evvy shuddered, sighing softly. Her skin tingled and her body filled with heat. She weighed all the reasons she shouldn't sleep with Sebastian Valentine against all the reasons she really, *really* wanted to.

They were stuck in a snowstorm and sharing a single bed in her small studio apartment. The Universe had handed this handsome, incredibly enticing man to her on a silver platter.

Wouldn't it be downright rude to reject the gifts the Universe was offering?

Because she, for one, could not afford to offend the great giver of all things.

Sebastian nuzzled Evvy's ear and fought the urge to press a slow kiss there. Because he knew that if he did, he'd want more. A kiss on her neck. A taste of her lips. The low, sweet murmur she'd made as his tongue had glided against hers two nights ago. To discover whether all of her skin was as smooth and silky as the soft skin low on her back.

He squeezed his eyes shut and heaved a quiet sigh before pulling away.

Evelisse stared at him, her chest rising and falling as if she'd been running. Her minty breath was soft and sweet, and those full, glossy lips of hers seemed to taunt him.

She slowly lifted a hand, her fingers barely touching his face as their eyes met. Evvy settled her weight onto his lap and leaned forward achingly slowly as if she was waiting for him to stop her.

Maybe he should have, but he couldn't bring himself to do it.

Yes, the two of them sleeping together could get messy when their families were so tightly connected. But he'd missed his chance with Evvy more than a year ago, and he'd been haunted by thoughts of her. Her mesmerizing smile. The contagious laugh that had sucked him in like a swirling wind whose pull he couldn't resist—despite his grumpy mood that night. The warmth and sweet floral scent of her glowing brown skin.

He hadn't been able to stop thinking about her. And maybe she'd been just as affected by him.

Perhaps this was what they both needed. To get their fascination with each other out of their systems. Then, in two months, when it was time for them to return to their respective cities, they could both move on. Or maybe...

Sebastian gently gripped the back of Evvy's neck and tugged her closer. She sighed quietly as their lips met, her soft, warm body molding to his.

This time, neither of them hesitated. Sebastian wrapped his arms around her waist, tugging her body tight against his as he glided his tongue along the seam of her lips, which tasted like apricot, before getting another taste of her warm, minty sweet tongue.

He placed his other hand gently at her throat, angling her head to give him better access to her mouth. His kiss grew hard and hungry, as did his dick pinned between them. Evvy ground her hips against him, ramping up his desire for her and making him want a taste of the valley between her thighs.

Evvy tugged her pajama top and bra over her head and tossed them onto the other side of the bed before resuming their kiss.

Sebastian flipped them, laying Evvy on her back as he hovered over her. Her loose curls spread out on the pillow around her like a halo. Her full breasts rose and fell with each shallow breath, and the stiff peaks seemed to strain for his touch.

He lowered his mouth over one of her hardened nipples, loving her little moan in response. As he licked and sucked the beaded brown tip, he was riveted by the erotic expressions that transformed her gorgeous face from one moment to the next. And the way her full lips parted with each inhalation.

Sebastian grazed her lips with his thumb as he continued to tease her nipple with his lips and tongue. Evvy sucked on the digit and the sensation went straight to his painfully hard dick. Made him desperate to know if the space between her full, lush thighs tasted as sweet as he'd imagined.

He pulled his thumb from her kiss-swollen lips and gently gripped her throat, applying only the lightest pressure as he grazed her nipple with his teeth.

He teased the other nipple with his tongue and then his teeth before kissing his way down her soft belly and planting kisses just above the waistband of her pajamas. He nipped the skin with his teeth as he slowly tugged down her pants and panties.

Evvy lifted her hips so he could pull them off.

"And you accused me of being impatient," he whispered against the bare skin just beneath her navel. Her belly shook with a nervous laugh as she ran her hands over his hair.

"I've been waiting a really long time for this." Her shy grin was sweet yet sexy.

"Baby, so have I." Sebastian trailed kisses over the narrow strip of dark reddish curls, inhaling her sweet, musky scent and relishing her reaction to each kiss. Finally, he parted her wet, glistening lower lips with his thumbs and swiped his tongue over the slick, swollen flesh.

"Sebastian." She moaned softly, her head lolling back as she thrust her pelvis forward, silently begging for more.

Sebastian gladly obliged, delving his tongue deep inside of her and reveling in her sweet, salty taste. He pressed greedy kisses to the soft, warm, sensitive flesh surrounding her pink center, following it up with gentle nibbles of his teeth that seemed to heighten her pleasure. He lapped at her center, craving more of her flavor. Driven by her growing murmurs and the increased motion of her hips as she moved against his mouth. Her hand applied gentle pressure to his head, guiding his eager mouth exactly where she wanted it.

He took every cue. Licked, sucked, nibbled, and tongue-fucked that beautiful pink pussy as she moved against him.

Evvy's free hand glided up her body and gripped her breast, pinching the taut brown nipple as her hips moved against him.

"You are so fucking sexy." He breathed the words between kisses to the hot, wet space between her thighs. Sebastian lapped at her center again. Teased her clit with his tongue.

Evvy gripped the bedding, her body tensing as she shattered, flooding his tongue with her sweet nectar. His reward for a job well-done.

He kissed her inner thigh, then slowly kissed his way back up her body, retracing the path he'd taken to paradise.

"You, sir, were amazing." Evvy pressed her hand to his cheek and smiled shyly, her cheeks and forehead flushed. She kissed the lips that tasted of her and glided her warm tongue along his.

"So were you," he whispered when he'd finally broken their kiss. He nibbled on her neck and her ear. "You taste so damn good. I could have you for breakfast, lunch, and dinner and do it all over again the next day."

The flush of her skin spread to the rest of her face and her chest. She snuggled against him, gliding her hand beneath his shirt and over the hair on his belly.

"Don't you dare threaten me with a damn good time

unless you're prepared to make good on that offer."
She glanced up at him through the mop of curls that
shielded one eye.

"Any time, any place." Sebastian grew painfully hard
as she traced the waistband of his pajamas.

Evvy lifted her head and flashed him a wicked smile
that made his chest swell and his heart thunder. She
pulled his shirt over his head, then trailed kisses all over
his chest before licking and teasing one nipple with her
tongue. She gently grazed his rock-hard dick with her
open palm, running it up and down his length as she
kissed his chest and nibbled at his sensitive nipple. Finally, she gripped him tightly through the fabric of his
pants, and the sensation rocketed up his spine.

Evelisse clutched the fabric on both sides of his waist
and tugged downward, but he placed his much larger
hands over hers.

"Sorry sweetheart, but I left the condoms back at
the inn."

A moment of disappointment flashed over her gorgeous face. It was quickly replaced with an impish smile
that filled his body with heat.

"We don't need them right now." Evvy kissed him
again, his hardened shaft pinned between them. Their
kiss was frantic and feverish. He ached for her so badly
that he was on the verge of making the trek, half-
dressed, across that bitterly cold walkway and into the
dark, frigid inn to retrieve those condoms.

Sebastian was seriously entertaining the thought
when Evvy broke their kiss and climbed out of bed. She
pulled him to his feet, her eyes locked with his. Evvy

dragged his pants and boxers down, his dick springing free of the confining fabric. Then she pushed him back onto the bed in a seated position.

"Fuck," Sebastian whispered reverently as Evvy dropped to her knees and took him inside her warm mouth.

It felt so damn good he was afraid he might explode right then and there. He sank his teeth into his lower lip, mesmerized by the sight of this gorgeous woman taking him down her throat, her head bobbing.

Sebastian gathered a handful of the wild, beautiful curls in his fist, not wanting to miss a moment of the action. He was glad Evvy hadn't managed to turn off the bedside lamp. Because watching her take him this way was one of the most titillating things he'd ever seen. And he hoped like hell that he'd get to see it again.

She pulled him from her soft, full lips with a pop. Then she glided her tongue from the base to the tip. When she worked him with her hand while sucking the tip again, his body stiffened and he cursed, warning her that he was on the edge.

Evvy pulled his pulsating flesh from her mouth just before he erupted, the creamy fluid spurting onto his thighs and her chest.

He leaned back on his elbows, his head feeling light as he tried to catch his breath. "*That* was fucking amazing."

Evvy flashed him a provocative smile that managed to be both impossibly sweet and incredibly dirty. When she made her way to the bathroom, every strike of her heel against the floor sent the most delightful bounce to the ass that still bore his palm prints.

Sebastian was completely spent and already dreaming of bending her over the bed and taking her from behind.

After they'd both gotten cleaned up, he put on his boxer briefs, and she donned a pink robe that hung about half an inch lower than those glorious ass cheeks—the sway of which had him hypnotized. He was thoroughly enjoying the little peeks of skin he got as she moved about the room.

"Suddenly, I'm starving again," Evvy declared as she pulled her wild coppery curls up into a ponytail that made him think of how he'd gathered her hair in one fist as she'd gazed up at him.

A shudder ran down his spine at the memory.

Sebastian stood behind Evvy and nuzzled her neck. "Are we talking about hunger for food or…"

"Both." Evvy giggled, and the sound made his chest swell. "But how about we have some leftovers and see where things go from there?"

He nibbled softly on her ear. "Sounds perfect."

Evvy pulled out the leftovers while Sebastian tugged on a shirt and watched her flit about the kitchen, humming softly as she took out slices of roast beef and a loaf of sourdough bread.

He looked forward to the next few days with the two of them getting to know each other better in every way imaginable. They were lucky. Things could've gone badly for them if that tree had fallen in any other direction. But a part of him felt luckier still to be hidden away from the world with this kind, beautiful woman who made him feel alive in a way he hadn't in so very long.

Thirteen

Evvy woke up the next morning momentarily disoriented by the woodsy, citrus scent that surrounded her, the soft snore, and the strong arm clamped around her waist. She lifted her head and glanced back at Sebastian, still sleeping soundly.

It brought an involuntary grin to her face, and butterflies fluttered in her stomach. The previous day's events ran through her head. From waking up to the sound of a tree falling to the incredible pleasure she and Sebastian had shared there in her bed. All of it felt improbable: like a fever dream.

Yet here she was, lying in her bed being spooned by Sebastian—whom she would've bet serious money was not the cuddling type.

Evvy lay down again, her back pressed against Sebastian's broad chest. None of this would've happened had they not gotten caught in this storm. But she could easily become accustomed to nights like the one they'd shared.

Was it selfish of her to hope they'd be snowed in for a few days?

And so much for her willpower. She hadn't lasted a single night before she'd given in to her growing desire for him.

Last night had been amazing, and she looked forward to the evening ahead. But a little voice in her head reminded her that this had been the result of extraordinary circumstances.

What would happen between them once the storm was over?

Evvy was shaken from her disconcerting ruminations by a soft kiss on her cheek, followed by one on her shoulder. The stubble on his chin scratched at her skin.

"Everything okay?" Sebastian kissed her neck. "You suddenly seem tense." He glided a hand down her thigh.

"I'm just worried about our families, who we can't get in contact with, and the inn. My sister has been dreaming about this inn for so long. We haven't been open three months yet and this happens."

"The inn is fine, just frigid," he reminded her. "And we did what we could to ensure that the pipes don't freeze."

"But what if they do? Or another tree crashes into the roof? Or—"

"Hopefully, none of that will happen." Sebastian turned her onto her back so he could meet her gaze.

As she stared up at him, she was reminded of how handsome this man was. "And if any of it does…that's what insurance is for," he reminded her. "In the end, they're all just things. What matters is that you're safe and so are your staff and all of your guests, because you had the foresight to send everyone home early."

"But not enough sense to leave myself." Evvy sighed. "Sorry I got you into this mess, Sebastian."

"I should be apologizing to you," he said. "You stayed because I was still here. And I stayed as long as possible because I knew we wouldn't see each other for a few days once the storm hit."

"You stayed at the inn another night just to have breakfast with me?" Evvy sat up with her back against the headboard.

Sebastian sat up too. "You find that hard to believe?"

She did. But Sebastian didn't need to know about her lifelong trust issues and struggles with self-worth. She'd been doing the work in therapy, but she still worked to conquer those childhood demons. And after she'd ended her relationship with Calvin, she'd taken up yoga and meditation because she realized that she needed to tackle her own issues before she could truly find happiness with someone else.

"I'm just glad we're both safe and that we have each other during this crazy storm." Evvy kissed his cheek, then climbed out of bed. "I'm gonna hit the shower."

"Okay." Sebastian seemed perplexed by her evasion of his simple question, but he didn't push the matter, and for that she was grateful.

Maybe he was disappointed that she hadn't been

willing to answer the question honestly. She felt badly about that. But she'd learned her lesson about investing in relationships that had no future. So she'd enjoy this little fling with Sebastian for what it was without making the mistake of expecting it to become anything more.

Evvy emerged from the bathroom and inhaled the scent of coffee and the delicious aroma of bacon. She looked around the corner. Sebastian was standing at the stove pouring pancake batter into a cast-iron skillet.

"That smells amazing. I had no idea you cooked." Evvy walked up behind him and wrapped her arms around his waist. "I'm impressed."

"Don't be. Not until you've tasted them." He grinned, then moved toward the cutting board, where he'd been slicing strawberries and kiwi.

"So you're a fan of kiwi now," Evvy said smugly.

"Stick with me, kid. I'll show you a few things." She winked.

"I'm pretty sure you already have." He handed her a cup of coffee, then went back to cutting the fruit.

Evvy's cheeks heated, thinking of last night. She'd been uncharacteristically bold and...*enthusiastic*. But after what Sebastian had done, she'd wanted to bring him the same kind of pleasure he'd given her.

She opened the fridge, then poured a splash of peppermint mocha creamer into her coffee. "I can finish up breakfast if you'd like."

"No, I'm good. You've been a gracious host these

past few weeks. This morning, I'm taking care of you," he said.

Evvy sat at the barstool opposite where he stood. "That's sweet of you, Sebastian. But caring for our guests is kind of my job."

"And you're damn good at it," Sebastian said.

"For three years, I was the personal assistant to a big-time director who also happens to be one of Hollywood's biggest man babies." Evvy shrugged. "Catering to demanding people is kind of what I do. *Did*," she added.

Everything had happened so quickly, she'd hardly had time to think about her decision to walk away from her job. Or how furious Fabian had been when she told him she hadn't intended on coming back.

"You aren't going back?"

"No." Evvy shook her head. "I've been trying to make a fresh start the past few months. Ended my relationship. Started meditating. Took up yoga. I'm eating better and exercising more regularly."

"That explains the even more banging body."

Evvy smiled, her tummy fluttering and heat rising in her cheeks. "Anyway, the only thing I hadn't changed was my toxic employer." She shrugged. "So when Kayleigh asked me to do this, it felt like a good time to cut ties. I'm not making as much here, but I'm not paying living expenses or utilities either. Gives me a chance to shore up my savings while I decide what I want to do next."

"Good plan." Sebastian flipped the pancakes. "But I got the feeling Kayleigh doesn't know you quit."

"She doesn't." Guilt knotted her gut. "Maybe I don't plan to go back to that particular job, but I plan to return to LA. I feel like I need to give acting one last honest shot. Kathy Bates, Jane Lynch, Steve Carrell… they were all around my age by the time they had their breakout roles."

Evvy realized how defensive she must sound, but she couldn't seem to stop herself.

"If Kayleigh knew, she'd never stop trying to convince me to stay."

"You're probably right." Sebastian's tone was measured. "But have you considered that perhaps *this* could be your next career?"

"Being an innkeeper?" She leaned forward, propping her chin on her fist.

"Why not?" Sebastian set down the spatula. "You make everyone around you feel special."

"Because I'm bringing them coffee or recommending a good mountain hiking spot?" Evvy snorted. "Kind of feels like the bare minimum."

"You're invested in each of your guests. They can sense that. And you have this light. You glow from within, and it's contagious. It's hard for even a generally grumpy guy like me to resist it." Sebastian flashed her a warm smile.

"Are you saying you find me mesmerizing?" Evvy batted her eyelashes playfully.

"Obviously." He winked. "But also that you have a gift for making your guests feel not only cared for but truly *seen*. Don't underestimate how important that is. I've watched you in action. What you do makes people happy. Including you." He smiled. "Something to think about."

"Thank you, Sebastian." She came around the counter and kissed his cheek. "I'm not saying I plan to stay, but I think I needed to hear that."

Evvy got out two plates while Sebastian removed the bacon from the oven and drained it on paper towels. He put two golden, fluffy pancakes onto each of their plates. Then he insisted that she take a seat while he cut up a banana and carefully arranged the slices of fruit on their pancakes along with a handful of blueberries.

She got out the maple syrup, and they sat down to eat.

"These are *amazing*, Sebastian. Don't tell Sofie, but your pancakes are even better than hers." Evvy speared a piece of each type of fruit to go along with her next bite of pancake.

"When we were young, we'd cook with my grandmother some Saturday mornings. Pancakes were my favorite, so she insisted I should learn how to make them myself. Otherwise, I'd run off with the first woman who could make a good pancake." Sebastian laughed, and so did Evvy.

"Your grandmother was a wise woman, and evidently, one hell of a cook."

There was a hint of sadness in Sebastian's smile. "My grandmother was a complicated woman, but in retrospect, I believe she loved us the best way she knew how. And I loved her, too."

"Is that why you feel compelled to stay at the firm? Because your grandmother would've wanted you to?" Evvy sipped her coffee.

"My grandparents would be rolling in their graves if they knew my dad had sold their company," he said. "But I get why the business felt like an albatross around my dad's neck. Why he felt compelled to sell it and do something he was passionate about." Sebastian nibbled on his bacon.

"And what do you really want to do, Sebastian?" Evvy asked carefully, aware of the disagreement they'd had yesterday around the topic.

Sebastian chewed thoughtfully. "If I'm being honest, my choices around school and career have been about two things." He ticked them off on his fingers. "Making my grandmother proud and making my mother regret leaving us. Which, now that I say them, feels pretty pathetic."

He hadn't answered her question, but after she'd sidestepped his earlier question, what right did she have to press him further on it?

"It's not pathetic to expect our parents and grandparents to genuinely care about us or to want them to be proud of us. That's what we all want." Evvy squeezed his hand, unsure of what else to say. She only knew he was in need of reassurance. She hoped he was feeling a little of the warmth and light he'd attributed to her earlier.

But maybe there was another way she could help lift his mood.

"Hey, I've got an idea. You game?"

Sebastian's eyes glinted with mischief, and one edge of that sexy mouth curved with a devilish grin that made her tummy flutter. "Oh, I'm definitely in."

Fourteen

"Am I supposed to be feeling something right now?" Sebastian cracked one eye open and peeked over at Evvy, who was also seated on the floor in a cross-legged position while the fireplace crackled, radiating intense heat.

"You're supposed to feel whatever it is you need to feel right now," she said.

"And the point of this is, again?" He opened his other eye and readjusted his position to alleviate some of the tightness in his hips.

Evvy's eyes opened, and she gave him a patient smile. Like a mother answering her five-year-old's tenth consecutive *But why, Mom?* question.

"Life can be loud and intense, our worries pervasive. Even when we try to sleep at night, the voices are still in our heads. Meditation is purposely giving yourself the time and space to just be calm and still. To feel however you feel without judgment. It's a way to re-center yourself and bring your focus back where it needs to be. On being your best self." Evvy smiled softly in response to his look of confusion. She reached over and squeezed his arm. "It's okay, Sebastian. Meditation isn't for everyone, and no one is necessarily good at it initially. I really struggled with it at first and gave up lots of times over the years. But I'm glad I stuck with it this time. It's been an essential coping mechanism for my anxiety. So I'm not surprised that your doctor recommended it."

"Okay, fine. I'll keep working on it." He squeezed his eyes shut and tried to quiet all of the pervasive thoughts running amok in his brain. It was a surprisingly challenging task.

He heard movement. Then Evvy slipped her much smaller hand into his open palm. Sebastian was startled at first. He opened his eyes, taking in the gorgeous woman who'd shifted the folded blanket she was seated on beside his.

Evvy smelled light and sweet—like a field of spring flowers. Her ruddy brown curls were piled atop her head in a loose bun. And her bare skin seemed to practically glow in the sunlight streaming through the window.

Sebastian threaded their fingers and gently squeezed her hand in his before shutting his eyes again. The tension in his shoulders slowly eased. The perpetual knot in his gut seemed to unfurl. He felt a sense of comfort and lightness he couldn't quite explain.

Finally, the timer on Evvy's watch sounded.

"That wasn't so bad, right?" She climbed to her feet, then tugged him to his.

"It wasn't," he admitted. "I don't know how much my knees and hips appreciate it." He laughed. "But I do feel surprisingly relaxed."

"Then it's a good thing we're doing yoga next." She placed a hand on either side of his hips. "Get those joints all loosened up."

"Funny you should mention loosening up joints. I've been thinking about that, too." He slid his arms around her waist. "But I had a different method in mind." Sebastian captured her lips in a slow kiss.

She tensed initially as if she was going to object to him interrupting their planned afternoon of meditation and yoga. But then the tension in her back eased, and she slowly melted into him as she fisted the back of his shirt.

"We're supposed to be doing a sun salutation practice next," she objected weakly between kisses. "It'll loosen your hips and shoulders and boost your mood."

"Yeah?" He tugged her shirt over her head, then followed it up with removing his own and tossing it onto a nearby chair. "So will what I have in mind."

He lifted her over his shoulder in a single motion, taking her by surprise.

Evvy kicked her feet in objection and laughed. "Sebastian Valentine, you put me down this instant!"

"Gladly, sweetheart."

He tossed her gently onto the bed, and she shrieked. Then he climbed onto the bed after her, thankful they'd made the earlier trek over to the main inn to check on the place and retrieve a few items.

Within seconds, they'd both shed their clothing and climbed under the blankets, his body covering hers. Sebastian slid his fingers into the hair at the nape of her neck as he resumed their kiss.

He devoured her mouth, his tongue gliding against hers as he reveled in the warmth and taste of her. It had been a long time since he'd kissed someone like this. With not only an intense longing but a pure sense of joy and abandonment. The euphoria of building intimacy with every brush of their lips.

The kiss escalated, heated and frenzied. As if neither of them could get enough. Finally, he trailed kisses down her neck and over her bare shoulder, loving the scent of her warm, fragrant skin.

Sebastian laved her beaded, dark nipples with his tongue, and her breathing elevated in response. Then he kissed his way down her belly and pressed delicate kisses to her apex, punctuated by little licks of her slick flesh.

Evvy placed a hand on his head, her legs falling further open as she tilted her pelvis, giving him better access to her slick, warm center. She whimpered with pleasure at each swipe of his tongue. But when he finally licked her clit, she cursed and squirmed, applying gentle pressure to his head as she arched her back. Begging him for more.

He obliged, spreading her with his thumbs and kissing, licking, and sucking the sensitive bundle of nerves and the surrounding flesh until she came hard, her body trembling and his name on her tongue.

Sebastian dragged himself back up her body and kissed her neck before retrieving the little foil packet from the nightstand drawer.

He tore it open and quickly sheathed himself, desperate to finally be inside of her—something he'd imagined more than he was willing to admit. He pressed the head of his erection to her slick center, inching his way inside. Each sensual murmur of hers was matched by a guttural groan of his own, both of them overwhelmed with the deliciously erotic sensations from their deeply intimate connection.

Evvy wrapped her legs around him, her heels digging into his low back as his hips moved slowly at first. Her short nails dug into his upper back as she held on to him tightly while he moved inside her. Each stroke felt more intense than the previous one. His pulse raced and his heart hammered in his chest as he hovered over her, varying the speed and direction of his movements in response to her reactions. He delighted in her soft moans, the arch of her back, and the seductiveness in her mesmerizing brown eyes.

Sebastian changed the angle of entry and the position of her leg, creating more friction against the tight bundle of nerves as he moved inside of her.

Suddenly, she gripped the bedding, her body stiffening and her core pulsing as she called his name again and again.

The sensation rippled up his spine, his hips thrusting harder and faster, as he chased the feeling building inside him like a volcano threatening to erupt.

Finally, it did.

A chain reaction of intense pleasure exploded inside

him like a fireworks finale on the Fourth of July. Sebastian cursed softly, Evvy's name on his lips.

He hovered over her, his breathing labored as he stared into her soft gaze. Her chest rose and fell as she searched his face. Evvy pressed a palm to his cheek, her sensual lips curving in an almost shy smile. She glided a thumb across his lower lip, then covered his mouth with hers.

Watching Evvy fall apart beneath him the way she had was the most deliciously sensual scene. And he was eager to experience it again.

Sebastian nuzzled her neck and kissed the outer shell of her ear. "If that was my reward for meditating, I'd do it every single day without complaint."

When he met her warm gaze and soft smile, they hinted at more than just desire. They radiated with a deep affection that made him flirt with fantasizing about the future.

What if they weren't just tucked away from the world on borrowed time? What if the friendship they'd been building since he'd arrived here and the closeness and affection they'd experienced the past two days was something they could have every day?

But they couldn't. Because they were both going back to their respective cities after the holidays. And as great as the time they'd spent together had been, it didn't change that. So why did that dose of reality hit him like a bucket of ice water being splashed over his head and make his chest ache?

"Sebastian, are you okay?" Evvy rubbed a palm on his shoulder. "For a moment you were gone." Her sweet face was filled with concern, and it made his chest ache even more.

Evelisse Jemison was everything he wanted, but he'd encountered her at the wrong place and time. A theme in his life. First it was his career. Now Evvy.

His body tensed and he was frowning again—something he hadn't done nearly as much since arriving in Magnolia Lake.

Sebastian kissed her cheek, then forced a smile. "I'm good, but I should take care of this. Be back in a sec."

"Okay." Evvy traced a finger down his chest and smiled. But the concern in her brown eyes indicated that she was unconvinced. Or maybe she was wishing that their situation was different, too.

Later that evening, Evvy stood in the kitchen making sangria while wearing Sebastian's T-shirt and a pair of panties. She tossed in two handfuls of diced apples before pouring some of the liquid over ice in two tall glasses.

Evvy carried their glasses to the bathroom, where Sebastian was soaking in the tub while reading a book—fiction this time. She'd honestly never seen a man reading in the tub before. But there was something incredibly hot about it. The kind of thing she'd add to a dating profile…if she had one.

Must love cuddling and reading in the bathtub on cold, snowy days.

"What you got there?" Sebastian's question pulled her from her temporary daze.

"Sangria." Evvy handed him a glass. "The name

is derived from *sangre*, the Spanish word for blood."
Evvy shrugged. "I figured it'll go well with your murder mystery."

"Legal thriller." He smiled, then took a healthy sip,
then another, draining half the glass. He set the glass
on the side of the tub. "Wow. That's damn good. I'm
gonna want a refill, for sure."

"Take this one. I can pour myself another." She
handed him the second glass, and he set it beside the
other. When she turned to leave, Sebastian caught her
hand.

"Is this a new service provided by Sweet Magnolia
Inn? Delivering themed drinks to guests while they
soak in a spa tub full of... What was that you put in
here again?"

"It's just a lavender-and-rose-scented bath salt I
created to make me feel better about needing to soak
away the aches and pains of forty-one-year-old hips
and knees," she admitted. "Why, should we add it to
the service menu, too?" Evvy teased.

"Definitely. But only for me." Sebastian tugged her
by the hand and pulled her into the tub, taking her by
surprise.

"Sebastian!" She slapped at his wet chest. "I *can-
not* believe you did that." Evvy wiped away the water
that had splashed onto her face and straddled him. She
wrapped her arms around his neck as she faced him.

"And I can't believe how amazing you look in that
wet T-shirt." He nodded toward her nipples protruding
through the clinging wet fabric. He nuzzled her neck.
"Can you say, hot as fuck?"

She giggled, and ripples of electricity trailed down her spine.

Evvy was quickly becoming addicted to spending time with Sebastian Valentine. It didn't matter if he was taking her to the highest heights in bed or if they were seated in front of the fireplace together reading in silence. She just wanted him there.

But her mind flashed back to the temporary panic on Sebastian's face after they'd made love that first time. The *oh no, we need to have a talk* look.

She already knew what it was he wanted to say. So she'd beat him to it and send the vibe-killing elephant in the room packing.

"Look, Sebastian, I just wanted to say that these past two days together have been amazing. If I had to get stuck in a snowstorm with someone, I'm glad it was you."

He handed Evvy her glass of sangria and then picked up his own, clinking their glasses. "I'll drink to that. Things would've gone very differently if I'd been trapped here with Daniel or Sofie." He chuckled. "They probably wouldn't have found my body until all of the snow thawed."

Evvy burst out laughing, then sipped her drink. "I told you, neither of them is mad at you. What can I say? You grow on a person."

"Like a mole?" Sebastian chuckled.

"Yes, but the really attractive kind that just adds character." She set her drink down after taking another sip, then leaned in and kissed him.

"Good to know." He broke their kiss and nibbled on

her ear. The sensation shot straight to her sex, pressed to his hardening length. "Anything else I should know?"

That's your opening. Take it.

"Yes." She sat up so that their eyes met. "I want you to know that I understand the nature of this…liaison. That once we leave this little cocoon, things will go back to the way they were before the storm."

"You mean like the night you kissed me?" Sebastian smirked.

"Okay, I did kiss you, but you leaned in first," she felt the need to clarify, slapping at his shoulder when he laughed. "You know what I mean, Sebastian. I'm just trying to say that you don't need to worry about things being weird. I understand that this was more about the moment than about us."

Sebastian frowned, seemingly deep in thought for a moment.

"I disagree," he said after a long, awkward pause. "Yes, I took advantage of the moment. But for me, this was very much about *you*, Evvy." Sebastian tightened his arms around her waist. "I realize that after the holidays, we'll both be headed back home. But until then…"

"Why don't we do more of this?" Her heart leaped and butterflies fluttered in her stomach. "I wouldn't object to that. But it'll be difficult to maintain a clandestine affair when my staff, my sister, and the guests are around. Mrs. McConley saw me coming out of your room and automatically assumed—"

"Why do we need to be clandestine about it?" Sebastian kissed her shoulder blade. "We're both grown and unattached. You're the boss, so you make the rules."

"I'm also responsible for setting the example for my employees." Evvy whimpered softly as he kissed the junction of her neck and shoulder. She seriously had zero willpower when it came to this man. "If I start dating the guests…"

"Not guests…" He nibbled on her ear. "Just me. That guy you had one amazing night with a year ago. Think of it as our snowbound second chance since I blew it before by not calling you."

Their second chance for what? A temporary fling that would leave her sad and heartbroken?

The questions caught in her throat because she already knew the answers. But if this was all they could ever be, maybe she should just enjoy the moment. She deserved a little bit of happiness, and so did Sebastian. Still, she should give herself some time and space to make a sound, thoughtful decision when she wasn't wet, half-naked, and pressed against Sebastian's deliciously hard body.

"Can I think about it?"

"Of course." Sebastian's half smile didn't quite reach his dark eyes. "But in the meantime, we should definitely take these off." He lifted the hem of the wet shirt, pulling it over her head and tossing it into the sink, followed by her wet lace panties.

Fifteen

Sebastian honestly didn't think he could be more content than he was right now. He and Evvy were lying in bed, reading their respective novels as they nibbled on a cheese tray and drank warm apple cider. Neither of them had spoken in nearly an hour. Yet he felt a sense of comfort and companionship he wasn't sure he'd experienced during the entirety of his marriage.

His phone sitting on the charger suddenly rang. He and Evvy exchanged surprised glances. Their cell phones hadn't been working for the past two days. Neither had the internet.

Sebastian picked up the phone. His younger sister's face filled the screen.

"Naya?"

"Sebastian! Thank God, you're alive!" Her voice broke, and she sounded teary. "Where are you? Are you okay?"

"I'm fine. I'm still at the inn. At the carriage house, actually." He glanced over at Evvy.

"Isn't that Evvy's place?" His sister's voice held a note of mischief.

"Yes," he confirmed, wondering how much of the conversation Evelisse could hear.

"You mean I have spent the past two days worried that you were wandering around out there in a snow-storm freezing to death when you've been at Evvy's place playing hide the salami this whole time?"

"Naya!" Their father's voice rang out. "There are children here."

"I know, Dad. That's why I didn't say S-E-X," Naya responded.

"Uncle Sebastian is having sex?" Harper asked in the background.

Evvy burst out laughing as she turned a page in her book. She shook her head. "Guess that cat is out of the bag."

That answered that. Clearly, she could hear every-thing.

Sebastian mouthed the word *sorry*, and Evvy snick-ered quietly. She kissed his cheek, then climbed out of bed and grabbed her phone, indicating that she planned to call her sister.

She stuck her feet into her fur-line boots, donned her winter coat, then made her way downstairs to the shop.

"We were stuck here when the storm rolled in early.

A tree fell, taking out the generator at the main inn. It came about two feet shy of falling onto my Beamer. We had no choice but to hole up in Evvy's studio apartment. The generator here is operational plus there's a wood-burning fireplace, and we've got plenty of wood. So we're fine." Sebastian ignored his sister's inquiry about how he and Evvy had been spending their time together. "How is everyone there?"

"We're all good. Dad's fine. Nolan, Laney, and Harper are here. And we've been able to keep in touch with Chandra and Julian because she took home one of our long-range walkie-talkies."

"Good." Sebastian sighed with relief. "How are the vineyards and the winery holding up?"

"The winery and the villa are fine. The workers did everything they could to prepare the vineyard for this storm. Dad, Nolan, and Laney have been monitoring everything."

"Me too!" Harper piped.

"Oh, and Harper here has been supervising them," Naya added. "She's so cute in her little snowsuit."

"Tell Dad I'm sorry I couldn't be there. Sounds like you could use the help." Sebastian replaced his bookmark and set his book on the table. "But as soon as the roads are clear, I'll be there. I'll help in any way you need."

"Thanks, Bas," Naya said, then added after a long pause, "I really was worried about you, bighead. I'm glad you're okay and that you're not alone."

"Same, Nye. Talk soon?"

"Hey, you never answered my question about—"

Sebastian shook his head as he ended the call. He'd worry about what he could or couldn't tell his family later. He just hoped that after the call with Naya, everything between him and Evvy would still be okay.

"I can't believe the two of you got stuck at the inn together and that a tree took out our brand-new generator and nearly destroyed Sebastian's car. That would definitely make our insurance premiums go up," Kayleigh said.

"I'm fine, too. Thanks, sis," Evvy deadpanned.

"Of course, I'm glad you're okay," Kayleigh said. "And I'm really glad that Sebastian was there with you."

"He helped me carry all of the perishables over to our backup fridge and freezer here in the carriage house and to secure the inn so nothing is damaged and the pipes don't freeze. Not to mention that he hasn't been able to stay in the room he's paying for. So I think we should comp his room for at least a week, if not more," Evvy said, rummaging through the shelving in Kayleigh's studio.

"Sure, of course. Just don't get carried away," Kayleigh warned. "Though maybe we should pay for a massage for the guy. His back must be killing him after two days of sleeping in one of those chairs in your apartment. Or did you two bring over one of the guest cots in the storage room?"

Evvy nibbled on her lower lip, silently pondering how to phrase her response.

"Neither," she said finally.

"Wait…you both slept in your bed?" Kayleigh asked, her voice a higher pitch.

Another long pause.

"Yes. It just seemed to make the most sense."

"And did you two sleep together or did you end up *sleeping* together?" Kayleigh asked.

"Yes and…yes." Evvy closed her eyes and pulled the phone away from her ear when her sister screamed.

"I knew it!" Kayleigh said excitedly. Then there was a sudden shift in her tone. "But now what? Does he plan to stay? Do you? Or would you ever consider—"

"We had sex during a snowstorm, Kayleigh. The man didn't ask me to marry him. Relax."

"Don't act like this is just about sex, Evs. The man hauled furniture for you."

"For you, actually," Evvy noted.

"Get real, sis. We both know why he *really* helped. Not to mention he'd already asked you out. So now you're saying this is…what…strictly a Snowpocalypse fling?"

"He wants to keep seeing each other while we're both in town." Evvy shrugged.

"And you don't?"

"I do, but…what if I do have feelings for Sebastian? If we continue this thing, those feelings are bound to deepen, right? So what happens when it's time for us to go our separate ways?" Evvy closed one cabinet and opened another.

Kayleigh sighed. "It'll hurt like hell. But let's be honest, seems like you're already there. So why not enjoy the remaining time you have together? After all, Chandra and Naya are trying hard to get Sebastian to join the winery. What if he—"

"He won't stay, Kayleigh." Evvy nearly whispered the words. "He feels he has something to prove still at their old company. Besides, I'm leaving, too."

"Or you could stay," Kayleigh said.

"I know you've been hinting that I could take over as the innkeeper. But you dreamed up this project, and you've looked forward to running the inn for a really long time."

"True. But even before I got hurt, I've been over-whelmed with everything at the inn," Kayleigh said. It was an admission Evvy knew couldn't have been easy for her sister. "When I made plans to run the inn myself, I hadn't expected business at the jewelry studio to take off the way that it has. I've decided to hire a full-time jewelry artist in addition to my current full-time assistant. Even that won't be enough. I could really use your help to run the inn, Evvy. Besides, you're really good at it. Have you seen some of the comments guests have been leaving? They're phenomenal. Every single review says they're looking forward to returning."

"That's terrific." Evvy recalled Sebastian's observa-tions about her being good at running the inn and how it seemed to make her happy. "But you selected a great staff. Mariana could easily step up to the role of inn-keeper if you needed her to. She's hardworking, bright, and eager to learn."

"Mariana is great and fully capable. But she isn't my big sister, Evs. And if I'm being honest, since I first considered opening the inn, a part of me hoped that one day you and I would run it together."

"You want me to buy into the inn? Kayleigh, I'm sorry, but I can't afford to do that."

"And I'm not asking you to. If you run the inn for the next two years, I'll continue to pay your salary. But at the end of it, you'll be a full partner—regardless of whatever the increased value of the inn might be by that time."

"And you'd just gift me half of the inn?" Evvy laughed. "Kayleigh, you can't be serious."

"I am."

"And Parker would be okay with that? After all of the time and money you've put into the inn?"

"Parker sits on the board at King's Finest. *I* own Sweet Magnolia Inn," Kayleigh said pointedly. "But of course, I value Parker's opinion, and we've discussed it. He knows this is what I want, and he's completely on board with it." There was a soft smile in her voice. "Look, I know you're dealing with a lot right now: power outages, fallen trees, hot grumpy guests sharing your bed…" They both laughed. "So there's no pressure to come up with an answer right away. But think about it, huh? And call at least once a day until we get dug out of this storm. I need to know you're okay."

"I will. Promise." Evvy finally located what she'd been looking for. "But first… I have one more favor to ask."

"There you are." Sebastian glanced up from stirring the hot chocolate on the stove when he heard Evvy come in. "I was just about to don my winter gear and gather a search party."

"But you decided you'd stop and make a meal first?" Evvy propped one fist on her hip and hiked an eyebrow. She held a canvas tote bag bearing the name and logo of the Sweet Magnolia Inn in the other hand.

Sebastian broke into laughter.

"You would've appreciated that thermos full of hot chocolate, though." He kissed Evvy. "And I did go looking for you after I ended my call with my sister. I heard you talking to yours. Thought you probably wanted some privacy." Sebastian turned off the stove and indicated the cloth bag. "More snacks?"

"No." Evvy removed her coat and switched from her boots to her slippers.

She pulled items from the bag, lining them up on the counter. A sketch pad. Graphic pencils, charcoal, Sakura Micron pens, and watercolor pencils. A manual pencil sharpener and erasers. She hung the empty bag on the back of the stool and offered him a sheepish smile.

"We're still stuck here for now, and you'll be on sabbatical for a while longer. I thought you might be motivated to draw again if you had the right tools." She shrugged.

"You pulled all of this together for me?" Sebastian's heart swelled with a wave of gratitude and affection that momentarily rendered him speechless. "I honestly don't know what to say except…thank you, Evvy. This was incredibly sweet. You must've raided Kayleigh's art supplies. Let me reimburse you for—"

"Absolutely not." Evvy waved a hand adamantly. "Think of it as an early Christmas gift from me *and* Kayleigh. An apology for the generator situation—"

"Which wasn't your fault," he noted.

"It's also a small token of gratitude for helping to transport all of the food and secure the—"

He hugged her tight, then kissed her. Finally, he extracted himself from their kiss and settled Evvy onto a kitchen stool. He poured the hot chocolate into two mugs and set one in front of her.

Evvy took a sip. "You made this from scratch?"

"I thought you could use something to warm you up."

"Another of your grandmother's recipes?" Evvy sipped more hot chocolate.

"Yes." He grinned.

"First those fluffy, delicious pancakes. Now the best hot chocolate I've ever had. What should I expect next?"

Sebastian cleared his throat, his pulse racing. "Actually, I'd like to ask you on a date."

"I can be mesmerizing," she teased. "So perhaps you hadn't noticed that we're literally snowed in here and can't go anywhere."

He chuckled, and it alleviated some of the tension in his shoulders. "My sister called back to remind me about our plans for a big family feast later this month. She wanted me to invite you."

"So Naya wants me there." Evvy sipped more of her hot chocolate, her brows furrowing slightly. "But do you want me there?" She set the cup down and studied him.

Sebastian kissed her open palm, then her wrist, then

the inside of her elbow. "I'd love it if you came to dinner with my family."

Evvy's tight smile revealed none of her gorgeous white teeth. But she nodded, draping her arms around his neck and pulling him in for a kiss. "Then I look forward to it."

"So does this mean we're officially dating for the duration of our stay in Magnolia Lake?" Sebastian kissed the shell of her ear.

"I guess it does." Evvy's smile was softer and more genuine. The tension in her body eased.

"Good." He swept her up in his arms, taking her by surprise. She shrieked, then giggled, holding on to him tightly as he carried her toward the bed they'd been sharing for the past two days. "I know just how I want to celebrate."

Sixteen

It was nearly two weeks since the storm of the century had hit Magnolia Lake and a little more than a week since the power had been restored. Evvy and Sebastian had been snowed in at the carriage house for two days without cell service—five without power. It had taken a full week from the start of the storm before the roads had been cleared.

Evvy had officially taken off her first day at the inn—at her sister's insistence. She'd slept in a little, reluctant to leave the warm bed she'd shared with Sebastian every night since the storm hit. They'd made love, and then he'd joined her for a little morning meditation, a sun salutation yoga practice, and a shower together before they'd gone their separate ways.

Sebastian had gone to spend the day at the winery

with his family—something he'd done nearly every day since the roads had been clear. And after more than a week of being shut down, Sweet Magnolia Inn welcomed back both employees and guests. Six of the inn's ten rooms were booked—including Sebastian's.

Evvy had suggested canceling his remaining reservation, but he'd insisted on keeping and paying for the room. Despite spending most of his time in her apartment.

Evvy had spent her morning running personal errands and enjoying being out in the world again now that the Cricketmobile's starter had been replaced. She went to the general store and a few of the new shops in the mixed-use retail space Cole Abbott had built. It had higher-end retail shops on the first floor of each building and townhomes on the second. Sometimes, it was hard to believe that this was the same little town she'd grown up in.

Magnolia Lake felt less isolated and rural now. It was still a small town, to be sure, but its footprint was expanding and its population was growing. Later that night, the town would launch its latest venture: the Magnolia Lake Christmas Market.

The market had been the brainchild of Kayleigh's mother-in-law, Iris Abbott. But Sebastian's father, sisters, and a few other shop owners and craftsmen in the area had also been instrumental in bringing the Magnolia Lake Christmas Market to life.

The snow had receded just in time for the opening of the market, which she was attending with Sebastian and his family later that night. The Sweet Magnolia Inn had booked several guests who'd learned of them because of the Christmas market. So Evvy hoped it would be a raging success.

After a trip to the pharmacy and the general store, Evvy dropped into a yoga class. Afterward, she bought turkey and bacon panini sandwiches, side salads, and giant sticky buns from the Magnolia Lake Bakery. When Evvy had entered Kayleigh's remote studio with the bakery's signature pink box, her sister had nearly toppled her by pulling her into a bear hug.

"You've been busy." Evvy surveyed the place after she'd set out their lunches. There were colorful sketches of new jewelry designs pinned to the walls and lots of sample pieces on one of the desks. "You're in quite the creative period. But I thought you were supposed to be resting." She took a bite of her sandwich and murmured with pleasure.

Magnolia Lake Bakery *never* missed. Their gourmet sandwiches and baked goods were always delicious.

"I know, and I am taking it easy, believe me. I sleep a good portion of the day. But there's something about knowing that you're there taking care of the inn… It puts my mind at ease and has really freed me up to be more productive in the few hours a day that I'm working in here."

"That doesn't sound like a hint at all." Evvy rolled her eyes.

"Then maybe I should say it louder. 'Cause that was absolutely a hint," Kayleigh said, and they both dissolved into laughter. "What? Subtlety isn't my gift. It's yours. You're much more patient with people than I am.

That's why I need you to run…no, to partner with me in the inn."

"Is this the real reason you wanted to spend the day together?" Evvy took another bite of her sandwich, one brow raised.

"Noooo," Kayleigh said with a guilty look and sing-song voice that indicated it was indeed her primary objective for this visit. "Can't I just want to spend time with my big sister? You have no idea how worried Parker and I were about you when we couldn't get through to you for days." Evvy squeezed her sister's hand. "I'm fine, sweetie. And thankfully, I wasn't alone. So let's not think about what could've happened."

"You're right. We shouldn't think about what might've happened. Let's talk about what did." Kayleigh shifted her eyebrows up and down and grinned mischievously. "I can't believe it took a whole-ass blizzard to get you two knuckleheads together."

"I know." Evvy put her sandwich down and licked a little of the homemade chipotle mayo from her fingers.

Evvy picked up her fork and stabbed some of her salad. A knot tightened in her gut, and suddenly her shoulders felt tense. When she glanced up at her sister, who was uncharacteristically quiet, a worried look marred the face that looked so much like her own.

"I thought you and Sebastian were getting along well."

Where did that question come from?

"We are," Evvy assured her.

"Then why do you look sad? Tonight is your first official date, isn't it? I thought you'd be thrilled."

"I am."

"Then why the furrowed brows?" Kayleigh bit into her sandwich, and a blob of chipotle mayo squirted onto the sandwich wrapper.

Evvy concentrated on her salad as she shoved the green leaf lettuce, tomatoes, and goat cheese around the small bowl.

"Evvy." Kayleigh put a hand over hers, halting her fiddling. "What's wrong? Talk to me."

Evelisse put down her fork and folded her arms on the table.

"Since Sebastian asked me out, I've been thinking about Calvin and why we spun our wheels for nearly six years before we flamed out."

"You aren't considering reconnecting with him?" Kayleigh cocked her head.

"No. But I've had a chance to do some honest reflection. I blamed him completely for the failure of our relationship. In truth, it was more like a sixty/forty split." Evelisse sighed. "The on-again-off-again dynamic… that was as much my fault as his. And the fact that we'd often break up just before the holidays…that was mostly me."

"Holidays are hard when you don't have any family of your own," Kayleigh said.

"You'd think I'd be eager to make up for all the disappointing holidays we had as kids. But being around other people's families at that time of year makes me feel like an intruder. My brain convinces me that they don't really want me there." Evvy dabbed her eyes with a napkin.

"I understand how you feel." Kayleigh squeezed her hand.

"How could you?" Evvy gently tugged her hand free. "You have Parker, and you're a bona fide member of the Abbott Family now."

"So are you," Kayleigh reminded her. "I know you don't believe that, but it's true. Duke has always looked out for us, Evs. Even when we didn't know it. And Iris asks about you and worries over you not wanting to join us for Sunday family dinners. Maybe you don't see it yet. But you are truly loved in this town, and you *are* part of this family. We all want you to stay. And speaking of family..." Kayleigh placed a hand on her belly. "Parker and I are pregnant."

"What? Oh my, God, Kayleigh. That's so exciting!" Evvy hugged her sister. "How far along are you?"

"About three months. I'm terrible at keeping track of my period. We discovered I was pregnant when they ran all those tests after my accident," Kayleigh admitted.

"You've been pregnant this entire time, and you didn't tell me?" Evvy pointed a finger at her sister.

"We wanted to wait until the second trimester," she said. "But don't say anything. We haven't told Parker's family yet. We plan to spring it on his parents at Christmas." She grinned.

"I'm so happy for you and Parker. You're going to be a mom, Kayleigh. And I'm going to be an aunt."

Evvy sniffled, wiping away more tears.

"I definitely didn't invite you over for a cry-fest." Kayleigh dabbed her eyes, and they both laughed. "But I'm really glad you're here. I don't want to pressure you or anything, but it would be nice to have my sister here for this."

"I know," Evvy said. "And I promise to consider it."

"Good." Kayleigh seemed satisfied for now. "In the event that you don't take me up on my partnership offer, when does Fabian expect you back in LA?"

Evvy froze for a moment, then chewed her mouthful of food slowly. How could she answer her sister's question without lying while also not telling her the whole truth?

"Fabian fired you, didn't he? "That bastard. I told you he didn't deserve you."

"And you were right. That's why I quit my job with Fabian," Evvy admitted. "I just didn't tell you because—"

"It'd give me one more reason to pressure you to stay." Kayleigh sighed. "Look, I really hope you'll stay, and I won't apologize for that. But you're my sister, and I love you. So I'll support you in whatever it is you want to do." Kayleigh squeezed Evvy's hand.

Evvy nodded, grateful that she and Kayleigh had reconnected.

And while she was glad she'd been having more honest conversations like this with her sister, she hadn't told Kayleigh the most surprising revelation she'd had thus far. That Sebastian was right. She did enjoy being an innkeeper—more than anything she'd done before.

Evvy loved being near her sister. And she enjoyed life in Magnolia Lake considerably more than she had growing up. But she'd also found unexpected bliss in being with Sebastian, who also seemed far happier.

Sebastian was far more relaxed than he'd been the day he'd trudged into the Sweet Magnolia Inn like some grouchy old bear who'd been prematurely awakened from hibernation. He'd softened a little. Frowned less, laughed more. And she enjoyed every moment they spent together, even though her heart ached, knowing they'd be walking away from each other in a few more weeks.

"If you're not ready to go full meet the family with Sebastian tonight, use me as an excuse. Say you decided to stay and keep me company so Parker could go to the winter market with his family."

"No, I should go. I want to go," Evvy added quickly. "Besides, I should be there to help man the table Mariana and I set up to promote the inn. But there is something you can do to help me."

"Anything," Kayleigh said. "Just name it."

Evvy read the text message that scrolled on her phone and smiled. The timing was perfect. "I'll be right back." Evvy went downstairs to open the door. She returned with two women, also sisters, who ran a mobile mani-pedi salon. The company specialized in serving the needs of those who found it difficult to get out to a salon.

Kayleigh was generally a no-fuss, no-muss kind of girl. She wore little to no makeup. And she rarely bothered getting her nails done because they got ruined while she was working with metals and other materials used in jewelry making. So Evvy's heart felt full when her sister's eyes lit up.

They spent the rest of the afternoon getting their

nails done, and she tried not to overthink all of the reasons she was so anxious about her date with Sebastian.

Sebastian snapped his last cuff link into place, put on his Armando Cabral boots, and donned his wool peacoat. Then he stuffed his car key fob into his pocket and left the room he rarely spent time in anymore. Since the catastrophic snowstorm, he'd spent most of his days over at Evvy's apartment and every night sharing her bed.

He loved everything about the time he'd spent with Evvy. From pleasure-filled moments of deep intimacy to quiet evenings cooking a meal together while talking about their pasts or reading together in bed. In two short weeks, Evvy's studio apartment had become the haven Sebastian hadn't been aware he so desperately needed.

He'd arise with Evvy early in the morning. They'd sit together and do twenty minutes of meditation, followed by exercise. Sometimes, he'd practice yoga with her. Sometimes he'd go over to the gym and do a couple of miles on the treadmill or one of the exercise bikes. If he was lucky, they'd grab a shower together and sometimes make love before Evvy had to start her day.

Sebastian had come to prefer the warmth and coziness of Evvy's space to the luxe room he was paying for. After Evvy left to care for the inn, he'd sometimes sit in one of the chairs in front of her wood-burning fireplace and sketch or draw scenes outside her window or pictures he'd taken of the vineyard. Then he'd spend the day at the winery.

Bas had been dead set against his father's decision

to sell the textile firm and put all of his time and resources into building up a rundown winery. But now he understood his father's need to be connected to his biological mother—whose family once owned the vineyards. And the more time Sebastian spent at the villa and the winery listening to his father relate fascinating facts he'd unearthed about both his mother's family and his father—King Abbott—the more he understood the draw of the place.

Nolan and his dad had been amateur winemakers prior to purchasing the vineyard. Chandra and Naya were quickly becoming winemaking connoisseurs, too. And with each trip he made to the winery, he learned more about the fascinating winemaking process. Harvest. Destemming and crushing. Pressing. Fermentation. Clarification. Aging and bottling. There was the business of branding, marketing, and distributing the wine. Then there were what he considered the winery's side hustles: the tasting room and hosting events.

Though the winery had been in business for decades, his family had owned it for little more than a year. Upgrading and rebranding the vineyards and winery was keeping his father and siblings busy. Yet, they'd never seemed happier.

Maybe there was something in the air in Magnolia Lake.

Sebastian stepped inside Evvy's apartment and inhaled the familiar fall scents that reminded him to take a slow, deep breath and relax.

He wasn't sure if it was the fresh mountain air, being near his family, the mindfulness routines, being with

Evvy, or a combination of the above that had improved the many symptoms of anxiety he'd suffered with increasingly over the past year. But he felt as if a weight had been lifted from his shoulders.

Nolan's words echoed in his head.

I know being CEO is what you've wanted for a long time. But bruh, this job is literally killing you. You've aged five years in the past year.

Harsh, but also true.

"Sorry about the wait. I spent the afternoon at my sister's getting glammed up." Evvy flashed her festively painted red nails and batted her eyelashes, bringing attention to her dramatic smoky eye shadow.

She wore a body-hugging gold sequin dress that highlighted her curves and made him fantasize about every inch of skin he'd spent the past two weeks memorizing. Sebastian wanted to slip his fingers into those coppery curls and pull her in for a kiss. But he knew better than to risk ruining her perfect pouty red lips.

"Give me a couple more minutes?"

"Take as long as you need, sweetheart." Sebastian kissed Evvy's cheek, inhaling the subtle floral hint of her perfume. He took a seat and grabbed his sketchbook, thumbing through it, careful not to get charcoal on his fingers.

"Your work is improving every day." Evvy put on one earring, then the other as she peered over his shoulder. "If you've got time, I could use a nice landscape on the wall." She hugged his neck, then grabbed her coat from the back of the chair.

Sebastian helped Evvy into her coat, and they made

their way to the car, hand in hand. The tree that had nearly crushed his vehicle was gone, and most of the snow had melted. He opened the door for Evvy and helped her inside before starting the car.

"I thought we were going straight to the market," Evvy said when he turned in the opposite direction.

"We're meeting my family for drinks at the tasting room first, remember? You don't need to be at the market at a certain time, do you?"

"No." Evvy flashed him a tight smile, then turned to look out the window.

He held out his open palm, and she slipped her hand in his, gripping it tightly. "You're not nervous about meeting my family, are you? Because they're looking forward to seeing you again, and I made Naya promise to be on her best behavior... for her."

A giggle burst from Evvy's pursed lips, and the tension in her grip eased the tiniest bit. "I wouldn't want your sister to be anyone but herself."

"You're definitely gonna regret saying that." Sebastian chuckled.

Normally, Evvy was an open book. But something was clearly bothering her, and she'd intentionally sidestepped his question about meeting his family.

He needed to do something to lift her mood, as she'd often done for him. Maybe music would help.

Sebastian released her hand to turn on the Christmas playlist Chandra had sent him because she insisted he needed to get into the holiday mood. The opening strain of "Let It Snow" by Boyz II Men and Brian McKnight filled the cabin of the car.

A genuine smile spread across Evvy's face, and her shoulders relaxed. "I love this song."

"Top-shelf Christmas jam," Sebastian agreed.

They sang along, followed by their bad karaoke editions of "This Christmas" by Donny Hathaway and "All I Want for Christmas Is You" by Mariah Carey. By the time they'd arrived at the villa, Evvy was all smiles.

She placed a hand on his arm before he got out of the car. "Thank you for that. You clearly realized that I needed it."

God, she was beautiful. Just seeing her face made him smile.

"So you *are* nervous about tonight." Sebastian took her hand in his. "Why? You've met them all before."

"It's not them. They're great. It's me. I get anxious around the holidays, especially when it comes to spending time with other people's families. It makes me sad about my own childhood," she admitted.

"Evvy, I'm sorry. I didn't know." He kissed her hand.

"There's no way you could have," she said. "I should've mentioned it before."

"Do you want to leave? Because if you'd rather spend a night in, we can turn around and go back right now. My family will be disappointed, but they'll understand." He'd wanted this night to be special for both of them. And he wanted his family to get to know Evvy and realize how wonderful she was. But not at the expense of her mental health.

"Thanks for understanding. But I can handle it. *Really*. Singing Christmas songs on the way here helped," she assured him. "But there is one other thing…"

"What is it?"

"Being introduced to a romantic partner's family typically means things are getting serious and you can envision a future with them. But that's not an option for us. So it's stirring up all of these conflicting feelings. Wishing we were something more. Recognizing we aren't and never will be. It's a little unsettling for me. But I want to do this, and everything will be fine. I just wanted to be honest with you about how I'm feeling."

Sebastian understood. It grieved him whenever he thought of how they'd eventually have to go their separate ways.

"If there was any chance for us to have a future together, Evvy, I'd jump at it. But in a few weeks, we'll be thousands of miles apart. I don't think either of us is interested in a long-distance relationship. So we don't have a lot of options here. Not unless you'd ever consider moving to Nashville."

Her beautiful brown eyes widened with surprise, momentarily. Then she shook her head, her curls bouncing.

"Then we should enjoy every single minute we have left together. Starting now." Sebastian kissed her cheek, hoping it would be enough to keep the deep, aching sadness they were both feeling at bay.

Seventeen

Sebastian stood at the festive dessert table ladling warm apple cider into two mugs for Evelisse and Mariana, who were stationed at the Sweet Magnolia Inn booth. The little red, green, and silver gift boxes Sebastian had helped Evvy fold and fill with tissue paper, premium chocolate, and a Sweet Magnolia Inn bottle opener key chain turned out to be a big hit. And if the number of tourists taking brochures, signing up for the newsletter list, and requesting bookings was any indication, the money Evvy had spent on the last-minute branding idea had been well worth it.

Evvy was better suited to her role as innkeeper than she gave herself credit for. And judging by the beaming smile on her face, she was definitely in her element.

When Mariana had been overwhelmed by the interest at their table, Evvy apologized for abandoning him, then ran over to help out.

"God, she looks amazing." He sighed quietly.

"She does indeed." His father chuckled at startling him. They stood together watching Evvy wearing that glittering gold sequin dress and a radiant smile. "Evvy looks mighty happy. Then again, so do you, son. You two are good for each other."

Sebastian didn't have the energy to argue the point with his father, especially when the old man was right. He shrugged. "Maybe we are, but the reality is that my life is in Nashville and hers is in LA."

"I hear that Kayleigh offered her full partnership in the inn if she stays and runs it for a couple years." His father took one of the warm mugs of cider in Sebastian's hand.

Sebastian poured another to replace it.

"Makes sense. She'd make an excellent partner in the inn." Sebastian hoped his father didn't notice how startled he was by the news. Why hadn't Evvy mentioned her sister's proposal? "But even if she accepts Kayleigh's offer, we'd still be hours away from each other. And neither of us is interested in a long-distance relationship." Sebastian groaned quietly. "Evelisse is an amazing woman, Dad. Believe me, if there was any way we could make a relationship work, I'd jump through fiery hoops to make it happen."

"Then maybe I can help you out, son." His dad grinned, his eyes glinting with the reflection of the colorful Christmas lights strung up around the space.

"Because I believe that we're ready to expand the facility and ramp up production."

"I really appreciate the offer, Dad. But—"

"I know your current salary is well above what we budgeted for the role of operations manager. But I'm a man of my word. I said that if you kids would give me three years to show you what we can do with this winery, I'd match your current salaries. I know I'd have to subsidize it a bit, but I'm willing to do that to bring you on board, son. The insight you've provided over the past few weeks has been *invaluable*. We could really use your help to push through this next phase of expansion."

This plea made by his father and siblings had always evoked an immediate *thanks but no thanks* response. But this time, he couldn't help imagining what it would be like to be here in Magnolia Lake full-time, getting to wake up to Evvy's gorgeous face every single morning and ending their nights reading together in bed or, even better, with her in his arms as he made love to her.

But that enchanting fantasy was quickly disrupted by the voice in the back of his head reminding him of how much time and effort he'd put into his current role. And of the employees who were counting on him to put a stop to the conglomerate's awful policy changes. The familiar feeling of dread and the churning in his stomach returned.

"That's an incredibly generous offer, Dad. But there are a lot of things I still need to accomplish at Valentine Textiles." Sebastian gave his father an apologetic smile. "I see your vision for the winery now, though.

And I'm behind you one hundred percent. I'll do anything I possibly can to help."

"I respect your decision, son." His father frowned and placed a hand on his shoulder. "But life is far too short, so don't waste it making the same mistake I did. Living up to someone else's expectations…it's no way to live. If I could do it all over again, I would've focused on doing more of what makes me happy rather than pursuing the things I felt I *should* be doing to meet someone else's approval."

"That isn't what you're doing now?" Sebastian raised an eyebrow. "Trying to strong-arm me into joining the new family firm?"

"Touché." His dad chuckled. "Building Valentine Vineyards together is my dream." He pressed a hand to his chest. "But it's structured so that each of us can find personal fulfillment by doing the things we're best suited for, the things that make us happiest. If you could find that here, I'd be thrilled. But if running the textile firm is what truly makes you happy, then I'll support that, too."

There was that gnawing in his gut again, and it felt like a vise tightened across his forehead. "I'll keep that in mind, Dad. Promise."

Sebastian took the mugs of cider over to Evvy and Mariana.

"You're the best." Evvy gave him a Hollywood kiss on the cheek, then whispered in his ear, "I'll definitely make this up to you when we get home."

Her brown eyes glinted mischievously, and his heart raced. Only he wasn't sure if it was because of all of the erotic visions playing out in his head right now or because she had implied that the apartment was *their* home.

And it pained Sebastian to realize that deep down, he wished that was true.

Evvy was lying in Sebastian's arms, her thigh draped over his. They'd barely gotten into the door before they'd torn each other's clothes off and made their way to her bed. The floor was strewn with their discarded clothing, including the designer dress and shoes she'd never have been able to afford had she not purchased them from a sample sale boutique.

Sebastian kissed her forehead and rubbed his large hand up and down her back, both of them enjoying the peaceful bliss of afterglow.

"Why didn't you tell me about Kayleigh's partnership offer?" Sebastian asked.

Evvy's chest tightened with guilt.

"Kayleigh just made the offer earlier today." She'd forgotten how quickly news traveled in a small town. "We were both focused on preparing for the kickoff of the Christmas Market tonight."

"True," Sebastian said, clearly unconvinced. "I guess I'm still a little surprised you didn't mention it."

"I'm sorry you had to hear it from someone else." She trailed a finger down his arm and gazed at him. "But I needed some time to process the offer in my head. Without everyone else's input."

"Have you made a decision?" he asked.

An involuntary smile spread across her face and she

nodded, her heart practically leaping in her chest. "Yes. I've decided to accept Kayleigh's offer."

"Evvy, that's great." Sebastian kissed her. "It's exciting that your relationship with your sister and with Magnolia Lake has really come full circle. And given the amount of business this place is doing already and the interest at the winter market, you two have got a hit on your hands."

"Thanks." She didn't need Sebastian's approval, but was reassuring to have it, just the same. Evvy lay on his shoulder again, breathing in his divine scent. "What you said about me being in my element and happy here—it got me thinking. The interest at the Christmas market tonight sealed the deal. Thank you for being so supportive."

"Of course, sweetheart. I'm thrilled for you both." Sebastian traced soft circles on her shoulder. "Which reminds me…my dad asked me to join Valentine Vineyards again tonight."

"Are you considering it?" Evvy tried her best to restrain the hopefulness in her voice.

There was a heavy pause, the thick silence filling the room and making her feel as if she was suffocating.

"Evvy, I wish I could stay. But I can't," Sebastian said finally. He dropped a gentle kiss on her forehead. "I'm just not ready to give up. Not when I know I can still have an impact on the company and on the lives of our workers. I'm sorry."

Sebastian wrapped his arms around her tightly, as if he was reluctant to let her go.

But he would. He'd all but made that clear. He wasn't

interested in moving to Magnolia Lake and pursuing a future with her.

When people show you who they are, believe them the first time.

The adage from the sage wordsmith Maya Angelou by way of Oprah popped in Evvy's head. Calvin had told her who he was—a man who hadn't wanted a serious commitment. And yet she's spent six years telling herself that it didn't matter while simultaneously hoping she could somehow change his mind.

It wasn't Calvin who'd been foolish. It was her. And now she was doing it again. Because deep down she'd been hoping that when Sebastian learned she was staying to help run the inn, he'd decide to join his family's business, too.

But no matter how strong their feelings for each other might be, it hadn't changed things for Sebastian. And it never would.

The only thing left to do was to enjoy every remaining moment of their holiday fling. And to ignore the little voice in the back of her head that kept chiding her for having fallen in love with another emotionally unavailable man.

Eighteen

Sebastian collected the last of his toiletries from Evvy's bathroom counter, zipped up his travel case, and stuffed it into his overnight bag. He set his bag by the front door. He'd take it down to the car with the rest of his things, already packed up from his room at the inn.

"Is that everything?" Evvy asked, her voice breaking slightly and the corners of her red eyes wet.

Sebastian swallowed hard and tried not to notice. "That's everything except my sketchpad."

He nodded toward the handmade, saddle-stitched, brown leather sketchbook cover Evvy bought him for Christmas from a leather goods artisan at the Magnolia Lake Christmas market. She'd had his initials embossed on the front cover. Inside there were pockets for his art supplies.

"Don't you forget this." She handed him the padded leather case. "And don't you dare stop drawing. You're *really* good, Sebastian. More importantly, you enjoy doing it. I love the incredible landscapes you made me for Christmas." She gestured toward his watercolor pencil drawing of the inn that she'd had framed and hung on the wall near the door.

The drawing of the Sweet Magnolia Inn exploded with vibrant fall colors—shades of red, orange, gold, and brown—that stood in stark contrast to the greenery of the coniferous trees that edged the property. The scene was just as he remembered it when he'd first arrived at the inn, and it was his best landscape to date. On the wall of Evvy's office over in the main building hung one of his earlier efforts: a charcoal sketch of the inn and carriage house at the height of the blizzard.

"Thanks for encouraging me to take up art again. And for nudging me to give meditation and yoga a try," he said. "It's made a big difference. You've made..." Sebastian sucked in a deep breath, his eyes stinging and his throat clogged with the kaleidoscope of emotions swirling inside his chest. He forced a smile. "*You've* made such a huge difference in my life in such a short time. I can't thank you enough, Evvy."

Sebastian shoved his free hand in his pocket, afraid that if he took her into his arms again, he'd never let her go.

They'd both known from the start that this moment would come. He'd spent the past few weeks mentally preparing himself for it. So why did every step toward that door make him feel that his still-beating heart had been ripped from his chest, thrown onto the floor, and stomped?

Because he'd been shaken by the depth of his feelings for Evelisse. Emotions he hadn't expected. Past romantic partners had accused him of never really opening up to them. At the time, he felt their arguments weren't justified. But now he realized that they'd been right all along.

Sebastian hadn't been willing to bare his wounds and share his insecurities with past partners. He'd held on to those things tightly for fear that seeing the version of him that was bloody and bruised from past trauma would diminish their perception of him. Ironically, the brick fortress he'd built around himself to hide the ocean of agony and self-doubt he was quietly drowning in was the very thing that had driven past partners away.

Something about Evelisse Jemison was so transparent and authentic. She was an open book about her past—even the ugly parts that were still bloody and raw. The honest conversations he and Evvy had shared while preparing dinner together or while luxuriating together in her spa bathtub had made him feel comfortable enough to let down those walls and be honest with her. But it also permitted him to be honest with himself in ways he hadn't before.

One thing Sebastian knew for sure. Because of their time together, his life would never be the same, and he was grateful for that.

"Good. I'm glad you'll have fond memories of our time together." She wiped the wetness from the corner of her eyes.

Sebastian's gut twisted, and fresh pain bloomed in his chest. Damn, he was going to miss waking up with Evvy in his arms, their morning routines, their open conversations over a good meal, and ending their nights together in bed.

"How could I ever forget my time with someone as special as you, Evvy?" Sebastian asked.

She turned her back to him, her shoulders shaking.

Sebastian dropped his leather padfolio onto the counter and took her into his arms, hugging her tight, though she'd tried to pull away from him at first.

"I'm sorry." Her words were muffled, and her tears wet his sweatshirt. "I promised myself that there would be no tears. That the end was always part of the plan. But I…" She broke into tears again, her cheek pressed to his chest.

Sebastian wanted to say something wise and comforting that would make Evvy feel better. But he wouldn't lie to her by promising that they'd see each other again. They'd talked through the scenarios. As their lives stood now, there was just no viable way for them to be together.

So why hadn't he come to terms with that?

Since he had no words to offer, Sebastian just held Evvy to his chest, comforting her the only way he could, as he tried to keep his own emotions at bay. He glanced around Evvy's apartment, still decorated for the holidays.

Ethereal white fairy lights were strung along the fireplace mantel, around the doorways, and near the ceiling. More white lights and exactly two dozen delicate ornaments circled the real spruce tree they'd picked out, hauled up her stairs, and decorated together. Something neither of them had done in years.

Sebastian glanced at the kitchen, where they'd eaten so many meals together and sometimes cooked them together, too. The fireplace they'd sat in front of and read their respective books. The bed that they'd shared.

This space always smelled of seasonal scents and good food. It was filled with warmth and light that stemmed from Evvy more than the raging fireplace they lit each evening. Here, he'd come to feel an overwhelming sense of peace and joy and what felt like love. More so than any other place else he could remember.

But it wasn't about the carriage house or the studio apartment itself. It was the woman he was holding now. The woman it broke his heart to walk away from.

Evelisse extracted herself from his embrace as she wiped at her reddened eyes with her sleeve. Her nose and cheeks were red, and her coppery curls bounced, as if in protest, with every movement.

"You've got a long drive ahead. I know you have to go." She handed him a small insulated bag. "I know it's less than four hours, but I packed you some water and a few snacks, in case you get hungry on the road."

Evvy was so loving and nurturing. She deserved someone better than him. A man who wasn't broken and still trying to figure his shit out.

"Thank you, Evvy." Bas forced a smile. "You realize you're far too good for me, right?"

"That isn't true." Silent tears streamed down Evvy's cheeks. She didn't bother to wipe them. Instead, she toyed with the diamond studs Sebastian had bought her for Christmas to wear in her second piercing, which she'd never seemed to have the right earrings for. "You are the perfect man for me, Sebastian."

"So you're into grumpy, anxiety-ridden dudes who sketch and have big, nosy families," Sebastian teased. "Noted."

"By the way, I'm really glad the relaxation techniques and lifestyle changes have eased your anxiety. But now that you're returning to work, those strategies alone might not be enough. There's nothing wrong with using medicine to alleviate the pressure. No reasonable person expects a perfect partner or employee. We want someone who is well-adjusted and self-aware—even if it takes therapy and anxiety meds to get there." She squeezed his arm.

Sebastian nodded, then hiked his overnight bag over his shoulder as she opened the door for him.

Evvy lifted onto her toes and kissed his cheek, then quickly closed the door behind him. As he made his way down the stairs, getting further away from Evvy, he'd never felt colder or more alone.

Evvy had climbed back into bed and clung to the pillow that still smelled of Sebastian's clean, woodsy, citrus scent. She sobbed, the tears falling harder and faster and her heart aching.

She was glad she'd had the presence of mind to take the day off of work. In this state, she wouldn't be good for anything.

Evelisse would permit herself today to mourn what

they'd lost. Then she'd get up in the morning, use a ton of concealer to hide the red splotches on her skin from all the crying, pull herself together, and get back to the work of building the business that she and Kayleigh now officially shared.

Her phone buzzed twice with text messages. The first was Kayleigh, asking if she was all right and inviting her over for dinner that night.

Her sister had probably asked Mariana to let her know the moment Sebastian left so she could text and check on her. The invitation was sweet, but she'd much rather be alone tonight.

The second message was from Sebastian.

Left a little something for you in the closet. Take care, gorgeous. And thank you for the most amazing three months of my life.

The text message was accompanied by a photo of a large red box with a silver bow on a top shelf in her closet. Evvy held the phone to her chest, moved by Sebastian's sweet message. Then she retrieved the gift. It was heavier than she expected. She placed it on the bed and lifted the lid.

Evvy's eyes widened, and she pressed a trembling hand to her open mouth. Beneath the first layer of tissue paper was a framed drawing. She lifted it from the box, studying it carefully. It was a watercolor drawing of her lying on her side, sound asleep. Through the window, the trees on the property were visible.

She hadn't seen this drawing before and had no idea

when he'd done it. Evvy hadn't seen Sebastian drawing many portraits. But this was absolutely stunning. Beneath another layer of tissue paper there was a smaller charcoal sketch, also framed. In it, she sat in front of the fireplace wearing pajamas and his gray-and-navy sweatshirt she'd commandeered. Underneath the final layer of red tissue paper was that same sweatshirt she was wearing in the sketch.

Evvy hugged the sweatshirt to her chest and cried, her shoulders shaking.

Maybe things with Sebastian hadn't ended the way she'd hoped. But she would never regret falling in love with him.

Nineteen

It was the first business day of the new year. But instead of feeling hopeful, Sebastian's heart was filled with dread as he pulled into the parking lot of Valentine Textiles and was greeted warmly by the guard at the gate. He pulled into the parking spot reserved for the company's CEO. The spot he'd envied, which had belonged to his father for years.

From the first day Sebastian had parked in this long-anticipated spot, it just hadn't held as much meaning as he'd anticipated. Because the rest of his family hadn't been there to celebrate the moment with him. And returning here now was even worse. What he felt was misery and anguish over being here when Evvy was back in Magnolia Lake—where most of his family was based.

When Sebastian awakened, he'd tried to follow the

same routine that he and Evvy had. Twenty minutes of meditation. A sun salutation yoga practice, which he'd become far better at. He'd taken time to eat breakfast and replaced his morning coffee fix with an adaptogen mushroom-based coffee alternative. Still, he could feel the tension rising in his chest and knotting his gut as he got closer to the firm. As he sat in his parked car now, his pulse raced, and the sound of his thumping heart-beat filled his ears.

Sebastian squeezed his eyes shut and concentrated on his breathing and the visual imagery Evvy had guided him through. Still, a band of tension tightened around his forehead and it felt as if his heart might explode.

We want someone who is well-adjusted and self-aware—even if it takes therapy and anxiety meds to get there.

Evvy's words echoed in his head. Sebastian reached into his inner suit pocket where he'd stored the little bottle of pills. But instead, he touched the card from Evvy that he'd placed there before leaving his house that morning.

Sebastian pulled the note card out and read it for what was probably the fiftieth time since he'd discovered it packed in the lunch container Evvy had sent him off with.

Thank you for coming into my life and showing me what it feels like to be truly cared for. And since I might never get another chance to say this: I love you, Sebastian. And I don't regret a moment of our time together. I only wish it had been longer. With a heart filled with love and joyful memories, I wish you a life filled with love, purpose, and true happiness.

Evelisse

Sebastian lay back against the headrest, his eyes pressed closed. Instead of finding comfort in Evvy's declaration of love and warm wishes, he felt a deep, bottomless ache in his chest at the pain of losing the woman who'd come to mean so much to him in a few short months.

Bas pulled out his phone, opened Instagram, and navigated to the Sweet Magnolia Inn page. Recent photos had included the inn all decked out for Christmas and some of the gorgeous breakfasts Sofie had created. But the latest post was a photo of Evelisse and Kayleigh with their heads full of coppery curls together as they held up glasses of bubbly, celebrating making their partnership official.

It reminded Sebastian of the photos in Evvy's apartment of Evvy and Kayleigh as kids and then again at Kayleigh's wedding. He wondered if the style and position of the shot had been intentional. Because it would look perfect sitting beside the other two photos.

He expanded the picture, then gently traced Evvy's lips with his thumb.

She looked happy, and he was thrilled for her. He understood why she'd been against coming to Nashville. But he desperately missed Evvy and the joy she'd brought into his life.

Sebastian glanced around the lot and swallowed

hard. But he couldn't seem to make himself grab the handle to get out of his car. He rubbed at the increasing tension in his forehead.

He could hear Evvy's sweet voice in his head.

Isn't the point of attaining the brass ring in your career that it's supposed to make you happy?

She was right, of course. And the job he was doing now didn't make him happy.

He wanted to make an impact. To leave a legacy of doing his best by his grandparents' company. But there was more than one way to approach nearly any dilemma. So maybe returning to his job as faux CEO wasn't the only way to accomplish that. He recalled his promise, the night he'd arrived in Magnolia Lake, to talk to his father if he needed help with work.

Well, it was time to make that call.

Sebastian started his car again, backed out of his parking spot, and headed for the exit. As he drove through those gates and back onto the streets, the band of pressure around his head eased, as did the tightness in his chest.

An involuntary smile spread across his face as he thought of the time he'd spent with his family back in Magnolia Lake and of the woman who'd turned his world upside down and made him believe in love again.

Evvy greeted two couples who'd arrived for the week. Then she went to chat with the group of retired widows who'd checked in the previous night. It was barely two weeks into the new year, and the inn was fully booked. They were excited about the prospects for the year ahead, and Kayleigh was already musing about the possibility of expanding.

Evvy should be thrilled. She *was* thrilled. And she had a wide grin frozen in place to prove it. Still, her gut was twisted in knots and her chest ached—as if there was a gaping hole where her heart once was.

She excused herself and returned to the front desk to fiddle with the knickknacks arranged along the back wall. She sniffled and discreetly wiped away the hot tears stinging her eyes and threatening to run down her cheeks.

"Get it together, Evelisse Jemison," she whispered angrily beneath her breath. "You always knew this is how things would end. Why are you being such a baby about this?"

"So we're at the point in the show where you're having full-on conversations with yourself." Mariana Rivera's tone was teasing yet empathetic. She placed a hand on Evvy's shoulder and offered a soft smile. She lowered her voice so only Evvy could hear her. "Today seems kind of rough for you. Why don't you take the afternoon off? We only have a couple more bookings scheduled to arrive today. I can handle it."

"Thanks, but I'd rather stay busy. Besides, my place seems so…empty now." Evvy sighed. "I think I need to be around people."

"All right." Mariana's big brown eyes were filled with empathy. "Then why don't you take lunch over to Kayleigh? She's been working all morning. She needs a break and something to eat, and so do you. I asked

Sofie to make lunches for both of you." Mariana nodded toward the kitchen. "Now go."

"Geez, you've been the assistant innkeeper for all of
a week, and already you're bossing me around," Evvy
teased, thankful Mariana was well-suited to her new
full-time role. "What I'm hearing is you don't want my
gloominess bringing the mood down." Evvy held up her
open palms. "Fine. I get it."

"It's not that," Mariana countered quickly. "I just hate
seeing you so sad. Maybe spending time with your sister in her studio will cheer you up."

"I'm sure it will." Evvy hugged the younger woman.
"Thank you, Mari. You're an excellent assistant and an
even better friend."

Mariana beamed, then walked to the door to accept
the weekly delivery of fresh flowers from the green-
house at Lockwood Farms—run and owned by Cole
Abbott's wife, Renee Lockwood Abbott.

Evvy thanked Sofie for the boxed lunches she'd prepared for her and Kayleigh. Then she took the covered
walkway to her sister's studio next door.

Being with Sebastian had shown Evvy what a truly
compatible relationship could look like. Too bad their
circumstances hadn't been as harmonious.

It felt as if every waking moment was filled with
thoughts of Sebastian. But for the sake of her sister and
friends, maybe she should at least pretend that everything was okay. Eventually, it would be.

But not today.

Today she was masking the pain of her broken heart
with a painted-on smile. And that's the way it would be.

* * *

Sebastian parked in his usual spot at the Sweet Magnolia Inn and threw his door open so quickly, he nearly forgot to put his BMW in Park. He turned off the engine, stepped out of the car, and filled his lungs with the crisp mountain air he'd missed so much.

He grabbed the large bouquet of flowers he'd picked up at Renee's nursery—the only stop he'd made since arriving in town. Then he hurried inside the inn.

"Mr. Valentine." Mariana, stood behind the front desk, surprised to see him. "What are you doing here? I mean…we weren't expecting you." Her cheeks flushed as she glanced around the space, then back at the computer in front of her. She clicked a few keys on her keyboard. "I'm sorry, but we're all booked this week."

"It's okay, Mariana." He honestly hadn't given much thought to where he would be staying. He only knew he needed to see Evvy again. That here in Magnolia Lake, surrounded by his family, was where he wanted to be. "I'll figure it out. I just really need to see Evelisse. Is she in the kitchen?"

"No, I sent her over to Kayleigh's studio half an hour ago. The two of them seem determined to work themselves to death without eating. Kayleigh is trying to make up for the time she lost with her arm broken, and Evvy…" Mari clamped her mouth shut and frowned. She folded her arms and cocked her head as she eyed him carefully. "Is Evvy expecting you?"

"No. And I'd like to surprise her. So please don't tell her I'm here."

Mariana was being protective of her friend whose heart he'd broken, even if he'd done so inadvertently. He would've felt the same.

"All right." Mari shook a finger at him. "But if you upset her—"

"I won't." Bas held up his open palms. "Promise."

"Okay." Mari sighed. She gestured toward the door with her head. "Go ahead. I won't say anything. But don't you dare forget your promise."

"I won't." Sebastian headed for the door leading to Kayleigh's studio and shop.

"Te arrepentirás si lo haces," she muttered behind him.

His high school Spanish was pretty rusty, but he was sure Mari had said something about him regretting it if he forgot his promise.

He didn't doubt it.

Bas opened the door to Kayleigh's shop, and a little bell tinkled overhead.

"Good afternoon. Can I…" Kayleigh emerged from the back on her knee scooter. Her eyes widened when she caught sight of him. "What are you—"

Bas held his index finger to his lips as he quietly approached the jewelry counter Kayleigh was standing behind. He glanced around the space, then mouthed the words, "Where is she?"

Kayleigh screwed up her face, pinching the gorgeous features, so reminiscent of Evvy's. She rolled from behind the counter and poked him in the bicep with one of the fingers of the hand no longer bound in a cast.

"You'd better not hurt my sister, Sebastian Valentine,"

she whispered angrily, her brown eyes blazing. "Either you're into her and you really want to do this, or—"

"I do," he said without reservation. "Getting to know your sister is the best thing that's ever happened to me. I realize that now, Kayleigh. And I won't screw it up again. I promise. Also, I've already been threatened by Mari. In Spanish."

"Sebastian?"

Both his and Kayleigh's attention snapped to where Evvy was standing.

She'd whispered his name as if she wasn't quite sure of what she was seeing. Her eyes were red and watery. She pressed a trembling hand to her lips.

Bas sucked in a deep breath, his chest suddenly tight. They'd only been apart for two weeks. So why did seeing her again make it feel so damn hard to breathe?

"Kayleigh, would you give us a moment, please?" Evvy asked.

"Are you sure?" Kayleigh hiked one brow as she flashed Sebastian her best hurt-my-sister-and-I'll-cut-you look.

"I'm sure. Please?" Evvy said.

Kayleigh humphed and rolled her scooter toward the back room of her studio, calling over her shoulder, "Fine, but if you need me, I'm just a call away. And I've got lots of tools. Heavy ones."

Evvy pressed a palm to her forehead and sighed. "Little sisters, right?"

"I don't know. I'm realizing now that they're a lot wiser than we give them credit for." Sebastian smiled, stepping forward. "Hey, beautiful."

"Hey, handsome." Evvy flashed the shy smile that always managed to simultaneously melt his heart and set his body on fire.

Sebastian swallowed hard, his throat dry. "Congrats on the official partnership on the inn. I saw it posted on social media."

"Thank you, Sebastian. And thank you for helping me realize what a good fit this is for me. But you didn't ride for hours to congratulate me, did you?"

"I've missed you desperately, Evvy." His gaze locked with hers.

She wrapped her arms around herself and regarded him warily. "Why are you here, Sebastian? You said you had unfinished business at your grandparents' company."

"I know." He cupped her face and stroked her cheek with his thumb. "But when I returned to Nashville, I thought about the conversations we had about doing the things that truly make us happy. I realized that my goals have shifted. Sitting at the head of that boardroom table isn't what I want anymore. More importantly, I can't fathom spending the rest of my life without you in—"

Before he could finish, she kissed him.

He slipped his arms around her waist and pulled her soft, warm body against his. Sebastian relished every curve. Greedily inhaled the coffee and coconut scent of her skin and the subtle vanilla scent wafting from her sleek curls.

Soon they were both lost in the heated, hungry kiss. As if it was life-giving water after a long, hot trek through the desert.

The repeated clearing of Kayleigh's throat was the only thing alerting them that she'd returned to the front lobby.

"Uh...hi." Kayleigh, who was now wearing a puffy winter jacket, mittens, and a colorful knit hat with ear flaps, raised her hand. "Still on the premises."

"Sorry, sis." Evvy wiped her lipstick from Sebastian's lips. Their eyes were locked even as she addressed her sister. "We forgot you were still here."

"Ouch." Kayleigh pressed a hand to her heart. "That hurts. Anyway... I just wanted you to know I'm closing up shop early today."

"But you were just working on a sketch," Evvy objected.

"Which I'm taking home to complete." Kayleigh patted the worn brown leather bag strapped across her body. The one that Evvy had given to their father a lifetime ago. "That'll give you two time alone." She glanced toward the ceiling and flashed a knowing smile. "Good to see you again, Sebastian." Kayleigh gave him the I'm-watching-you gesture. "Just don't forget what I said."

"I won't." Sebastian nodded. "Promise."

"Love you, sis." Kayleigh gave Evvy a big hug.

"Love you, too." Evvy squeezed her sister tight before releasing her. Then she slipped her hand in Sebastian's and led him up to her apartment.

Twenty

Evvy climbed those stairs as fast as her legs would take her with Sebastian's hand clasped firmly in hers. The moment they were in her apartment, she kissed him again. And in a matter of seconds, they shed their many layers of clothing and ended up in her bed. There was very little time for speaking.

After they made love, she put on the teakettle.

Sebastian slipped his boxers on and got the fireplace started. Then they snuggled together in bed, her cheek against his broad chest.

She missed Sebastian's warmth, his scent, and the comfort of lying in his arms. She missed how being with Sebastian made her feel. *Loved*, even if he had yet to say it.

"So…when you said you came back here to be with me…"

"I meant just that." Sebastian sat up against the headboard. Evvy did the same. Sebastian lifted her chin, his eyes locked with hers. "I am totally, completely, and irrevocably in love with you, Evelisse Jemison."

Evvy's heart swelled, and her eyes stung with tears. Sebastian sounded so sincere. She felt every single word he'd uttered deep in her soul. Still, the familiar feelings of fear and doubt she'd been nursing her entire life slowly seeped in and started to take root.

Her past was littered with broken promises. Words fervently uttered but seldom meant.

I love you's from past boyfriends that turned out to be empty words. The parents whose responsibility had been to love them unconditionally. Promises of movie and television roles that never materialized.

What makes Sebastian any different? the little voice in her head whispered.

"Evvy, did you hear me?" Sebastian touched her arm.

"I did." Evvy forced a bright smile and threaded their fingers. She searched his dark eyes. "You mean so much to me, Sebastian. I want you in my life. But I need to know I can trust what you say. So if you're only saying you love me because of the note I wrote…"

"I'm saying I love you because I do, sweetheart. But I didn't think I should say it if I wasn't prepared to make the hard choices I needed to make to prove it."

Evvy squeezed his hand, mimicking the squeeze of her heart in her chest as Sebastian regarded her, his eyes filled with emotion. "Really?"

"Really." He dropped a soft kiss on her lips. "I thought I could walk away and go back to my life. Just be grateful for the incredible memories." He shrugged. "But all I could think of was you. I enjoy being with you, Evvy. And I love that you completely get me, but you're also not afraid to challenge me in ways that make me think and grow as a person. The honest talks we had made me come to terms with some of my childhood and relationship trauma. Made me realize that I want and deserve a love like this, as long as I'm willing to do the work. And baby, I am. Because I've never been happier than I am when I'm with you."

Evvy's eyes welled with unshed tears, her heart thudded in her chest, and her hands trembled. "Are you saying... Do you mean..."

"I'm here to stay." Sebastian wiped the wetness from her cheek.

"What about your unfinished business at your grandparents' company?"

Walking away from his job as CEO and his life in Nashville was a life-changing decision. Evvy needed to know that this wasn't a knee-jerk reaction.

"I desperately wanted to be the CEO of my family's company, but for all the wrong reasons. *You* helped me realize that. And I will always be grateful to you for it." He kissed the back of her hand. "As for the unfinished business... I handled that, too."

"How?"

"This morning, I held a press conference outlining the reasons I resigned from the company, including the proposed adoption of anti-worker policies in direct op-

434 SNOWBOUND SECOND CHANCE

position to how our family has always treated our workers. From the calls I received from some of my staff, the company is already shifting its position on some of the changes. Maybe I burned a bridge with the conglomerate, but hopefully, it'll make things better for the employees I'm leaving behind."

"That took courage, Sebastian. I know it couldn't have been easy, but I'm proud of you." She cupped his cheek. "I know your family is, too."

"Thanks," he said. "I swallowed my pride and consulted with my dad on how to handle the situation. The press conference was his idea."

"Then I'm surprised you're not with your dad now celebrating," she said.

"Once the press conference was over, I hopped into my already packed car and drove straight here. You were the person I wanted to tell more than anyone. Because you mean the world to me, Evvy. I've spent most of my life closed off and resentful about my mother abandoning us. So much so that I think I'd started to feel almost dead inside. It was my way of coping. But being with you helped me realize that's no way to live. I deserve to be happy. And being with you genuinely makes me happy. I don't ever want to be without you again."

Evvy could no longer hold back the tears that had burned her eyes and clogged her throat from the moment Sebastian declared his love for her

"I don't want to be apart again either." She smiled. "I'm doing work that I love. I finally appreciate the little town I grew up in. My relationship with my sister is in the best place it's ever been, and I'm going to be an aunt. Yet the moment you got in your car and drove off, I was heartbroken and miserable. Because I love you, Sebastian. And I want a life with you, too. But part of me is terrified," she admitted.

"Why?"

"No one has ever made this kind of sacrifice for me. Part of me is celebrating that you just gave up your entire life in Nashville for me. And part of me is thinking…*holy shit*. This man rearranged his entire life plan just to be with *me*."

Sebastian chuckled, pulling her closer. "And is that a bad thing?"

"No, it's a beautiful, wonderful, magnanimous gesture for which I am truly appreciative." Evvy settled her head on his shoulder.

"And this makes you wary because…" The tenor of his voice was warm and calm.

She sat up again. "What if you don't like living here in Magnolia Lake? What if things don't work out at the winery? I don't want you to wake up one day and resent our life together because you gave up everything to be with me."

Evvy could feel the panic in her chest rising. Her father had married her mother when she'd gotten pregnant with Evvy. But he'd resented his life as a husband and a father. And he'd drowned himself in a bottle of whiskey every night to escape the weighty responsibilities he'd never really wanted. Evelisse was terrified that she'd one day look into Sebastian's eyes and see that same anger and resentment.

"Sweetheart, I would gladly have given up all of that

just to be with you." Bas pressed a lingering kiss to her lips, then stroked her cheek. "But if you want the absolute truth, I did this for me. I resigned from my position and put my house up for sale because being here with you and working with my family…that's what *I* want." He tapped his chest. "I did it because this is what makes me happy. Not because of pressure from you or my family. All right?"

Evvy nodded, and Sebastian was a blur as tears streaked down her face.

"Please tell me those are tears of happiness." He kissed her damp cheek.

"They are." The tears fell faster. "I love you, baby."

He gave her a watery smile as he laid her down and hovered above her. "And I love you, too."

Sebastian kissed her, held her, made love to her. And for the hours they spent together, holed up in that apartment, it felt as if there was no one else in the world except the two of them.

There was no one in the world she'd rather be with.

Epilogue

Sebastian stood at the window of the carriage house, sipping his morning adaptogen-blend latte that had replaced his daily four cups of coffee. The deciduous trees on Sweet Magnolia Inn's property were radiant in the morning light, decked out in their fall finery: leaves of red, orange, and gold. It'd been little more than a year since that crisp autumn afternoon when he'd first arrived at the inn and one year exactly since a blizzard had blown into Magnolia Lake and forever changed his life.

He closed his eyes and inhaled deeply, thinking of everything that had transpired over the past year. He'd reconnected with Evelisse. They'd gotten caught up in an unprecedented snowstorm together, and it had turned out to be his snowbound second chance. Not only his second chance at a relationship with the woman he'd

spent the previous year regretting his missed opportunity with. It had also given him a second chance at
finding love and happiness.

That meant he'd had to finally let go of all the things
that no longer served him: the job he didn't really want,
the house he'd purchased as a last-ditch effort to save
his marriage, and a busy, stressful life that didn't bring
him joy. Sebastian's current state barely resembled the
man he was a year ago, and he was grateful for it.

He was by no means perfect, and he still struggled
with occasional moments of anxiety. But he was at
peace with himself and a lot more patient than he'd
been a year ago. Though his little sister, Naya, still
seemed to have a gift for annoying him and testing the
limits of his newly achieved serenity.

"You lit the fireplace." Evvy wrapped her arms
around him from behind. Her fingertips dug into the
abs that were far more toned than they had been a year
ago. A happy by-product of the yoga practice he'd maintained for the past year.

"I know it's not particularly cold today," he said.

"But lighting the fireplace is the perfect way to kick
off the anniversary of the Snowpocalypse. And playing hooky today so we can lounge in bed together all
day was a brilliant idea." She kissed his bare shoulder.
"Thanks for letting me sleep in this morning."

"After watching the girls last night, I figured we
could both use the extra rest." He chuckled.

Chandra and Julian, Nolan and his fiancée Delaney,
Parker and Kayleigh, and several other members of the
Valentine and Abbott families had attended a recital

at the new Magnolia Lake School—a microschool Savannah, Zora, and Renee had formed so their children could attend school locally rather than being bussed to the next town. He and Evvy had volunteered to babysit his toddler niece, Autumn, and Kayleigh's infant daughter, Jemma. They'd enjoyed spending time with their nieces. But by the end of the night, they'd both been ready for a long, hot bath and a long night of sleep.

"Then again, spending all day in bed with the woman I adore? That's never not a good idea." Sebastian set his cup down and turned to face Evelisse. He hooked his arms around her waist.

"Hmm… No arguments here." She purred softly as he trailed kisses down her neck. "But I thought we might emerge at least once to grab some dinner."

"Already got that covered," he said. "How about having lunch and dinner delivered to us instead?"

"You think of everything." Evvy settled her hands on the waistband of his pajama pants, slung low on his hips. She was wearing the top to his pajamas and little else. She glanced up at him, her expression more serious. "Is that why you were so deep in thought the past few days? I was worried something was wrong."

"Everything is perfect, Evvy." He kissed her, slow and sweet. "A part of me was worried it was too perfect," he admitted. "That I'd eventually find a way to fumble this relationship."

"And?" The smile that lit her brown eyes indicated she already knew his answer.

"This has been an amazing year for both of our families. The inn is doing incredible business. So much so that you and Kayleigh are seriously considering expanding to accommodate twice as many guests. The winery has increased production and nearly doubled our distribution channels. You have a brand-new niece, and Nolan and Laney are engaged. I'm drawing again—"

"You're doing a lot more than just drawing, Sebastian." She gestured to the art that filled the walls of the space: sketches that were more personal to them. "You're a working artist who regularly sells pieces. And your idea for having the paint-and-sip events and showing the work of regional artists at the tasting room… I'm not sure you understand just how big that's been to a lot of the rural artists around here. And personally sponsoring a booth for regional artists at the Magnolia Lake Christmas Market this year. That's incredibly generous of you." Evvy practically beamed.

He loved that they were supportive of each other both personally and in their careers. And he never took for granted what a gift it was to have someone like Evelisse in his life.

"I've never been this happy, Evvy." Sebastian cupped her cheek. "And I owe so much of the good in my life to you."

"I can't take credit for that." Evvy grinned. "You made the choice to pursue a different path, and you're doing the work required—physically and emotionally. I'm just grateful that I get to be a part of that journey. And baby, I am so damn proud of you. Because I know it isn't always easy."

"Being with you is one of the easiest things I've ever

done," Sebastian said. "And any work I needed to do on myself…it was absolutely worth it."

Learning to be more honest with himself and open with her had definitely required some effort, including self-care and therapy.

"I'm not saying you changed me," Sebastian clarified. "But you challenged me to face some hard truths about myself and what I wanted out of life. For that, I will forever be grateful." He kissed her again.

Evvy was stunning: forty-two and fine as hell. He woke up each morning eager to spend time with her, however they could fit it into their busy days. And he looked forward to all of the adventures they had in store. He couldn't imagine not having Evelisse in his life.

"I love you, sweetheart. More than anything in the world." He stroked her cheek.

She smiled, her eyes welling with tears. "I love you too, baby."

"Marry me?"

The words tripped out of Sebastian's mouth, taking him by surprise. He wasn't an impulsive man. He planned his life and thought through his decisions. But the moment he'd articulated the words, he realized how sincerely he meant them. He had no doubts about his feelings for Evvy or that he wanted to spend the rest of his life with her.

Evelisse's eyes widened, and she pressed a hand to her mouth. "Did you just…propose?"

Shit. He was bungling this proposal.

"I did, and I'm doing a terrible job at it. I should've waited until we were out to dinner with our families or something. I should already have the ring. And I definitely should've gotten down on one..."

"*Yes*, Sebastian." Evvy's voice was soft and tears ran down her cheeks, despite her bright smile. "I can't wait to marry you."

It took a moment for her acceptance to register in his brain. But when it did, his heart expanded in his chest, and his vision clouded with joy and gratitude.

Sebastian kissed Evvy, lifting her into his arms and carrying her to the bed they'd shared for the past year. He made love to the woman he would always be grateful to for giving him a second chance at love and happiness. And he would love her until the end of time.

* * * * *

To follow the Valentine Vineyards future adventures, join Reese Ryan's newsletter mailing list here: https://www.reeseryan.com/subscribe/.

HARLEQUIN
PLUS

Try the best multimedia subscription service for romance readers like you!

Read, Watch and Play.

Experience the easiest way to get the romance content you crave.

Start your **FREE TRIAL** at
www.harlequinplus.com/freetrial.